BANE COUNTY

Forgotten Moon

J R RICE

Silver Canyon Press

for Aimee

Abandon all hope, ye who enter here.
—DANTE ALIGHIERI, 1320

The devil's best trick, is to persuade you that he doesn't exist.
—CHARLES BAUDELAIRE, 1864

Those who cannot remember the past are condemned to repeat it.
—GEORGE SANTAYANA, 1905

CONTENTS

Title Page
Dedication
Epigraph
PREFACE   5
INTRODUCTION   6
PROLOGUE   10
CHAPTER 1   15
CHAPTER 2   33
CHAPTER 3   59
CHAPTER 4   76
CHAPTER 5   97
CHAPTER 6   115
CHAPTER 7   130
CHAPTER 8   158
CHAPTER 9   177
CHAPTER 10   193
CHAPTER 11   210
CHAPTER 12   234
CHAPTER 13   263
CHAPTER 14   286
CHAPTER 15   306

EPILOGUE

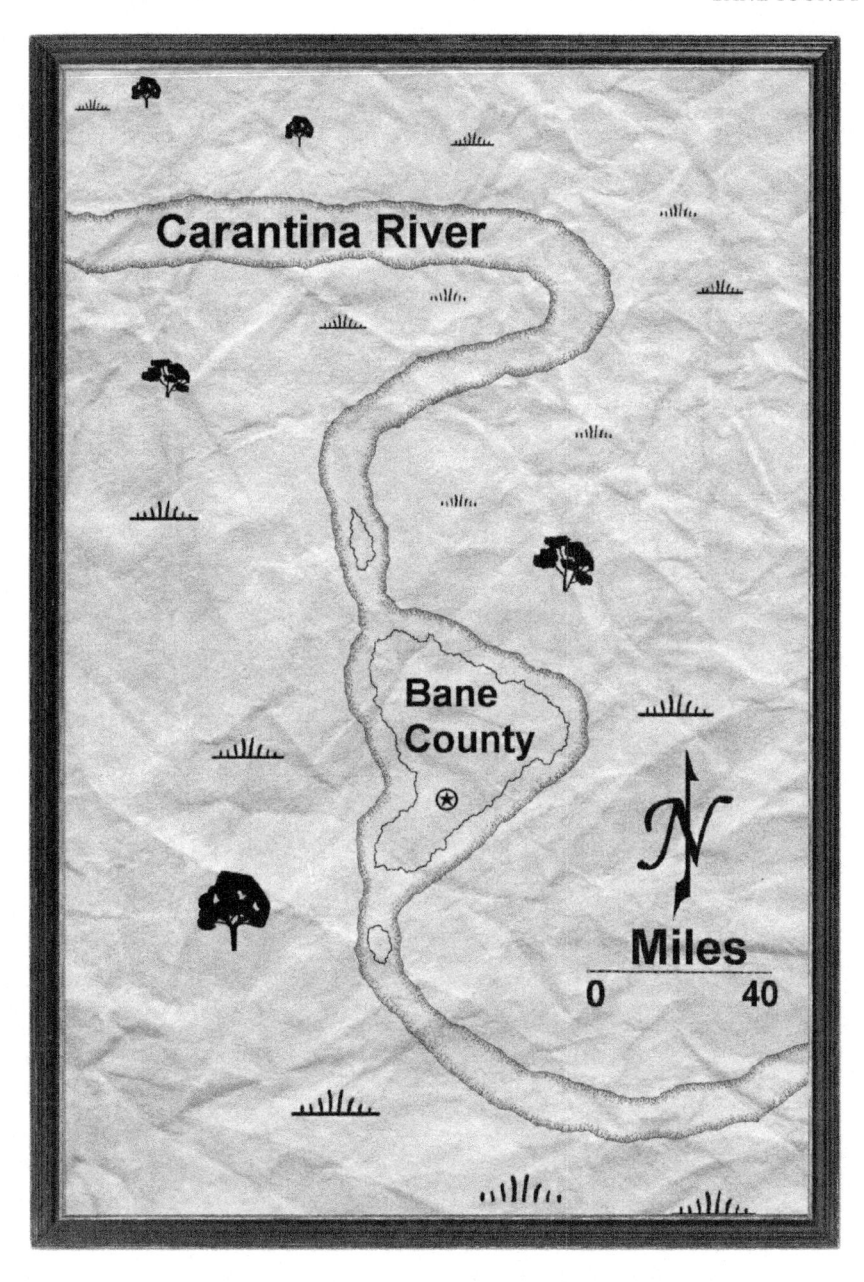

BANE COUNTY

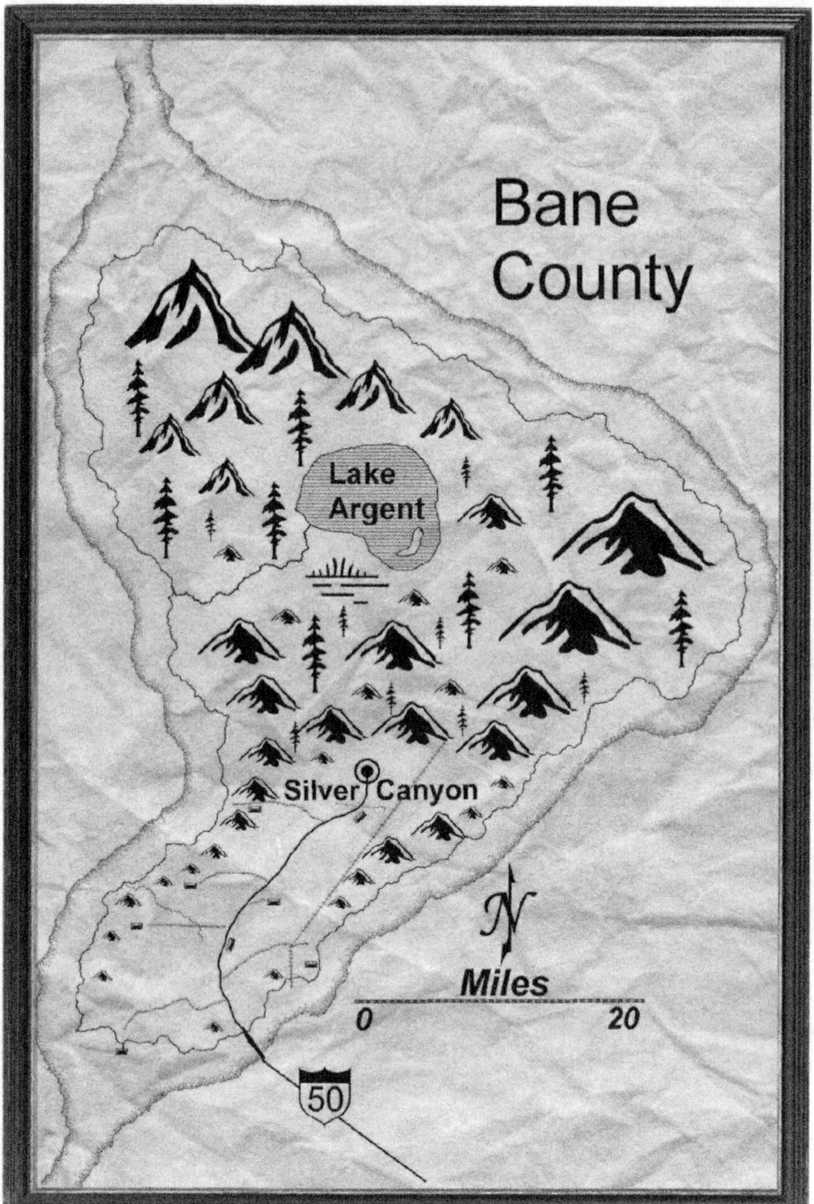
Bane
County
Lake
Argent
Silver Canyon
N
Miles
0
20
50

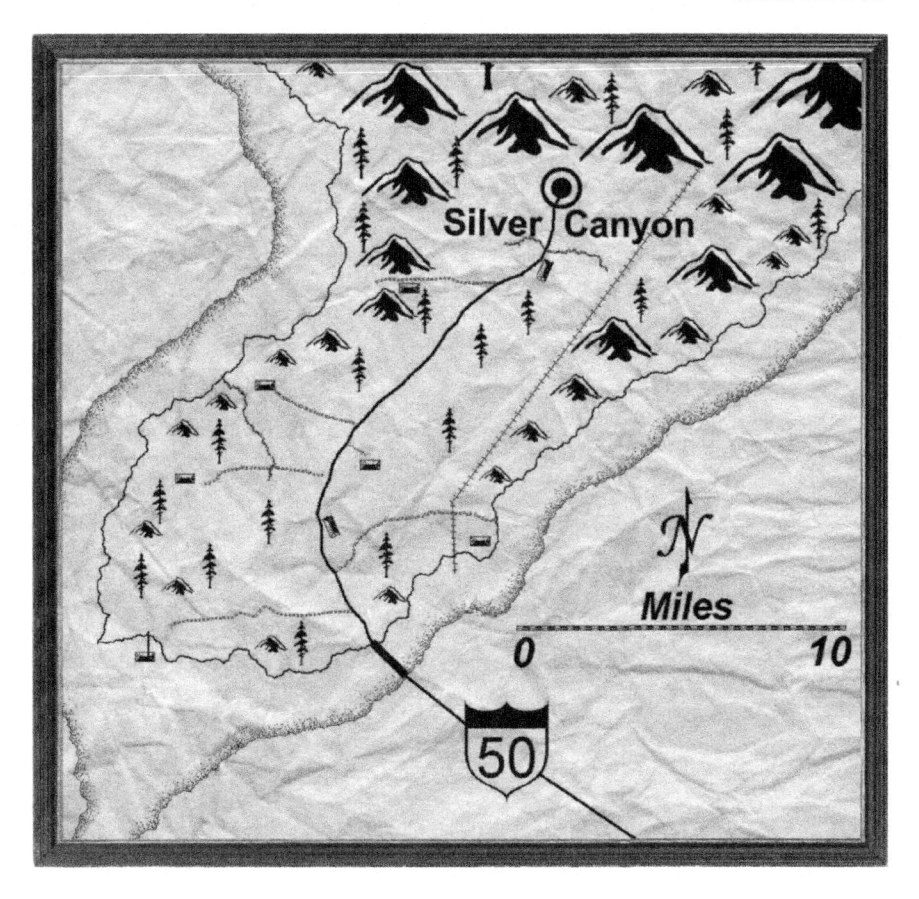

BANE COUNTY

PREFACE

A Cautionary Tale

BECAUSE AT ONE POINT IN MY LIFE, many years ago, I was the parent of two impressionable young children, and because I know that some individuals have no stomach for tales of horror, I felt compelled to forewarn prospective readers—or their parents—of the nature and substance of this novel.

While the story contains no scenes of deviant or sexual behavior, there is a smattering of coarse language and four-letter expletives; though nothing that you couldn't find in a PG-13 rated movie.

On the other hand, the tragic and gruesome demise of both man and beast, and the pain and emotional turmoil that follows, is somewhat prevalent throughout the story; and in a few cases, the graphic descriptions can be quite explicit.

In short, the story is one of suspense and mystery, of discovery and terror, and of the horrifying realization that not all *things* that go bump in the night are imaginary.

So, having been forewarned, and if you choose to continue, please allow me to offer the following historical introduction and set the stage for our journey into darkness—to a remote small town at the edge of a vast wilderness.

Welcome, to Bane County.

J R RICE

INTRODUCTION

Historic Bane County

BANE COUNTY was completely surrounded by water. It wasn't a tropical island in some distant ocean; it was a river-island, formed by a long anabranch of the mighty Carantina River.

Sixty miles long, and forty miles wide, the large river-island of Bane County was almost the size of Delaware, and was located in a remote rural area, far removed from any large city or town.

For the most part, Bane County was unpopulated. The bulk of its landmass consisted of rugged mountains covered with dense forests. Only in the southernmost part of the county—where the mountains ended and a large canyon opened into grasslands—could you find the small populace of Bane County.

The Town of Silver Canyon—the only town *in* Bane County—was home to just under two thousand residents, and like any other small town, everyone knew each other.

In 1878, a prospector by the name of Eugene Howell discovered silver in the mountains of Bane County. Howell—an avid explorer—had been surveying a large cave-system, when he came upon a sizable vein of silver ore. Soon after, the Canyon area near the mountains had become a large mining camp, and the Town of Silver Canyon was born.

A hand-drawn cable-ferry had been built, providing access

to and from the river-island; but a bridge quickly replaced it, as mining companies and private prospectors flooded into the canyon.

As ore production increased, a train trestle and railway spur were constructed, connecting Silver Canyon to the Union-Pacific mainline, and train cars filled with silver ore flowed from Bane County.

Then, in 1896, tragedy struck. A tremendous wildfire engulfed Silver Canyon and destroyed the entire town; not a single structure survived. Survey maps and property deeds for the entire county were incinerated during the intense blaze, casting the region into total chaos. The carnage of the disaster was unspeakable, and it claimed an untold number of lives.

Even though the survivors of the fire were hesitant to speak, news of the conflagration spread quickly. Gossip and rumors were rampant. Various stories of fire-and-death abounded, ranging from the mundane to the surreal; and some of those stories—the ones whispered by hesitant lips—*those* stories, became legend.

In the weeks following the fire, mining operations halted, and eventually ceased altogether. The dwindling ore reserves hadn't warranted a resumption in production. A small handful of survivors—those willing to remain—began the slow and arduous process of rebuilding the Town of Silver Canyon.

Five years later, in 1901, President William McKinley was shot by an assassin and mortally wounded. Upon his death, Vice President Theodore Roosevelt had been sworn into office. Roosevelt—considered by many to be the country's first *conservationist* President—created the nation's premier wildlife refuge.

In 1903, by executive order, the Pelican Island National Wildlife Refuge had been established on the Atlantic coast of central Florida, the first of its kind. By the end of Roosevelt's second term in office, he had issued 52 executive orders, establishing wildlife refuges in 17 states and 4 territories. The large river-island of Bane County had been one of those territories.

In 1905, about ninety percent of Bane County—over one million acres—was annexed by the government, and the Silver Canyon National Wildlife Refuge had been established. Only the southern tip of the county—the large canyon area south of the mountains—remained as private property.

It was the geographical uniqueness of Bane County that had caught Roosevelt's eye. The rugged fault-block mountains —some as high as 6000 feet—shaped and carved over eons, sculpted by ancient glaciers. Giant old-growth forests, so dense and green they were virtually impassable. A large, subalpine lake that encompassed over fifty square miles of crystal-clear water, and a labyrinthine warren of interconnected caverns that spanned the entire refuge.

The abundant verdure of the mountainous river-island was nourished by orographic rainfall, and its diversity could rival that of any South American rainforest. Rare plants and animals abounded within the unique microclimate, with many species still undiscovered.

Over time, Bane County had become somewhat popular due to the wildlife refuge. Each year, hundreds of backpacking enthusiasts flocked to the secluded region, eager to explore its pristine, untouched wilderness. In addition to backpackers, the rare flora and fauna of the area were a Mecca for scientists: biologists, botanists and speleologists—just to name a few— visited the region on a year-round basis to collect scientific data and search for new species.

No roads existed inside the one-million-acre wildlife refuge, and it was not a recommended destination for the average tourist. Only highly experienced, able-bodied individuals were encouraged to enter the grueling and sometimes perilous terrain.

In addition to the treacherous landscape, the wildlife refuge also remained littered with hundreds of abandoned silver mines, however, due to the lack of survey maps—and the heavy regrowth of the forest—the whereabouts of most of these mines were unknown.

While it was unlawful for a person to enter an abandoned mine, many thrill seekers were willing to take the risk. Exploring an old mine could be extremely dangerous and it wasn't unusual for people to go missing from time to time.

In fact—during some years—it was quite common.

PROLOGUE

Winter 1878

A DENSE, LOW-LYING FOG HUNG IN THE DISTANCE. A murky harbinger of death, it spread across the land like a funeral pall, heralding the coming slaughter.

Today would be the young one's first kill.

Moving silently across the canyon floor, concealed within the waist-high grass, he edged closer to his prey. Keeping his chest low to the ground, he crawled on his belly, gliding stealthily through the cold, dank weeds. Plump drops of early-morning dew clung to the tall grass, beading each blade like gemstones, shimmering in the orange light of dawn.

Slowly inching forward—parting through the grass—a continual cascade of dewdrops showered him. His body soaked, unaffected by the harsh elements, he focused only on the kill.

The shrill bugle of a bull elk resonated across the canyon, his presence obscured by the cottony shroud of mist. The young one moved into position, lying patiently in wait behind a large thicket.

A tiny field mouse scuttled across the ground in front of him, stopping only inches from his nose. Motionless, the little mouse cowered with fear, his bulging, black eyes searching for an escape. With a momentary loss of focus, the young one cocked his head and studied the small creature.

Again—much louder—the bull elk bugled in the distance; it was closer now, the time to attack was near. Hidden behind a thorny briar, the young one rose to his knees, peering through the thick underbrush. Through the morning murk, he watched the herd of elk. They had come down from the northern mountains to graze in the verdant canyon. There, in their midst, was the large bull, his towering antlers reached to the sky.

Within the dense thicket, the young one rose cautiously to his feet, heart pounding in his chest. The attack needed to be perfect—and it *would* have been—were it not for the appearance of an unexpected breeze.

One of the elk released a high-pitched bark; she had caught the scent of a predator on the wind. The entire herd reacted, their eyes searching for danger, unsure of which direction to run. Now, out of time, the young one leapt from the thicket and attacked the bull elk.

He raised his bow and loosed an arrow. Slipping through the morning mist the arrow struck home—hitting the elk's ribcage, it punctured his lung. The massive elk flinched at the arrow's sting, and then galloped away with the herd.

Behind the young Indian boy, the proud cries of his father were heard; they echoed across the canyon. The young boy looked back at his father, a huge smile on his face; he knew he had done well. Quickly, the boy turned and raced across the canyon floor, pursuing the wounded elk through the grasslands.

They followed the blood-trail north, to where the elk had re-entered the mountains. The young boy looked to his father, and then sadly hung his head. He was heartbroken. He knew they couldn't follow the wounded elk into the northern mountains; it was against tribal law.

The mountains to the north were forbidden. Every tribe of the Indian nation knew the legend of this canyon; the elders had passed it down since the first dawn. The mountains north of the canyon were the hunting grounds of the *Ba'cho Najin*: the Standing-Wolf.

The Standing-Wolf was an ancient creature who existed long before the Great Spirit created man. It was a fierce, gigantic beast, much larger than the Great-bear. It walked upright, on two legs and ran faster than the pronghorn antelope. Sleeping in caves by day, deep within the earth, it waited for darkness to fall. The Standing-Wolf was a ruthless hunter of men, and would devour anyone who entered his lands.

The legend told of a foolish young brave who decided to hunt in the mountains north of the canyon. Knowing the Standing-Wolf slept by day, the young brave believed it safe to invade its land. After the hunt, he traveled many miles back to his village, believing he had outwitted the mighty beast.

That night, the creature followed the young brave's trail across the canyon and attacked his village. The men of his tribe fought the Standing-Wolf, but their spears and arrows could do no harm. Only a few women and children that fled into the riparian forest had survived, the rest were slaughtered by the beast.

The boy and his father wouldn't make the same mistake as the foolish young brave. They would never follow a wounded elk into the northern mountains. There were plenty of elk in the canyon, and there would be other days to hunt.

In the distance, the bray of a complaining mule could be heard, followed by a scolding voice—the voice of a white-man. The boy and his father quickly concealed themselves in the rocks, behind a large thorn-bush. They couldn't allow this white-man to see them. If he did, they would have to kill him. Then again, they might kill him anyway. No white-man was allowed to enter the sacred canyon.

As the white-man rode past, they saw that he didn't wear the bluecoat of the soldiers. His buckskin clothing was dark and wet—soaked while fording the deep river. He sat astride a tall, roan stallion, tugging at the reins of an overladen pack-mule who complained and followed reluctantly.

Resting under his hand was a Winchester 1876 Centennial, it sat sideways across his saddle. The big-bore repeating rifle instilled a healthy level of fear and respect in all those who saw it. This was the first white-man they had seen since leaving the reservation, and that was five winters ago.

The small tribe of Indians had been living in the secluded canyon, hiding from the bluecoats who searched for them. They had been lied to by the double-tongues, and forced to live on a reservation; but they had refused, escaping to the distant canyon.

They traveled far to take refuge in the hidden canyon, a sanctuary known only to the tribes of the nation. It was a land completely surrounded by a mighty river—cloaked from prying eyes. No white-man had ever seen the hallowed canyon, or even knew of its existence.

The canyon was a secret place, a holy place, a place that was drenched in tribal lore. It was the one place thought safe to hide—and it *had* been safe—until just that moment. Seeing a white-man after all this time, was a bad sign. Soon, the bluecoats might be coming, too.

The letters E. HOWELL were stenciled on a wooden crate strapped to the mule's back, but they couldn't read the white-man's words. They only knew it wasn't the same symbols as used by the soldiers.

Suddenly, the young boy was overcome with dread. He watched in disbelief, as the white-man rode unknowingly into the northern mountains. He looked to his father with pleading eyes, as if to say, "*We should warn him*," but he knew they could not.

No white-man could ever know that his tribe lived in the

hidden canyon. A white-man would tell the bluecoats; then, the pony-soldiers would come, and force them back to the reservation.

As the white-man disappeared into the dark, forbidding forest—into the hunting grounds of the Standing-Wolf—the boy's father felt a sense of relief.

There was no need to kill the white-man, he realized. *Perhaps, this hadn't been a bad sign after all.*

As the boy and his father continued on to their village, the boy asked, "What will become of the white-man, Father?"

His father replied, "The Standing-Wolf will take him."

The boy nodded, and then asked thoughtfully, "Why is the Standing-Wolf here, Father? Why does he choose to live in *these* mountains?"

His father smiled and mussed his son's hair. "The Standing-Wolf lives here for the same reason we do," he said, "... because it's a good place to hide."

CHAPTER 1

Autumn 1953

IT WAS A CLOUDLESS SEPTEMBER AFTERNOON when Gladys Rickman set out from her farmhouse down the long dirt road that led to her mailbox on Ranch-Road 10. Gladys was spry for a woman of sixty-seven, and she moved quickly, like a woman on a mission.

"It better be there," she warned.

Up ahead in the road, her dog, Rusty—a large tan-and-black bloodhound—stopped and looked back at her. Gladys was annoyed. In fact, she was hotter than a billy-goat's ass in a pepper patch, and she didn't care who knew about it.

"It should've been here *days* ago . . . lazy, no-good mail-service," she grumbled. Laboring forward, she left a trail of dust in her wake.

As she spoke, Rusty stared at Gladys and cocked his head with concern. He was very protective and her tone was making him uneasy. Gladys made a habit of talking to herself on a regular basis and Rusty knew her every mood by the tone of her voice.

When she arrived at the mailbox, Gladys jerked open the door and quickly looked inside. "Well, it's about time."

She smiled and pulled her new Farmer's Almanac from the box. Gladys had ordered another copy of the publication last month, replacing the one she forgot outside the night of the big rainstorm.

Rusty had found the lost book the next morning, while patrolling the garden. He had retrieved the remains and brought them to Gladys, but when the almanac fell from his mouth, it had landed like a giant spit-wad. She didn't know whether to laugh or cry upon seeing the remnants of her book, but she still praised Rusty for his thoughtfulness.

On the long walk back home, Gladys riffled through the pages of her new almanac. "I'm almost certain it happens tonight," she muttered.

She thumbed through the book until she found the information she sought. "It *is* tonight," she said, with a pleased smile. "September 23—tonight is a *true* harvest moon."

Gladys only remembered a couple of times in her life when a full moon took place on the night of the fall equinox—making it a *true* harvest moon.

A *regular* harvest moon happened every year. It was simply whichever full moon took place *nearest* to the fall equinox. But a *true* harvest moon—when the full moon and the fall equinox took place on *exactly* the same night—well, that only happened a few times each century. This was *truly* a special night.

Rusty had noticed the cheerful tone of Gladys's voice and loped back down the road to investigate. He sat at her feet and cocked his head, a perplexed look on his face. She looked down at him and spoke in an animated, playful tone.

"We're working in the garden tonight; won't that be fun?"

Rusty always became overly excited when Gladys spoke playfully. He reared up on his hind legs, put his front paws on her shoulders and licked her square on the mouth.

"Ugh, get down," she sputtered. "I'm too old to have a huge dog jumping on me."

Rusty hopped down, ran a circle around Gladys barking, and

took off for the house as if his tail was on fire. She laughed and shook her head. *That dog is nuts,* she thought.

By the time Gladys finally arrived back at the house, Rusty had lost all patience. He had been sitting on the front porch watching her for what seemed an eternity. As she stepped onto the porch Rusty gave a muffled bark, as if to say, *what took you so long?*

Gladys chuckled and wagged her finger at the impatient hound. "You just hold your horses," she chided. "A half-mile is a long walk for an old lady. We'll get started in a little while after I've rested a bit."

Gladys walked across the porch toward a pair of old rocking chairs. She stepped past the first chair with reverence and sat in the smaller chair at its side. Rusty lowered his head somberly and followed her, lying down between the two chairs. He rested his head quietly on his paws and stared out into the garden. Gladys put her hand on Rusty's back and patted him gently.

"I miss him, too, boy," she said wistfully. "I miss him, too." Rusty didn't move, he just breathed a heavy sigh, and then closed his eyes.

Gladys's husband, Bill, had passed away earlier that year, and now, it was just her and Rusty on the Rickman farm. Her children had long since moved away to the big-city, and only came back to visit her on the holidays. They were constantly asking her to sell the farm and come live with them in the city, but Gladys would never sell the farm. She had worked this land for over fifty-two years, and the land itself had been in the Rickman family for almost seventy-five. Her children just couldn't seem to understand the importance of history.

Lester Rickman, her husband's father, had given the land to Gladys and Bill as a wedding gift back in 1901. The two-hundred-acre-plot was located in Bane County, about ten-miles south from the Town of Silver Canyon.

Her father, Eugene Howell, was the man who first discovered silver in Bane County, back in 1878. Why, if it weren't for Gladys's father, the Town of Silver Canyon might not even exist.

Her father had started the region's first silver mine, and for many years it had been very prosperous. Sadly, though, he had died during a fire in 1896, and the mine eventually closed.

Even though Gladys was only ten-years-old at the time, she still remembered the night her father died. Standing with her mother in the backyard of their home, miles from town, they saw the haunting glow of flames on the distant horizon. It wasn't until the next day—when news of the fire had reached them—that she learned of her father's death.

Gladys knew she'd never leave her farm, regardless of how many times her children asked. There was just too much family history in Bane County—and history should *never* be forgotten.

THE SUN WAS BEGINNING TO SET when Gladys removed her gardening tools and baskets from the shed, preparing for the evening harvest. It had been her and Bill's tradition to work late into the night during the harvest moon, bringing in the crops.

When the harvest was complete, they would always open a bottle of Gladys's homemade blackberry wine to celebrate. She and Bill would sit talking and laughing until the wee hours of the morning. Those were some of the happiest memories of her life.

Tonight would be her first harvest moon without Bill, and she was determined to keep the tradition going to honor his memory. The fact that tonight would be a *true* harvest moon, made it even more special.

"Okay, Rusty, garden patrol," Gladys announced.

Rusty had been raring to go. He jumped up and headed straight for the garden. Walking up one row and down the other, he sniffed under every plant. For years, it had been Rusty's job to check the garden for snakes and other threats to Gladys. It was his duty to protect her and he took that very seriously. When Rusty finished his rounds and felt it was safe, he would always look over at Gladys and bark.

Woof . . .

"Thank you, Rusty," she said, praising his diligence. Gladys loved Rusty with all her heart; to her, he was family.

She entered the garden and began harvesting the Indian corn, while Rusty kept diligent watch. From time to time, he would walk up and down the rows again, rechecking for any danger.

About a half-hour into the harvest, a brilliant, yellow moon rose above the treetops of the neighboring forest. Gladys stopped her work and took a moment to admire the spectacular sight. "I don't think I've ever seen a bigger or brighter full moon. It's almost as bright as daylight out here, Rusty."

At the mention of his name, Rusty looked up briefly, but went straight back to patrolling. After admiring the moon for a moment, Gladys moved on to harvest the squash.

Time flew by, and the moon rose higher and higher into the lofty night sky. A light breeze had begun to blow from the direction of the forest. It was a cool breeze and sent a chill over Gladys. "Brrr . . . I'm going inside to grab a sweater. I'll be right back, Rusty."

Rusty glanced at her, but something else had just caught his attention. A strange scent was in the air coming from the forest. A scent that Rusty had never smelled before—a fetid scent. He raised his nose high into the air and sniffed deeply. A soft, involuntary growl rumbled in his chest.

Rusty walked slowly toward the forest with his nose raised high into the wind. He lowered his head and searched the tree line for any movements or sounds that didn't belong. The scent was growing stronger, and getting closer.

Something bad was coming—and it was coming fast.

A large figure appeared at the edge of the forest about a hundred yards away, it crept slowly from the dark shadows that pooled beneath the trees. Rusty's heart raced as adrenaline coursed through his body. An angry growl formed in his chest, hackles bristling.

What was this thing, a man? It stood upright like a man, but it was taller—much taller. It just stood there at the edge of the forest, staring toward the house. Rusty froze in place, his eyes fixed on the strange creature; a threatening growl radiated from his chest... and then—it happened.

From behind him, Rusty heard his name.

"Rusty! Where are you?" Gladys hollered loudly, from the front porch.

He spun around to face her and gave a single bark, as if to say, *be quiet!*

When he looked back, the creature was moving forward, straight for the house—straight for Gladys. Rusty ran toward her barking frantically, trying to make her understand: *get in the house!* He stopped at the edge of the garden and placed himself between Gladys and the strange beast.

Rusty stood guard, growling, as the creature came closer and closer; what was this thing? It wasn't charging forward and it wasn't trying to remain hidden. It was just calmly walking toward the house, completely free of fear. As the huge beast neared the house, Rusty heard a loud gasp from behind him.

"Oh, my God!" Gladys cried, when she caught sight of the

horrible creature.

Her heart jumped in her chest and her knees buckled; she couldn't believe what she was seeing. Faint with fear, she grabbed hold of a porch post to steady herself.

Gladys had heard the stories, ever since she was a little girl—everyone had—but she never believed they were true. Only crazy people—superstitious old fools—actually believed in the legend. It was just a myth, folklore, a scary bedtime story told to naughty children to make them behave.

Dear God, it's true . . .

She slowly backed away toward the front door, calling for Rusty to come with her. He ignored her plea; all of his senses told him this thing was dangerous, deadly. It had to be stopped before it got to the house—before it got to Gladys.

He lowered his head and moved menacingly forward—baring his teeth and growling viciously—but his actions had no effect on the creature. It continued walking calmly toward the house. Rusty now knew: the only way to stop this thing would be to kill it.

The creature was over eight-feet-tall with a rangy, muscular body. Its dark, rugose skin was covered with a sparse layer of long, mangy hair the color of gray moss. The beast's massive hands extended to its knees, and its long, spindly fingers were tipped with huge, hooked claws. An enormous snout filled with sharp, jagged teeth and massive fangs drooled with anticipation. Pointed ears rose atop its matted mane and coal-black eyes peered from its hideous face. Its filth-covered body reeked of rotting flesh, and the putrid stench pervaded the air as it continued tromping forward.

Rusty's muscles tensed as he prepared to charge. Everything else faded away as he focused on bringing down the beast. He could no longer hear Gladys's calls urging him back—nothing else existed. In his mind's eye, there was only him . . . and the beast.

Rusty exploded forward in a thunderous rage. He closed the distance between him and the enormous creature in mere seconds. At the last possible moment, his powerful hind legs drove him upward at incredible speed. He opened his mouth and lunged for the beast's throat . . . but it slapped the dog to the ground and held him there with one of its massive clawed hands. Rusty struggled violently to free himself, but the hideous creature pinned him to the ground with little effort.

Over the sound of Rusty's vicious growls and snapping teeth, Gladys cried out in a furious rage. "Let him go, you werewolf son of a bitch!"

The beast jerked its head around and glared into Gladys's eyes, his razored teeth almost mimicking a grotesque smile. While she watched, the werewolf swiped his taloned fingers across Rusty's throat and severed the dog's head.

"NO!" she screamed.

Gladys turned and ran toward the front door, but stumbled and fell, her legs weak with fear. Pulling herself up, she limped through the doorway and locked it behind her.

Outside, the beast knelt over the dog, lapping the warm blood that flowed from its body, but this wasn't the luscious liquid he craved. Rising to his feet, the werewolf stalked toward the house, compelled by a voracious desire for human flesh. Stepping onto the porch, the massive creature loomed outside the front door, waiting, savoring his coming meal.

Inside the house, Gladys ran to the hall closet where her husband had kept his guns. Her heart pounding, she grabbed a double-barrel shotgun and clutched it tightly. Opening the breech, she looked inside.

Empty . . .

Gladys rummaged frantically through the closet, searching for the box where her husband had stored his ammunition.

She finally spotted the shoebox on the top shelf, just out of reach. Jumping as high as she could, Gladys caught the edge of the box with the tip of her finger and toppled it over. Ammunition crashed to the floor and scattered everywhere. Dropping to her knees, she quickly scavenged through the pile of loose ammunition until she found two 12-gauge shells. Using the shotgun for support, Gladys pulled herself to her feet. Her hands were trembling with fear and rage as she struggled to slip the shells into the gun.

"I'm gonna kill that rotten son of a bitch," she snarled, slamming the guns breech shut with a loud click.

Trying to swallow her fear, Gladys gripped the shotgun tightly and strode resolutely into the living room. The werewolf stood waiting, just outside her front door. The height of the monstrous creature was so great, that only its chest was visible through the door's window. Gladys stood in horror, as the giant beast slowly lowered its head and pressed its hideous, wolf-like face against the glass. A sickening, bloody drool flowed from its rancid mouth and trickled slowly down the windowpane. Gladys knew it was Rusty's blood.

As if to announce his arrival, the beast dragged its long, hooked claws down the doorframe, causing an unbearable scraping noise. Slicing like wood-chisels, each claw left a curly shaving in its wake, as they carved deep grooves into the wood.

Without warning, the werewolf smashed into the door with tremendous force. Wood splinters and broken glass showered the room as the door exploded. Gladys screamed and tried to cover her face with the shotgun, as glass and wood peppered her body.

The enormous beast ducked his head under the doorframe and entered the room, just as Gladys aimed the shotgun at his chest and pulled the trigger. A small flame danced from the shotgun's muzzle, as a loud blast sent a round of #6 birdshot into the beast. The impact of the shot caused the werewolf to stumble back, smashing his head into the top of the doorframe. Stunned and infuriated, he started to move forward, but Gladys quickly aimed and unloaded her second barrel into the beast, knocking him out the door and flat onto his back.

Now, in an uncontrollable rage, the creature sprang to his feet and released an immense, unearthly roar, causing her to drop the shotgun and cover her ears. As the werewolf re-entered the house and stalked toward Gladys, she fell to her knees crying and began to pray. She wasn't asking God to save her, she was asking Him to forgive her sins. Gladys knew she was about to die.

The werewolf reached down and wrapped a clawed hand around her throat; she coughed and sputtered violently as the beast lifted her high into the air. Tightening his grip, she was unable to scream, and her feet dangled helplessly above the floor. Drool poured over the creature's black lips as it stared hungrily into Gladys's eyes. Leaning forward, the werewolf cocked his head and rubbed his filthy, wet nose across her cheek, snuffling her hair. He relished the smell of fear.

With his other hand, the beast dragged a single claw across her stomach. It sliced through cloth and skin like a straight-razor as he disemboweled her.

As Gladys's body began to go into shock, she could hear the wet splattering sound of entrails falling to the floor. Reaching a clawed hand inside of her body, the beast ripped out her liver and raised it to his fetid mouth. As she slipped into darkness, Gladys's final image was that of the werewolf devouring her liver.

Dropping her lifeless body to the floor, the creature knelt and began his frenzied feast. He devoured his prey greedily, gorging himself on the succulent flesh and organs. The horrific sounds of ripping flesh and snapping bones filled the night, as Gladys's body was torn to shreds. Blood and gore painted the room, as the beast wallowed and reveled in his butchery.

Rising from the blood-soaked floor, the werewolf moved outside into the night; his hair and body drenched in Gladys's blood. Much like a wet dog, the beast shook himself, flinging blood and small gobbets of raw flesh from his hair. A macabre, moonlit halo surrounded the creature—a fine mist of blood that sparkled in the cool night air as it drifted slowly to the ground.

His rancid black tongue slurped and savored every drop of blood as he cleaned his long, spindly fingers. Using his spiked teeth, he picked small gobs of flesh from beneath his long claws, relishing each tiny morsel as if it were the last course of an evening meal.

Raising his soulless, black eyes to the heavens, the werewolf searched the night sky for his irradiant master. The *true* harvest moon beckoned covetously from the starry sky; it called to him relentlessly.

The moon reflected brightly in the eyes of the beast with an eerie, demonic glow. Like apertures in the furnace door of Hell —his eyes blazed with raging amber fire.

Drawing a deep breath, the creature released a thunderous howl that echoed for miles through the darkness; then skulking across the moonlit field, he disappeared into the dense, shadowy forest.

FOUR DAYS PASSED before a neighbor noticed a circle of buzzards flying over the Rickman's house and contacted the Bane County Sheriff's Office.

Deputy Dalton Morrow was sitting in his car at CB's Drive-in eating lunch when the call came across the radio.

"Base to car three, can you read me, Dalton—over?"

It never fails, he thought. *Every time I stop for lunch, that woman calls me.*

"Yeah, I read you, Delores. Go ahead—over."

"Dalton, we just got a call from Pat's gas station out on Highway 50. Pat said somebody told him they'd seen some buzzards flying by the Rickman's house over off Ranch-Road 10. The sheriff wants you to go out there and have a look—over."

Well that just figures . . . somebody sees a damn buzzard, and it's the end of the world.

"All right, tell the sheriff I'm on my way. Oh and Delores . . . you didn't happen to ask Pat who it was that reported this, did you—over?"

"Uh . . . no, Dalton, I didn't. But, I can call him back if you want—over."

I swear . . . that woman couldn't pour water out of a boot if the directions were written on the heel.

"No, don't worry about it. I'll stop in and talk with Pat myself while I'm out there."

Jesus Christ—a buzzard! What's next . . . be on the lookout for squirrels?

Dalton took a final bite of his foot-long chili-cheese-dog and slid it back into the bag. Then he headed south on Highway 50.

After about fifteen minutes, he turned off the highway and made his way down Ranch-Road 10. When he veered onto the dirt road leading to the Rickman's house, a sick feeling came over him. Deputy Morrow had been a lawman in Bane County for almost twenty years, and he had learned to trust his instincts. He could see a wake of buzzards feeding in the field, and a dozen more of the wretched, black vultures were circling overhead. Dalton knew without a doubt—this was gonna be bad.

Parking his car in front of the Rickman's house, he stepped out and slipped on his Stetson hat. "Mrs. Rickman!" he hollered. "Bane County Sheriff's Office."

He was making his way toward the buzzards on the ground, when he noticed the front door of the house had been smashed in. Dalton reached down and slipped his .45 Long Colt from its holster. He eased the hammer back one notch, half-cocked.

"Bane County Sheriff's Office!" he shouted, again.

His thumb still resting on the hammer, Dalton lifted his revolver partway and turned a slow circle, surveying his surroundings. He wanted to make damn sure that he was alone. Continuing toward the buzzards, he stomped his feet and yelled. "Get . . . get-on, you smelly bastards." When the buzzards cleared, he saw it was a dog they were eating.

Damn . . . where the hell is your head?

Dalton turned and walked toward the house. As he drew near, he noticed the huge bloody footprints on the front porch. He dropped to one knee to have a better look. They were bigger than any man's footprint and appeared to have claws for toes.

What the hell . . .

Rising to his feet, he moved slowly toward the doorway. His eyes widened at the giant claw marks carved into the doorframe. Dalton traced the contour of the deep grooves with his finger.

Jesus Christ . . .

From out on the porch, he could hear the plangent buzzing of flies inside the house. The place was a shambles: blood and gore were everywhere. When Dalton entered and saw what was left of Mrs. Rickman, it took all his strength to keep from retching up his lunch.

"Sweet Mother of God," he intoned.

She was torn to shreds—what was left of her—and pieces

were strewn all around the room; large bones laid bare and gnawed upon. Across the room, the pointed shade of a large floor-lamp was festooned with entrails and swarming with metallic-green blowflies. It looked like some sort of, grotesque Christmas tree.

Dalton lowered the hammer on his revolver and holstered it, then made his way cautiously across the room. It was like moving through a minefield. Blood and gore squished underfoot, sticking to the soles of his boots. It held each step in place like flypaper.

Slowly moving forward, he watched a large barn-rat scuttle across the room and disappear beneath the couch; its blood-boltered body was dark and wet.

Using his bandana, Dalton picked up the blood-encrusted shotgun from the floor and opened its breech. He saw that both shells had dented primers. Pulling the empty hulls from the gun he saw the #6 stamped on their side.

Well . . . at least she got off a couple of shots, he thought. *Even if, it was only birdshot.*

Flies and maggots covered the entire room, buzzing, and crawling, and writhing through the carnage. One small piece of remains had been so filled with maggots it actually crept across the floor, as if reanimated by some evil, demonic presence.

The stench and horror inside the house became more than Dalton could endure. Saliva flooded his mouth and he felt as though he would vomit. He laid the shotgun on the floor and hurried outside into the front yard.

For a long moment, Dalton stood in place, frantically wiping his bloody boots on the grass. Finally, he removed his Stetson and squatted down, trying to clear his head. The stench of death seemed to permeate his very soul. He took a deep, cleansing breath and exhaled through his mouth. Staring toward the dense forest, he shook his head despondently.

"What in God's name am I gonna say to her family?" he breathed.

Slipping on his hat, he pulled a can of Copenhagen from his pocket and took a dip. He worked the small bolus of tobacco between his cheek and gum for a moment, then pursed up his lips and spat on the grass.

Well, shit . . . guess I better call it in.

Hoping he wasn't out of radio range, Dalton hopped into the car and shut the door. He keyed the button on the microphone a couple of times and gave it a try.

"Car three to base . . . Delores this is Dalton, can you read me —over?"

Mixed with static, a woman's tinny voice came over the radio. "Go ahead Dalton, I can read you—over."

"Delores, I need you to get Sheriff Cooper for me. Right away, please—over."

Smacking her chewing gum, Delores turned and hollered across the small office. "Tom, Dalton's on the radio!"

Sheriff Tom Cooper flinched at the sound of her voice and looked up from his paperwork. "You don't have to shout, woman. I'm not deaf," he hissed.

"Well, you sure seem deaf enough when I ask you to do chores around the house," she sniped.

The sheriff smiled and gave a little wink to his wife as he took the microphone from her hand. "Go ahead, Dalton."

"Sheriff . . . I need you out here at the Rickman farm right away. Mrs. Rickman's been . . . well . . . there's been an animal attack—over."

An uneasy look came across Sheriff Cooper's face. "What the heck happened, Dalton—over?"

Not wanting to discuss the gory details over open airwaves, Dalton shook his head impatiently. "Tom . . . I really need you to come out here and see this for yourself—over."

Sheriff Cooper smiled at his now-nervous wife and gently squeezed her hand to reassure her. "All right, Dalton. Just stay put, it'll take me about fifteen minutes to get out there."

Dalton leaned back in his car seat and tried to relax.

Stay put . . . where the hell would I go?

He stared nervously toward the shadow-painted forest, and then looked over at the smashed front door. Dalton thought about the giant footprints he had seen and the claw marks on the doorframe. His mind began to imagine what kind of horror Mrs. Rickman must have faced.

It sure is quiet out here . . .

With an unexpected shudder, fear scampered down Dalton's spine like a furry-legged spider and his skin pebbled with goosebumps. He reached over his shoulder and slammed down the door lock, then slipped his Colt out of its holster and sat it on the seat beside him.

Just in case . . .

When Sheriff Cooper finally arrived at the Rickman farm, Dalton walked over to greet him.

"What the hell's going on out here?" Tom asked, shaking Dalton's hand, but before he could respond, the sheriff headed toward the front porch.

"Hang on a minute," Dalton said, grabbing Tom's arm. "I need to tell you something before you go over there."

"Tell me what?" Tom asked; surprised by the hand that was gripping his arm.

"Now just bear with me, Tom," Dalton pleaded, releasing his grip. "Do you remember way back when—must be, almost twenty years ago—soon after I joined the sheriff's office and we had all those animal attacks around the Silver Canyon Wildlife Refuge?"

Tom's face lost all expression, caught off guard by the old memory. "Yeah, I remember."

"And do you remember the last body we found, right before Christmas?"

Tom shifted his feet, appearing impatient at the line of questioning. "Yeah, I remember, Dalton—where are you going with this?"

"Do you remember the strange footprints we found?"

"What the hell does *that* have to do with *this*?" Tom barked.

Dalton motioned with his chin toward the front porch. "Go have a look."

They moved to the porch and squatted next to the footprints. Tom saw blood everywhere as he glanced through the open doorway.

"Je-sus wept," he intoned.

Fixing his eyes on the footprints, Tom shook his head in disbelief. "It can't be . . . how in the *hell* is this possible?"

Dalton placed a hand on Tom's shoulder. "They're exactly the same as the ones we saw in the wildlife refuge almost twenty years ago—I'll never forget those footprints as long as I live."

Tom nodded his head slowly in agreement. "You're right, Dalton. They're the same footprints."

Even though Tom Cooper was the sheriff, Dalton seemed to take control of the situation and began cautioning him. "The last time this . . . *thing* showed up, fifteen people were either killed, or went missing," he pointed out. "We need to warn people, Tom—tell them to stay inside their homes at night. People need to keep their doors locked and their weapons loaded."

Tom made his way to the demolished front door and looked inside. He stared in horror at the remains of Gladys Rickman's mutilated body and the shotgun lying beside her on the floor; he shook his head despairingly.

"I don't think that'll do much good, Dalton . . . I don't think that'll do much good at all."

CHAPTER 2

Summer 1991

BRYCE McNEEL was confused—stunned, actually. Why had *he* been chosen for this task? There were certainly more qualified people readily available—professional people, skilled people, people who could accomplish this task *without* being killed.

It made absolutely no sense, where was the logic? What could possibly be gained by asking him to risk his life? *Reckless*—that's what this was—*reckless*. A total disregard for the safety and welfare of others.

"Come on, Bryce, we ain't got all day," Grandpa McNeel hollered, from his perch atop the tall wooden fence surrounding the corral. Sitting to the left of Grandpa McNeel was Doc Waggner, the best—and only—livestock veterinarian in Bane County.

"Just talk to him, son," Doc Waggner encouraged calmly, from the safety of his perch.

Bryce glared at the two old men; they looked like a pair of greedy old turkey-buzzards waiting for something to die. He couldn't decide which one was more infuriating: his grandpa, with his big, jack-o'-lantern smile, or Doc Waggner and his crooked grin; with one corner of his mouth raised, he looked like a hooked fish.

"Quit your dithering, we've got a fence to build," Grandpa

McNeel hollered.

"All ri—" Bryce started to yell, but then thought better of it. He remembered where he was and quickly lowered his voice. "All right!" he hissed softly.

Standing inside the corral with Bryce was Happy Jack, Grandpa McNeel's prize-winning bull. Happy Jack was a *Chianina*, a breed first imported from Italy back in the 1970s. It was pronounced, *kee-a-nee-na*, but however you said it, Happy Jack was enormous.

He stood six-feet-tall from his withers to the ground and tipped the scales at 3300 pounds. He outweighed a *Ford Taurus* automobile by 250 pounds—the only *other* type of bull that even came close to his weight-class. He was steel-gray on the front half of his body, and faded to white toward the rear. His hair was short-and-slick and showed the ripple of every muscle as he moved.

Happy Jack was a purebred breeding bull and Grandpa had been selling his services to other ranchers for years. Earlier that day, however, Happy Jack had taken it upon himself to do a little *unauthorized* breeding.

Apparently, Grandpa's herd of Black Angus heifers had been tempting Happy Jack with their buxom bodies and insistent lowing. Beguiled by their feminine charms, he had no other choice but to answer their siren call.

Despite the taut, six-strand barbed-wire fence between Happy Jack's paddock and the south field, he had decided to pay a social call on the horny heifers. When you weigh-in at 3300 pounds, a barbed-wire fence is more of a *suggestion* than a deterrent.

With the promise of sweet-feed, Grandpa had managed to lure Happy Jack away from his bovine debauchery, and back to the corral where he could inspect his injuries. The barbed wire had caused several deep scratches and lacerations to his legs and underbelly, urging Grandpa to call Doc Waggner. After examination, Doc had said no stitches were needed, but an antibiotic injection would be a good idea. That's when Doc handed a large, stainless-steel syringe to Bryce.

Wait—what?

Happy Jack stood opposite Bryce in the corral with his head held low to the ground—pissed. Not only had Grandpa taken away his girlfriends, he had only given him a single handful of sweet-feed for his trouble.

"Just clap him on the neck a couple times, then slip him the needle, son. That way, he'll never feel a thing," Doc said, with a snicker.

"I don't think he *wants* to be clapped on the neck," Bryce pointed out nervously.

Happy Jack lifted his head and bellowed loudly, popping his tail from side to side; he pawed at the ground and snorted, raising a cloud of dust. Bryce took a step back.

"Stand your ground, son," Grandpa urged, trying to fight back a fit of laughter.

"Let him know who the boss is," Doc added, with a snort.

Both of the old men began to laugh so hard they almost fell off the fence. Bryce glared at the two old codgers. "Sadists," he accused.

To Grandpa, Doc asked, "What'd he call us?"

To Doc, Grandpa replied, "Hell if I know. I don't understand half the words that boy uses; he's too damn smart for me."

Happy Jack had lost all patience. He lowered his head and lunged forward, lifting Bryce off the ground, knocking him backward about fifteen feet. He landed flat on his back with a hard, hollow thud, air blasting from his lungs.

To Grandpa, Doc commented, "Good thing we de-horned ol' Happy Jack, huh?"

Grandpa pursed his lips and nodded the affirmative.

Happy Jack stalked over to Bryce—who was still lying on his back with the wind knocked out of him. The massive bull loomed over him, sniffing at Bryce's head with his giant, wet nose.

"Help," Bryce squeaked.

A huge pink-and-gray tongue slurped across Bryce's face as Happy Jack began slobbering all over him.

"I think that bull loves the boy," Doc affirmed dryly.

"Well, that's enough fun for one day," Grandpa announced, as he and Doc hopped down from the fence.

"Fun?" Bryce wheezed, trying to fend off the giant tongue of his newfound friend.

Grandpa walked across the corral, grabbed the large bag of sweet-feed, and began shaking it noisily. "Happy Jack," he called.

The big bull gamboled across the corral and buried his snout in the feedbag. Doc walked over to Bryce—who was still lying on his back wheezing, sputtering and wiping slobber from his face. Doc bent over, looking down at the boy, he still wore his crooked grin. Looking up through bleary eyes Bryce tried to focus, and offered a half-dazed smile.

Doc was a tall, gangling old man who was as thin as a rail. He always reminded Bryce of the actor, *Vincent Schiavelli*, who played "Mr. Vargas" in the movie, "Fast Times at Ridgemont High"—although; Doc Waggner's wife looked *nothing* like *Lana Clarkson*.

"I'll take that, son," Doc said. He reached down with his long, skinny arm and pried the stainless-steel syringe from Bryce's hand—he still held it in a vise-like death-grip.

Doc sauntered across the corral, syringe in hand, to where Happy Jack was enjoying his sweet-feed. As Bryce watched,

Doc clapped the bull twice on the neck muscle and injected him. Happy Jack never even flinched.

"Well, I'll be damned," Bryce muttered, dusting himself off. "Those two old farts suckered me."

"Come on, Bryce, let's head to the house," Grandpa said, with an impish grin. "We'll fix that fence first thing in the morning. Happy Jack can stay in the corral tonight."

Bryce just smiled, shook his head and hobbled toward the pickup truck.

THE NEXT MORNING, BRYCE McNEEL awoke to the smell of bacon and coffee. The taunting aroma drifted through the entire house, urging him out of bed. Outside, he could hear the loud crashing sounds of his grandpa loading something heavy into the pickup truck. Bryce knew he should already be out of bed—outside helping his grandpa—but it was still summer break, and he only had a few more days left to sleep-in.

School would be starting again right after Labor Day, and even though summer was over, Bryce was looking forward to the new school year. Two days ago, on August 29, he had turned seventeen, and in a few days, his senior year of high school would begin.

Bryce attended school in the Town of Silver Canyon, which was about eleven miles north of his home. He lived with his grandparents on their twelve-hundred-acre cattle ranch located in Bane County. Bryce's parents had died in a house fire when he was only four-years-old, and other than a few faded memories, he had no real recollection of them.

The old rusted gas pipes of a faulty propane system had been the cause of the fire, and even though Bryce didn't really remember his parents, it still pained him to think of it; a fiery explosion was no way for a person to die.

From the kitchen, he heard his grandma's voice: "Bryce . . . get your butt out of bed before I come in there and snatch you bald headed."

Growing up in the south, Grandma had a real way with southern sayings, and Bryce didn't think a day had ever gone by when he hadn't heard a new one. His all-time favorite was the time she burned her hand on the kitchen stove and shouted: *"Well, shit-fire and save the matches!"* Bryce thought he was going to bust a gut laughing, mostly because his grandma never cursed . . . well, rarely.

He rolled over and looked at his alarm clock: *6:32 a.m.* "I'm up Grandma, just give me a minute."

By all accounts, Bryce McNeel appeared to be a typical red-blooded country-boy. He stood six-feet-tall and weighed-in at a well-toned one-seventy. He had corn-flour blue eyes, light brown hair, and a farmers-tan on his face and arms —from always wearing a T-shirt while working in the sun. His callused hands and strong muscles were the hallmark of any person who worked on a cattle ranch—tossing around seventy-pound bales of hay all day will have that effect on a person. Yes, by all accounts, Bryce was a typical corn-fed country-boy.

However, there was *one* thing about Bryce McNeel that made him very unique. He was—for lack of a better word—a genius. Bryce had a perfect 4.0 GPA, and he had scored off-the-charts on every test they threw at him. He could've graduated high school and started college years ago, but he preferred not to stand out from his peers. It was very important to Bryce that he appeared to be, just a regular guy.

Unlike most seventeen-year-old boys, who covered their bedroom walls with posters of fast cars, and scantily clad young girls. Bryce's walls were covered by bookshelves, filled with every type of book imaginable. He was exceedingly studious and craved knowledge; a great deal of his spare time was spent reading. While his memory wasn't completely eidetic, he could absorb information like a sponge, and had astonishing recall.

Bryce rolled out of bed and fell into his button-fly jeans. He slipped on a T-shirt and some white tube-socks, and then pulled on a well-used pair of work boots. As he did every morning, he touched the picture frame that sat atop his bureau and smiled wistfully; it contained a photo of his parents—Brian and Lori.

He completed his daily ensemble with a tattered, green-and-yellow John Deere cap and a ragged pair of leather work-gloves, and then shuffled lazily toward the kitchen.

"Mornin', Grandma. It *sure* smells good in here." Bryce exaggerated the tone of his compliment, knowing that he was late getting out of bed.

Grandma McNeel primmed her lips, slid her glasses down her nose and looked up at Bryce—she was almost a foot shorter than he was. "Do I look like a biscuit to you?" she asked dryly.

"Ma'am?" Bryce answered, furrowing his brow.

"I said do I look like a biscuit?" she repeated.

"Uh . . . no, ma'am?" Bryce replied, still unsure where this was going.

"Then quit trying to butter-my-butt with compliments and go sit down and eat your breakfast." She jabbed him in the ribs with a plate of food.

"Yes, ma'am," Bryce said, chuckling.

He took a seat at the kitchen table, making sure to remove his hat. Behind him in the kitchen, he heard his grandma snickering as she filled a large paper bag with sandwiches and drinks.

"When you're finished eating, go help your grandpa," she said. "He's heading out to fix the fence Happy Jack knocked down over by Cedar Creek, and he shouldn't be lifting those heavy spools of wire and fence posts all by himself."

"Yes, ma'am." Bryce spoke around the food in his mouth, quickly polishing off a plate of eggs, bacon, and biscuits-and-gravy.

He kissed his grandma on the cheek and thanked her for breakfast. As he hurried out the door, he picked up the bag of sandwiches and grabbed another biscuit—clenching it between his teeth.

Walking toward the barn—biscuit in mouth—Bryce started slipping into his work-gloves. "Mornin', Grandpa." He mumbled around the biscuit. Grandpa McNeel looked up and began to chuckle.

"Well . . . good afternoon, sunshine," Grandpa quipped. "If you're finished with your beauty sleep, you can go fetch a posthole digger, a box of fence staples and a one-ton come-along from the barn."

"Yes, sir," Bryce said, and hurried into the barn. Grandpa McNeel was always giving him a hard time over *something*—but it was all just good-natured fun.

"Grab my big claw-hammer, too," Grandpa hollered. "It's in my workshop." The barn was an immense structure, three-times the size of the house, and was divided into several large rooms. Grandpa's workshop was closest to the front of the building and contained every hand-tool and power-tool known to man. He even had tools that were used to repair broken tools.

After the truck was fully loaded and they were about to leave, Grandpa said he needed one more thing. "Let's go, Snip," he called. From out of nowhere, a brown-and-white bird-dog leaped through the air and landed in the back of the pickup.

Grandpa fired up the old truck and they trundled through the woods for about a mile. Winding through trees and gullies, they followed a teeth-rattling cow trail at speeds of no more than 15 mph. Even at that low speed, the bumpy terrain managed to slam Bryce's head into the vehicle's roof several times.

"Dang, Grandpa. When are you gonna put some new shocks on this antique?"

"If it ain't broke . . ." Grandpa replied, using only half of his favorite old adage. He maintained a white-knuckled grip on the steering wheel of the jouncing vehicle, as they pitched and yawed down the trail.

Grandpa's old truck was a 1966 International Harvester, and with a curb weight of almost six thousand pounds, it plowed through the woods like an Abrams battle tank. The truck had been green at one point in its life, but now it was mostly rust, Bondo, and brown primer. Grandpa jokingly called the color "camouflage."

They exited the forest into a broad open field, and coasted the old truck down a long, grassy declivity to the edge of Cedar Creek. Without hesitation, Snip hopped out and began sniffing around.

Grandpa McNeel stepped out of the truck, removed his tattered old cowboy hat and wiped his forearm across his brow. There was about forty yards of fencing that was down, and the barbed wire was a tangled mess. Happy Jack had pushed through the fence near a corner, so he had not only destroyed the paddock fence, he ripped up the fence along the creek-bottom, as well.

The section of fence along the edge of the creek was extremely old, and the bottom of the posts had rotted away in the moist soil. When Happy Jack had pulled on them, the posts snapped off at the ground, and now the entire section would need replacing.

Snip began barking near some brush along the fence line,

so Grandpa and Bryce headed over to have a look. They heard what Snip had found long before they saw it; the rattling was unmistakable. There, tucked under the edge of a large rock was a huge rattlesnake; it blended perfectly into the dry leaves. Snip growled and held point on the deadly snake.

Not long ago, a large rattler had bit Grandpa on the leg while he was replacing the leather-packing in an old windmill. Grandma had rushed him to Doctor Milstead's clinic in Silver Canyon for treatment; he was laid up for over a week. Ever since then, Grandpa always brought Snip along. Snip was an excellent snake-dog.

"Bryce, go grab my snake-charmer."

"Yes, sir," Bryce replied, jogging over to the truck.

What Grandpa so affectionately referred to as his *snake-charmer*, was in fact, a sawed-off shotgun; a single-shot 20-gauge, to be exact. The barrel had been sawed off to about fifteen-inches in length—which was about three-inches shy of legal—and the wooden stock had been trimmed to form a pistol-grip.

Bryce retrieved the weapon, handed it to his grandpa and then commanded Snip to back off. Grandpa didn't waste any time. He walked over to the deadly snake, pointed the gun and fired; the noise was deafening. A giant fireball burst from the tiny barrel's muzzle, as a large cloud of dirt, leaves and shredded rattlesnake exploded into the air.

Grandpa offered Bryce a knowing smile. "Works ever' time."

Bryce's Grandpa was tougher than a fifty-cent steak, the epitome of a *true* cowboy. He was what Bryce referred to as: old-man-tough. The kind of toughness derived from a lifetime of hard work on a cattle ranch.

He was sixty-five-years-old, with a lanky, bandy-legged build, and his sun-hardened skin was as dark and tough as leather. His close-cropped hair was mostly gray, with a small patch of red on top, a subtle intimation of his Scottish heritage. If you were meeting him for the first time, you might even think him feeble—nothing could've been farther from the truth.

Bryce recalled one Saturday afternoon, a couple of years back, when he and Grandpa had been watching a heavyweight-boxing match on TV between *Evander Holyfield* and *Michael Dokes*. ABC's *Wide World of Sports* was a weekend tradition in the McNeel household, and they never missed an episode. The program's melodramatic introduction featuring the spectacular crash of ski jumper *Vinko Bogataj*, always brought to mind the second-half of the show's iconic catchphrase: "The thrill of victory . . . *and the agony of defeat.*"

When the match ended, Bryce had commented that speed and power were the traits of a good boxer, but Grandpa contended that being able to take a punch was the determining factor. After a brief debate, Grandpa proposed they put it to a test. He would allow Bryce to punch him in the stomach, to prove that taking a punch was more important than speed or power. Bryce thought it was a bad idea, but his grandpa had insisted.

Grandpa stood at the ready, but Bryce was hesitant, afraid to throw the punch—he didn't want to hurt his grandpa. Bryce was strong; apart from his chores on the ranch, he worked-out daily with free-weights and even had a heavy punching bag that hung from the rafters of the barn.

"Just throw the dang punch," Grandpa demanded.

"Okay," Bryce said reluctantly.

He drew back, and punched his grandpa in the stomach with everything he had. Even though he was wearing the gloves that he used when he worked the heavy-bag, it was like punching a brick wall covered with an inch of padding.

Bryce stepped back, shaking his hand in pain. "Ow . . .

man . . . I think I busted my wrist."

Grandpa chuckled and patted him on the back. He said, "You'll be okay there, speedy. Now, slip off those gloves and let's get something to eat. I'm hungry."

Bryce never saw his grandpa in the same light again.

Refocusing on the task at hand, Bryce glared at the barbed-wire fence and shook his head. "Well this is a godawful mess. Rebuilding this old section along the creek is gonna take a while, Grandpa."

"Aw, it ain't as bad as it looks," Grandpa said. He rested his hand on Bryce's shoulder.

"How old *was* this fence anyway?" Bryce asked, noticing the rusted wire, and old, rotted posts.

Grandpa rubbed his chin whiskers and thought. "Well . . . let's see. I built this fence back at the end of 1953 and its 1991 now, so that's . . . almost thirty-eight years."

Bryce nodded. "That's pretty old"—he pondered a moment and then asked—"How can you remember exactly what year you built this fence?"

Grandpa lifted an eyebrow at the implication.

"I mean . . . I'm not saying you're senile or anything," Bryce quickly clarified.

Grandpa laughed and clapped Bryce on the back. "Well," he said, "I remember when I built this fence because"—he paused suddenly, realizing he was about to open a door that ought to remain closed—"1953 is a year I'll never forget."

"Why is that?" asked Bryce.

Grandpa slipped a hand into the back pocket of his jeans and looked down, scuffing at the ground with the tip of his pointy-toed boot. He looked as though he was trying to decide if he should answer. "Well . . . that's a long story, son," he finally replied.

Bryce glanced over at the forty yards of downed fence, jerked his thumb over his shoulder and said, "I think we got some time, Grandpa."

Grandpa offered a weak smile and nodded. Then breathing a heavy sigh, he said, "Well . . . all right, but one condition: don't mention this to your grandma, it'll just upset her."

Bryce was surprised at the stipulation, but he agreed, and Grandpa began the story. He knew that his grandpa loved to joke around, and at times, could be quite the fabulist; but when Bryce saw the steely appearance of Grandpa's face . . . he knew this tale was no joke.

It was near the end of September back in 1953. I had been looking for a young calf that had gone missing and I ended up down here by the creek. It had only rained once that summer, about a month earlier, and the creek-bed had almost dried up. I saw the calf's tracks in the mud, leading across to the other side. Cedar Creek is the property line between our ranch and the old Rickman farm.

I followed the calf's tracks across the creek and through the forest for about three hundred yards. I found her just past the tree line in an open field. That's when I saw all the buzzards circling over the Rickman's house. I knew right away—something bad had happened.

I threw a rope around the calf's neck and led her home to her mother. We didn't have a phone at our house back in those days, no one did, and so I got in my truck and drove over to Pat's gas station on Highway 50. I told Pat what I'd seen and asked him to put a call in to the sheriff's office.

The next morning, Deputy Dalton Morrow came by our house to tell me what had happened to Mrs. Rickman. By the look on his face, I knew it was gonna be bad. I remember sending your dad and your Aunt Ellen into the other room with your grandma. Your dad was only two-years-old at the time, but Ellen was six, and I wanted to make sure they didn't hear. To be honest, I didn't want your grandma to hear what happened either; she knew Mrs. Rickman.

What he told me was hard to believe, but I had known Dalton Morrow for many years, and he wasn't the kind of man who made up stories.

He told me that Mrs. Rickman had been attacked by some kind of large animal; that it had ripped her to pieces and eaten most of her. He said whatever attacked her had broken through her solid-oak front door and had left large claw marks on the doorframe. He said the claw marks were enormous—unlike anything he'd ever seen before—and they were carved deep into the wood, almost like the flutes of a column. He also found a 12-gauge shotgun—with two shots fired—lying on the floor next to her body. Apparently, it hadn't done much good.

The most unbelievable thing he told me, however, was about the bloody footprints that he found. He said the footprints were bigger than any man's footprint and they had claws for toes. What's more, Dalton said he'd seen those exact same footprints before.

As he continued, I remember he pulled out a can of Copenhagen to take a dip. I could see his hands shaking as he opened the can and his face became pale. There was fear in his eyes, and he wasn't the type of man who scared easy.

Dalton said he'd checked the files for details the night before, and back in 1934, between September and December, fifteen people had been killed—or went missing—around the Silver Canyon Wildlife Refuge. He said some kind of large animal had ripped them to shreds and eaten them. He told me that he and Sheriff Tom Cooper had seen those exact same footprints in the dirt around the body of one of the victims. I remember seeing a chill come over him as he remembered the incident. When he finished, he shook my hand and headed out to inform all the neighboring farms and ranches about what had taken place. It was what happened next, that would haunt me for the rest of my life.

During the three months that followed, eleven more people died—or went missing; the ones they found were torn to shreds. These *weren't strangers, you understand; we knew some of those people. They were our friends and neighbors. It was the same as what Dalton Morrow said happened back in 1934, right down to the giant clawed footprints.*

The week after Christmas in 1953, your grandma made me come down here and build this fence, so no more cattle could cross the creek to the Rickman farm ever again. I haven't set foot on the other side of Cedar Creek in almost thirty-eight years.

"So," Grandpa concluded, "that's how I know exactly what year I built the fence."

Bryce's jaw had dropped, his mouth was agape, and his eyes couldn't have opened any wider. He was stunned. He had no idea that something like this had happened right here in Bane County.

"Good God," Bryce exclaimed, "what do you think it was? What do you think killed all those people?"

Grandpa McNeel hesitated; he peered at the ground. Finally, he said, "Aw, it doesn't matter—that was a long time ago. Anyway . . . you probably wouldn't believe me if I told you."

"Come on, Grandpa, what do you think it was?"

Grandpa McNeel took off his hat and leaned in toward Bryce, as if he were imparting a secret. He looked into his eyes with all sincerity and said, "It was a werewolf."

GRANDMA McNEEL stood in front of the stove cooking supper while Grandpa sat at the kitchen table going through his coin collection. He had been collecting old coins for most of his life and he had dozens of quart-size Mason-jars filled with coins sitting on shelves out in the barn. On occasion, he would bring several jars into the house, dump them onto the kitchen table, and look up each one in his book of rare coins.

Bryce sat quietly across the table from his grandpa and watched as he went through his collection. He still didn't know how to feel about his grandpa's story—especially the part about it being a werewolf that had killed all those people.

Bryce had laughed, saying that he didn't believe in such things, but Grandpa seemed to take umbrage at his laughter, and then wouldn't discuss it any further. After that, they had just focused on getting the fence built. Now, Bryce was baffled as to why his grandpa would say such a ridiculous thing.

He said it with such absolute certainty, Bryce remembered.

"Nathan," Grandma McNeel barked. "Will you *please* move those dang coins so I can set the table for supper?" Anytime she used Grandpa's first name, you knew she meant business.

"Sure thing ... Blanche, sweetie," Grandpa replied. He offered a broad, exaggerated smile.

Here we go, thought Bryce.

Grandpa had just upped-the-ante. By using Grandma's first name, along with a pet name, and framing it with a fake smile, Grandpa had thrown down the gauntlet.

Grandma mumbled something under her breath; something about, wiping that shit-eating-grin off of his face ... and we were off to the races.

Bryce's grandparents really enjoyed bantering with each other, and he always looked forward to the nightly event. Bryce sat back in his chair, smiled and followed the play-by-play. At least for the time being, he had forgotten about his Grandpa's werewolf comment.

Later, during supper, Bryce had been acting somewhat reserved and picking at his food. He just couldn't stop obsessing over Grandpa's story.

"Why aren't you eating?" Grandma asked. "Are you feeling sick to your stomach?"

Bryce looked up, unsure of what to say; his grandpa was quick to respond for him. "I think he's just a little tired from rebuilding the fence today . . . aren't you, Bryce?" Grandpa offered him a conspiratorial glance.

Bryce nodded and smiled. "Yeah, I'm fine."

Just then, there was a quick rap at the door and Bryce's first-cousin, Jackson Campbell, strolled into the house.

"Hey Grandma, hey Grandpa . . . what's up, Bryce?" Jackson said, lifting his chin.

Grandma immediately asked, "Have you had your supper yet?"

Jackson patted his belly. "Yeah, I already ate," he said. "I just came by to see if Bryce wanted to take a cruise in my new car over to Silver Canyon. Tonight's dollar-movie night at the Rialto and *Young Guns II* is playing."

Bryce rose from the table with great alacrity. He was eager to do anything that might take his mind off Grandpa's preposterous tale.

"You bet . . . y'all mind if I go?" Bryce asked.

Grandma looked at Jackson suspiciously and primmed her lips. He was wearing a sleeveless *Ronnie Montrose* "Rock the Nation" t-shirt that depicted a woman with breasts like traffic cones. "What's it rated?" she asked.

"It's PG-13," Jackson said, grinning. "Plus, we already saw it last year when it first came out. They're just replaying it for dollar-movie night."

Grandma was always skeptical of Jackson and his plans. She considered him the black-sheep of the family. She always worried that he might get Bryce into trouble, somehow.

Bryce was a clean-cut and dutiful young man; he minded his manners, and did extremely well in school. Jackson, on the other hand, wore his hair in a lank mullet past his shoulders, loved T-shirts emblazoned with offensive depictions—that he *always* cut the sleeves off of—and he barely passed his classes. Grandma finally agreed and pulled five dollars from her purse for Bryce.

"That's okay, Grandma. I've got cash," said Bryce. He earned a good allowance for all the work he did around the ranch each week.

"Just take it," she said, stuffing it into his shirt pocket.

"Okay, thank you," Bryce said, chuckling.

"You boys behave and don't be too late coming home," she said.

They agreed and headed out of the house with Grandma in tow. She poked her head out the door and hollered after them. "You boys be careful."

"Okay, Grandma," Bryce said. He smiled and shook his head at how much she worried.

Grandpa McNeel watched his wife. "They'll be fine, Blanche," he assured her. "Bryce is a smart kid, smarter than both of us put together; you worry too much."

"It's not Bryce I'm worried about," she said, "it's Jackson. That boy is too wild. Sooner or later, he's gonna get Bryce into trouble."

"Stop your worrying and come here," said Grandpa, patting his hand on his lap. "We got the house to ourselves for a change."

Grandma lowered her chin and peered at him over her glasses. "Oh, really?" she said, with a devious little smile.

BRYCE McNEEL AND JACKSON CAMPBELL were both seventeen, but Jackson was four months older. The two boys had spent their entire childhoods together, and were much more than first-cousins; they were best friends—brothers.

Most people said they favored each other. They were about the same height and build, had similar features and both were as tough as nails. However, there was no mistaking Jackson, with his long dark hair past his shoulders and his constant bad-boy attitude.

Although both of them were nearing the age of adulthood, they were still just children in many ways. Growing up in a remote area like Bane County, could lead to a very sheltered life. Then again—in other ways—growing up in the country could turn boys into men more quickly.

Jackson's mom, Ellen, was Grandma and Grandpa McNeel's daughter, and she was married to Grady Campbell, Jackson's dad. Jackson and his family lived on a farm about a mile north of Bryce's house. Jackson's dad was a long-haul truck driver, so he was gone quite a bit, but his mom was always around.

Jackson had just bought an awesome 1987 Camaro IROC-Z. It was jet-black with a tinted T-top roof, extra-wide rear tires and a custom side-exit exhaust system. Over the past few years, the original owner of the car had spent a great deal of time and money customizing the vehicle, but apparently, he had to sell it for financial reasons.

Jackson had been working part-time for Don Davis at the Western Auto store in Silver Canyon for the past year, and saving all his money. Then, a few days ago, his dad finally agreed to help him buy the car.

They drove far enough away from their grandparents' house so no one would hear, and then Jackson floored the accelerator. The Camaro's souped-up engine roared like a freight train as they rocketed forward.

"Holy shit! This thing moves," Bryce shouted, his voice muffled by the thundering side-pipes.

"You haven't seen jack-shit. Wait until we get out on the

highway and I open this baby up; it's got over 250 horses under the hood."

When they reached the highway intersection that led to Silver Canyon, Jackson stopped the car and turned to Bryce, a devilish grin on his face. "Hold on to your balls, buddy."

When he floored it, the small-block 350 V8 smoked the rear tires and they jumped forward like a racehorse out of the gate. Bryce slammed back into his seat so hard he thought he'd end up in the trunk. After what seemed like only four or five seconds—but was probably more like fifteen—Bryce glanced at the speedometer and saw the needle passing 100 mph. He had no doubt that the car could reach the 140 mph mark if Jackson pushed it.

"Jesus Christ," Bryce yelled, his grin was ear to ear.

Jackson took his foot off the gas and backed it down to 65 mph. "All right, that's enough. I better keep it near the speed limit before I get a ticket and my old-man takes the car away."

Bryce shook his head laughing and drummed his hands on the dashboard. "That was awesome; this car hauls ass!"

Jackson smiled. "Yeah, she's a screamer; and it's got a custom sound system too!"

Bryce smiled; the custom stereo system was probably what had sold Jackson on the car in the first place. While Bryce's bedroom looked like the Library of Congress, with more books than anyone could count, Jackson's room looked like the distribution-center for a large chain of record stores. Rock 'n' roll music was Jackson's passion, and his immense collection of hard-rock and heavy-metal was endless.

Jackson reached down and popped a tape into the cassette deck. It was the new *Metallica Black Album*; the song, "Of Wolf and Man" blasted over the speakers. The two boys bobbed their heads and rocked-out for the eleven-mile-trip over to Silver Canyon.

They arrived at the Rialto Theater about fifteen minutes before the show started and headed straight to the concession stand, loading up on popcorn, drinks and candy. Jackson grabbed his usual box of *Red Hots* while Bryce opted for the *Milk Duds.* As they made their way up the staircase toward the rear balcony, they were surprised to see that the theater was nearly empty; dollar-movie night was usually crowded.

The construction of the old Rialto Theater had taken place in the late 1920s, during the movie-palace era, and its opulent, art-deco interior was truly a remarkable sight. Its rich colors and bold geometric designs were in sharp contrast to the rustic-style buildings of Silver Canyon. Even though the theater was relatively small, the high, bas-relief ceiling gave the room a strange ethereal feel, like that of a large cathedral.

Just before the lights lowered, Bryce recognized a few people from school. He smiled cordially and offered a quick wave. Even though he and Jackson had seen the movie the year before, it was still great fun. It was loaded with action, gunfights, and funny dialog. Emilio Estevez was hilarious as *Billy the Kid*.

One of their favorite scenes had been when *Billy* shot a deputy with a shotgun loaded with eighteen dimes and said: "Best buck-eighty I ever spent." Bryce and Jackson roared with laughter, even though, they had heard the line before.

They also enjoyed the scene where a woman walked out of a whorehouse butt-naked, told the town to kiss her ass, and rode away on her horse. When she showed her naked ass, Jackson gave a loud whistle that echoed across the theater; in his defense, though, it *was* a nice ass.

When the show ended, they exited to the parking lot, laughing and repeating funny lines from the movie.

"You wanna cruise around town for a while before we head home?" Jackson asked.

"Sounds good," said Bryce.

As Jackson unlocked the car door, they heard shouting from the other side of the parking lot, where three people were standing beside a car. Two of the individuals were girls that Bryce recognized from school—he had seen them inside the movie theater before the show started. The third person—the one making all the noise—was a young man who looked familiar, but Bryce couldn't put a name to the face. He wasn't able to make out what the argument was about, but both girls appeared frightened. Then, without provocation, the guy reached out and slapped one of the girls.

"Oh shit . . . here we go," Jackson muttered. He looked down and shook his head.

Like a fan at a sporting event, Jackson readied himself. He leaned against the side of his car, folded his arms and waited, anticipating the show to come. He knew *exactly* what was about to happen, he'd seen it a dozen times before. For as long as he had known Bryce, one irrepressible trait remained perfectly clear: Bryce *hated* bullies!

Whenever Bryce saw a bully picking on someone who couldn't defend themselves, he would, "resolve" the situation. At least, that's what Bryce had called it once. A couple of years back, under similar circumstances, Bryce had told Jackson, "*Hold on a minute while I 'resolve' this situation*," and the expression stuck; or at least, in Jackson's mind it had.

"Pardon me for a moment," Bryce said calmly. "I'll be right back."

He made a beeline across the parking lot, honing in on the bully like a guided missile. As he neared the group, Bryce called out, "Hey!"

When the guy saw Bryce approaching, he turned and walked out to meet him. Trying to appear tough, he said, "Well-well, what do we have here? Just what the fu—"

Bryce landed a left-jab to the guy's nose—then another. He followed with a powerful right-cross to the chin. The guy dropped to the ground like a sack of feed—he never even twitched. The entire situation was *resolved* in less than five seconds.

The sharp, intermittent sound of a lone person slowly clapping their hands echoed across the parking lot. Jackson followed up his listless applause with a long, shrill whistle. Finally, he shouted: "Can we *go* now?"

Bryce turned to the girl, and asked. "Are you okay?" He could see that her eyes welled with tears, and her cheek was flushed.

Both girls were staring at the young man on the ground with their mouths open; he was still out cold.

"Uh-huh," the girl finally managed.

"Is this your car?" Bryce asked.

"Uh-huh," the other girl responded, still staring at the bully sprawled on the ground.

"Are you all right to drive?" he questioned, further.

"Uh-huh," she replied numbly.

Apparently, *uh-huh* was the extent of their vocabulary abilities at this particular moment in time.

Finally, one girl asked, "What about—"

"Sleeping Beauty?" Bryce interrupted. "He'll be fine."

The two girls looked at each other briefly and then smiled at Bryce.

"Well . . . okay then," Bryce said, very matter-of-factly. "Drive safe."

He took a few steps backward, sketched a perfunctory salute, then turned and sauntered back to the car.

The girls—still dumbfounded—watched as Bryce swaggered off, as if nothing had happened. After a moment, they got into their car and slowly drove away.

When he arrived back at Jackson's car, Bryce wore a smug smile across his face.

"Did you 'resolve' the situation?" Jackson asked, in a smart-ass tone.

Bryce just continued to smile.

"I am *so* disappointed in you." Jackson said drolly. "I *hope* you're proud of yourself."

"I feel *just* terrible," Bryce said, feigning regret. "I'm all broken up over the entire incident."

"Yeah, I can see that," Jackson said snidely. He motioned to the bully who was now sitting up and looking confused. "Looks like your boyfriend's waking up."

"Good. Now let's get the hell out of here before he says something else and I have to kick his ass again."

Starting the car, Jackson burned-rubber out of the parking lot and headed up Main Street. He turned and looked at Bryce, glaring at him sternly. "And Grandma thinks that *I'm* the troublemaker!" he complained.

The two boys stared at each other impassively for a moment—then burst out laughing. They drove north until they reached the end of Main Street and turned onto Howell Avenue. Howell was the street that ran along the edge of the Silver Canyon National Wildlife Refuge—or as all the locals called it, "The Refuge."

"Have you ever eaten at one of these Gypsy restaurants?" Jackson asked, motioning to the businesses along the street.

"No, I never have," said Bryce.

"The food must be good, though; all the tourists eat there."

"Yeah, and they're close to The Refuge," Bryce added, gesturing at the large parking lot at the game warden's office.

You could always get an idea of how many people were inside The Refuge by how many cars were in the parking lot overnight.

Bryce and Jackson knew The Refuge like the back of their hands; they had grown up hiking in its vast wilderness. On a few occasions, they had even been offered money to act as guides for tourists, but they always declined. Playing nursemaid to a bunch of citified backpackers was not their idea of a good time—at any price.

As they drove past the main entrance, Bryce thought about Grandpa's story, and the people who had died. He wondered if Jackson knew about the killings, but he decided to keep it to himself.

They cruised around town talking, laughing and listening to music until it was time to leave.

"I guess we better start heading back," said Jackson.

Bryce nodded. "Hey, do you want to go over to Grandpa's cabin tomorrow and go fishing?"

Many years ago, Grandpa had built a log cabin on some land he owned along the Carantina River. He only used it during hunting season, or when he needed a little peace and quiet. It didn't have electricity, but it had a sink and hand-pump inside, for running water. It was comfortable, built like a rock and had a huge, stone fireplace with a cast-iron crane for cook-pots. As long as you didn't mind using an old, stinky outhouse—and a *Montgomery Ward* catalog for toilet paper—it was the perfect hangout.

Jackson thought for a second. "Sure, I'm off work tomorrow. Fishing sounds great. I'll pick you up in the morning." He cranked up the stereo and they jammed-out to *Van Halen* all the way home.

As they drove down the dark highway—drumming their hands to the music—neither of them realized just how much their lives would begin to change tomorrow.

CHAPTER 3

Ghost House

IT WAS A GLORIOUS SUNNY MORNING. Jackson Campbell walked out the front door of his home and headed for his new car; fishing with Bryce was exactly what the doctor ordered for this beautiful day. He'd been listening to his parents argue all night and was ready to get the hell out of Dodge.

Jackson's dad, Grady, had just returned home from another long-haul trip across the country, and as usual, he was unwinding with a few beers. Jackson's dad never drank when he was on the road; he took his job as a truck driver very seriously. However, when he came home he liked to drink. Jackson's mom, Ellen, on the other hand, hated her husband's drinking; it was always a constant source of friction.

Jackson couldn't understand why his mom hated it so much that his father drank; it wasn't as if his old-man was a drunk. He didn't get belligerent or angry when he was drinking; in fact, Jackson thought his dad was a lot more fun to be around after he'd had a few beers. Regardless, he was just glad to get out of the house and away from the constant bickering.

As Jackson drove his new car along the road to his grandparents' house, he popped an old *Foghat* tape into the deck, jamming-out to the song, "Slow Ride." He had removed the tinted-glass panels from his Camaro's T-top; wind and sunshine filled the inside of the car as he roared down the highway, tapping his hands to the music.

When he arrived, Bryce was out front, going through his fishing gear. "What's up, Bryce?" Jackson hopped out through the car's T-top roof without opening the car door.

"Just getting my shit together."

"Bring your .22; there're a lot of snakes at the river."

"Already planning on it."

Bryce went back into the house, and after a moment, emerged with his Ruger semi-automatic .22 rifle. "Pop the hatch."

Carrying his gear toward the rear of the car, Bryce smiled at the open T-top; it was the perfect day for a convertible. As he placed his rifle into the back of the car, he double-checked the safety, and noticed that Jackson had brought his rifle, as well.

Both boys hopped into the car through the T-top—without opening the doors—a move made famous by *Burt Reynolds* in the movie, "Smokey and the Bandit."

"Let's hit it," said Jackson, firing up the loud engine. Moments later, they turned onto the highway and headed toward their grandpa's cabin.

Bryce dug through the glovebox, until he found an old *Boston* tape; he popped it into the deck. The song, "Smokin" kicked off.

"I brought some sandwiches and chips, but let's stop here at Pat's gas station and grab a six pack of Dr. Pepper," Jackson said. He veered off the highway into the gravel parking lot, grinding his tires to a stop.

Pat's store was older than the hills; and Pat, himself, wasn't much younger. It looked more like a junkyard than a gas station. There were old wrecked cars, and pieces of scrap-metal scattered everywhere; Pat lived in a small cabin out back.

They entered the old clapboard building through a spring-mounted screen door that squeaked noisily and slammed shut behind them. Walking across the creaking, plank-wood floor, they made their way to an old Kelvinator soda-chest and slid back the top. The NEHI BEVERAGES logo on the old chest was rusty and faded, and the compressor made a loud clunking sound, but the sodas were the coldest in the county, almost frozen.

The boys brought the six-pack to the checkout counter and sat it next to the ancient cash register. Bryce tossed two dollars on the countertop. Pat stood glaring. He was a grumpy, old barrel-chested man, wizened and wrinkled, with a face like cured beef. Grandpa had once told Bryce that the old man's name was actually *Felix*; the nickname "Pat" was short for his last name, which nobody could pronounce. After a moment, with a few loud clicks and a resounding *ka-ching*, he rang up the soda.

"That'll be a dollar-eighty," he said, with a deep, gravelly voice.

The two boys turned their heads to face each other, a smile growing on their lips. Then, in perfect unison, they chorused: "Best buck-eighty I ever spent"—quoting the movie from the night before.

Laughing all the way back to the car, they hopped in through the roof without opening the doors—like *The Bandit*—and spun gravel as they raced out of the parking lot, music blaring.

Pat just stared at the floor and slowly shook his head. "Those damn kids must be smoking the pot."

After a few miles, they turned onto a paint-chipping gravel road with a surface like a bent washboard. Winding through the forest for about three miles, the road finally came to a dead-end at the bottom of a hill near the Carantina River.

They grabbed their gear and headed south, moving along a heavily bowered pathway next to the river. After about five hundred yards, they came to a clearing, and their grandpa's old log cabin. It sat on a hilltop overlooking the Carantina River;

near the remains of an old wooden train trestle entangled in vines. The old trestle had collapsed into the deep river many years ago; large pylons and timbers could still be seen rising up from the murky depths. Even though the wood of the old trestle was more than a century old, you could still smell the creosote oozing from its pores.

The tracks of the old railway spur ran all the way to The Refuge, once used to haul silver ore from the mines. The old-timers called this fishing spot *Trestle Hole* and it was notorious for large-mouth bass and yellow-catfish.

They found a small, sandy clearing at the edge of the river and put down their gear. Bryce started going through his tackle box to find his favorite bass lure. It was a yellow broken-back jitterbug covered in black spots. He put it on his line and cast it into the river where it landed near some pylons.

Bryce let the lure float for a few seconds, then gave it a quick little tug and slowly started to reel. He continued giving little tugs and slowly reeling, until... *Wham!* A bass jumped into the air with the lure in his mouth.

"Yeah, that's what I'm talking about," Bryce hollered. He reeled in the fish, but it was too small, about one pound, so he dropped it back into the river.

As Jackson watched him release the fish, he noticed a bruise on Bryce's knuckle. "How's your hand feeling?"

Bryce glanced at his hand. "It's all good," he said, flexing his fingers.

"You really walloped that guy last night."

"Yeah, well, he shouldn't have slapped that girl."

"No doubt," Jackson agreed, "assholes like that get what they deserve."

Bryce nodded and cast his lure into the river again.

Jackson sat quietly for a few minutes, fishing, and then he

looked over at Bryce with a sly smile. "You know, that girl was kind of cute."

Bryce looked at him and furrowed his brow. "What girl?"

"The girl you saved, numb-nuts; the one who got slapped."

Bryce smiled and nodded. "Yeah, her name is Wendy, something-or-other. I've seen her around school."

"You should ask her out," Jackson said dryly. "Who knows, you might even get laid for once."

"For once," Bryce said indignantly. "I've been laid before."

"When have *you* ever been laid?" Jackson scoffed.

"A couple of months ago," Bryce said. Then he lowered his voice and finished softly, "with Karen Jenkins."

"Karen Jenkins!" Jackson roared. "She's almost two years older than you."

Bryce was grinning like a Cheshire cat, with an equal amount of pride and embarrassment.

"Why am I just hearing about this now?" asked Jackson.

"Because, it's none of your damn business," Bryce said, "and if you tell a single soul—I swear, Jackson—I'll kick your sorry ass."

"Who am I gonna tell?" Jackson said, feigning innocence.

"I mean it, Jackson! You keep your damn mouth shut," Bryce warned.

"All right—all right," Jackson said. He raised his hands, surrendering. "... Karen Jenkins?"

The boys sat on the riverbank fishing and lolling the day away. They talked, and laughed, and caught several large fish for Grandma's frying pan. It was a perfect day to mark the end of summer; school would be starting the day after tomorrow.

Jackson reached into his tackle box and removed a small,

silver flask. He unscrewed the top and offered it to Bryce.

"What's that?" Bryce asked.

"This—my friend—is some fine Kentucky sippin' whiskey."

"Where the hell did you get whiskey from?"

"My dad's liquor cabinet."

"He's gonna bust your ass when he finds out," said Bryce.

"No way," said Jackson, "I only took a little, and I filled the bottle back up with water. He'll never miss it."

Jackson held the flask out to Bryce. "Have a taste," he said, nudging it closer.

"I'll pass," said Bryce.

"Come on Bryce; quit being such a boy-scout all the time. Have a drink for Chrissake, it ain't gonna kill you."

Bryce took the flask and had a swig; he grimaced and gave a whistle. "Wow, that's some stout shit."

Jackson smiled, took a big gulp, and proffered the flask again.

"Nah, I'm good."

Jackson shrugged and then swigged down the remainder of the flask.

"You'd better slow down on that shit, it'll rot your liver," said Bryce. He was smiling when he said it, but he had true concern for his cousin. His Aunt Ellen had complained about Jackson's father drinking too much, and alcoholism ran in families.

Jackson didn't know the whole story about his father's drinking. It had been kept very hush-hush and Bryce had only learned of it by accident—an overheard conversation. On a few occasions, Jackson's dad had become violent with his mom. It was something that parents tended to hide from their kids, and Bryce wasn't sure if that was good, or bad.

Just then, something caught Jackson's eye out in the water.

About twenty-five yards away, a huge water moccasin had curled up in the warm sun atop some partially submerged timbers.

"Bryce, look over there," Jackson whispered. He squinted an eye and aimed down his finger like the barrel of a rifle.

"Holy shit, that's a cottonmouth," Bryce said quietly. He slowly reached over and grabbed his .22 rifle; it leaned against the large walnut tree beside him. He took careful aim at the snake's head.

"You got him?" asked Jackson.

"Oh yeah . . . I got him," Bryce said, flicking off the safety. He exhaled slowly, and then gently squeezed off a shot from the small-caliber rifle.

Pop!

"Perfect head shot," Jackson shouted, as the snake dropped into the water.

"Man, he was a monster. I sure would've hated to run into him if we were swimming."

Trestle Hole was also a popular swimming area that people frequented during the hottest months of summer. The boys knew of a young girl that was bitten by a cottonmouth while swimming there a few years back; she almost died. Venomous snakes were a serious threat, and they were always eliminated on sight. While cottonmouths *were* rare to Bane County, Bryce figured there were enough non-venomous snakes around to keep the ecosystem in balance.

Jackson and Bryce were both excellent shots with a rifle, or with any weapon, as far as that went. They had grown up with guns and had been hunting since they were in grade school. They both knew how to track an animal, and how to stay down wind so it wouldn't smell them. They even knew how to follow the blood-trail of a wounded animal.

"Are you about ready to head home?" Jackson asked.

"Yeah, but let's go up to the cabin and fillet these fish before we leave. You know how much Grandma hates it when we clean fish at her house."

Jackson chuckled and agreed; he pulled the large stringer of fish from the river and they made their way up the hill. As they began cleaning the fish, Bryce decided to share his grandpa's story.

"Has Grandpa ever told you anything about the old Rickman farm?" Bryce asked.

"You mean the old ghost house?"

Bryce furrowed his brow. "Ghost house?"

Jackson smiled. "Yeah, my mom told me once that the old Rickman house was haunted. She said that somebody was killed there—or something like that—a long time ago. You know how Mom is: she's superstitious about that kind of crap."

Bryce nodded, but continued questioning. "So . . . Grandpa never told you the story about what happened to Mrs. Rickman?"

Jackson stopped cleaning his fish and looked over at Bryce. "What story?"

Bryce told him everything; exactly as Grandpa had told him the day before, including the part about the werewolf. When he had finished, Jackson actually looked a little spooked, but only for a second, he wrinkled his lips and shook his head.

"A werewolf," he said incredulously. "That's a load of horseshit. Grandpa was just pulling your leg."

"No, he wasn't," Bryce assured. "He was being dead serious."

"What—and you believed him?" Jackson scoffed. "You believe a werewolf killed Mrs. Rickman?"

"Hell no," said Bryce, "not a werewolf. But, *something* killed her, and all those other people."

Jackson still wasn't convinced. He thought that Grandpa was probably full of shit. "I'll tell you what, let's go over to the old Rickman house and check it out for ourselves."

Bryce raised an eyebrow, surprised by the suggestion. "Really?"

Jackson nodded. "Sure, why not . . . you're not scared, are you?"

Bryce frowned indignantly. "Don't be an idiot."

Jackson smiled. "Well, all right then; let's go check it out."

BRYCE AND JACKSON RETURNED to their grandparents' house, gave the fish fillets to Grandma, and then headed straight for the door.

"We're going squirrel hunting down by the old pecan grove, Grandma," said Bryce. "We'll be back before dark."

"The old pecan grove?" For some reason, Grandma seemed to balk at the idea at first, but then she said, " . . . Okay, you boys be careful."

As soon as they were out of sight, the two boys cut through the woods and made their way to Cedar Creek. By the time they arrived, it was nearing sundown.

"Let's make this quick, it'll be dark in less than an hour," Bryce pointed out. He tried not to seem anxious.

"We've got plenty of time," said Jackson, playing it cool.

They crossed over the new barbed-wire fence Bryce and Grandpa had built the day before and went down to the edge of the creek. The water was only about chest deep, so they took off their boots and clothes and held them above their heads, along with their rifles, in order to wade across. They moved cautiously through the bramble and bracken that lined the creek bank and entered the water.

"Yikes!" Bryce gasped. "This water's freezing."

Reaching the other side, they dressed quickly, and then worked their way along a sinuous path through the darkening forest. It was getting late, and the thick forest canopy blocked what little sunlight remained. Although they would never admit it to each other, a creeping disquietude had overtaken them. Every time a twig snapped or a rabbit scurried through the leaves, they would swing around and point their rifles in the direction of the noise.

After about three hundred yards, they came to a tree line and exited the dense forest into an open field. It was much brighter out in the open and both of them felt more at ease. Across the field, about a hundred yards away, they saw the old Rickman house. Without uttering a single word, the two boys moved quickly across the field, as if compelled by some strange, unknown force.

When they neared the house, they saw that it lay in ruins, nothing more than a dilapidated, old shack. There were holes in the roof and walls, and the front porch was sagging, about to collapse. Vines embowered the rotting walls, growing through holes and missing windows, and waist-high weeds surrounded it. The old house stood alone, as cold and silent as an empty grave; they could see why Jackson's mom had called it "haunted."

"Look at that," Bryce said, pointing to the ridge of the roof. "It looks like it was struck by lightning." The gable of the old house was black and charred, crumbling.

"It's a wonder it didn't burn down," said Jackson. " . . . Rain must have put it out."

They made their way to the front of the house and stood side by side in silence; the entire place was *extremely* creepy.

With great apprehension, they stared across the weed-covered front porch toward the open doorway. It was near sunset, and darkness cloaked the old house's interior. Their hearts raced, trying to gather enough courage to enter. They looked to each other for a brief moment, then back at the dark entrance; Bryce decided to go first.

He moved tentatively toward the front porch, each step slow and unsteady in the thick weeds. As Jackson watched, a mischievous grin came over his face; he couldn't pass up this opportunity.

Jackson drew a deep breath and shouted: "Mrs. Rickman!"

Bryce nearly jumped out of his skin. He turned, glaring, and stormed back to where Jackson stood. He drew back, and punched him in the shoulder with everything he had. "You asshole!" Bryce hissed.

Jackson was laughing hysterically and rubbing his arm. "Ow! Shit . . . all right . . . let's go in together."

Jackson was family and Bryce loved him like a brother, but he wasn't always the sharpest tool in the shed. Grandma had once said, *"If Jackson ever has an idea . . . it'll die of loneliness."*

They waded through the weeds growing through the floorboards of the front porch, and moved slowly toward the doorway. Just as they were entering the dark house, Bryce saw something.

"Holy shit," he exclaimed, "look at this!" Along the length of the old doorframe, you could still see the deep claw marks.

"Son of a bitch," Jackson said. He rubbed his hand over the deep grooves cut into the wood.

"Just like in Grandpa's story," Bryce admitted nervously. He couldn't believe what he was seeing.

Jackson was stunned; he just stood there, rubbing his hand over the giant claw marks. "A werewolf killed Mrs. Rickman?"

he said, in a hushed tone. He wasn't sure whether he was asking a question or stating a fact.

"Look at the size of these things," Bryce remarked. He traced the contours with his finger. "What could have done this—a bear?"

"Bigger than any bear I've ever seen," Jackson protested.

There was a loud *crash* and the floorboards began to shake violently; pieces of the old house started to collapse.

"Shit!" they chorused.

They bolted off the front porch into the weed-choked yard, then turned and raised their rifles. After a long, fearful moment of aiming their guns at the dark house, they finally realized that nothing was coming for them.

"It was just a possum or a coon, or something crawling around under the house," Jackson said breathlessly.

"Yeah . . . that's all it was," Bryce agreed. His heart was pumping a mile-a-minute.

Out of nowhere, a strong gust of wind blew through the old house and swirled around them in the grass.

"Let's get the hell out of here," Jackson urged.

"Good plan," said Bryce.

Together they hightailed it across the open field, back toward the tree line of the forest. They moved like a military unit on high alert; rifles partially raised, keeping a 360-degree view of their surroundings at all times.

Loping across the field, the wind continued to swirl around them, grasping at their legs and feet; it seemed to follow them relentlessly. Bryce noticed a sorrowful moaning sound that carried ever so faintly on the wind; it seemed to be coming from the old Rickman house.

It's just the wind soughing through holes in the old house, Bryce assured himself.

He was about to ask Jackson if he, too, heard the moaning, when as suddenly as it had arrived, the wind abated. A tomb-like hush surrounded them. The only sound they heard was the scuffling of their boots as they moved through the withered grass.

When they arrived at the tree line of the forest, it was much darker than before. The sun was setting fast and they were both extremely skittish. As he entered the dark forest, Bryce chanced a final glance at the old house. He saw a strange ethereal light flickering in one of the windows—it appeared to be, a candle.

What the hell . . . It must be the sun reflecting off a piece of broken glass, Bryce figured, trying to reconcile the strange apparition.

They bounded through the dark forest at a fast pace, struggling to see in the dim light of the setting sun. A gauzy blanket of mist had formed on the forest floor, obscuring their footpath in a milky cloud. As Bryce stumbled forward, trying to find his footing in the thick layer of purling mist, the roots and vines on the forest floor took on the appearance of writhing serpents and slithering worms. In fact, the entire forest seemed to come alive with a dark, malevolent presence.

Trudging forward as fast as possible, they had the uncanny feeling that something followed them. There, in the shadows, just out of sight—something lurked in the darkness. Whatever it was, it stayed parallel to their path, keeping pace with their every move. It was something dark, a shadow among shadows, and everywhere it went—faint whispers seemed to follow it.

They never clearly saw or heard anything, but they knew it was there. They could feel it—deep in their gut—something was *watching* them.

Something—*wanted* them.

The sun had already set by the time they arrived at Cedar Creek; they could barely see the water.

"You cross first, I'll cover," Jackson told Bryce.

"I'm on it," Bryce replied, racing to undress.

He quickly pulled off his boots and clothes and waded across the creek while Jackson aimed his rifle into the dark forest. There was no complaint of frigid water this time; in fact, he didn't even notice.

Bryce clambered up the creek bank and dressed quickly, then turned and pointed his rifle into the darkness.

"Go, Jackson, I've got you covered," Bryce hollered.

After Jackson made it across, the two boys double-timed it through the darkness without saying a single word until they saw the lights of home. For some reason, after they had crossed the water, they felt safer. As if, the thing following them had stayed on the other side of Cedar Creek.

Looking out her kitchen window, Grandma McNeel saw the boys walking quickly toward the house. She hollered at them through the open window. "You boys ready for some fried fish?"

Bryce and Jackson both flinched at the sudden sound of her voice, and felt foolish for being so jumpy. "Sure, Grandma, that sounds great," said Bryce.

Grandma McNeel saw how nervous and out of breath they looked; she smiled slyly and questioned them. "Where are all the squirrels?"

Bryce and Jackson gave each other a confused look, and then remembered they were supposed to have been squirrel hunting. "We didn't see any," Jackson offered.

Grandma McNeel peered at the two boys over her glasses. "Mm-hmm . . . I see," she said with a skeptical frown. She always knew when they were up to something.

After supper, they helped Grandma clean up around the kitchen. Taking part in a familiar routine was strangely comforting and helped take their minds off everything. When Jackson was ready to leave, Bryce walked him out to his car. Neither of the two boys was ready to talk about what they had just seen, so instead, they just made small talk.

"Got any plans for Labor Day?" Jackson asked, opening his car door and taking a seat.

"Nope, just need to get a few things ready for school."

"Are you still planning on heading off to college after high school?"

"You bet," said Bryce. "I'm really looking forward to college."

"You always did like school a lot more than me."

"Are you still planning on getting your commercial license and driving big-rigs like your old-man?" Bryce asked.

"That's the plan."

But that *wasn't* the plan. Jackson hadn't told anyone his *actual* plan, not even his best friend. He thought if people knew, they would try to stop him. Jackson had decided to join the military.

Six months earlier, the U.S. military had decimated the Iraqi army and liberated the country of Kuwait in just four short days. Operation Desert Storm had been the most decisive victory in U.S. military history. As a result, patriotism and military enlistment was at an all-time high.

Don Davis—Jackson's boss at the Western Auto store—had been an Army Ranger in Vietnam, and he and Jackson had talked at great length about military service. So, after much deliberation, Jackson had decided that he, too, wanted to be an Army Ranger; and considering his proficiency with firearms, and excellent physical condition, there was no doubt he would excel.

Jackson would turn eighteen a month before he graduated high school. He would enlist, and head to boot camp, right after graduation. That was his *actual* plan, but he was keeping it to himself.

Jackson closed his door and started the car. Driving away, he hung his head out the window and shouted to Bryce. "I'll pick you up first thing Tuesday morning for school."

Bryce waved goodbye and walked back to the house.

THAT NIGHT, a warm summer breeze blew through Bryce's bedroom window; it brought with it the aroma of cedar and the faint chirring of crickets. He lay in bed—deep in thought—considering the claw marks he had seen at the old Rickman house, and the story his grandpa had told.

He no longer had any doubts about his grandpa's story; he had seen the proof. Some type of large animal had killed Mrs. Rickman.

But not a werewolf, he thought, shaking his head. *This wasn't some Hollywood movie—Lon Chaney Jr. hadn't been running around the countryside back then eating people—this was real life.*

"It had to be a bear," he thought aloud. "A really *big* bear. Nothing else could have made those claw marks."

What still bothered Bryce, however, was whether something had actually followed them through the forest from the old Rickman house. Had Jackson conjured some malign spirit—the ghost of Mrs. Rickman—when he shouted her name; or had they just imagined the entire thing?

"Don't be ridiculous," he muttered, "there's no such thing as ghosts."

But what about the candle I saw in the window? He mused, *and the moaning sounds?*

"It was just the sun reflecting on a broken pane of glass," he said. "And the moaning I heard was just the wind."

There was nothing in the forest, he decided. *It was just my overactive imagination.*

Staring out the window, Bryce could see the dark woods in the distance. He watched as tall, wind-stirred trees swayed back and forth in the night breeze. The moon was low in the sky and shined brightly through their boughs, casting long, mottled shadows across the field. As the trees creaked and twisted in the windy darkness, black shadows crept and writhed across the ground. Bryce thought once again of the dark forest on the other side of Cedar Creek—and of the faint whispering of the shadows.

An unbidden shudder raced through his body, as the rimy hand of fear touched an icy finger to his spine. He jumped out of bed, ran to the window and slammed it shut.

With a loud squeak, he twisted the old metal latch and locked the window. As he closed the curtains, he realized—this was the first time he had ever locked his window.

Bryce went over to his gun rack, grabbed his deer rifle and popped out the magazine to make sure it was loaded. He slapped it back in place and quickly chambered a round. Checking the safety, he placed the weapon gingerly against the headboard of his bed for quick access.

This is ridiculous, he thought. *We're talking about something that happened thirty-eight years ago. I'm just being stupid.*

Feeling a little more secure, Bryce climbed back into bed and tried to get some sleep. He chuckled, thinking of the rash-of-shit Jackson would give him if he ever found out that he had locked his window, and was sleeping with a loaded weapon.

CHAPTER 4

Forgotten Moon

SILVER CANYON HIGH SCHOOL was located just off Main Street near the center of town, and today, it was bustling with activity. It was the first day of the new school year, and for the one hundred and sixty students in attendance, it was total chaos.

A black Camaro IROC-Z roared into the school's parking lot with the old *Aerosmith* song "Back in the Saddle" blasting at full volume. Everyone watched as Jackson and Bryce hopped out of the car and headed toward the building.

Various young girls who had gathered in front of the school greeted the boys; Bryce and Jackson were both quite popular with the young ladies of Bane County.

"Good morning, Bryce."

"Hi, Jackson."

Bryce responded obligingly to each girl with a wave and a smile, while Jackson—with his ever-present bad-boy persona—gave only a lift of his chin.

Inside the school's main hallway, the two boys weaved through the yammering crowd, working their way toward the assembly hall. As Bryce squeezed through the packed hallway, he felt a hand grab his arm; he turned to find a young girl smiling up at him. It was the same girl from the parking lot of the movie theater.

"Hi," Bryce said, smiling, a little taken aback.

"Hi, yourself," she said, with a diffident smile. "I never got a chance to say thank you for what you did, so . . . thanks."

"Forget about it. That jerk had it coming."

"Well . . . anyway"—she paused—"Hey, I'm working as a carhop at CB's Drive-in now. You should come by and see me—I mean—if you have time," she finished timidly.

"Definitely," said Bryce. "That's a cool place to work. They have great burgers and you get to wear roller-skates."

"By the way, I'm Wendy—Wendy Walker," she said, with slightly more confidence.

"Nice to meet you; I'm Bryce McNeel."

"I know," she said coyly.

"Well, all right then—Wendy Walker," he said, with a nod. "I'll see you later." He gave her a quick wink, then turned and jogged down the hallway to catch up with Jackson—who waited with a huge grin on his face.

"Just, shut up, Jackson," Bryce said, smiling. "Not a word. Not. One. Word."

Jackson just held up his hands and kept smiling as they continued down the hallway.

After all the details of class schedules, locker assignments and other trivialities were resolved, Bryce and Jackson went their separate ways to their assigned classrooms. Bryce's first period class was Biology; it was his favorite class—he figured it must be in his genes.

Over the years, Bryce's grandparents had told him all there was to know about his mother and father. Both his parents had been field biologists with the U.S. Fish and Wildlife Service and they had worked primarily inside The Refuge.

His parents met in college and had married right after

graduation; Bryce was born a year later. He had been four-years-old when his parents were killed in a house fire, and Bryce often wondered how his life might have been different if his parents hadn't died. Grandma and Grandpa McNeel had given Bryce an excellent life, and he loved them with all his heart; but he still wondered how things might have been different.

THE DAY WENT BY QUICKLY, and after school, Bryce and Jackson met in the parking lot.

"How'd it go?" asked Bryce.

"Well—Mrs. Jenner sent me to have a little 'talk' with the principal about my 'wardrobe selection.'"

Bryce blinked, "You're joking."

"No—as funny as that is... Mr. Burrows said my T-shirt was 'risqué and suggestive' and that I should 'rethink my choice in apparel'."

Bryce issued a loud laugh. Jackson was wearing an *Aerosmith* T-shirt that depicted a scantily clad woman with large breasts on an elevator, and the words "Going Down" inside a speech bubble; and as always, Jackson had cut the sleeves off.

"And how was *your* day?" Jackson said drolly.

"Good. It's gonna be a great last year," Bryce replied.

Jackson shook his head and hopped in the car. "Like I said, you always liked school a lot more than me." He reached over and popped an old *AC/DC* tape into the cassette deck. The song, "If You Want Blood" blasted over the speakers as they squealed tires out of the parking lot.

Before heading home, they decided to head over to the Dairy Treat and grab a root-beer-float. The two boys sat at an old rickety picnic table enjoying their drinks, then after a while, they began to talk about their visit to the old Rickman house. It was the first time they had spoken about the events of two days ago, and now that some of the edginess had worn off, their discussion had been mostly light-hearted. It felt good to talk about it, and by the time they hopped into the car to head home, they both felt a lot less anxious.

THE FIRST THREE WEEKS OF SCHOOL were uneventful and went by quickly. Bryce was enjoying his senior year and easily maintaining his perfect 4.0 GPA. In fact, he had never been happier.

He and Jackson had stopped worrying about Grandpa's werewolf story and their visit to the old Rickman house. They had talked about it on numerous occasions and had concluded that a huge bear made the claw marks they had seen. They also decided that what happened in the dark forest had been nothing more than their overactive imaginations.

Although they had agreed to forget about the entire incident, neither of the boys mentioned the fact that a tiny flame of uneasiness still guttered inside each of them.

Bryce had turned his focus entirely to school, his grades, and deciding which college to attend. It had always been his dream to attend a top university and experience life in a large city. He had already started the process of applying to several schools, and with his grades and abilities, all of them would accept him. Everything was progressing exactly as he had planned.

However, what Bryce didn't realize was that life was about to change for the people of Bane County. While Monday, September 23, 1991 had seemed like any other cool autumn afternoon, tonight, something very rare would take place.

Most people around Silver Canyon hadn't realized that today was the fall equinox; or that tonight, there would be a full moon. In fact, tonight would be the first *true* harvest moon to rise over Bane County in a very long time.

Of course, only the old-time farmers followed such things, and there were fewer and fewer of them around each year. Over the ages, the *true* harvest moon had become, a forgotten moon.

※

ROBERT MILLER TAPPED HIS HAND on the steering wheel of his new Range Rover, and lip-synced to an old *Creedence Clearwater Revival* song on the radio. The yellow stripes of Highway 50 had become a monotonous blur after two hours of driving along the desolate highway.

Elisa Brooks, Robert's fiancée, sat barefooted in the passenger seat, resting her feet on the dashboard, painting her toenails. As she squinted, focusing on her little toe with the tiny brush, the tip of her tongue emerged from the corner of her mouth.

Robert smiled, giving her a sidelong glance. *Damn she's cute*, he thought, *I'm a lucky man. I just hope she doesn't get that crap on my dashboard.*

"Are you laughing at me?" Elisa asked, noticing his glance.

"No, not at all," Robert replied. "I was just thinking what a lucky man I am to be marrying such a beautiful woman."

"Aw, you're so sweet—and so full of shit. You were thinking, 'I hope she doesn't spill polish on my new Range Rover.'"

"*Our* new Range Rover," Robert corrected. "We're getting married in three weeks."

"God, 'three weeks'," Elisa repeated. "We'll never have everything ready in time. I can't believe I let you talk me into a week-long camping trip."

"You're gonna love it," Robert said. "Plus, we needed a break;

your mother was driving me nuts."

Elisa swatted his arm. "What about *your* mother?" she countered. "Did you see the table cloth pattern she picked out? It looked like a florist threw-up on a table."

Robert guffawed. "Yeah, those *were* pretty hideous."

Elisa noticed a large, blue road sign ahead, strategically positioned in front of a small store. "LAST GAS FOR 109 MILES," she read aloud. "Where the heck are you taking me?"

Robert smiled, "I told you this place was in the hinterlands; there's a *whole* lot of nothing out here."

"And you've been there before?"

"This'll be my fourth time. It's amazing, you're gonna love it."

"So, tell me about it, what's it like?" Elisa asked.

"I can do better than that," said Robert. "Look in the glovebox; I've got a huge travel guide that tells all about it."

"Where'd you get that from?" she asked, digging through the glove compartment.

"Well, I know how much you like keepsakes, so I called and asked them to mail it to me."

Elisa smiled at Robert; he was so thoughtful. It was one of the things she loved about him. She removed the booklet and looked at the cover: "Historic Bane County," she read aloud.

Elisa curled her legs up in the large leather seat of the Range Rover, mindful not to smudge her freshly painted toenails, and sat quietly reading. Whenever she found something of interest, she shared it with Robert.

"So," she said, "Silver Canyon National Wildlife Refuge is located in Bane County."

"Mm-hmm," Robert agreed.

"Well," Elisa added, "did you know that Bane County is an

island?"

"An island?" he said, furrowing his brow.

"That's right," she noted. "It says right here: 'Bane County is a large river-island almost the size of Delaware'."

"Really?" said Robert, "An island?"

"Yep, it says that it's, 'sixty miles long, and forty miles wide, and that it's completely surrounded by the Carantina River and its anabranch, the Little Carantina'."

"What the hell's an 'anabranch?'" Robert asked.

"Well, I'm not exactly sure," she admitted. "But looking at this map, the Carantina River appears to fork; it encircles the county and then rejoins again—creating a river-island."

"Huh, I knew there were rivers on both sides of the county, but I never realized that it was *completely* surrounded."

"Yep, it also says that the wildlife refuge is over a million acres."

"That, I knew," he said. "The place is immense. You could spend your entire life hiking in there and never see the same place twice."

Elisa squinted at the book and then chuckled. "The outline of Bane County is shaped like a pork-chop," she said, showing the map to Robert.

"Yeah, you're right," he said, giving a quick glance, "it does look like a pork-chop."

"And except for the little bone at the bottom"—Elisa continued with her pork-chop analogy—"the entire thing is the wildlife refuge."

"That little bone," Robert said, joining in her analogy, "is where all the people live; in reality, the canyon area is about eight miles wide, and twenty miles long."

"How many miles is the wildlife refuge?" Elisa asked.

"It's roughly forty miles wide, and forty miles long; about sixteen hundred square miles."

"Wow."

"Yeah, it's huge."

Elisa continued to read quietly for some time and appeared to be quite fascinated with the information. When they finally reached the edge of Bane County, Robert pointed to the Carantina River.

"Look," said Robert.

"Oh, it's so beautiful," she breathed.

They passed over the long bridge into Bane County and followed the highway north through the canyon. As Elisa looked out her window, she saw a green-and-white road sign that read: SILVER CANYON 18 MILES.

Elisa marveled at the picturesque setting: the pastoral grasslands and gentle rolling hills, the heavily forested areas that lined small creeks and streams, and mile after mile of small farms and ranches. At one point, they even passed an enormous, knobby field of pumpkins nearing time to harvest. It was like stepping back in time and it gave her a warm and peaceful feeling.

However, when her eyes came to rest on the cloud-tipped mountains in the distance, that peaceful feeling changed to one of apprehension.

"Is that the wildlife refuge?" she asked, pointing to the mountains on the horizon.

"Yep," said Robert. "That's it."

"Do you suppose we'll meet any wild animals?"

"You mean like—lions and tigers and bears?"

She swatted him on the shoulder. "I'm serious. Are there any dangerous animals in the wildlife refuge?"

"Well, there *are* timber wolves and bears in the wildlife refuge," he admitted, "but, they're really afraid of people and stay deep inside the interior. The only animal we *might* see is a mountain lion—I hear they can be curious—but they're afraid of people, too. They would never attack two full-grown adults. They're more afraid of us than we are of them."

"Are you sure?"

"Positive," Robert said. He touched her leg gently and met Elisa's eyes. "I promise."

Elisa smiled and nodded hesitantly.

"We'll be there in less than fifteen minutes," said Robert, "and I know the perfect place to have lunch."

"Where?"

"You'll see," Robert said, smiling. "You'll see."

Robert and Elisa walked into Cătălina's Café and found a booth next to a window. Robert had been planning their hiking trip through the Silver Canyon National Wildlife Refuge for weeks and wanted them to have a good meal before they started living off beef jerky and trail mix for the next week.

He knew the north side of Silver Canyon had several good Gypsy restaurants and that you could even have your fortune told. When they arrived and he told Elisa his plan, she seemed very excited; Robert loved to see her smile.

The menus were already on the table, so they began looking at their choices.

"So, this is Gypsy food?" she asked quietly, not knowing if the term "Gypsy" was a racial epithet.

"I think people refer to it as 'Bohemian' food," said Robert. "I'm not sure whether or not 'Gypsy' is considered a slur."

An attractive young woman, about seventeen- or eighteen-years-old approached their table. Her long, black hair and radiant, pale-blue eyes accentuated her traditional Gypsy garb.

"How may I help you?" she asked. Her smile was captivating.

"What do you recommend?" asked Robert.

"The roast pork and stuffed dumplings are very good," she assured.

Robert and Elisa looked at each other and nodded. "Oh, and can we also have some kolache for dessert, please?"

The young woman fixed them with a knowing look. "But, of course. You must have kolache and coffee," she insisted, with a pleased smile.

The meal was amazing and they ate until they nearly burst. They sat contently for a while chatting, laughing, and finishing their coffee, and then they asked for the check. As Robert paid the bill, Elisa asked the young woman where she could have her fortune told.

"Cătălina, my great-grandmother can tell your fortune," she offered, gesturing to the doorway at the rear of the café draped in beads.

Elisa looked at Robert and tugged at his arm. "Come on, let's try it."

Robert nodded and they followed the young woman to the back of the restaurant. Passing through the bead-covered doorway, they made their way up a narrow, creaking staircase to a quaint little apartment atop the restaurant.

Cătălina Pătrașcu was a hundred and two years old. She had long flowing hair as white as snow, and her coriaceous face was as dark and creased as a tanned hide. She sat at a small table holding a white Manx cat on her lap, and appeared as if she had been expecting them. In fact, she seemed a bit impatient, as if she had been kept waiting.

The young woman spoke quietly into her great-grandmother's ear. "Străbunică, this lady would like you to *'see'* for her."

Cătălina nodded her head knowingly and waved away the words. The young woman lifted the cat from her great-grandmother's lap and stood behind her. She motioned for Elisa to come forward. The old woman's hands were horribly deformed, misshapen by rheumatoid arthritis. As Elisa moved to the table, she met the old woman's eyes.

Cătălina's piercing gray eyes were a bottomless pool; they seemed to look right through Elisa, and she found it very disquieting. The old woman stared at her intently, without saying a word, until Elisa began to squirm uncomfortably. Robert was about to suggest they come back another time, when the young woman spoke quietly.

"You must pay first, or the spirits will be angry." She motioned to the small bowl on the table. Robert wrinkled his lips and nodded, then placed a twenty into the bowl.

Cătălina had come from the old country when she was just a little girl and spoke with a heavy Romani accent. "Sit, please and show me your hands. Your palms—show them to me, please."

Elisa took a seat across the table from the old woman and proffered her hands. Cătălina gazed unyieldingly into her eyes as she spoke.

"Your left hand shows your past and all those who you carry with you," she explained. "Your right hand unveils your future, that you may choose your path."

Cătălina reached her decrepit hands across the table and took Elisa's left hand in hers; she flinched slightly at her touch. The old woman closed her eyes briefly—then spoke.

"You are alone. No brother, no sister," Cătălina asserted, as she opened her eyes.

Elisa was stunned; she looked at Robert with wide eyes. "She's right, I'm an only child."

Cătălina continued to hold Elisa's left hand and again closed her eyes. After a moment, she nodded to herself and smiled.

"Your father wishes he could be at your wedding," she imparted.

Elisa quickly pulled her hand from Cătălina's grasp. "My father died last year," she said sharply.

Cătălina gazed at Elisa with caring eyes; she smiled reassuringly and offered a single nod. Elisa was shocked, her heart was racing, how could this woman have known these things? She looked at Robert for reassurance, and then slowly put her hands back on the table.

Cătălina reached across and took Elisa's right hand in hers, and closed her eyes. A startled look came over the old woman's face; she quickly released the hand and pulled back, eyes wide with surprise.

"Where are you going?" Cătălina asked abruptly.

Stunned by the old woman's reaction, Elisa became confused. "What do you mean?"

She asked her again, more forcefully. "Where are you going?"

Elisa became nervous and defensive; she met Robert's eyes for a brief moment and then answered the old woman. "We're going backpacking in the wildlife refuge."

Cătălina began shaking her head and rose shakily to her feet. "No!" she commanded. "You will not—you must not!"

The young woman rushed to her great-grandmother's side and tried to calm her. "Străbunică, what's wrong?"

The old woman's eyes rolled white and she began to intone with trancelike repetition. "Tonight it comes . . . tonight it comes!"

Elisa had become extremely upset and wanted to leave immediately. Robert took her arm and drew her away from the old woman's table. They hurried down the stairs and left the café with Elisa in tears.

As they walked out the door, toward the parking lot of the wildlife refuge, they could still here Cătălina's voice in the distance. "Tonight it comes..."

Elisa leaned against the Range Rover crying. Robert put his arms around her and tried to console her.

"What the hell was *that*?" she demanded.

"She's just some crazy old bitch, forget about it," Robert said.

"Well how the hell did she know I was an only child, and that stuff about our wedding and my father?"

"It was just lucky guesses, that's what these Gypsies do."

"She said we shouldn't go into the wildlife refuge—let's just go home, Robert, please."

"I'm not gonna let some fruitcake old lady ruin the trip I've been planning for weeks. It's all just a big show they put on for money."

Robert held Elisa close and kissed her cheek. "Let's just put on our backpacks, and head into the wildlife refuge like we planned. Okay, sweetie?"

Eventually, Elisa conceded; she nodded and smiled. "You're right," she said, wiping the tears from her cheeks. "I'm being ridiculous. We shouldn't let some stupid Gypsy fortune teller ruin our vacation."

"That's my girl," Robert said, with a kiss to her forehead. "We still have a few hours to find a good campsite before dark."

Robert helped Elisa slip on her backpack, gave her a kiss and reassured her once again that everything would be fine. He made sure he locked the Range Rover and headed toward the main entrance and game warden's office.

From the sidewalk on other side of the street, Cătălina and her great-granddaughter watched the two backpackers walk toward the forbidding forest.

"Devla go with them," Cătălina said quietly. She rubbed the silver amulet that hung around her neck.

The old woman turned slowly and her great-granddaughter helped her back inside.

"You did what you could," her great-granddaughter assured.

"They will not be seen again," Cătălina said sadly. "From this day forth, they will live with those who whisper."

"Those who whisper?" the young woman questioned.

"The souls of those killed by the *Neuri* can never rest," she imparted. "They are cursed to walk the earth—as whispering shadows—for all-time."

The young woman had heard her great-grandmother's stories of the hideous creature she referred to as the *Neuri*, and the possible fate of the two backpackers was not something that she cared to consider.

Near the main entrance of the wildlife refuge, Robert and Elisa entered the warden's office. Bruce Fletcher, the local game warden, greeted them.

"Good afternoon folks, how can I help you?" asked Bruce.

"We need a one-week camping permit," replied Robert.

"All right; have you been here before?" the warden inquired.

"Yes, a few times."

"So, you're aware it's pretty tough terrain then?" Bruce said, looking at Elisa.

Great, Robert thought, a*nother person trying to talk my fiancée out of going.* He glanced at Elisa's face and could see the concern building.

"Yeah, like I said, I've been here before and it's getting kind of late, so, if we could, please . . ." Robert said impatiently.

"No problem, that'll be thirty-five dollars."

Robert quickly filled out the form, paid the game warden and headed for the door. As they were leaving, the game warden told them to be careful and asked that they stop by his office to sign-out when they returned in seven days. That way, he'd know they had made it back safely. Robert agreed and he and Elisa headed into the wildlife refuge.

As soon as they entered the forest, Elisa noticed a change. It was cooler in the forest and the brightness of the sun didn't penetrate the thick canopy. Small dapples of light made their way to the forest floor along brilliant sunbeams that swirled with tiny insects and motes of dust.

"It's so green," Elisa said, with amazement. "It's almost blinding." She looked up at the canopy and turned in a slow circle. The profusion of flora was breathtaking. A green epiphytic moss embowered everything: trunks of trees, boulders and rocks, even the forest floor. Large ferns and lichens sprang from every crevice.

The sounds of town quickly faded away, as the smell of pine and cedar surrounded her; and there was another scent, as well, the musty organic smell of detritus and dirt. It reminded Elisa of her rose garden in the spring, when she would weed and turn the soil, adding mulch and fresh topsoil to the beds.

The familiar aroma somehow calmed her apprehension of the forest, allowing her to appreciate the amazing beauty. She listened to the calming sounds of birds warbling and chirping, as they flitted from tree to tree. High in the canopy, she heard the trilling of insects and the occasional rustle of leaves as large boughs swayed in a light, fitful breeze.

"It's so beautiful," she said, taking Robert's hand.

"I told you," he said. "Just wait, it gets better."

"I don't see how."

They pushed on through the dense forest, winding through giant trees that towered above them, like mighty Titans of old. It was like entering a new world. Civilization slowly faded away and the woods grew thicker around them, as they moved deeper and deeper into the verdant wilderness.

By sunset, Robert and Elisa had hiked several miles into the dense forest and stopped to make camp near a small pond at the base of a high cliff. Small rivulets of water sprang from the ancient rock-face, trickling down along water-carved runnels. At the base of the cliff, the water formed a small, pellucid stream that meandered aimlessly across the meadow and emptied into the pond.

Robert was proud of himself for finding such a perfect little glade, with fresh running water for cooking and bathing. He dug a fire-pit and encircled it with large stones, then collected a large supply of firewood from all around the campsite. Starting a fire, Robert placed pots of water to boil for their evening meal of dried beans and rice, along with a pot for coffee.

As Robert prepared dinner, Elisa busied herself with setting up their tent and sleeping bags, and organizing the campsite. She was a bit of a neat-freak, and believed a campsite should be well ordered and tidy. She even picked wildflowers for the tent, placing them in an old rusted can she found in the grass.

After dinner, they sat on a blanket by the placid waters of the small pond, drinking coffee and watching the moon ascend above the tall trees across the water.

"I've never seen the moon look so beautiful," Elisa said. "It's amazing."

"I know. It's so bright, you don't even need a flashlight," Robert said. "Now, aren't you glad you didn't listen to that crazy old Gypsy woman?"

"I am. This vacation is perfect." She rested her head against his shoulder. After finishing their coffee, they went back to the tent, snuggled into their doublewide sleeping bag, made love, and fell blissfully asleep.

Several hours passed, and they awoke to find the fire had dwindled and the night had grown much colder.

"It's freezing," Elisa said, shivering.

"I'll go put some more wood on the fire," said Robert.

He got dressed, crawled out of the tent and stirred the hot coals. Placing the last small piece of kindling into the pit, he restarted the fire.

"We need more wood," said Robert. "I'll be right back, sweetie."

"All right," Elisa said. "I'm going to heat some water for tea."

Robert walked into the forest to gather more firewood, while Elisa readied a pot of water for a cup of evening tea. The moon was now high in the sky and shined so brightly that Robert didn't bother bringing his flashlight.

He had already scavenged all the firewood around the campsite, so he needed to walk farther into the forest to find more wood. To keep track of his location, he would occasionally look back through the trees toward his campfire. After moving some distance into the woods, he looked back, and could barely see the ardent glow of his campfire in the distance. As he gathered the wood, Robert suddenly noticed a horrible smell in the air.

God, it smells as if something died around here, he thought.

As he bent down for another piece of wood, Robert heard a loud rustling up ahead. He strained his eyes, trying to see what was making the noise; a formless shadow seemed to move in the brush.

"Hello . . . is anybody there?" Robert asked timidly, trying to focus his eyes on the shadowy form. Again, the shadow moved, leaves crunched underfoot.

"Who's there?" Robert said, with more conviction. "This isn't funny." He was still unable to see clearly, still uncertain if something was actually there . . . until it stepped out of the shadows into the moonlit forest and a gigantic silhouette unveiled.

The moonlight reflected brightly in the werewolf's eyes; they burned through the darkness like blazing amber flames. Beneath the beast's gaping mouth, swirls of hot breath condensed into the cold night air.

Robert's eyes now focused, he could clearly see the grotesque creature approaching him. For a brief moment, shock overcame his body; his feet were rooted to the ground. His voice froze in his throat and he couldn't bring himself to scream. Finally, he dropped the firewood and ran; he ran as fast as his feet could carry him, toward the tiny speck of light in the distance—his campfire.

His heart pounded against his ribs like a jackhammer as his body shifted from shock to fear. His muscles burned like fire as an overload of fear-pumped adrenaline coursed through his veins. As the light of his campfire began to grow larger in the distance, he didn't dare look back. His panic-stricken brain could only process one word: "Run."

At first, Robert could only hear his own rapid heartbeat pounding in his ears, but the sound of his heart was soon overridden by another repetitive sound—a sound coming from directly behind him. It was the sound of large feet, pounding into the forest floor as they jogged effortlessly behind him. Warm puffs of hot breath began pulsing against the back of his neck and he could hear the slavering sounds of a ravenous maw. A final massive burst of adrenaline fueled his terror. He released a long, ineffable scream that rang-out through the darkness—just as he was grabbed and thrown to the ground.

When the ghastly sound of Robert's scream reached Elisa's ears, she leapt to her feet, dropping her cup of tea into the dwindling fire; a hiss of steam burst from the guttering flames. She had never heard such a primordial, agonizing cry. It was a horrific, visceral scream of anguish, like the frantic wailing of a dying animal. A long, thunderous scream had pierced through the night—and then . . . silence.

Robert?

Rigid with fear, Elisa stood in silence, peering into the night. What once seemed like a brightly lit, moon-bathed forest—a verdant wonderland—was now a dark and menacing wilderness. A godforsaken place where inky-black shadows seemed to flow and knit together, consuming the forest and expelling the moonlight—a place of pure, unspeakable evil.

Only a moment ago, Elisa's life with Robert had been wonderful and full of promise. Now, gripped by fear, she couldn't move, she didn't know what to do.

Elisa was unaware of the horrors yet to come—it was only Robert's *first* scream that she had heard.

The werewolf rolled Robert onto his back, pinning him to the ground with a huge clawed hand. The beast had been right behind him the entire time, toying with him, a cat playing with a mouse. Robert began to scream hysterically, begging and pleading at the top of his lungs as he looked into the hideous face of the beast staring down at him. The werewolf cocked his head from side to side, listening with *great* pleasure to the tormented screams of its quarry. Drool flowed in torrents from its gaping mouth onto Robert's chest, as the beast *lusted* for its first mouthful of flesh.

Horrid screams of anguish echoed through the canyons as the werewolf swiped his razored claws across Robert's chest. The sweet coppery aroma of fresh blood poured from the flayed skin. The beast reveled in the torture of his prey.

The hellish screams only fueled the werewolf's hunger; the beast dragged his claws across Robert's stomach and eviscerated him; a skein of intestines poured from his body. The shock of seeing his open stomach spilling onto the ground stopped Robert's screams—but only for a moment. When the creature jammed its clawed hand inside his body and pulled out his liver, he relinquished an immense final scream of torment—a tortured scream that echoed through the canyons, even after Robert's heart had stopped beating.

The werewolf yearned to feast on his kill, but he knew there was more prey nearby that couldn't be allowed to escape. As the beast stalked toward the lambent flames of the campfire in the distance, the thrill of the hunt and the anticipation of the kill once again fueled his irrepressible lust for human flesh.

Elisa stared vacantly at the tiny flames of a dwindling campfire; their flickering reflection capered numbly in her eyes. Her arms wrapped tightly around her knees, she pulled them tight against her chest, rocking back and forth in a mindless daze. The horrifying sounds of Robert's vicious mutilation still echoed in her mind. The unspeakable horror of being forced to listen to Robert's torturous death had pushed Elisa's mental being far past its breaking point, and into a trance-like, fugue state of insanity.

When the werewolf stalked into the campsite, Elisa didn't scream; she just stared blankly at the towering beast. Her body shaking, she mumbled the same phrase repeatedly.

"Tonight it comes—tonight it comes," she intoned, rocking back and forth.

Not until the beast grabbed her by the throat, lifted her into the air and shook her violently, did she finally awake from her trance-like state. She screamed hysterically. Elisa had momentarily regained her sanity—just in time, to be eaten alive.

Miles away, sound asleep in her bed, an old Gypsy woman sat bolt upright and screamed. A young woman ran to her bedside and found her great-grandmother sitting with her eyes rolled white. Only three words passed her lips before she finally awoke.

"Tonight it comes," she whispered.

The werewolf knelt over Elisa's lifeless body and gorged on her tender flesh. He pulled succulent organs from the cavernous maw that had been her ribcage, and feasted until he could eat no more.

Moving to the edge of the pond, he dropped to all fours and lapped at the cool waters until he had slaked his thirst; then, raising his fiery eyes to the *true* harvest moon, the werewolf released a loud, terrifying howl into the darkness, a nightmarish roar that resounded for miles.

The entire forest fell silent.

Killing more prey than he could consume, the beast collected the remainder of his quarry, and carried their bodies deep within the secluded forest, back to his hidden lair; the ambrosial flesh would not be wasted.

CHAPTER 5

Wife's Tale

SEPTEMBER HAD COME AND GONE in the slow-moving town of Silver Canyon; deciduous trees stood nearly bare along Main Street, their fallen leaves a testament to the coming winter. A dry and rainless summer had led to an early fall, and it seemed much later than October.

Golden-orange and rusty-red, the leaf-strewn sidewalks of Silver Canyon looked like the cloth-patterns of a holiday table—a table that waited unknowingly for a hungry visitor.

The ebb and flow of a gentle north wind moved through the streets, filling the morning air with the aromatic scents of cedar and pine. Large wind-swept leaves skittered slowly down the sidewalk; dry and brittle, their sharp edges scraped and scratched across the concrete like the claws of a great beast.

On the edge of town, Bryce McNeel pulled his grandpa's truck into a parking space next to Beckman's Feed and Ranch Supply and turned off the engine; the old truck sputtered twice, and then clunked to a stop. He lifted up on the handle and shouldered into the door; with a loud squeak and a pop, it flew open.

Stepping out of the truck, Bryce paused for a moment and lifted his face toward the bright morning sun. He closed his eyes and let the warm rays pour over his skin. Yawning noisily, he placed his knuckles into the small of his back and arched. After several relaxing pops, he reached into the truck and grabbed his list of supplies.

Across the street, he spotted Reverend Stubbs mowing the lawn in front of the Silver Linings Gospel Church; he gave Bryce a big wave.

"Mornin' Reverend," Bryce hollered, across the street. He was glad to see that the old preacher was busy with his yardwork; otherwise, he'd be listening to the "we haven't seen you in church lately" speech. When they were small boys, Bryce and Jackson had attended Sunday school at the old church on a regular basis, but later in life, they had become what the more devout churchgoers referred to as "backsliders."

Bryce's eyes wandered to the old cemetery next to the church. When they were little, Jackson used to dare him to run to the other side and back. The place still gave him the creeps. Many of the old graves in the cemetery were from 1896, the year the entire town had burned down.

Reverend Stubbs's church was the oldest building in Silver Canyon. It had been the first structure erected after the fire. Survivors of the tragedy had built the new church atop the old stone foundation of the original, and supposedly, it was an exact replica.

One day after Sunday school—Bryce recalled—Jackson had convinced him to sneak into the old church's cellar. It had been full to the rafters with old crates, and furniture, and all manner of junk. The ancient stone walls were black with soot from the historic fire, and the entire room had been seething with large, hairy spiders. Bryce shuddered at the old memory and brushed a hand over his arm, as if wiping away something hairy that crawled there.

Refocusing on his task, Bryce closed the truck's door with a loud, squeaky slam, and then bent over to pull down and straighten his pant legs. His jeans tended to ride-up over his boots whenever he drove Grandpa's truck; trying to work the clutch in the old vehicle, was like leg-wrestling with an East-

German gymnast.

Each Saturday morning, Bryce drove to Silver Canyon to purchase supplies for the ranch, a leisurely errand that he always enjoyed. He would stroll around town, window-shopping and talking to friends, and then have an early lunch at the Buckhorn Café before heading home.

Bryce walked into the feed store and headed to the back counter where old man Beckman stood on a ladder stocking shelves; the syrupy-sweet smell of grain and feed pervaded the air in the old wooden building. He sketched a lazy salute toward the two old-timers that were playing checkers atop an old rain-barrel in the corner. They gave Bryce a quick nod and then refocused on their game.

"Mornin', Mr. Beckman. How're you doing today?" Bryce said cheerfully.

Without turning around, Beckman answered. "Well, I ain't had my mornin' coffee yet, and nobody's been shot so far—I reckon I'm doing okay."

"Glad to hear it," Bryce said, grinning. He knew that Beckman had most likely downed a whole pot of coffee since daybreak. "I'll leave my list here on the counter and be back after lunch to settle our account."

"All right; we'll have your truck loaded up and ready to go by the time you get back."

Bryce exited the feed store into the cool morning air and headed up Main Street. He smiled at the scarecrows and pumpkins, and the other fall decorations that adorned the sidewalks of the small town, in preparation for the upcoming harvest festival; the annual street fair was always a lot of fun.

He walked past the post office and Reilly's IGA Grocery store, and then stopped to look in the front window at Pickett's Bookstore. He tapped on the glass and offered a quick wave to Mr. Pickett. Bryce suspected that *his* purchases alone, had kept the small bookstore's ledger in-the-black over the past decade.

Continuing up Main Street, he turned suddenly and veered across the street to the Dairy Treat, then slyly made his way next door to Nichols' Barbershop. He had spotted Doc Waggner through the large, plate-glass window at the front of the shop. Doc was sitting in the barber's chair getting a shave, and Bryce thought this would be the perfect time for a little payback for the incident with Grandpa's prize-winning bull. Bryce furtively poked his head through the barbershop's door to launch a sneak attack.

"Hey, Mr. Nichols!" Bryce shouted.

Mr. Nichols, who currently held a straight-razor to Doc Waggner's throat, flinched, tossing shaving cream into the air.

"Christ Almighty, Bryce!" Nichols exclaimed. "You made me nick Doc's neck."

Both men glared at Bryce, wondering why he had a shit-eating-grin plastered across his face.

"Just clap him on the neck a couple of times," Bryce advised. "That way, he'll never feel a thing." He quickly ducked out of the doorway and headed up the street. Behind him, he heard Doc Waggner release a loud volley of laughter, followed by a deep snort.

Bryce just smiled and continued toward CB's Drive-in. He had been hoping that Wendy Walker would be at work this morning. He'd decided to ask her out on a date—mostly, because Jackson wouldn't shut the hell up about it. However, he also thought she seemed like a nice person who was worth getting to know a little better.

Wendy was roller-skating around from car to car, delivering food and drinks; Bryce thought she looked cute in her short-skirted carhop uniform. He sat on a picnic table, between the two rows of cars, and waited for her to come take his order. At the table next to him, two old men sat playing dominoes, drinking coffee and bickering over the rules as old-timers usually did. Bryce always got a kick out of eavesdropping on ruminant old geezers chewing-the-cud.

"Hi, Bryce," Wendy said, skating over to see him.

"You're pretty good on those skates."

"Thanks, it's actually kind of fun," she admitted. "Do you want something to eat? The breakfast tacos are pretty good."

"No thanks, just a cherry-Coke."

"You got it."

"I like your earrings," Bryce complimented. He had noticed the large jade-and-silver dragonflies that dangled from her ears. "Those are really cool."

"Thanks," she said, with a faint blush, "my mom gave them to me for my sixteenth birthday."

"They're gorgeous," he said. Then, "Hey, I was wondering—would you like to go see a movie with me next Friday?"

Wendy's face beamed. "What's playing?" she asked, pretending as if she actually cared.

"That new *Denzel Washington* flick, "Ricochet" starts next week," Bryce said.

"Oh, I love him," she said, not sure who the heck *Denzel Washington* was. "But, I don't get off work until 9:30 p.m. on most nights."

"That's cool, we can catch the late-show," he said. "It usually doesn't start until around 10:00 p.m."

Wendy jotted her phone number on the back of an order pad and gave it to Bryce. "Call me," she said, smiling, then skated off to get his drink.

While Bryce waited for his soda, he noticed old man Brown across the street in front of the Woolworths five-and-dime store. He was sitting alone on a bench talking to himself, and as usual, he was holding a brown paper bag with a bottle in it.

Tom Brown was the town drunk, and was shunned by most of the townsfolk. Bryce, on the contrary, felt compassion for the old man, and tried to help him whenever he could. He could be a bit crotchety at times, and his discursive and rambling narrative could be a little hard to follow, but Bryce still enjoyed the old fellow's company.

Brown had a frail and haggard appearance, and his complexion was always sallow and clammy. The grizzled stubble that covered his gaunt cheeks hadn't seen a razor in weeks and his nose was florid from alcohol abuse. His baggy clothes were worn and bedraggled and he was always in serious need of a bath—another reason people treated him with disdain.

He always reminded Bryce of a scrawny version of *Walter Brennan*, the actor who portrayed, "Stumpy" in the old *John Wayne* western "Rio Bravo."

Bryce's grandpa had said—when they were young men—Tom Brown had been a good friend of his; but, when Tom's wife died, he'd crawled into a whiskey bottle and never came out again.

Brown was by no means destitute or homeless, in fact, he owned a great deal of land in Bane County; though his once beautiful ranch-house was now nothing more than a ramshackle pile of lumber from decades of neglect. The old shack abutted the edge of the canyon, not too far from the McNeel Ranch, buried in weeds and falling to pieces.

Like Bryce's grandpa, Tom Brown had been a successful rancher in the early years; but he no longer raised cattle. He leased his land to other ranchers to graze their stock; and what little money he earned he frittered away on whiskey.

When Wendy returned with Bryce's cherry-Coke, he asked for a cheeseburger to go—hold the pickles.

"Did you decide you were hungry after all?" Wendy asked.

"It's for a friend," said Bryce. He motioned to the old man across the street.

A rising smile of admiration grew on Wendy's face as she turned and skated back to the kitchen. When she returned, Bryce paid the bill and forced her to accept a nice tip.

"I'll call you later to make plans for the movie," Bryce said.

"Okay." She watched him walk across the street toward the old man on the bench, a huge smile on her face.

Each time Bryce saw Tom Brown—which was most Saturdays—he would bring him something to eat. Invariably, the old fellow looked emaciated, as though he hadn't eaten in a week.

To ensure that the meal didn't appear as charity, Bryce always had an excuse for giving him the food. It was more of a game the two of them played, to keep up appearances. Bryce knew his old friend was no fool.

"Hello, Mr. Brown," Bryce hollered, as he crossed the street.

"Why, it's young Master Bryce," Brown slurred, looking up through bloodshot eyes. "And how are you this fine day?"

"I'm doing well, Mr. Brown," Bryce said. He walked over and sat on the bench. "I was wondering if you could help me out with something."

"Why, certainly," he said, trying to speak clearly, "always happy to help out the young folks."

"I ordered too much food, and I don't want it to go to waste," he fibbed. "Do you think you could take this cheeseburger off my hands?"

"Well, I do hate to see good food go to waste," Brown said, taking the bag. He poked his nose inside the paper sack and took a deep whiff, then looked over at Bryce through bleary eyes and asked, "Pickles?"

"No pickles," Bryce said, smiling. He knew the old man hated them.

Brown nodded, closed the bag and set it aside for later; he never ate in front of Bryce. "How're your grandma and grandpa doing?"

"Oh, they're doing just fine, Mr. Brown," said Bryce. He always called him "Mister" Brown, instead of Tom. Bryce thought it was important to treat the old man with deference, to show he was worthy of respect.

"I've been meaning to stop by and see your grandpa," he said, "but"—he paused, looking away—"I don't drive much anymore."

Bryce knew he had lost his driver's license for drunk driving years ago. "Well, I'm sure he'd love to see you," Bryce fibbed, again.

His grandpa had told him that he had tried to help Tom many times over the years, with no success. Now, he just couldn't bear to see his old friend anymore.

"You know," Brown said, staring vacantly ahead, looking at nothing in particular. "My wife and your grandma were best friends."

Bryce was astounded at the old man's statement. He had spoken with him on dozens of occasions, and not once, had he ever mentioned his wife. Bryce had always hoped that—at some point—he would be able to help his old friend ease his sorrow, and regain some semblance of his former life. Now, with that one statement, he thought—perhaps—this was his chance.

"I didn't know that," Bryce said cheerfully. "When was it that your wife passed away, Mr. Brown?"

The old man took a long drink from his bottle of whiskey and wiped his mouth with his shirtsleeve. "1953," he said. "October 21, 1953."

Bryce's heart jumped into his throat and his face became flushed. He felt as though his voice had seized and he was unable to speak. His grandpa's story about 1953 came flooding back to him: *"Eleven more people had been found dead, or went missing,"* Grandpa had said, *"People they knew, friends and neighbors."*

Dear God, Bryce thought. *Had Mr. Brown's wife been one of those people?*

When old man Brown noticed that Bryce had stopped talking, he turned to face the boy. When their eyes met, he realized that Bryce had been startled. "You know something, don't you?" he said lucidly. Brown was no longer slurring his words. In fact, he sounded quite clearheaded. "Did your grandpa tell you something about what happened back in 1953?"

Bryce nodded slowly and thought about how he should answer the question. The last thing he wanted to do was use the word "werewolf."

"Yes, sir; he told me a little," Bryce admitted. "Grandpa told me that the lady who owned the farm next to us—Mrs. Rickman—had been killed by . . . some kind of animal. He also told me that several more people had been killed, or went missing, over the months that followed."

"Poor Gladys," Brown said mournfully. "I had forgotten all about her."

"Gladys?" Bryce questioned.

"Gladys Rickman," he said. "She was the first one to die."

"Oh," Bryce said, nodding. "I never knew her first name."

"After Gladys died, it seemed like, almost every week someone else would go missing—or worse—they'd find a body torn to shreds. Then, almost a month after Gladys—my Sally disappeared."

"Sally. That was your wife's name?" Bryce asked.

He nodded and once again stared vacantly ahead. Bryce thought he noticed a fleeting smile cross the old man's lips, for just a second, as he remembered his wife. "She was so beautiful," he said, thinking back. "Did you know she was Native American?"

"No, I didn't," said Bryce. He offered a kind smile.

"Yep, full-blooded; her hair was blacker than a raven's wing and her caramel-colored eyes were as big as the moon." Brown was actually smiling now as he spoke; Bryce had never seen him smile.

"She must have been lovely, Mr. Brown," he said kindly.

The old man took another drink of whiskey and sat quietly for a moment. Then, he said something completely unexpected: "My wife was gathering pecans with your grandma the night she disappeared."

"What?" Bryce said. He drew out the word, stunned by the revelation.

"Sally and your grandma were gathering pecans at the old grove," he said. "Afterwards, they went their separate ways—but, Sally never made it home."

Bryce didn't know what to say, he was speechless. Now he knew why his grandpa didn't want him to mention the story to Grandma. Why Grandpa had said: *"It'll just upset her."* His grandma's best friend had ended up the same as Mrs. Rickman.

Bryce thought back to the day he and Jackson had said they were going squirrel hunting at the old pecan grove, and how Grandma seemed to balk at the idea at first. Now he knew why.

"When I went looking for Sally," the old man went on, "all I found was her basket of pecans, about a half-mile from our house. It was just—sitting there . . . covered in blood."

Without realizing it, Bryce had cupped his hand over his

mouth. He saw that the old man's hands had started to shake and unbidden tears welled in his eyes; he put his arm around his old friend's shoulders. "I am *so* sorry, Mr. Brown," he said consolingly.

He smiled at Bryce and nodded. "You're a good boy, son."

"You gonna be okay, Mr. Brown? Can I do anything for you?" Bryce asked sincerely.

"I'm fine," he said, forcing a smile.

At that point, Bryce figured he should end their conversation; he could see his old friend was exhausted. "All right," Bryce said, patting him lightly on the shoulder. "I better be heading out; I've got a few errands I need to run."

As Bryce stood and turned to walk away, Brown asked him a question: "You wanna hear something strange?"

Bryce didn't know if he could handle any more strangeness today, but he obliged the old man. "What's that, Mr. Brown?"

"The day before she disappeared, Sally told me she knew what had been killing people. It was part of some old Native American legend."

"What did she say it was?"

"She called it: the *Ba'cho Najin*," he said, staring vacantly ahead once again. "It was some kind of . . . giant wolf or something; I really didn't pay much attention. Sally was full of old superstitious legends, and I never put much stock in that sort of thing—at least—I didn't back then.

The old man twisted in his seat, turning to meet Bryce's eyes; he had a dour look about his face. "The strange thing is," he recounted, "the night Sally went missing, I heard a howl come from deep in the forest. It was an ungodly roar that came from Hell itself. I don't know what it was—and I hope to God I never find out."

Bryce was trying hard to hide the surprise that washed over

his face; he attempted to make light of what he had just heard. "Boy, you weren't kidding, were you, Mr. Brown?" He chuckled nervously. "That's definitely strange."

The old man took a long drink of whiskey and faded back into a detached, vacant stare. Bryce could tell he had finished talking. "You take care of yourself, Mr. Brown," Bryce said. "I'll see you soon, okay."

The old man nodded and offered a feeble wave.

Bryce turned and headed up Main Street to the public library; he had special-ordered a book and wanted to see if it had arrived yet. He couldn't believe the story he had just heard.

Jesus—another damn monster-wolf story, he thought, *first Grandpa, and now Mr. Brown. What the hell happened back in 1953?*

When Bryce entered the library he saw Agnes Furman, the town's librarian, sitting at her large curved desk; she met Bryce's eyes and smiled.

Agnes was a pale and willowy woman, in her mid-sixties, and was always dressed immaculately. Her long, gray hair coiled perfectly into a crisp chignon, and her graceful aquiline features always reminded Bryce of a beautiful, majestic bird. Standing, she removed her horn-rimmed glasses, allowing them to dangle on the long, silver chain around her neck.

"It's here," Agnes said exuberantly, "all the way from the Harvard University Library."

She scampered across the room to retrieve the book; her excitement made her nimble for a woman of her age. Agnes was fond of Bryce; she felt a certain kinship with him, a shared passion. He had the same voracious appetite for reading that she possessed, and that was a rare thing in Bane County.

Agnes held the book in front of her and admired the binding; it was quite old: *North American Cicadas by William Thompson Davis.*

"It's a compendium of scientific field studies from the early 1900s," Bryce noted.

"I see," Agnes replied, "it should be quite fascinating."

"I needed some additional information for a biology report I'm working on."

Glancing furtively around the library, she leaned in toward Bryce. "You know," Agnes whispered conspiratorially, "I'm not supposed to let this leave the library."

"I'll guard it with my life," he whispered, and gave her a wink.

She smiled and handed him the book.

Bryce thanked her and was about to leave when a thought occurred to him: "Say, Agnes . . . you wouldn't have anything on old Native American legends, would you?"

She glanced upward and pondered a moment, then said, "Nothing comes to mind, but we can order something."

"No, that's all right," said Bryce. "I was just curious about something."

Agnes nodded, and then said, "You know who you should talk to?"

"Who?"

"Sam Nightfeather."

"Sam Nightfeather," Bryce repeated, nodding his head in concurrence. "I hadn't thought of that; great idea."

"I have my moments," Agnes said proudly.

Bryce had never met Sam Nightfeather personally, but he had heard about him for years. He was a Native American healer that was well known for his herbal remedies.

Nightfeather had been taught by his father—and his father before him—and many of the old-timers around Bane County swore by his elixirs and poultices. Even Bryce's grandma used

Nightfeather's herbal teas whenever she had a cold.

He was rumored to be somewhat of a recluse, and lived in a small fishing cabin at the southern tip of Bane County, near the confluence of the Carantina and Little Carantina rivers. If anyone knew about old Native American legends, it would be Sam Nightfeather.

"I think I'll drive out there tomorrow and see him," Bryce said.

"Have you met Sam before?" Agnes asked.

"No, but he knows my grandma."

"Take doughnuts."

"Doughnuts?"

"Oh, yes"—Agnes assured him—"from Hattie Mae's Bakery. Sam Nightfeather hates strangers, and he's as likely as not to run you off with a shotgun. However, he also has a huge sweet-tooth, and Sam loves Hattie Mae's doughnuts. If you show up with a box of her doughnuts, he'll let you through the door."

"Good to know," Bryce said, chuckling. "Thanks for the tip."

Bryce said his goodbye and made his way out of the library, continuing up Main Street with his new book in hand. Over in the town square, he noticed Sheriff Culley and Deputy Bennett speaking to a group of men in front of the sheriff's office. They appeared to be organizing for something.

Crossing the street, Bryce strolled into the Buckhorn Café to have an early lunch before returning to the feed store. He took a seat at the lunch counter and waited for Adelaide to take his order.

"The usual, Bryce?" Adelaide hollered, from the other end of the counter.

Bryce smiled and nodded, he always had the chicken-fried steak. "What's going on over at the sheriff's office?" he asked.

Adelaide made her way over to Bryce and sidled up to the counter. "The sheriff's putting together another search party," she said, shaking her head. "A couple of tourists got lost in The Refuge again. Now Sheriff Culley's got to go find the idiots. Damn tourists; he ought to make them pay a fine for hauling their keisters out of there."

"Your tax-dollars at work," Bryce said, chuckling. Adelaide was one of the orneriest old ladies that Bryce knew—but she sure made a *mean* chicken-fried steak.

After lunch, Bryce returned to the feed store, settled his account with Mr. Beckman, and then headed for home. When he arrived back at the ranch, he parked the old truck next to the barn to unload the supplies.

Before getting started, Bryce decided to take a little reading break. He walked over to the old maple tree, and cleared a spot to sit. The ground was covered in a thick layer of rusty-orange leaves. Leaning against the trunk of the ancient tree, he opened his new book and entered the world of cicadas.

Inside the house, Grandma McNeel stood at the kitchen sink washing dishes and listening to her favorite *oldies* station on the radio. As *Sam Cooke* crooned, "You Send Me" she swayed slowly back and forth, slow-dancing to the music. Watching his wife from the other room, Grandpa McNeel smiled and crept up behind her; he slipped his arms around her waist.

"You better be mindful of who you're sneaking up on," she giggled, brandishing the large butcher knife she was scrubbing.

"I see your point," Grandpa said dryly. " . . . Have you seen Bryce?"

Grandma motioned out the window above the sink toward the old maple tree. "He's been out there about an hour now."

Grandpa kissed his wife on the neck, and gave her a little slap on the tush; as he headed out the door, he glanced back.

Grandma wagged the tip of the butcher knife at him.

"You better watch those hands, mister," she warned, with a devilish grin. "One of these days, you might pull back a nub."

Grandpa gave her a wink, then walked out to the maple tree and sat down next to Bryce. "What are you studying?"

"The seventeen-year cicada," Bryce replied, not taking his eyes off the book.

"You mean locusts?" Grandpa questioned.

Bryce closed the book and met his grandpa's eyes with a smile. It was always fun when they discussed science. Grandpa pretended to be simple-minded, but in actuality, he was extremely intelligent.

"That's a common misnomer," Bryce answered. "A lot of people refer to cicadas as locusts. But, a *true* locust is actually a type of short-horned grasshopper that has a proclivity to swarm at a certain stage in its lifecycle."

"Is that so?" said Grandpa. "And cicadas—what makes them so unique?"

"Well," Bryce offered, "to start with, they have a lifespan of seventeen years. The majority of insects only live for a few days or weeks."

Grandpa pursed his lips and nodded as he listened intently.

"When cicada eggs hatch, the larvae—they're actually called nymphs—fall from the trees and burrow into the soil. Then, they attach themselves to a root for sustenance, and remain dormant for seventeen years. Then, like clockwork, billions of cicadas emerge all at once. Over the next few weeks, they molt and mate and lay their eggs; then the cycle begins anew."

"They should have named them *Rip Van Winkle* bugs," Grandpa quipped. "So why do they hide underground for seventeen years?"

"Well, there's a lot of debate over that question in the

scientific world," Bryce admitted.

"But, you have a theory," Grandpa stated, with a knowing smile.

"As a matter of fact . . . I do," Bryce said ardently.

Bryce and Grandpa turned to face each other for a more serious conversation.

"When you introduce a billion cicadas into the food chain, the predators—birds and small mammals—who feed on cicadas have a heyday. More food means more offspring, and that leads to an overabundance of predators. If the cicadas were to reemerge over the next few years, they would be decimated by this new overabundance of predators—before they could mate and lay eggs. Eventually, they'd become extinct. So . . . they wait—for seventeen years—for the lifespan of those extra predators to run out: most birds and small mammals have a lifespan that's shorter than seventeen years."

"Smart bugs," said Grandpa. "That's an impressive theory."

"Thanks," said Bryce. "But, there's another factor, as well. The next time the cicadas emerge, none of the existing predators will know what they are—they've never seen a cicada before. It'll take a little while for the predators to realize that the cicadas are a food source. And that small advantage will give the cicadas a little extra time to mate and lay their eggs before becoming a meal."

Grandpa pondered that for a moment, and then said, "So, the cicadas hide underground until the old predators die off, and the new predators don't even know that they exist—and that keeps them safe from attack . . . at least, for a while."

"Yeah, pretty much."

"Excellent theory—you sold me."

"Well, let's hope my biology teacher feels the same way," Bryce said. "My report's due the end of next week."

"I wouldn't worry about that," said Grandpa. He stood and wiped the leaves off his rear. "Let's unload the truck and go get cleaned up for supper."

They walked over to the pickup and started hauling bags of feed into the barn. Bryce could see that his grandpa was still mulling-over their discussion as he worked.

Finally, Grandpa said, "Wouldn't it be something, if the roles were reversed?"

"What do you mean?"

"What if the seventeen-year cicadas were the predators—instead of being the food source?"

"I'm not sure I understand what you mean," Bryce said.

"Ah, don't worry about it. I'm just thinkin' out loud." He tossed the last bag of feed into the barn. "Let's head in and get cleaned up for supper."

Bryce knitted his eyebrows at his grandpa's notion for a moment, then shrugged it off and headed for the house. Tomorrow, he had a busy day planned.

CHAPTER 6

Legend

THE FOLLOWING MORNING, Bryce borrowed Grandpa's truck and headed toward Silver Canyon; his first stop would be Hattie Mae's Bakery for a dozen doughnuts. He hadn't mentioned to his grandparents that he was going to see Sam Nightfeather; he just said he needed a few things from town.

On Sundays, many of the businesses in Silver Canyon were closed, but the bakery was open seven days a week. Hattie Mae did a brisk business on the weekends, especially on Sundays after church let out.

The bakery was located on Hubbard Street, which ran parallel to Main, and you couldn't miss the building. It was painted pink-and-white in a candy-stripe fashion, and all of Hattie Mae's baked-goods came in a cardboard box with the same color pattern.

Bryce parked on the street beside the bakery, and even from outside on the sidewalk, it smelled like heaven. The doughnuts had just come out of the deep fryer as Bryce walked through the front door and he eagerly ordered a dozen. They were warm, shiny, and thick with glaze; even though Bryce had already eaten breakfast, the mouthwatering aroma caused his stomach to growl. All of Hattie Mae's pastries came in a baker's-dozen, so Bryce ordered a cup of coffee to go and kept one doughnut for himself.

He fired up the old truck and headed south. On his way out of town, he noticed Jackson's car parked in front of Western Auto. He was working today, as he did most every weekend. Western Auto was another of the few businesses that were open on Sundays.

Sam Nightfeather's cabin was a little over twenty miles away, at the southernmost tip of Bane County. Bryce had never been there before, but he knew the way, only one road led to the confluence of the rivers, and Nightfeather's cabin was located where that road ended.

Bryce traveled south along the highway until he came to the bone-jarring, gravel road that led through the forest toward Nightfeather's cabin. The road was little-traveled, and became worse the farther he drove. By the time he reached the end, the road had become nothing more than two dirt ruts buried in high grass.

Bryce parked the truck and continued by foot, he could see the roof of a cabin just beyond the tree line. He waded through the waist-high grass with his pink-and-white box in hand and exited the riparian forest onto the sandy banks of the Carantina River.

To Bryce's surprise, Sam Nightfeather's fishing cabin wasn't located at the edge of the Carantina; it was over the river. Nightfeather's cabin was at the end of a long wooden pier about ten feet above the water.

What a great fishing cabin, Bryce thought, as he made his way to the entrance. He strode up the steep wooden stairs to the top of the pier and headed down the long narrow walkway toward the cabin. The pier was about four-feet-wide, and built without handrails; a person could easily fall off the edge into the water. Sheathed with thin wooden planks, the deck of the pier creaked and moaned with each step forward, and Bryce nervously slowed his gait along the rickety pier.

He thought about what he might say to Nightfeather when

they met; saying that he was there to ask a bunch of crazy questions probably wouldn't go over too well. If Bryce expected to get the answers he wanted, he would need to be humble and respectful, and say something intelligent—something unique.

"That's far enough, white-boy," a voice called, from the cabin.

Bryce looked up to find the muzzle of a double-barrel shotgun protruding through a partially cracked door.

"Uh, Mr. Nightfeather, sir," Bryce said shakily. "I'm Bryce McNeel. Uh, you know my grandma, Blanche McNeel?"

The barrel of the shotgun remained trained on Bryce. "Why are you here?"

Bryce thought once more, about what he should say. He held the box of doughnuts a little higher. "Mr. Nightfeather, sir. I'm only here to listen . . . and to learn—sir."

After what seemed like an eternity, the gun barrel slowly disappeared back inside the cabin and the door opened; Sam Nightfeather stepped outside and motioned for him to come forward. Bryce made his way down the pier with a nervous smile on his face; he stopped a few feet from the door.

Nightfeather eyed the pink-and-white box in Bryce's hands. "What's in the box?"

"Doughnuts," he said, proffering the box to Nightfeather.

"Doughnuts, huh," Nightfeather said, pursing his lips. "What for?"

"Uh, w-well," Bryce stammered. "I, uh, brought them for you, sir."

Nightfeather paused, looking Bryce in the eye. Finally, he said, "You know . . . a while back, some of my relatives back-east had a white-man come to their door with a box of goodies . . . next thing you know . . . they didn't own Manhattan any more."

A single laugh burst from Bryce's mouth and then he clamped his lips together tightly; he wasn't sure if it was a joke. There was a long, uncomfortable silence, and then Bryce shrugged timidly and added, "They're fresh?"

Nightfeather glared at him impassively—then he began to laugh. "I'm just messin' with you, kid. Come on in." He turned and walked back inside the cabin.

Relief washed over Bryce as he relaxed his body and started to breathe again; he followed Nightfeather inside. While the cabin was small, it was tastefully furnished and had a warm and inviting feel; it was much nicer inside than out.

"Have a seat at the kitchen table, Bryce," Nightfeather offered. "I'll boil some water for tea."

"Thank you, Mr. Nightfeather."

"My father was Mr. Nightfeather," he said. "Just call me Sam."

Bryce smiled. "Okay—Sam."

Sam Nightfeather wasn't what Bryce had expected at all. To begin with, he was much younger than he had imagined, only forty- or forty-five-years-old. He was trim and muscular with long black hair that he wore in a ponytail and he seemed very well spoken.

"So . . . you're Blanche's grandson," he said—and then added—"the *smart* one. Your grandma sure brags on you. How is she? I haven't seen her in a coon's age."

"She's doing well, sir—I mean—Sam."

"That's good," Sam said, smiling. "She's a great ol' gal." He made his way back to the table with two mugs of tea, sat down and opened the box of doughnuts. "Hattie Mae sure makes a *mean* doughnut."

"I already had one driving out here," Bryce confessed, sipping his tea.

Sam nodded and said, "So what's all this 'I'm here to listen and learn' crap?"

Bryce chuckled. "Yeah, I'm not real sure where that came from," he admitted. "Then again, I've never had a shotgun pointed at me before, either."

"Wanna know a little secret?" Sam asked, talking around the large bite of doughnut in his mouth. "It wasn't even loaded."

"You're sh— kidding me," Bryce revised.

"Nope," Sam said, chuckling, "I shit you not."

Bryce laughed. "You scared the hell out of me."

"Well, that's kinda the point, ain't it?" he said dryly. "When a person's staring at the business-end of a shotgun, I've always found that an unloaded gun is just as intimidating as a loaded one."

Bryce nodded. "You've got a point."

"Anyway," Sam admitted, giving a sly wink. "I wouldn't actually shoot someone—I mean—unless I *had* to."

Bryce nodded. *This guy is great*, he thought, smiling. *I see why Grandma likes him.* He took another sip of tea.

"So, why *did* you drop by?"

Bryce sat his mug of tea on the table. He said, "Well, I was hoping you might be able to give me some information about an old Native American legend, Sam."

"Really?" he said, taking another bite of doughnut, "which legend?"

Bryce said, "Have you ever heard of something called: the *Ba'cho Najin*?"

Sam Nightfeather stopped chewing his doughnut; his face had lost all good-humor. "Who the *hell* told you that name?" he said curtly. "And don't tell me that you read it somewhere, 'cause it's not written in any book."

Bryce was shocked at Sam's sudden change in demeanor. It

seemed as though Nightfeather considered this subject taboo. "Tom Brown told me the name," Bryce answered, "and I'm sorry if I—"

"Sally!" Sam Nightfeather interrupted. "She must have told her husband the name—the fool—and now, after *all* this time, that damn drunk goes and tells you."

"Hey," Bryce said sharply, "there's no call for that. Tom Brown's an okay guy; he's just had a—hard life."

"I'm sorry, Bryce, but you don't understand," Sam insisted. "First of all, don't *ever* say that name again. If you utter the name of the beast, you risk summoning it. Just call it what it is: a werewolf."

Nightfeather's strong reaction to his question caught Bryce completely off-guard; he didn't know how to respond. Apparently, he had broken some sort of rule about, not speaking a name, and Nightfeather had become extremely agitated. However, for some reason, the only thing that Bryce managed to say was, "a werewolf?"

Sam frowned at him and shook his head, then walked into the kitchen and grabbed a bottle of beer from the fridge. He opened it, tilted his head back and took a long, gulping pull. When he lowered the bottle, he pointed it at Bryce and wagged the tip like a scolding finger. "You're asking questions about shit you shouldn't be meddling with, boy." He took another gulp of beer.

Bryce opened his mouth to express his regret and try to explain, but Nightfeather swallowed and continued his rant.

"Why the hell are you asking about this anyway?" Nightfeather growled. "This is none of your concern."

Bryce hesitated, to make sure Sam had finished speaking, then he said, "Mr. Nightfeather, sir—Sam—I'm really sorry if I offended you, it certainly wasn't my intent. The only reason I asked about this was . . . well . . . about five weeks ago, my grandpa told me this story about something that happened back in 1953—something bad. Then, yesterday, Tom Brown told me even more of the story, and he mentioned the legend. I was just . . . curious—sort of, filling in the blanks."

"Just curious, huh?" Nightfeather scoffed, shaking his head in disbelief. He downed the dregs of his beer, threw it noisily into the garbage can and grabbed another; he headed toward the back door. "Come with me."

Bryce followed Nightfeather out the door and onto the back porch. Like the pier, the porch had no handrails, and he got the distinct impression that Nightfeather was about to push him into the river. Instead, Sam pointed to a couple of old Adirondack-style chairs and told him to take a seat.

They sat quietly, gazing at the confluence of the two mighty rivers; the view was breathtaking. The silence lengthened until Sam took a sip of his beer and said, "You didn't tell your grandparents that you were coming here today, *did you*?"

"No . . . I didn't," he confessed.

Sam frowned, and with an exaggerated nod, he said, "All right . . . tell me about your grandpa's story—and *don't* leave anything out."

Bryce agreed and began to recount the story. When he finished, he told Sam about the claw marks he and Jackson had seen at the old Rickman house. He had been tempted to omit the part about the whispering shadows in the dark forest —after all, it had only been their imagination—but, he had agreed not to leave anything out, and so he didn't. When Bryce told Sam about the shadows and the whispering they had imagined, Nightfeather's eyes had widened.

"Wanagi Nuni," Sam said softly, gazing out at the river, "the lost spirits of those killed by the beast."

Lastly, Bryce recounted Tom Brown's story from the day before; he made sure to not to mention the name that had upset Sam earlier. When Bryce had finished, Sam sat quietly, gazing at the river. Finally, he hung his head, sighed loudly and said, "Well . . . shit."

"Sam," Bryce said respectfully. "I apologize if I'm overstepping my bounds—but—would you please tell me just what the *hell* is going on here?"

"Listen," Sam said, meeting Bryce's eyes. "I may follow the old-ways—in keeping with tribal traditions—but I'm not some, superstitious nutcase. Hell, I've got a B.A. in Philosophy from Stanford for Chrissake."

Bryce lifted his eyebrows in surprise. "Really?" he said, "from Stanford?" It was one of the Universities on Bryce's shortlist.

"Yeah . . . let's keep that little tidbit between us, okay?" Sam urged. "I've got an image to maintain."

Bryce shot him a puzzled look, and then slowly nodded.

"My point is: you need to take what I'm about to tell you seriously," Sam demanded.

"I will," Bryce promised.

"I'm not going to bore you with the entire legend," he began, "because—quite frankly—a lot of it is superstitious fodder; I'll only tell you the parts you need to know."

Nightfeather paused to gather his thoughts, and then he met Bryce's eyes. "It was told to me by my elders, that after the first dawn, the Great Spirit created a treaty between man, and the beast whose name is not spoken. The land north of the canyon belonged to the beast, and no man could enter his hunting grounds.

"The legend told of a foolish brave who entered the northern mountains to hunt—breaking the treaty. That night, the beast followed the brave back to his village and slaughtered his entire tribe; only a few women and children survived.

"After this great tragedy, the treaty was once again

reinstated; and the borders of the beast's hunting grounds were never breached again—at least—not until the white-men came.

"It was said that when hundreds of white-men arrived and began destroying the forest, digging giant holes into the ground in search of silver, the beast crawled deep within the earth, hiding from those who would defile his hunting grounds.

"Year after long year, the beast remained hidden. Languishing in the cold, torpid blackness of the abyss, forced to endure the constant sounds of men: pounding, digging, and destroying his forest; they tormented him endlessly. Day after long day, he was tortured, his anger and rage and hatred growing, until finally—he was consumed. There, in the darkness, insanity transformed him, his tortured mind now craving and hungering for the bloody taste of vengeance.

"Then, on a night when the moon shone as brightly as the sun, the beast rose from the stygian darkness, eager to exact his revenge. Driven by an insane lust for human flesh, he began his reign of terror.

"One by one the beast stalked his prey, beginning with those who would not be missed—those who were alone. The beast always remained hidden; no one who saw him had ever lived. In fact, his greatest strength was that no one knew he existed.

"Prey that doesn't know it's being hunted—is always the easiest to catch."

"As more and more people died or disappeared, men started to become wary—they began to believe that a beast may indeed exist. So, knowing his time had come to an end, he crawled deep within the earth once again; and there, he waited—year after long year.

"He waited for people to forget—to forget that he had ever existed. He waited for the time when he would rise again—to hunt the flesh of men."

Sam Nightfeather's eyes were on Bryce during the entire story; he now sat back in his chair, gazed at the river and took a long sip of beer.

Bryce sat stock-still and wide-eyed, facing Sam's chair; he was brimming with questions, but knew he should broach each one carefully, so as not to offend. "That's quite a story," he said. "Thank you for sharing it with me."

Sam's only response was another sip of beer.

"Sam"—Bryce continued cautiously—"earlier you used the term 'werewolf,' is that what the beast in your story is supposed to be?"

Sam turned to look at Bryce. He said, "That's what all the old-timers called it—including my grandfather—the actual translation means: Standing-Wolf. I guess 'werewolf' is as good a description as any."

Bryce gathered his thoughts for a moment, and then he said, "Please don't take this the wrong way, Sam. But, are you saying that you believe this creature actually existed at one time?"

Sam continued to gaze at the river. "No ... that's not what I'm saying," he said. Nightfeather twisted in his chair, turning to meet Bryce's eyes. "I'm saying—it *still* exists."

Bryce fixed Sam with a "you-must-be-kidding-me" look, but he didn't utter a word; the last thing he wanted to do was offend him. "So all those people that were killed back in 1953," he asked intently. "You're saying they were killed by this creature?"

He gave Bryce a quick nod, then rose from his chair and downed his last sip of beer. "I think that's enough questions," he said. "My advice to you is: leave this alone, kid—before someone gets hurt, or worse."

Bryce was disappointed—he still had dozens of questions—

but, he tried not to show it; he knew it was time for him to leave. He rose from his chair and shook Nightfeather's hand. "Okay, Sam," he said, smiling. "Thanks for taking the time to speak with me."

"Sure thing kid; be sure to tell your grandma I said hello."

Bryce smiled and nodded, then turned to admire Nightfeather's cabin. "You know," he said, changing the subject. "I really like your cabin, how's the fishing here?"

"Don't know," said Sam, "never tried."

Bryce frowned and raised a dubious eyebrow.

"I hate fish," he insisted, his lips wrinkled with distaste. "I'm more of a meat-and-potatoes kind of guy."

Bryce chuckled. "So why live in a fishing cabin if you don't like to fish?"

"Who said this was a fishing cabin?" he asked. "There're lots of reasons to live on the river. Do you like to swim?"

"Yeah," Bryce said, nodding. "I like to swim."

"See?" Sam said. "There's a reason. I love to swim, and it's healthy for you; swimming keeps you alive."

"I guess I see your point."

They walked back through the cabin and headed out the front door. Bryce looked down the long pier and said, "You should put some bracing underneath those planks, your pier is a bit rickety.

"Nah," Sam said, "its fine. My grandfather built that pier almost sixty years ago; those planks are made from white oak. They'll be here long after I'm gone. Plus, as much as I like Hattie Mae's doughnuts"—he patted his belly—"It helps me keep an eye on my weight."

Bryce laughed and gave a quick wave, then turned and made his way down the long pier. From his cabin, Sam watched until Bryce disappeared behind the bosky riverbank. He no longer wore his jovial smile; the look that now painted Sam Nightfeather's face was one of grave concern.

ON THE DRIVE HOME, Bryce began to muse about Nightfeather's story; he was still surprised that a simple question had created such an ordeal. As the old truck jounced along the bumpy gravel road back to the highway, he considered something that Nightfeather had said. "It still exists?" Bryce muttered. He frowned and shook his head. "Why would he say that?"

Nightfeather had said that he wasn't a superstitious person, and Bryce now knew that he was an educated man.

"He has a B.A. in Philosophy from Stanford," he thought aloud, smiling. "You never can tell about people." His smile was short lived, however, as he once again frowned at the absurdity of the situation.

Bryce had no idea why he was so damn intrigued with something that had happened thirty-eight years ago—but he was—and he was determined to get to the bottom of it.

The gravel road finally ended, and he turned the old truck onto the highway. As he began to accelerate, the tiny pebbles that had gotten stuck in his tire treads began to tick and clack against the pavement; it sounded like a playing-card in the spokes of a child's bicycle. By the time he reached highway speed, most of the pebbles had dislodged and were pinging and ricocheting around inside the wheel-well like a pinball machine; until they shot out like a bullet. Tailgating was never much of a problem in rural areas, at least, not if people valued the glass in their windshields.

While Bryce headed north along the highway, back toward the ranch, he tried to rationalize what he had learned over the last five weeks. If he didn't somehow quantify this puzzle, it was going to drive him nuts.

"Okay," he wondered aloud, "what do we know?" Bryce created a mental fact-sheet—a problem-solving technique that he used.

According to Grandpa, twelve people died, or went missing, thirty-eight years ago, in 1953; and they had found the huge footprints and claw marks of an unidentified predator. The footprints were identical to those found in 1934, when fifteen additional people had died, or went missing. Grandpa said that the predator had been a werewolf.

According to Tom Brown, his wife, Sally, had been one of the people killed by this unidentified predator, back in 1953, though he never found her body. Brown also heard a strange howl the night his wife disappeared, and claimed his wife said the predator was a giant wolf—she even told him its name: the Ba'cho Najin.

At this point, Bryce paused his thought process for a moment and reflected on something Sam Nightfeather had said: *"If you utter the name of the beast, you risk summoning it."* Tom Brown's wife had told her husband the predator's name the day before she went missing.

He shook his head—*that's ridiculous*—and refocused on his mental fact-sheet.

According to Sam Nightfeather, the predator was a Standing-Wolf—or a werewolf—and it was an animal indigenous to The Refuge. He said that when mining operations had begun, back in the late 1800s, the predator went underground, where it stayed for many years—until finally, it went insane.

Sam had said that when the predator finally emerged, it began killing people in an act of revenge—and that it always remained hidden. He said the predator's greatest strength was that no one knew it existed, and that when people became wary, the predator went underground again, where it waited for many years—waited for people to forget it had ever existed.

Nightfeather had also commented on the whispering shadows Bryce and Jackson imagined—calling them: Wanagi Nuni—the lost spirits of those killed by the beast.

Bryce shook his head. Ghost stories weren't something he was willing to consider.

Finally, Sam Nightfeather, a well-educated man, who claimed he wasn't superstitious, had said, "It still exists."

Bryce knew that forming a theory, or even a simple hypothesis, from such a hodgepodge of conjecture would be a shot in the dark, but he had to try.

"Maybe it was some type of unknown species that existed back then," he surmised aloud. "Most legends have at least *some* basis in fact."

If a large predator wanted to hide, Bryce figured, *there would've been no better place than The Refuge—one million acres of some of the toughest, unmapped terrain on planet earth. The Amazon, the Congo, Southeast Asia—none of those jungles had anything on The Refuge.*

He had read books on cryptozoology, and while the majority of them were nothing more than pseudo-scientific bullshit, he knew that hundreds, if not thousands of new species were found each year throughout the world, even species thought to have been long extinct.

The discovery of mountain gorillas in the Virunga region of East Africa in 1902—only eighty-nine years ago—was a prime example of a large, unknown species going unnoticed. Before their discovery, there were only local legends of giant monsters who lived in the mountains.

In 1910, rumors spread of a gigantic, man-eating dragon that lived on a small island in the Indian Ocean. The story told of a pilot who had crash-landed his newfangled flying machine in the sea, and swam ashore on the remote island. When he was finally rescued, the incredible tales of being chased by giant monsters were thought to be the mad ravings of a lunatic. It wasn't until 1926—only sixty-five years ago—that an expedition returned with live specimens of the Komodo dragon.

Perhaps, what early Native Americans had referred to as a Standing-Wolf had been nothing more than an unknown species of some kind—not an evil monster that was hell-bent on revenge.

Bryce turned off the highway onto Ranch-Road 11 and headed down the final stretch of road for home. There were many questions still left unanswered, and much of what he knew didn't make any sense. At any rate, it would have to wait until tomorrow; he had several chores he needed to complete before supper.

When he parked the old truck next to the barn door, Bryce noticed the large pile of feedbags they had unloaded. *What had his grandpa said about the cicadas yesterday?*—he thought back—*'Wouldn't it be something, if the roles were reversed? What if the seventeen-year cicadas were the predators, instead of being the food source?'* Something about his grandpa's notion still gnawed at him.

As he headed out to finish his chores, Bryce wondered what Jackson would say tomorrow, when he filled him in on the events of the past two days.

CHAPTER 7

Missing

IT WAS A FOGGY OCTOBER MORNING when Grandpa McNeel and his dog Snip walked outside to get the Monday morning newspaper. It was still dark outside, but the horizon was alight with shades of pink and orange. Snip looked up at his master with anxious eyes.

"Go get it," Grandpa commanded.

Snip bolted toward the road and started sniffing around the high grass near the mailbox. He quickly located the paper and brought it back; Snip knew what his master held in his hand.

"Good boy," Grandpa said. He handed him a slice of crispy-fried bacon.

Grandpa brought the paper back inside, tossed it on the kitchen table and went over to the stove to pour another cup of coffee. He sat down at the table, blowing on the hot brew and opened the morning paper to the front page:

SILVER CANYON GAZETTE—MONDAY, OCTOBER 7, 1991.

Search Continues for Missing Backpackers.

Robert Miller and his fiancée Elisa Brooks entered the Silver Canyon National Wildlife Refuge on Monday, September 23 at approximately 3:00 p.m., after purchasing a one-week camping pass at the game warden's office, and were due back on Monday, September 30. When they didn't return as scheduled, their families filed a missing person report.

On Friday, October 4, after the mandatory three-day waiting period had expired, search and rescue efforts for the missing backpackers began.

The mandatory waiting period was enacted in order to limit the number of unnecessary search and rescue efforts initiated by worried family members. It is very common for campers to extend their stay for a few days without prior notification.

Sheriff Neil Culley and Deputy Wayne Bennett led the search for the missing backpackers, and were able to locate their campsite on Sunday, October 6. The backpackers, however, were nowhere to be found.

Sheriff Culley stated that blood and torn clothing had been found in and around the campsite, suggesting a mountain lion or other large predator may have attacked one or more of the missing backpackers. Sheriff Culley also noted that The Refuge consisted of over one million acres (sixteen hundred square miles) of impassable, rugged terrain, and that heavy rains last week would make locating the individuals exceedingly difficult. The search for the missing backpackers will resume today and will continue until further notice.

There was a large photo of the sheriff, and another smaller one of his deputy and several volunteers.

Sheriff Neil Culley has been with the Bane County Sheriff's Office since 1974 when he replaced retiring-sheriff Tom Cooper. Deputy Wayne Bennett has been with the sheriff's office since 1980 when he replaced retiring-deputy Dalton Morrow. Both Culley and Bennett are highly trained experts in SAR (Search and Rescue).

Anyone with information about the missing backpackers should contact the Bane County Sheriff's Office.

Grandpa McNeel folded the newspaper and laid it on the table. Sitting back in his chair, he took a sip of coffee and sighed.

If those poor people are dead, he thought, *I sure hope it really was a mountain lion that killed them.*

Grandma McNeel walked in the door and went to the sink to wash her hands; she had just finished throwing feed to her chickens.

"Is there any *good* news in today's paper?" she joked.

"Oh, just the same old stuff," he replied, not wanting to upset her with news of missing backpackers.

Bryce walked into the kitchen and grabbed some biscuits and bacon from the stovetop.

"Do you want me to make you some eggs?" Grandma asked.

"No thanks, Grandma, this is plenty," he said. "Jackson will be here any minute to pick me up for school."

As Bryce made his way out the door, Grandpa got up from the table and followed him; the newspaper was tucked furtively under his arm.

"Hey, Bryce, come here a second," Grandpa called.

"Yes sir?" he said, turning around.

"I want you and Jackson to steer clear of The Refuge. There's been some kind of animal attack over there and a couple of people are still missing."

Bryce's eyes widened when he saw the stony-faced appearance of his grandpa. Five weeks ago, when he had told Bryce the story about what happened back in 1953, his grandpa had fixed him with that same somber, unwavering stare.

Before he could respond, Jackson drove up and laid on his horn. Bryce flinched and turned to see his cousin waving him to the car.

"Let's go," Jackson hollered. "We're burnin' daylight."

Bryce waved to Jackson, then turned back to meet Grandpa's

steely eyes.

"Take this with you," Grandpa said, handing him the newspaper. "I don't want your grandma to see it; and don't forget what I told you. Steer clear of The Refuge."

Bryce took the newspaper and nodded. Without saying a word, he turned and jogged to Jackson's car and hopped in.

"What the hell was *that* all about?" Jackson asked, seeing the startled look on Bryce's face.

"Grandpa just told me that two people were attacked by some kind of animal in The Refuge . . . and now they're missing. He told us to steer clear."

Jackson's face took on the same startled expression as Bryce's. "Shit."

Jackson put the car in gear and headed for school. The *Pantera* song "Cemetery Gates" played quietly in the background and neither boy spoke a word as Bryce quickly read the news article. After he finished, he told Jackson about Tom Brown's story from two days ago.

"He said it was a giant wolf?" Jackson scoffed. "You know the old guy's a drunk, right?"

Bryce bristled at Jackson's rude statement. "Yeah, well, that's not all." He filled Jackson in on his trip to Sam Nightfeather's cabin the day before.

"Man. This shit's getting weird," said Jackson. "Did you talk to Grandpa about what Tom Brown and Nightfeather told you?"

"No. I didn't," said Bryce. "I figured, why bring up a sore subject."

Jackson nodded and said, "I mean . . . all that other shit happened way back in 1953. That was"—he paused a long moment to do the math in his head—"thirty-eight years ago. There's no way the same animal attacked *those* two people." He pointed to the newspaper.

The two boys met eyes, but Bryce still hadn't responded.

"... Right?" Jackson demanded.

"Yeah, I guess so," Bryce said. "Hell, I don't know. This whole thing's creepin' me out."

"Yeah, well, join the fuckin' club," Jackson offered. He reached over and cranked up the tunes.

Those tiny flames of uneasiness that had been guttering inside each of them for the past month—were now burning brightly.

***

Early Monday morning, Sheriff Neil Culley sat leaning back in his chair with his feet propped on the corner of his desk, sipping his morning coffee. He liked coming into the office early, before things got busy—not that things ever got *busy* in Bane County.

Culley unfolded the morning paper and frowned as he saw his own face staring back at him. They had used the stock-photo from his election campaign three years ago. *Like a deer in headlights,* he thought, shaking his head.

He tossed the newspaper onto his desk next to a stack of paperwork. There was no need to read the article, he knew more about the story than the newspaper did. Culley had spent the last three days searching for the lost backpackers in The Refuge.

This shit sure piles up quick when I'm gone, he thought, looking at the stack of papers.

Irene Murphy, the night dispatcher, walked out of the back-office and moved slowly toward the front door. Irene answered the phones at night and forwarded any emergencies on to the sheriff or his deputy. There weren't many emergencies in a small town, so Irene's job mainly entailed drinking coffee, doing crossword puzzles and jotting down the occasional message. She had been working a lot of extra hours over the past few days, due to the ongoing search for the lost backpackers. She looked tired as she shuffled toward the front door to head home.

"Good morning, Sheriff," Irene said.

"Goodnight, Irene, goodnight," Culley sang jokingly. It was the lyrics to an old blues song by *Lead-Belly*.

Irene feigned laughter on her way out the door. *Is he ever gonna come up with some new material?* She wondered.

Bane County—and the Town of Silver Canyon in particular—was a peaceful place, and there wasn't much crime to speak of; two lawmen were generally all that was needed to handle the workload. However, with the missing backpackers, things had gotten a bit hectic.

After about an hour, Culley had managed to wade through about half the paperwork on his desk, when an old gray-haired man with a cane walked through the door. He wiped his feet on the rug and hung his old Stetson hat on the rack. The old man looked across the room and made eye contact with Sheriff Culley.

"Well, hello there, Deputy," Culley hollered.

Former Deputy Dalton Morrow had been retired for over eleven years, but everyone around Silver Canyon still called him "Deputy." Back in 1974, when Sheriff Tom Cooper retired, and Culley became sheriff, Dalton had continued as his deputy, until retiring in 1980. Now, at seventy-six-years of age, he had served nearly forty-six of those years as a deputy sheriff in Bane County.

"I'm glad I caught you, Culley," Dalton said. "I figured you might be out in The Refuge looking for those lost backpackers." Dalton made his way across the room to the coffee pot and lifted a large Styrofoam cup from the stack to pour himself a cup of black coffee.

"No, not today," Culley said dryly. "I've got more important business that needs tending to." He motioned to the stack of paperwork on his desk.

Dalton offered a wide grin and scratched doggedly at the back of his balding pate. "I can see that." He sipped his coffee and walked over to shake Culley's hand.

"I sent my deputy, Wayne Bennett, along with a few volunteers out to the wildlife refuge to continue the search. We've been at it since Friday," Culley added.

Dalton sat down in front of the sheriff's desk and continued sipping his coffee.

"So, what brings you in today, Dalton?" Culley inquired.

"I read in the paper this mornin' that you thought a mountain lion might've attacked those backpackers. I wanted to know exactly what you found in that campsite." Dalton had never been one to beat around the bush.

"Well, normally I couldn't talk about an ongoing investigation in any great detail," Culley hedged. "But, since you're a former deputy, I can make an exception"—then he added—"this information *is* confidential, you understand."

Dalton nodded the affirmative and took another sip of coffee. *Culley's such a damn stickler,* he thought.

"Yesterday morning, a little before noon, Deputy Bennett and I finally located their campsite," Culley began. "There were heavy rains inside The Refuge last week, so they were pretty hard to track; a lot of evidence most likely got washed away.

"There was a woman's blouse and blue jeans on the ground next to the fire-pit, ripped to shreds and soaked in blood. Even after the heavy rains, you could see where blood had stained the ground; it was definitely a kill-site.

"We did a 360-degree perimeter search of the campsite, out to about two hundred yards. East of the campsite, about fifty yards out, we found a second kill-site. A large area of grass was disturbed, and there were more shredded clothes; you could see there had been a lot of blood on the ground.

"My personal opinion: there's no chance in Hell that either of those people survived the attack. There was just too much blood loss. But . . . I still don't have any bodies—so—we'll keep looking."

"Did you notice anything . . . *unusual* around the campsite?" Dalton asked.

"Unusual? No . . . not that I recall," Culley said, thinking back.

Dalton nodded slowly and met Culley's eyes, wanting more.

"Well . . . there *was* this strange footprint near the edge of the pond," Culley remembered.

A concerned look came over Dalton's face. He said, "What *kind* of footprint?"

"It was probably nothing," Culley said dismissively. "You know how rain can wash out a track and change its shape—make it look bigger than it really is. That's all it was."

Dalton stood up and looked down at the sheriff's desk. He said, "Can I borrow that legal pad and a pencil?"

Culley furrowed his brow and nodded, curious what the old man was up to. Dalton swallowed the dregs of his coffee and sat the empty cup on Culley's desk. He picked up the pad and pencil and began to sketch. When he had finished, he handed the drawing to Culley.

Dalton said, "Did the footprint you saw by the edge of the pond look like this?"

A look of complete surprise washed over Culley's face. He said, "How in the *hell* do you know what that footprint looked like?"

Dalton sat back down and sighed heavily. The old man's face had taken on a grim, ashen appearance. "That's a *long* story."

"Well, I sure as *hell* wanna hear it." Culley demanded.

Dalton pulled out a can of Copenhagen from his shirt pocket and took a dip. He reached for his empty Styrofoam cup on Culley's desk and spat in it noisily. Culley winced, grimacing at the disgusting sound.

"Well," Dalton began. "It all started for me back in 1934 when we had a series of animal attacks around The Refuge. Between September and December of that year, fifteen people died, or went missing; and right up until we found the last body, we thought a mountain lion was responsible.

"Sheriff Tom Cooper and I saw those clawed footprints in the dirt," Dalton said, pointing to the sketch, "all around the last body. We had no idea what kind of animal made them, but we knew—whatever it was—it had killed all those people. After December, the killings stopped, and Tom and I just tried to forget that we'd ever seen those footprints.

"Then, in September of 1953, it all started again. The same animal killed a woman by the name of Rickman at her home, ten miles south of here. Sheriff Cooper and I found the same clawed-footprints on her front porch—they were an exact match. The front door of her house had been smashed in, and there were giant claw marks on the doorframe. I also found a double barrel 12-gauge, with two shots fired, lying next to her body on the floor. Over the next three months, eleven more people died, or went missing; the same way it happened back in 1934.

"In 1972, we had nine missing person cases between September and December, and you know as well as I do, that's an unprecedented amount. We didn't find any blood or bodies, so it wasn't front-page news, but I know in my heart that the same animal killed all those people.

"Now, the killings have started again," Dalton warned. "You saw the clawed footprint yourself. I'm telling you: there's gonna be a lot more killings and a lot more missing people before the end of the year; and it won't be because of any damn mountain lion."

"Come on, Dalton," Culley pleaded. "Give me a break. I grew up around here listening to the same bullshit monster-stories that you did. Old-timers have been talking about a big, hairy creature that lives in those mountains for as long as anybody can remember. You *can't* be telling me that you think—*what*?—a *werewolf* is responsible for the missing backpackers?"

"I don't know *what the hell* it is," Dalton exclaimed, his dander starting to rise. "What I *do know* is that some kind of large predator lives in those mountains . . . and it's *hungry* again."

As Dalton rose to his feet to leave, Culley posed a final question: "Why do you think we didn't find any bodies?" Culley asked snidely.

"Well, the way I figure," Dalton offered, "it just killed more than it could eat—so, it hauled off the leftovers to its meat locker."

Culley smirked and shook his head.

"Now, let me ask you a question," Dalton said. "Did you find a single mountain lion track—*anywhere*—around that campsite?"

Culley didn't answer the question. Instead, with a condescending tone, he said, "All right, Dalton; thanks for stopping in, you take care now."

"That's what I figured," Dalton muttered knowingly. Then he headed toward the door. As he slipped on his Stetson, he gave Culley a final warning: "Keep your eyes open, Culley—there's a storm coming."

Sheriff Neil Culley sat at his desk smiling and shaking his

head. *That senile old son of a bitch is crazier than a shithouse rat.*

He picked up the sketch Dalton had drawn of the footprint and stared at it, pondering. *How in the hell did he know what that footprint looked like?*

Culley tore the page from the pad and placed it in the bottom left-hand drawer of his desk. That was his file-13 drawer. It was the type place a person would store information about an Elvis sighting or a second gunman on the grassy knoll.

"I don't have time for this bullshit," Culley proclaimed, slamming the drawer shut. He started going through the paperwork on his desk again.

After another hour, Culley had almost caught up on his paperwork, when two women came through the front door. A young lady helped an old, snowy-haired woman walk across the room to Culley's desk.

"Can I help you ladies?" Culley asked, standing up to greet them.

"My great-grandmother has information about the two people who were killed in the wildlife refuge," the young woman answered.

Culley shook his head. "They haven't been declared dead, ma'am, the search is still ongoing."

The old woman met Culley's eyes. "They are dead."

Culley walked around his desk and joined the two women. He said, "I'm sorry, who are you?"

"This is my great-grandmother, Cătălina Pătrașcu, and my name is Mariana."

"And why does your great-grandmother believe these people are dead?" Culley asked.

"No person can escape from the *Neuri*," Cătălina insisted.

Culley got a confused look on his face. He said, "I'm sorry—

the what? The *new-ree,* and just who is this *new-ree* person?"

"The *Neuri* is no person. The *Neuri* is the ancient one, a demon from the underworld; it is the eater of men!" Cătălina raised her voice. Mariana put an arm around her great-grandmother and tried to calm her.

"All right now, let's just calm down," Sheriff Culley said softly. He gently herded the two women toward the front door. "Thank you both very much for coming in and we'll keep an eye out for any . . . man-eating demons, and the like. Y'all ladies have a good day now, bye-bye."

Closing the door, Culley laughed quietly. *The crazies are coming out of the damn woodwork today.* As he made his way back to his desk, he once again heard the door opening. *Oh, hell,* he thought, *what now?*

Culley turned to find Harriot Drucker, his secretary, coming through the door; she worked part-time a few days per week. Under his breath, he muttered, "Oh, thank God."

"Good morning, Sheriff," Harriot said cheerfully. "How's your day going?"

"I think I'd rather be back out in The Refuge," he said dryly.

IT WAS 9:30 P.M. WHEN WENDY WALKER finished her shift at CB's Drive-in and made her way to the women's locker room to change clothes. She really disliked her carhop uniform, she thought it looked tacky, and there was no way she would *ever* walk home wearing it.

All day long, she had been listening to customers' gossip about the missing backpackers. It seemed like every time she delivered a burger someone asked if she'd seen today's paper, and after hearing it for the umpteenth time, she was sick of it. She couldn't care less about missing backpackers; people got lost in The Refuge all the time. Eventually, they always showed up again. Right now, the only thing on Wendy Walker's mind was her upcoming date with Bryce McNeel.

After she finished changing, she put her roller-skates back on and headed out the door; the only thing she carried with her was a pair of sneakers. Wendy knew her trip home would be faster if she skated down the sidewalk to the edge of town. She could coast down the long, gentle slope of Main Street the entire way. From there, she would change into her sneakers and walk the rest of the way along the highway. Wendy's house was just under a mile from the edge of town, and the walk only took about fifteen minutes.

As she coasted down the long, empty sidewalk, the brisk night air washed over her; she held out her arms as though flying, slaloming back and forth. The streets of Silver Canyon were quiet this time of night and she mused about her upcoming date with Bryce. It was only four days away—and she had *nothing* to wear.

When she reached the edge of town Wendy removed her skates, slung them over her shoulder and slipped into her shoes. The remainder of her journey home would be along the unlit highway that led out of town. It was the same stretch of road she had walked to-and-from school each day for years, and she had made the trip at night on countless occasions.

As she strode briskly down the brush-lined highway, away from the sheltering lights of town, Wendy began to notice that the night seemed much darker than usual. The lonely stretch of road appeared to fade and vanish into the distance; like a tiny ribbon of asphalt that dipped into an inky-black well. There was no moon in the hazy night sky, and the pale dusting of stars seemed faint and distant.

At first, Wendy gave little thought to the deepening gloom, she continued along the highway without concern. However, as the lights of Silver Canyon fell farther and farther behind— the darkness eventually consumed her.

Wendy's pace began to slow as the world before her took on the appearance of a tangible black shroud, a thick, palpable darkness that seemed to cling and crawl across her skin as she moved through it.

As if by instinct, Wendy raised her arms, feeling her way through the darkening gloom. Even her own hands appeared faint and indistinct as they reached timidly into the void. Wendy had never known a night so black.

Once, when she was a small girl, her family had visited Carlsbad Caverns in New Mexico. While inside the cavern, the tour guide had turned off the lights, to show visitors what *true* darkness looked like. Only *that* darkness, what she had experienced deep inside the cave, only *that* was blacker than the night where she now found herself.

Wendy's breathing had become labored and anxious. With each shuddering breath, it felt as though black air was filling her lungs. Even though she moved at a slow gait, her pulse had begun to surge and she could feel her heart drumming in her chest.

"Everything's fine," she breathed. "There's nothing to be afraid of."

The faded white stripe that fringed the lonely highway was her only visible guide, and even *that* was almost indiscernible. Wendy stared intently at the road beneath her feet, her eyes fixed upon the faint white stripe. After plodding forward for what seemed an eternity, the stripe curved and the guardrails of a bridge appeared. She had made it to Shambles Wash, a small seasonal creek that ran along a heavily wooded ravine. The bridge was the half-way-point of her journey; she was almost home.

Even though she moved blindly along the dark and desolate highway, reaching the half-way-point had eased her anxiety. Sliding her hand atop the guardrail, she started across the ravine, her gait now faster, and more confident.

Beneath the bridge, she could hear the soughing of the wind, as it swept through the deep ravine. The haunting sound carried the subtle impression of voices; a susurrant chorus, offered up by the inky-black trench. Wendy gasped, and ran to the end of the bridge. Then, taking a deep breath, she continued on, following the faint white stripe through the darkness.

A loud cracking sound, like a branch breaking, came from the gulf of darkness behind her; large rocks and scree tumbled down the side of the ravine next to the bridge. Wendy gasped and quickly spun around, roller-skates falling to the ground. Her skin pebbled with goosebumps as she stared blindly into the darkness.

The sound of snapping branches and crumbling rocks rose from the depths; it was the sound of something large, clambering up from the deep ravine.

Instinctively, Wendy began backing away from the ominous sound; she paid no attention to the direction she traveled. As leaves began crunching under her feet, she found herself gone from the shoulder of the highway and standing on the grassy verge.

Realizing she'd left the road, Wendy began to panic. The white stripe of the highway had been her only visible guide. Now, with the menacing sounds from the ravine coming closer, she had completely lost her bearings. Not only was she blinded by the darkness, she had no idea which direction was home.

As Wendy struggled to see through the fuliginous murk that seemed to swarm around her, the sounds from the ravine faded. Whatever had been scaling the cliff had finally reached the top. A deathly silence surrounded her. Wendy's blood ran cold, and her heart felt frozen in her chest. She had no idea which way to turn, which way to run.

In the darkness—silence was horrifying.

A repulsive stench, like rotting flesh pervaded the air; Wendy cupped a hand to her nose. From the brush behind her, she heard the rustling of branches. She gasped and spun around, facing the ominous sound. She lifted her hands, holding them in front of her, as if to push back what lurked in the shadows. She could barely see her own fingers through the pall of darkness.

Wendy's breathing had become rapid and shallow as she gaped into the shadowy gloom. Seized by fear, she was petrified, her body trembled and shuddered violently; her heart thudded in her chest, threatening to explode.

The sound from the darkness shifted, it now came from behind her again. Grass and leaves rustled and gravel crunched underfoot. Wendy gasped and swiveled to meet the sound emanating from the inky pitch.

It was circling her; whatever it was—it was circling her.

"Who's there?" Wendy tried to shout, but her voice caught in her throat, as if her words were made of dust.

The sound moved around her, circling closer, tightening the noose. A tiny scream, no more than a squeak, escaped Wendy's lips. Once more, she whirled around, facing the sound; it was behind her again. She jutted her hands into the darkness, trying to force back the hidden terror.

Wendy could hear the deep, raspy breathing and ponderous footsteps of the thing that was stalking her. She wanted to scream, but she had forgotten how. She opened her mouth, but fear had stolen her voice.

She lifted her hands into the sable abyss, reaching and probing, turning in a slow circle, following the sound as it moved, creating an imaginary barrier between herself and the thing that lurked in the darkness.

The sound grew closer, and the darkness became tangible; as Wendy reached her hands forward, she found purchase on the towering black shadow that stood before her. Long, matted hair entangled her fingers.

Yanking back her hands, she tried to scream, but her feeble cry wedged in her throat. The enormous dark presence that loomed over her began to emerge. Wendy slowly lifted her eyes, focusing on the large, slavering maw directly above her head; putrid drops of slobber rained down upon her face.

As a deep, guttural growl sent tremors through Wendy's body, her eyes rolled white, and she crumpled to the ground like a ragdoll.

A HALF-MILE AWAY, Vivian Walker stood on the front porch of their colonial-style home, staring at the dark and desolate highway. When her daughter, Wendy, had been late coming home, she began to worry, and had been standing vigil for the last twenty minutes.

Vivian knew she was being ridiculous, and overprotective, nothing bad ever happened in Silver Canyon; it was the type place where people didn't even lock their doors at night. Wendy—and every other kid in town—walked around Silver Canyon all the time, day or night, with never a worry or care; it was just that kind of town.

Nothing bad ever happens here, she assured herself.

For what seemed like the twentieth time, she peered through the screen door at the large wall-clock in the entryway. Taking a final puff from her cigarette, she stubbed it out in the soil of a potted plant on the porch.

"10:25 p.m.," she muttered. Vivian knew that CB's Drive-in closed at 9:30 p.m. and it never took Wendy more than twenty minutes to walk home. Thirty minutes tops, if she dawdled, and she knew better than that.

Feeling somewhat uncertain, Vivian walked into the house, grabbed her purse and keys, and pulled the Chrysler Town & Country from the garage. She didn't know which emotion she felt more, anger or worry; regardless, Wendy was grounded for a week.

Chuck would pick this week to be out of town, she thought, frustrated that her husband was away on business.

As Vivian headed down the long driveway, she switched on the van's high-beams for better visibility; the night was exceptionally dark. She turned onto the deserted highway and headed toward Silver Canyon.

There was rarely any traffic along Highway 50 this time of night. In a small town like Silver Canyon, the joke was, "they roll up the streets when the sun goes down."

Vivian trundled slowly along the night-cloaked highway, the bright headlights of her mini-van slicing through the gloom. Traveling at 25 mph, it would only take a couple of minutes to reach the edge of town—it was just under a mile—and from there, CB's Drive-in was less than half a mile up Main Street. Her eyes scanned both sides of the brush-lined highway, searching every shadow for her daughter.

As she approached the bridge at Shambles Wash, Vivian's headlights reflected brightly off something at the edge of the road. Applying her brakes, she drifted the van onto the shoulder, edging toward the luminous object. As the van rolled slowly forward, Vivian leaned over the steering wheel, trying to get a better look. When she finally realized what she was seeing, a startled gasp burst from her lips.

Slamming on the brakes, Vivian threw the van into park, and flung open the door. She raced to the front of the vehicle and stared in disbelief. There, on the side of the dark, desolate highway, was a pair of white roller-skates—Wendy's skates.

Vivian stood rigid with fear, her feet rooted to the asphalt. Her mind began to race as her face flushed with heat. She wanted to call out, but there was no air in her lungs, she had forgotten to breathe.

"Wendy," she gasped feebly. Then—taking a deep breath—"WENDY!"

Panic-stricken, Vivian Walker ran frantically up and down the highway yelling her daughter's name into the darkness; with each desperate shout, she became more and more hysterical. The only sound the night offered was the drumbeat of her heart. Finally, she ran to the railing of the bridge and stared into the stygian darkness below.

"WENDY!" she screamed, and then sobbed uncontrollably. Her voice echoed along the dark cliffs of Shambles Wash and faded into the distance.

Catching her breath, Vivian started to regain her senses, and realized that she needed help. Racing back to her van, she jumped inside and slammed it into gear. Loose gravel shot from beneath the vehicle as she squealed and smoked her tires across the asphalt, making her way back home in a matter of seconds.

Careening madly up her driveway, Vivian veered off the side and cut across her front lawn, heading straight for the front door. At the last possible moment, she slammed on the brakes and slid to a stop, cutting deep ruts into her freshly mowed grass. She bolted from the van and raced through the front door toward the phone. Then, with some semblance of rational thought, Vivian called the Bane County Sheriff's Office.

Within minutes, Deputy Wayne Bennett had rushed to the scene. He found Vivian Walker standing alongside the lonely highway, holding her daughter's roller-skates tightly to her chest, waiting, sobbing. As she explained to Deputy Bennett exactly what had happened, her voice quavered uncontrollably; then, she broke down and cried.

Using the spotlight on his cruiser, as well as, a bright handheld lantern, Deputy Bennett spent over an hour searching the entire area. There was no sign of a struggle anywhere: no torn clothing, no blood, no discernable footprints or scuff marks, and no tire tracks—save for those left by Vivian's van. There was absolutely nothing that indicated a crime had taken place. Wendy Walker had just . . . vanished.

THE NEXT DAY, news of Wendy's disappearance was all over town, including the Silver Canyon High School. Information flowed through a small town like a sieve. Everyone was shocked that something like this could happen in Silver Canyon. There was talk of a deranged psychopath, cruising the roads of Bane County, abducting young girls.

Bryce and Jackson couldn't help thinking that a psychopath might not be responsible for Wendy's disappearance. Yesterday, they had learned of two backpackers that had gone missing, after some kind of animal attack, and now—Wendy vanishes.

"This shit's getting out of hand," said Jackson, as they made their way across the school parking lot.

"I know," Bryce agreed. "I can't stop thinking about Grandpa's story, and what Tom Brown and Sam Nightfeather told me."

"I keep thinking about those damn claw marks we saw at the old Rickman house," Jackson added.

Bryce nodded his head, thinking, staring ahead at nothing in particular. "Let's stop at Shambles Wash on the way home," he said. "I want to have a look around."

"Really?" Jackson said, a bit taken aback by the suggestion. "Okay." He fired up the Camaro and headed for the highway.

A few minutes later, they arrived at Shambles Wash, and

pulled off the road onto the verge. The two boys sat quietly for a moment, then Jackson killed the engine and they stepped out of the car.

It seemed unnaturally quiet beside the highway—save for the occasional rush of a passing car—and knowing that Wendy had disappeared from this exact location less than twenty-four hours ago was somewhat unnerving.

They walked out onto the bridge and leaned on the guardrail, looking down into the deep ravine. Neither of them had said a single word since they arrived. The entire place had a strange, funereal feel about it, as if they should only speak in hushed tones.

Finally, Jackson broke the silence. "You doin' okay, Bryce?"

"Yeah, I'm good."

"I mean, I know you liked Wendy and all."

"Actually," Bryce said, "I barely knew her. We were going to the movies this Friday."

"Yeah, I know . . . I can't believe this shit. It doesn't seem real."

Jackson pulled a silver flask from his jacket and offered it to Bryce.

"Nah, I'm okay."

"If there was ever a time for a drink, it's now," Jackson insisted, edging the flask closer.

Bryce took the flask and had a sip, then passed it back. Jackson took a sip, and then poured a shot of whiskey into the ravine.

"To Wendy," Jackson offered.

"To Wendy."

As the boys watched the shot of whiskey plummet into the deep ravine, splashing on the rocks below, they noticed something unusual.

"Did Deputy Bennett go down into the ravine to search?" Jackson asked.

"I don't know," said Bryce. "I just heard they searched the area and didn't find anything."

They were both peering at the rocky wall of the ravine and moving toward the end of the bridge for a closer look.

"He *must* have searched the ravine," Jackson insisted. "You can see where someone rappelled down the wall. See all those fresh scuff marks and broken branches?"

Bryce was already nodding his agreement when he noticed the four parallel scratches on the rock-face at the top of the ravine. His mind immediately flashed back to the claw marks at the old Rickman house.

"Maybe Bennett *didn't* rappel down," said Bryce, pointing to the large scratches. "Maybe something else, climbed out."

When Jackson saw the claw marks, he had the same thought as Bryce—the old Rickman house—but he didn't want to believe it.

"No way," he said. "One of the broken branches must've done that when it fell."

"Maybe so," Bryce agreed, "but you have to admit."

"Yeah," Jackson said. "Definitely creepy."

Looking closer, Jackson caught a glint of sunlight reflecting off something in the grass. "What's that?" He pointed to the edge of the ravine.

"What?"

"There's something shiny in the grass over there."

"Where?"

Jackson hopped over the bridge railing and moved toward the ravine's edge. "Do you see it?"

"Yeah, I see it now," Bryce said. "It's about four feet to your left." Then he added, "Be careful, that edge could crumble."

"Yes—Mom." Jackson spoke in a mocking tone.

"I'm serious, Jackson. If you fall in, I'll leave your scrawny bahookie down there."

"Hmm," Jackson breathed. He reached down and grabbed the shiny object.

"What is it?"

"A dragonfly."

"What?" Bryce said. He jumped over the railing and moved quickly toward Jackson.

"It's a piece of jewelry or something."

"Let me see that," said Bryce, taking the piece into his hand. His eyes widened. "Holy shit, Jackson . . . this is one of Wendy's earrings."

"You've got to be fucking kidding me."

"I wish I was," said Bryce, "and look at the wing."

Jackson took a closer look. "Damn . . . that's dried blood."

"Yeah, it is," he said somberly. "We need to take this to the sheriff's office—right now."

They quickly made their way back to the car and headed into to town. A few minutes later, they walked into the sheriff's office and found Deputy Bennett sitting at his desk.

They introduced themselves, even though both boys had met Bennett before. They explained that they were friends of Wendy Walker, and that they had stopped at Shambles Wash on the way home to have a look around. Then they gave him the earring and pointed out the blood.

"Damn," Bennett exclaimed, looking at the earring. "Where was it?"

"Near the edge of the ravine, at the southwest corner of the bridge," said Jackson.

Bennett shook his head and wrinkled his lips, disgusted with himself. "I can't believe I missed this. I even gave the entire place a second going-over early this morning."

"It was really hard to see," Jackson pointed out. "I'd have never seen it, if the sun hadn't hit it just right."

The boys talked with Bennett a while longer and then headed toward the door. As they were about to leave, Jackson decided to ask Bennett a question. He was afraid of the answer he might get, but he elected to ask it anyway. "Deputy Bennett?" Jackson said.

"Yeah, son?"

"When you searched the area, did you go down inside the ravine?"

"No," Bennett said. "I just looked down from the bridge. Why do you ask?"

"No reason," Jackson said. "Just curious." He gave a quick wave and headed out the door.

"Did you hear that shit?" he asked Bryce, "Bennett said he didn't go into the ravine."

"Yeah, I heard," said Bryce. "You still think a falling branch made those scratch marks?"

"Fuck if I know," said Jackson. He fired up the loud engine and dropped it into gear. "I don't know what to think about any of this shit."

As Jackson headed for the highway, Bryce popped an old *Blue Öyster Cult* tape into the deck. When they drove past the bridge at Shambles Wash, Bryce noticed the road sign on the bridge with the ravine's name.

"Do you know the meaning of the word 'shambles'?" Bryce asked.

"Sure, it means 'messy'. My mom tells me that my room is a shambles all the time."

"Yeah, that's true," Bryce agreed, "but, it has an older meaning too: a 'shambles' . . . is a slaughterhouse—a scene of great carnage."

"Are you shitting me?"

"Nope, I shit you not."

Jackson blinked. "Well, thank you, Bryce . . . thank you for that enlightening little addition to this otherwise completely *fucked-up day*. It's not like I wasn't *freaked-out* enough over this shit."

"Sorry," Bryce said. "It just sort of, slipped out."

They drove for a few minutes in silence, then Jackson said, "So, what the hell are we saying here, Bryce? Are we saying that Wendy and those two backpackers were killed by some kind of monster? The same monster that killed Mrs. Rickman over thirty-eight years ago?"—he paused—"Because, if *that's* what we're saying here, then . . . well . . . Shit!"

"Dude, I have *no idea* what we're saying here," Bryce admitted. "All I know is that some seriously weird shit is going down; and *none* of it makes any sense."

"So, what the hell do we do now?" Jackson asked.

"I'm not sure," said Bryce. "I guess we just . . . keep our eyes open."

"Yeah, well . . . being well-heeled might not be a bad idea either."

When Jackson suggested that they carry a gun, it seemed strange; but then again—these were strange days.

IT WAS THE MORNING OF OCTOBER 23 and with Halloween a little more than a week away, the students at Silver Canyon High School were thinking about what costume they would wear to the upcoming masquerade dance. It had been fifteen days since Wendy Walker's disappearance, and for most people in Silver Canyon, the shock of the terrible tragedy had begun to fade somewhat; more than anything, people were just trying to get on with their lives.

For Bryce and Jackson, the disappearance of Wendy Walker and the two backpackers in The Refuge still weighed heavily on their minds. Jackson had made good on his suggestion of being well-heeled; he had taken to keeping a small .38 Special revolver under the driver's seat of his car.

Bryce had been keeping an ear out for all the town gossip, and an eye on the local newspaper. He had even stopped by the game warden's office on several occasions, to enquire about people visiting The Refuge. Warden Fletcher had found it a bit strange that Bryce kept dropping by to look at his sign-in sheet.

"Why do you care so much about who's in The Refuge?" Fletcher had asked him.

"Oh, I . . . um, it's for . . . a school project," Bryce had stammered; he was a lousy liar. "I'm doing a report on tourism . . . for my political science class."

"Politics, huh? Well, good luck with that," Fletcher had scoffed, handing Bryce the sign-in sheet.

Over the past two weeks, all the visitors to The Refuge had been day-trippers—people who hiked for the day, but didn't camp overnight—all except for one group: a biology professor and three graduate students from USC San Diego had purchased an extended camping permit for two weeks, and were heading to Lake Argent.

Lake Argent was a large, subalpine lake located at the center of The Refuge, a popular destination for scientists of all disciplines. It was located in a hanging valley at an elevation of about three thousand feet, and the diversity of flora and fauna found there was unequalled anywhere in the world.

Bryce and Jackson had hiked to the distant lake on numerous occasions, and even for an experienced woodsman, the twenty-mile-hike to the center of The Refuge would've taken at least two full days; the terrain was extremely grueling.

The group had entered The Refuge twelve days ago, and even *if* something bad had happened, they wouldn't be overdue for another two days. No matter how hard he tried, Bryce couldn't quell the sense of foreboding, that something terrible had befallen the group.

When he informed Jackson of the people heading to Lake Argent, he, too, had felt uneasy. Then, Jackson suggested something to take their minds off the issue. *"Deer season's open,"* he had pointed out, *"let's just focus on that."*—and so they had.

It was true, opening day of deer season had always been the highpoint each fall that they eagerly anticipated. When Bryce and Jackson exited school that afternoon, they could feel the excitement in the air. There hadn't been any missing people over the past two weeks—at least, none that they knew of—so their spirits were high as they headed home that afternoon.

"Which deer stand are you going to use?" Jackson asked.

"I want the old tower-stand near the highway."

"Cool. I'm gonna use the log-stand out past the old storage barn; I'll walk there from my house, then we can meet-up after dark."

"Sounds good; let's hit it."

As they turned onto the road, Bryce rummaged through the glove-box and found a cassette tape; he looked at the cover: *Nazareth* "Hair of the Dog." The artwork depicted a pack of scary, long-fanged dogs, or some such thing.

"Where'd you find this?" asked Bryce.

"Dave's Record Hut, where else?" It was the only place in Bane County where you could buy, sell, or trade rock 'n' roll music. Jackson was one of their best customers; his collection of classic rock 'n' roll was endless.

"I love these guys," Bryce said, "they're from Scotland." With a name like "McNeel," he would.

Bryce popped in the tape and the song, "Changin' Times" kicked off.

They would have no idea how appropriate their choice in music had been, until later that night.

CHAPTER 8

Hunter's Moon

BRYCE MCNEEL WALKED TO THE GUN RACK in his bedroom and removed his deer rifle. He popped out the magazine and tossed it on the bed, then slid back the spring-loaded bolt and checked the chamber. Laying the rifle gently on his bed, he admired it. The weapon was *truly* a cold-steel work of art.

It was a Remington model 7400 autoloader with a blued-steel barrel and glossy walnut stock. It was a .30-06 Springfield, and was topped by a Leupold 3x9 variable power scope. He had taken several deer in the past at well over three hundred yards with this powerful rifle.

Bryce slipped on a pair of camouflage coveralls and his hunting boots, and then pulled a small hunting pack from the closet. He grabbed his bone-handled hunting knife, a box of ammunition, a flashlight and a small spray-bottle of *Old Pete's Original Indian Buck Lure*. After stuffing everything into the pack, he filled a small canteen with water and headed for the door.

"My freezer is empty," said Grandma, as Bryce walked through the kitchen. "I expect you to fill it."

"I'm gonna do my best," he said, with a wink.

Bryce loved deer season; he walked outside into the crisp autumn air and took a deep, cleansing breath. There wasn't a cloud in the sky. The old tower-stand near the highway was about a one-mile-walk through the heavily-wooded forest and it would take him about twenty or thirty minutes to get there; he needed to move as cautiously and quietly as possible.

Before leaving, he took out his spray-bottle of *Buck Lure* and sprayed the tops and bottoms of his boots along with his coveralls. That way, if a deer got downwind, or crossed the path he had walked, it wouldn't recognize his scent as human; he would be invisible. Finally, Bryce sprayed his rifle with a light mist of *Buck Lure*, to mask the smell of gun oil; deer associated that with humans, as well.

It was about two hours before sundown when Bryce left home. He slapped the magazine into his rifle and pulled back the bolt to chamber a round. Checking the safety, he slung the rifle over his shoulder and made his way silently through the forest. Deer began foraging about thirty minutes before sundown, so Bryce always tried to arrive at his deer stand at least an hour beforehand. It lessened the chance of spooking a herd of deer along the way.

The old tower-stand was a small wooden box that rested atop stilts about twenty-feet above the ground. It was located at the edge of an old live-oak grove, which overlooked a large open field. Acorns from the ancient trees covered the ground and brought deer and other wildlife from miles around.

Live-oak trees weren't indigenous to Bane County. There was a rumor that an expeditionary party for the Spanish explorer Francisco Vázquez de Coronado had brought the acorns to Bane County around 1541; they had been gathered in southern regions to use as feed for the expedition's livestock. Inadvertently, the explorers had planted trees along the way.

Many of the giant trees were hundreds of years old; however, no one knew if the rumor was true. Coronado's own journal stated that several of his scouting parties had disappeared without a trace, so their exact routes were unknown.

The deer stand's painted exterior had a leaf-like camouflage pattern; it blended perfectly into the treetops. While live-oak trees were not *true* evergreens, they kept the majority of their leaves year-round.

When he arrived, Bryce sprayed more *Buck Lure* all around the deer stand and then climbed the twenty-foot-ladder to the small wooden box at the top. He opened the door on the back of the stand and stepped inside; taking a seat on the swivel-chair that was bolted to the floor. It was a close fit inside the stand, about the size of a small walk-in closet: five- by five-foot square, with a six-foot ceiling; but it made for a perfect shooting platform.

The backside of the stand—where the door was located—faced into the dense treetop, so there was no need for a window. The other three sides were spanned by narrow shooting-windows, furtively draped with camouflage netting.

The view from the front and left windows of the stand faced a vast open field, about five hundred yards across. Through the right side window, you looked down a long, narrow right-of-way, a broad swath that had been cut through the forest to run electrical powerlines.

The clearing of the right-of-way was about fifty yards in width, and ran for about seventy-five yards in a straight line. There, it curved sharply, and went down a steep hill toward the highway. The powerlines ran down the center of the swath, and dense forest hemmed both edges.

Bryce sat in total silence for the next ninety minutes. He had seen several squirrels, a large covey of quail, and even a flock of wild turkeys—but not a single deer. A tired sun had fallen below the treetops, casting its final golden rays skyward. Gazing out the left window of his deer stand, Bryce marveled at the amazing colors in the western sky. Feathery wisps of dark-violet clouds skirted the horizon, their edges ablaze with fiery orange light.

Darkness gathered. Songbirds finished their farewell to the light, as crickets and frogs welcomed the night. There were always sounds in the forest, but the melodious din of sunset always offered the greatest ensemble.

The snap of a twig, and the crunch of dry leaves reached Bryce's ears—something moved through the forest. He turned quietly and peered down the right-of-way. About forty yards away, four deer moved warily from the dense forest into the clearing. Bryce's eyes slowly lifted to the eastern horizon; above the deer, a full moon was rising over the treetops.

He hadn't realized there was a full moon tonight, but at this particular moment, it was a welcome sight. Its pale-yellow glow filled the right-of-way, and held back the dusk, improving visibility. Bryce quietly raised his rifle, peering at the deer through his scope; he dialed down the magnification until he could see more clearly; they were all does.

For the most part, he still had moderate visibility, but the orange backlight of the western horizon was failing quickly. If a buck didn't step out of the forest to join his harem soon, Bryce would have to call it a night.

He watched the herd hopefully for the next ten minutes, but in the failing light, it had become more and more difficult to see through his scope. In the moonlight, Bryce could still see with his naked eyes—he had excellent night vision—but rifle scopes tended to magnify the darkness as much as the object they were focused on; a clean shot was no longer possible.

Bryce was about to head home, when he saw the herd of deer shudder and spin around toward the forest; something had spooked them. Almost immediately, the deer turned and bolted across the clearing of the right-of-way and vanished into the shadowy forest.

No sooner had the deer disappeared, than Bryce heard something large moving through the forest behind him. Whatever it was, it moved quickly and made a great deal of noise. He could hear the dull thud of heavy footsteps stomping through the forest, and the sound of small trees being uprooted. Branches creaked and snapped, as brush was trampled underfoot.

Bryce listened anxiously to the unnerving sounds as they came closer and closer. He had spent his entire life in the forests of Bane County, and wasn't aware of any animal that moved through the forest with such raw power—not even a really pissed off bear.

He sat stock-still, his heart hammering against his ribs. Whatever had been moving through the forest had stopped; it was now directly behind his deer stand. A strange hush filled the night, as if the entire forest was holding its breath.

In the eerie stillness that surrounded him, Bryce heard a sound that chilled him to the bone: it was the sound of something sniffing, snuffling—searching. There wasn't a window in the back of the deer stand, and even if there were, Bryce wasn't sure if he could've looked.

A nauseating, putrid stench—like the rotting carcass of a long-dead animal—assaulted his nose, causing him to grimace. However, before Bryce could raise a hand to his nose, it started moving again, running and smashing its way through the dense forest. Whatever this thing was, it moved quickly along the edge of the right-of-way, and stayed hidden in the trees.

Bryce peered nervously out the window of the deer stand. The thing was heading east toward the highway, and if it crossed the clearing of right-of-way, he might be able to get a look at it. The full moon rising above the trees lit the clearing perfectly.

As the crashing sounds moved farther away, they suddenly came to an abrupt stop. A huge, hairy figure bolted across the right-of-way at blinding speed, crossing the fifty-yard-clearing in less than two seconds.

Bryce gasped. *Holy shit . . .*

His heart jerked violently in his chest as a shot of adrenaline burst into his bloodstream. The thing was huge—*enormous*—and it moved on two legs. *Nothing moves that fast*, he thought. *It cleared fifty yards in less than two seconds—and on two legs.*

Bryce's heart was hammering, his body shaking from the overload of adrenaline in his system; he couldn't think straight. He lifted his eyes to the full moon above the trees—a single word entered his mind: "werewolf."

A terrifying thought suddenly occurred to him: *what if it comes back?* The beast hadn't caught his scent because of the *Buck Lure* he had sprayed everywhere. He needed to get the hell out of there—fast. Bryce grabbed the small flashlight from his pack and switched it on.

Nothing—he had forgotten to check the batteries—*Shit!*

He scrambled down the dark ladder as quickly as possible and made for home. Patches of moonlight pierced the thick canopy, lighting the forest well enough to see, but it also cast dark shadows everywhere. As Bryce headed through the night, he kept constant watch over his shoulder. There were always sounds in the forest—small animals scurried around—but tonight, every noise seemed to come from behind him. Fear surged through his body. *Was the giant beast tracking him, was he being hunted?*

Enveloped by darkness, his mind drifted back to the forest near the old Rickman house, and the whispering shadows that had followed him and Jackson—that was nothing, compared to the fear he now felt.

He bounded through the moon-dappled forest as fast as possible, wary of the torpid, black shadows that pooled beneath each tree. The journey home seemed endless; he huffed and panted, his legs burned from the exertion. Finally, a small flicker of light appeared in the distance—his grandparents' house—a tiny beacon of hope in the darkness.

A sudden noise came from behind him—this time he was certain. It moved quickly, he could hear the crunching of dried leaves underfoot. A massive surge of adrenaline fueled his fear as his heart jolted against his ribcage. Bryce bolted through the night, running as fast as he could—and he kept running—until he reached his grandparents' house.

Grandpa McNeel was sitting on the back porch, and saw Bryce running toward the house. Concerned, he walked out to meet him. "What the heck are you running from?" Grandpa asked. He could see the panic in the boy's eyes.

Gasping for breath, Bryce tried to answer him. "Grandpa," he panted. "I saw something... I saw the werewolf!"

Suddenly, it came out of the darkness right toward them. Bryce and Grandpa both gasped and recoiled in fear.

"What the heck's wrong with you two?" Jackson asked, stepping into the light. "And why were you running from me?"

Bryce gaped in disbelief. "That was *you* behind me?"

Jackson stared at him curiously, furrowing his brow. "Yeah... who'd you think it was? We said that we'd meet up after dark... remember?"

Bryce's eyes widened—*Jesus*—he had completely forgotten that Jackson was on the other deer stand, only a half-mile away.

Jackson said, "When it got too dark to see through my scope, I walked over to meet you. I saw you climbing down from your stand—I was about a hundred yards to your west—but you took off as if your hair was on fire. I've been on your tail ever since trying to catch up."

Bryce met Jackson's eyes and blurted out, "I saw the werewolf."

Jackson blinked. "What?" He turned to Grandpa, a look of

disbelief on his face.

To Bryce, Grandpa said, "Now just calm down, son, and tell us what happened."

Bryce took a deep breath and tried to calm himself, and then he said, "About twenty or thirty minutes after sundown, I was watching some deer in the right-of-way to the east, but something spooked them and they took off. Then, I heard something big come crashing through the woods. It headed down the right-of-way toward the highway, but it stayed in the trees, so I couldn't see what it was. But then, it crossed the clearing right in front of me, about forty or fifty yards out"—Bryce paused to take a breath and compose himself—"I saw it Grandpa . . . it was enormous, and running on two legs; it was fast, *really* fast . . . it was the werewolf."

Jackson interrupted, saying, "It was probably just a bear, Bryce."

"Bears don't run on their hind legs, or cross fifty yards in less than two seconds," Bryce snapped. "Do you know how fast that is? About 70 mph, it wasn't a damn bear, Jackson!"

Jackson held up his hands in a placating fashion. He said, "I'm not saying you didn't see something, Bryce; but, it was dark out there, and two seconds is a pretty quick glimpse."

Bryce met Jackson's eyes with a flinty glare that could've burned a hole through steel.

"Look," Jackson clarified. "I'm just saying: there's no such thing as a werewolf."

A loud, terrifying howl echoed through the darkness; a hellish roar that pebbled their bodies with goosebumps and filled their souls with fear. It was the stuff of nightmares.

Together, they looked to the full moon above the trees, then back to each other. Grandma McNeel opened the back door, peering at her husband. Her eyes were wide, and filled with fear; she appeared as though she had heard that same terrifying howl once before.

Grandpa tried to speak calmly, and cover the fear that worked its way into his voice. "Come on boys, let's head inside."

Bryce and Jackson moved quickly through the doorway, while Grandpa gave a final look into the darkness; then he closed the door and locked it.

Once inside, Bryce turned to Jackson and said, "Did you spray yourself down with *Buck Lure*?"

Jackson nodded. "Yeah, I soaked myself down like always, why?"

Bryce sighed. "You have *no idea* how lucky you are."

Jackson furrowed his brow. "Tell me what you saw, *exactly*."

The two boys walked into the living room and leaned their deer rifles in the corner, then took a seat on the couch. Bryce took a deep, calming breath. "I couldn't make out any fine details," he began. "It was too dark; but I saw its outline perfectly: it was enormous, at least seven- or eight-feet-tall, and it had a long snout, definitely canine. It was covered in hair and had long arms and legs; and the way this thing bulldozed through the forest, it must have weighed at least a thousand pounds"—he took a deep breath—"I swear to you, Jackson, it moved on two legs; and I've never seen anything move that fast. It was faster than a pronghorn—way faster."

Jackson nodded. "I believe you, Bryce. I believe that you saw this thing. But, I'm having a real problem with calling it a werewolf."

"Look, Jackson," Bryce clarified, "I'm not saying that I think some *person* turned into a werewolf because it's a full moon tonight. This thing isn't a person, and I don't think the full moon has anything to do with it. Wendy Walker disappeared fifteen days ago, and that would have been a *new* moon. This thing is an animal, something no one has seen before. But trust me, Jackson, if you saw this thing—you'd have called it a werewolf, too."

Grandpa walked into the living room and sat down with the boys.

"Is Grandma all right?" Bryce asked.

"She's fine, son," Grandpa said. "She's just having a rest"—he paused, looking at the two boys—"now, I need you to tell me *exactly* what you saw?"

Bryce went over the details of what he had seen for his grandpa; and then he told him about their trip to the old Rickman house, and about his meetings with Tom Brown and Sam Nightfeather. Finally, Bryce told his grandpa about his connection to Wendy Walker, how they'd found her earring and given it to Deputy Bennett.

Grandpa had been surprised by everything he'd heard, but he tried not to show it. He'd read about the missing girl in the newspaper a couple of weeks ago, but hadn't realized Bryce's connection to her, or known about the earring.

"Well," Grandpa said casually, "looks like you two *Hardy* boys have been pretty busy."

"I'm sorry I didn't tell you about everything sooner, Grandpa," Bryce said. "I just didn't think it was all that important at the time."

"Don't worry about it, son," said Grandpa. "It wouldn't have made any difference either way."

Silence filled the room for a moment, then Bryce said, "Grandpa . . . I've told you everything we know"—Bryce gave Jackson a sidelong glance, looking for support—"I think you owe us the same courtesy."

Grandpa raised his eyebrows at Bryce, a bit surprised at his bold demand. He pondered the request for a short moment; the faint nodding of his head gradually became more distinct. Finally, he said, ". . . Okay."

Grandpa rose from his chair and moved furtively across the room, he glanced at the bedroom door. His wife was resting and he didn't want their discussion to be overheard.

Bryce met Jackson's eyes briefly, surprised by their grandpa's peculiar behavior.

Grandpa took his seat again and said, "There's lots of old legends about Bane County—just like the one that Sam Nightfeather told you; and they all have one thing in common: a giant, hairy creature that lives in The Refuge—a creature that likes to eat people—a werewolf."

"I was only eight-years-old in the fall of 1934, but I still remember hearing people talk about all the deaths—fifteen people, dead or missing. Most people said a mountain lion had been killing people; that's what my parents had believed. The old-timers, however . . . they had claimed a werewolf was responsible. I remember my mother telling me that those people were just trying to scare me, and there was no such thing as a werewolf. Then, just before Christmas, the killings stopped; and after a few months, everyone had forgotten all about it.

"But in late September of 1953, Deputy Dalton Morrow came to see me—and the killings began again; twelve people, dead or missing by Christmas." Grandpa paused, shaking his head sadly. Then he lowered his voice. "Your Grandma and Sally Brown met at the old pecan grove down by the river. I remember telling Blanche that I didn't want her to go—what with all the killings and missing people—but you know how your grandma gets when her mind is made up."

Bryce and Jackson both nodded knowingly.

"I made her take my revolver, and she swore that she'd be home long before dark—which she was—but Sally Brown had stayed behind to gather more pecans. To this day, your grandma blames herself for not staying with Sally, or at least, for not forcing her to head home."

"It wasn't her fault," said Bryce.

"I know," said Grandpa. "Tom Brown even assured her that she wasn't responsible, but she just can't forgive herself. Sally was her best friend. That's why I don't talk about this stuff around your grandma; it's just too upsetting for her."

Both boys nodded somberly.

"There's one more thing," Grandpa added. "You know how Tom Brown said he heard a howl the night Sally disappeared?"

Bryce nodded.

"Well," said Grandpa, meeting their eyes. "The night Sally disappeared, your grandma and I heard that same howl . . . and it sounded just like the one we heard a few minutes ago."

Bryce's and Jackson's eyes widened. "Jesus," they said.

"I've always had a feeling that this . . . *thing* was real," said Grandpa. "But, nobody's ever laid eyes on it—at least—nobody that lived . . . not until now." He raised his eyebrows at Bryce.

"I can't believe this shit," Bryce said. He cringed, realizing he had cursed. "Sorry."

Grandpa chuckled. "That's putting it mildly."

"How is it that I've lived here my entire life, and I've never heard about these legends?" Bryce asked.

"People are superstitious," Grandpa said. "They don't like to talk about this stuff. I guess they figure: the more you talk about something, the more likely it is to happen."

"Does that include you?" Bryce asked, but his grandpa didn't respond. He thought back to what Nightfeather had said about, *"not uttering the name of the beast."*

"Why now?" Jackson interjected. "This thing hasn't been around since 1953. Why does it show up now?"

"That's a good question," Bryce said, turning to his grandpa. "Have there been any other strange animal attacks that you know of since 1953?"

"No," Grandpa answered abruptly. He didn't even need to think about it. He had been keeping an eye out for animal attacks for the past thirty-eight years. "There've been a few incidents with mountain lions over the years, but none that resulted in death; and the victims always identified their attacker."

"What about people going missing?" Jackson asked.

"Yeah," Grandpa said, scratching at his chin whiskers. "Every now and then, people *have* gone missing in The Refuge"—he paused, thinking back—"in fact, now that you mention it, in the fall of 1972, there was a rash of people that went missing. I remember the year because your mom and dad"—he motioned to Bryce—"graduated college and got married that next spring, in 1973.

"I recall seeing it in the newspaper, and finding it a bit strange, but I never paid much mind to it; I have no idea if it's related to this. There was never any blood or other evidence found that suggested an attack. I would've definitely noticed that. I remember it seemed like every few weeks someone else had been reported missing, but—"

The phone began ringing in the kitchen: two long-rings, then a pause, followed by two long-rings again. When you lived in a rural area like Bane County, it wasn't possible to have a private phone line; you shared a party-line with several other households. When a call came in, it rang at everyone's home. In order to distinguish one subscriber from another, homes were assigned a unique ring cadence; distinctive patterns, such as: two short-rings, two long-rings, one-long and one-short ring, and so on, would identify which home was being called.

To make a call, a party-line worked like any other phone—as long as the line was clear—but if you wanted to place a call to someone who was on the same party-line as you, things got a little bit tricky. You had to dial their number, and then quickly hang up the receiver. Then, all the phones on the party-line would begin to ring with the distinctive ring-pattern of the person being called; when the ringing stopped, you knew they had answered. Then, you picked up your receiver and said hello. There was never any privacy on a party-line, and eavesdropping was always a problem—they were a constant source of gossip.

Grandpa walked into the kitchen to answer the phone; two long-rings meant the call was for him.

"Hello," he answered. "Hello . . . ? Oh, hi, hon'—yeah, he's here—uh-huh—all right, I'll tell him—bye-bye, sweetie." Grandpa hung up the receiver. "Jackson, that was your mom, she says to get your butt home right now; your dad just got in, and he wants to talk to you."

Jackson raised his eyebrows. "Okay?"

"What's that all about?" asked Bryce.

"Hell if I know," Jackson muttered. "I need a ride. My car's still at the house and I'm not walking back in the dark."

"No doubt," said Bryce. They both grabbed their deer rifles, and headed for the door.

"I'll be right back," said Bryce, I'm gonna run Jackson home." He only lived about a mile away.

Outside, Snip barked at something in the shadows.

"Hang on a minute, boys," Grandpa said. He opened the door and stepped outside. He stood quietly, and peered into the darkness for a long minute. It was quiet, almost too quiet; but there was nothing there. He called Snip into the house for the night. "Okay, boys, be careful; and keep your eyes open."

Bryce and Jackson made their way to the truck, hopped in, and headed down the dark road. The two boys had no idea that something watched them from the shadows.

THAT NIGHT, AS THE MOON ROSE above the night-draped forest, the beast moved south, compelled by an endless hunger for human flesh. Over the last ten days, the creature had feasted on the four humans who had invaded his lake, high in the mountains. He had hunted them, one-by-one, night-by-night, with no fear of being seen. The slow-moving humans had traveled too far inside his hunting grounds; they could no longer escape on foot. They were trapped, like cattle in the stockyard of a slaughterhouse.

The humans had scattered like frightened little mice when they saw the beast. They ran through the forest in every direction—each one—lost, screaming and alone. It made great sport for the beast, and he had reveled in the slow and relentless pursuit, night after night.

His hunting grounds now devoid of human prey, he headed south, deep into the canyon. He moved quickly, crashing through the dense forest, unconcerned by the noise that he made. His keen sense of smell was so acute, he could easily detect humans from miles away—long before their feeble ears ever heard him coming.

The werewolf came to an abrupt stop, raising his long snout high into the air; a strange scent was in the forest. Even though it was still miles away, the curious scent drew his attention and drove him to move faster. The scent wasn't a human, or any other animal he recognized; it was something different, something new.

In addition to the strange scent that pervaded the air, he also smelled a herd of deer, but they weren't the quarry for which he searched. He only hunted prey that screamed and begged.

As he moved closer to the strange scent, he heard the hooves of deer bolting across an open field, fleeing for their lives. The beast stopped once again, raising his nose, sniffing, snuffling—searching. The strange scent was everywhere; it was no longer captivating, it had become confusing, infuriating.

Then, another scent came to the beast, from miles away; it was the scent of a human. He could smell its flesh, its sweat, and its blood. Once again, the beast bounded through the forest, moving quickly toward his new prey; his gaping maw drooled at the thought of warm human blood.

JAMES CLARK couldn't believe his bad luck. He had promised his wife that he would be home before dark, and here it was, a half-hour after sundown, and he was stuck on the side of the highway trying to fix a flat tire.

She's gonna kill me, he thought. *Yep... I'm a dead man.*

Tonight was their nineteenth wedding anniversary and he knew his wife had been preparing a special anniversary dinner for them. James had left work early that afternoon—as planned—and had stopped by Reilly's IGA Grocery store to buy a nice bottle of wine and a large bouquet of flowers. Then, he stopped by Cooter's Bar—for just one beer.

One beer had turned into two, then two turned into four, and before James knew it, he had gotten himself into an exponential world of shit. He stumbled out of Cooter's just after sundown, figuring that he would only be a little bit late coming home; that was before he hit a pothole about twelve miles out of Silver Canyon and blew-out his rear tire. Now, he was stuck changing a flat tire in the dark, getting his good clothes all sweaty and greasy—and the fact that he was half-crocked, and seeing the world through beer-goggles, wasn't helping matters any.

James staggered back to the rear of his old car and popped open the trunk; it was a 1964 Lincoln Continental, with suicide-doors and a midnight-black paint job. It was the exact same model as the one *Flounder* had borrowed from his brother in the movie, "Animal House." It was his pride and joy—mint condition.

He grabbed his lug-wrench and loosened the nuts on the driver's-side rear tire, then pulled the jack-stand out of the trunk. The '64 Lincoln used the old-style jack that hooked around the outer bumper and your lug-wrench doubled as a jack-handle.

What the hell is that smell? James grimaced, and sniffed at the cold night air. *Did I run over a skunk?*

As he began to ratchet the jack-handle up and down, it made the familiar *click-click click-click* sound, and started to lift the car off the ground. When the car was high enough to remove the tire, he stopped working the jack—but, oddly enough, he still heard the *click-click click-click* sound . . . coming from behind him.

The dim taillights of the old car lit the road with a faint, red glow, and it took a moment for his eyes to focus on the dark shadow that slowly moved toward him. At first, James didn't realize what he was seeing; he squinted his eyes toward the crimson-hued darkness. He couldn't comprehend the large clawed feet that were tapping against the asphalt with each step forward. *Click-click click-click.*

When the werewolf came completely into view, James Clark screamed; a wet warmth bloomed in his trousers. Holding his lug-wrench, he threw it at the beast. Without so much as a flinch, it bounced off the creature's chest and jangled onto the asphalt. James turned, and ran down the highway screaming.

The beast was on him within seconds; with a single swipe of its razored hand, the werewolf sliced open his back. James landed face down at the edge of the highway, motionless, his spinal cord severed. The creature stood above the man growling, kicking his paralyzed body, goading him to run, and disappointed that the hunt had ended so quickly.

Gasping for breath, James struggled to move, his body had already gone into shock; he no longer remembered where he was, why he was laying on the ground, or why he couldn't move. He only had the use of his left arm and he clawed at the ground instinctively, trying to pull himself forward.

The headlights of the old Lincoln illuminated the horrific roadside tableau: a giant gray beast looming over a lacerated body. Moisture rose from the warm, open wound, condensing into the cool night air like steam from a kettle; then disappearing into the darkness—a spirit departing its body.

The werewolf fell upon the man, jamming its clawed hands deep inside the open wound. With a single thrust, the beast pried open his back, bones snapping and popping like the flames of a crackling fire. A final blood-curdling groan filled the night air.

The werewolf dipped its greedy snout inside the man's body and devoured the succulent organs. In a ravenous frenzy, it ripped him limb-from-limb, gulping down the warm flesh in large, un-chewed chunks.

After he had eaten his fill, the beast made his way into the shadowy forest. Raising his head to the night sky, he released an immense, hellish roar that was heard for miles. Then, he headed north, back to the safety of his hunting grounds.

Bounding through the moon-bathed forest, the beast once again encountered the strange scent; but this time, there was a human scent, as well. He sniffed at the forest floor, and then stopped at the edge of a clearing. The werewolf looked up, cocking his head at a strange wooden box high in the trees. The beast suddenly realized that there had been a human inside the box, and somehow, the man had remained hidden. A great anger arose within the creature; no human had *ever* deceived him before.

The werewolf followed the strange scent trail through the forest until he came to a house. Listening from the shadows, he could hear the voices of several humans inside. The strange scent was everywhere. He wanted to attack, rip them all to shreds, but knew it was too risky. He didn't know how many humans were inside the house—one of them might escape; he couldn't risk revealing himself. Remaining hidden-and-unknown was more important than revenge. He would wait for another time to kill this human, a time with no chance of escape.

A small dog began to bark, he had seen the giant creature lurking in the shadows. The back door opened and a man peered into the darkness, but his weak eyes couldn't see the beast. As the man called the dog inside the house, other humans exited and drove away. The werewolf growled quietly, it was still too risky, too many unknowns. He turned and disappeared into the shadowy darkness. The beast would remember the strange scent and the one who had deceived him. This human's time would come soon enough.

CHAPTER 9

Believer

HE HAD BEEN ON THE ROAD for almost two weeks and Grady Campbell would soon be home. As he drove his tractor-trailer rig down the final stretch of Highway 50 toward his farm, he noticed a car on the side of the road with its trunk open. He downshifted and slowed the big-rig to see if someone needed help. With a moaning, metallic squeal and the hiss of air-brakes, he brought his semi to a stop alongside the old car.

At first, Grady thought the car had hit a deer. There was blood and entrails everywhere, and the remains of a carcass at the edge of the road. However, when he looked closer, he saw a man's face staring back from the steaming pile of flesh.

Holy shit...

Grady quickly switched his CB radio over to emergency channel 9 and called for help.

"Emergency, can anyone read me—over?"

After a brief pause, he got a reply. "This is Deputy Wayne Bennett with the Bane County Sheriff's Office. What is your emergency—over?"

"This is Grady Campbell; I'm out on Highway 50 near mile-marker 12. There's a dead body on the side of the road out here, next to a car with a flat tire. He's torn all to hell—looks like something... *ate* this guy—over."

Another brief pause. "Okay, Mr. Campbell, I can be there in about ten minutes, just stay put—over."

"Stay put my ass! Something just *ate* this guy ... and it might still be hungry. I'm out of here." Grady hung the microphone on its hook, put the big-rig into gear, and headed for home.

Deputy Wayne Bennett flipped on his emergency lights; the high-pitched wail of his siren filled the night as he raced down Highway 50.

What had Grady Campbell said? Bennett pondered. *Something ate the guy?*

Bennett knew Grady Campbell, and if this were some kind of prank, there would be hell to pay. However, when he arrived at the scene, all thoughts of pranks evaporated.

Shit ... that's James Clark's old car, he realized.

Bennett parked his cruiser alongside the '64 Lincoln; he could already see the blood and gore splashed across the asphalt. He eased out of the car with his hand resting on his pistol, and quickly surveyed the surroundings. Grabbing a couple of road-flares from the trunk, Bennett tossed them onto the highway, then cautiously made his way to what was left of James Clark's body.

The remains were strewn at the edge of the road about twenty feet in front of the car, and they were well lit by the headlights. Bennett clasped his hand over his mouth as he drew near.

Sweet Jesus—grant me strength ...

He had never seen anything like it. There was nothing left of the man: legs and arms had been ripped from their sockets, flesh devoured, bones crunched and gnawed upon, and the impression-marks of large teeth were clearly visible. What remained of the torso had been hollowed out, the organs consumed. The only identifying factor that remained was the man's blood-spattered face—a face that Deputy Wayne Bennett recognized.

"James Clark," Bennett breathed, "Je-sus Christ." He had feared that Clark was the victim when he first saw the old car, but now he was certain.

Clark's face stared back at him from the roadside, his blood-filled mouth and milky-white eyes were both open, frozen in a final silent cry of horror and disbelief. Bennett turned and quickly walked back toward his cruiser. Just as he reached for the door handle his body suddenly convulsed; he bent over and retched his dinner out onto the highway.

I'm never eating Mexican food again, he vowed, spitting. He glanced at his watch. *Irene should be at the office by now.*

He got on the radio and contacted Irene Murphy, the night dispatcher, and told her to call Sheriff Culley. As usual, Irene wanted all the juicy details.

"Just tell him it's an emergency and have him meet me near mile-marker 12 on Highway 50," Bennett said curtly, and then he hung up the microphone.

He walked to the rear of his car, took a couple more road flares from the trunk and threw them onto the highway. Fortunately, there was never much traffic on Highway 50 in the evenings.

Bennett grabbed his camera, hung it around his neck and headed back to the remains. He hated to document such a gory scene, but it was necessary. There was no doubt in his mind that this was an animal attack, but until the sheriff signed off, he had to treat it like a crime scene.

He began snapping photos from every angle while he waited for Sheriff Culley to arrive. He could see what appeared to be animal tracks all around the body, but the rough asphalt and gravel at the edge of the road made them hard to discern.

As he made his way around the scarlet heap that was once James Clark, he saw a single bloody track farther up on the smooth pavement. When he moved closer to take a photo, his eyes widened; Bennett had seen this same footprint once before.

A little over two weeks ago, while searching for two lost backpackers in The Refuge, he had found the strange footprint. It had been located at the edge of a small pond near the backpackers' campsite. Sheriff Culley had dismissed the footprint, claiming that rain had washed it out, changing its shape, and making it appear larger than it actually was. Bennett had felt differently about the footprint. The edges were too crisp and clean, not wallowed out by rain, but he had kept his opinion to himself.

He snapped several photos of the strange footprint; then, for a size reference, he placed a dollar bill on the road next to it and snapped a few more. Maybe Sheriff Culley wouldn't dismiss the evidence quite so quickly this time.

Seeing the strange footprint for a second time had convinced him that some type of large predator was killing people in Bane County. He had no idea what he was dealing with, but he was certain of one thing—it wasn't a mountain lion. Now, he needed to convince Culley of that fact, so they could enact some sort of plan to deal with this threat.

In the distance, Bennett heard the keening wail of a siren; Sheriff Culley was arriving.

This should be interesting, he thought.

SATURDAY MORNING, THREE DAYS AFTER James Clark's death, Deputy Wayne Bennett and Sheriff Neil Culley sat drinking their morning coffee at Tammy's Roadhouse. Culley hadn't been impressed with the bloody footprint on the highway; he had said that it just looked like blood-splatter to him. Later that evening, when Culley had delivered the bad news to

James Clark's wife, he told her that a mountain lion had been responsible.

"Dammit, Culley, we've got a serious problem here," Bennett demanded. "First, we had those two backpackers go missing, and we *both* know they're dead. Then, we had Wendy Walker, that young girl who disappeared while walking home. Now, James Clark is dead. That's four people in three weeks, Culley."

"I can count," Culley groused.

"I had lunch with Dalton Morrow yesterday," Bennett added. "Dalton said he stopped by the office to see you after the backpackers went missing—said you weren't very interested in what he had to say."

Culley looked down and shook his head. "Je-sus Christ, Bennett . . . please don't tell me you believe that senile old bastard's story about a werewolf running around Bane County eating people."

Bennett stood his ground. "Dalton may be seventy-six years old, but his mind's as sharp as yours. You and I both saw that footprint at the edge of the pond, and then again on the highway the other night.

"No, I don't believe it's a werewolf; but I do think there's a damn big predator out there—and it's *not* a mountain lion. Dalton Morrow has dealt with this thing before, and we should be listening to what he has to say."

Culley smirked and said, "Well, answer me one question, Bennett. If there's some kind of giant predator running around Bane County eating people, how come nobody's ever seen it before?"

Bennett looked Culley straight in the eye and said, "Lots of people have seen it, Culley—but nobody's ever lived long enough to tell about it." He threw two dollars on the table, and stormed out of the roadhouse.

Culley sat quietly, finishing his coffee. *A werewolf,* he

thought, *what a crock of shit.*

❊

ABOUT THE SAME TIME as Bennett and Culley were having-it-out at the roadhouse, Bryce McNeel was standing in front of his bathroom mirror brushing his teeth. He had been developing a theory about the werewolf and was heading into town to visit the public library to do a little research.

Over the past three days, Bryce and Jackson had been trying to come to terms with everything that had taken place. Jackson's dad, Grady Campbell, had been the person who first found James Clark's body and contacted the sheriff's office. He had told the two boys about his gruesome discovery that same night, when Bryce gave Jackson a ride home.

Bryce had been horrified at the news, though he tried not to show it. He knew that the creature he had seen earlier that night had been responsible for the man's death. He had watched as the werewolf sprinted across the right-of-way, heading straight for the highway.

While Bryce had been running through the dark woods, toward the safety of his grandparents' house, the werewolf had been ripping James Clark to pieces and devouring him. Bryce had become nauseous just thinking about it.

Jackson's dad had thought a mountain lion must have killed the man, so the boys had just agreed with him and left it at that; the last thing they wanted to do was start a discussion about the werewolf.

At school the next day, everyone had been talking about the man killed on the highway, as well as, the disappearance of Wendy Walker and the two backpackers earlier in the month. The people of Silver Canyon were starting to connect-the-dots, but nobody knew the truth. Most people thought that a killer mountain lion was on the loose, but a few whispered darkly of an escaped lunatic.

Bryce knew the latter theory was closer to the truth and wanted to tell people what he knew, but they would've called him crazy. Each night after sundown, Silver Canyon and the rest of Bane County had become a ghost town. No one went out after dark. People were afraid, although they weren't exactly sure of what.

That morning when Bryce arrived at the public library the entire place smelled of lemons, he found Agnes Furman polishing the tables and chairs.

"Morning, Agnes," Bryce said, smiling.

Agnes put away her spray polish and rags and met Bryce at the front desk. "You're up early," said Agnes, returning Bryce's smile. "What's on the agenda this morning?"

Bryce hesitated for a moment, and then said, "I have a rather... unique request."

Agnes smiled. She almost looked giddy; the time she spent with Bryce was usually the highlight of her day. "What are we working on?"

"Do you have any books about... werewolves?" he asked quietly.

Agnes lifted her eyebrows and her voice dropped to a whisper. "That request isn't as unique as you might think," she said. "You're the second person to ask me for a book about werewolves today."

Bryce's eyes widened.

Agnes pointed to a man sitting at a table in the very back of the library. "That gentleman is looking at the only book about werewolves that we have. Perhaps, you could ask him to let you see it when he's finished?"

Bryce turned and looked at the man. He hadn't noticed him when he entered the library; he almost appeared to be hiding.

Bryce made his way to the back of the library, surprised that someone else had asked for a book about werewolves. The man was sitting with his face to the wall, but as Bryce drew closer, he recognized him.

"Excuse me, Deputy Bennett, sir?" Bryce said quietly.

Wayne Bennett quickly closed the book and turned it over, hiding the title. "Can I help you, son?" Bennett appeared flustered, caught with his hand in the cookie jar.

"Can I talk with you for a minute, sir?"

Bennett recognized him now. He smiled and motioned to a chair. "Sure, Bryce, pull up a chair; what can I do for you?"

Bryce sat down, took a deep breath, looked Bennett straight in the eye and said, "I saw what killed that man on the highway the other night."

Wayne Bennett's face lost all expression. "Exactly, what was it that you saw, Bryce?"

He reached across the table and flipped over the book Bennett was concealing: *The Werewolf, by Montague Summers*. He tapped his finger on the name of the book. "It was a werewolf."

Bryce began telling Deputy Bennett about what had happened on the deer stand, and how the werewolf couldn't smell him because of the *Buck Lure* he had used. He told how he'd watched the beast cross the right-of-way, heading straight for the highway, and how fast the giant creature had been.

Then, with as much detail as possible, Bryce began telling Bennett everything that he and Jackson had learned over the past eight weeks. His grandpa's story about 1953, the huge claw marks they had seen at the old Rickman house, Tom Brown's addition to his grandpa's story; he even told Bennett about the rash of missing people in 1972 that his grandpa had talked about. Finally, Bryce told him about the legend that Sam Nightfeather had shared.

He listened intently to everything Bryce had to say, and when he finished, Bennett said, "I believe you, son."

A wave of relief washed over Bryce. "Thank God. I figured you'd think I was crazy."

Bennett shook his head and smiled. "I don't think you're crazy, son. I'm already a believer; I know this thing is real."

"I can't tell you how happy I am to hear that," said Bryce.

Bennett smiled and tapped his finger on the book he was reading. "Understand: I don't think this thing is an *actual* werewolf, it's just some kind of animal no one has seen before. The Silver Canyon Wildlife Refuge is over a million acres; that's sixteen hundred square miles of extremely rough terrain. It wouldn't be very hard for something to remain hidden in a place like that."

"That was my thought, exactly," said Bryce, "but, trust me, Deputy Bennett, if you'd seen this thing, you'd have called it a werewolf, too."

Bennett twisted in his chair and looked over his shoulder. Agnes was the only person in the library and she was busy polishing tables. "If I share some information with you about this thing, will you keep it just between us?" Bennett asked.

"Jackson is part of this, too," Bryce reminded him. "He was the one who found Wendy's earring. He'd be here right now, except, he had to work this morning, at Western Auto."

Bennett chuckled. "Okay, you can tell Jackson."

"And my grandpa, too," said Bryce, "but that's it, no one else."

"And your grandpa," Bennett agreed, with a sly smirk.

Bryce smiled. "Sorry, but, they're as much a part of this as I am."

Bennett nodded and then began telling Bryce what he had learned. "Yesterday morning, I got a phone call from former Deputy Dalton Morrow. He asked me to meet him for lunch at the Buckhorn. He said that he had some information I needed to know about.

"I have to admit, I had a hard time believing what Dalton told me at first, but after spending most of last night digging through old records at the sheriff's office, I now believe everything he said." Bennett reached into the satchel that sat next to his chair and removed a file folder. He opened it and slid a piece of paper across the table.

Bryce's eyebrows lifted. It was a sketch of a strange looking footprint.

"Dalton Morrow drew that while we were having lunch yesterday," Bennett pointed out.

The sketch was similar to a human footprint, except the heel was a bit narrower, and it had five toes that were all about the same size; the toes were also exceedingly long and pointed—like claws. Bryce knew from his grandpa's story that Dalton Morrow had been the first person to find the footprints.

"Is this what Dalton said the footprints looked like?" Bryce asked.

Bennett nodded. "Dalton said he saw that footprint back in 1934, and then again in 1953." He pulled a photo from the folder and slid it across the table. It was a photo of the bloody footprint on the highway near James Clark's body. It looked just like the sketch.

"Holy crap," Bryce said. He was gaping at the dollar bill that Bennett had used for a size reference. "How big is that thing?"

"Just over eighteen-inches-long," he said somberly, meeting Bryce's eyes.

Bryce's mouth fell open even farther. "Damn." He saw the other photos in the folder. "What are those?"

Bennett closed the folder and slowly shook his head. "You don't want to see those," he said. "It'll be etched into your brain for the rest of your life. Some things, Bryce . . . you just can't unsee. Trust me—I know."

Bryce gave a weak smile and nodded. "Have you found anything else?"

"Well, I can tell you that your grandpa was right about 1972," he confirmed. "There were nine missing people between September and December; and that's an unprecedented amount. Dalton Morrow said he had no doubt that the same animal had killed them. However, what doesn't make any sense is the timeline: 1934, 1953, 1972 and now, 1991, why such a long time span between occurrences?"

Bryce nodded slowly, thinking. *What do 1934, 1953, 1972 and 1991 all have in common*, he asked himself. After a long minute, Bryce said, "They're all multiples of nineteen."

"How's that?" said Bennett.

"Nineteen," said Bryce. "There's nineteen years between each occurrence."

Bennett did the math. "You're right," he said. "Nineteen years, but why? What's so special about nineteen years?"

Bryce grinned and slapped his hand on the table. "It's a nineteen year cycle," he said. "I'll be right back." Bryce trotted across the library to the encyclopedias, grabbed the volume labeled "M" and headed back to his table.

"What are you up to," asked Bennett.

"Meton," said Bryce.

Bennett furrowed his brow. "That's Greek to me," he said.

"Exactly," said Bryce. "Meton of Athens was a Greek astronomer in 432 B.C." He opened the encyclopedia and showed Bennett the page.

Bennett cocked his head and lifted an eyebrow.

"You see," Bryce said, tapping on the page. "The Metonic

Cycle is a nineteen-year lunisolar calendar."

The look on Bennett's face became more confused. Bryce closed the book and opted for a different approach. "When's your birthday?" asked Bryce.

"February 23."

"Okay. Let's say that on the day you were born, there was a full moon," Bryce suggested. "There wouldn't be another full moon on your birthday until you were nineteen years old."

"Really?"

"That's right. It takes nineteen years for the moon to complete its cycle through the heavens and return to the *exact* same place-and-time in the sky again."

"Huh. You learn something new every day," Bennett said. "But, how does that relate to our werewolf."

It made Bryce smile when Bennett called it a werewolf. "Well," Bryce pointed out. "Sam Nightfeather said a couple of things that caught my attention. The legend says, 'The beast crawled deep within the earth,' and 'Year after long year, the beast remained hidden.' Now, to me, that sounds like an animal that's hibernating in a cave."

Bennett nodded slowly. "Yeah . . . yeah, I suppose so."

Bryce reflected for a moment, and then added, "Another thing Nightfeather said was: 'On a night when the moon shone as brightly as the sun, the beast rose.'"

"What do you think that means?" asked Bennett.

Bryce rubbed his chin. "The attacks always began around the end of September, right?"

"Yeah, that's right," said Bennett.

Bryce nodded. "Hang on a minute." He made his way across the room to talk with Agnes. "Agnes, do you have a current copy of the Farmer's Almanac?"

"Yes," she said, gesturing across the room. "It's over on that rack with all the other annual and periodical publications."

"Great. And do you archive copies of past years?"

"Certainly."

Bryce borrowed a pencil and paper from Agnes and jotted down three years: 1972, 1953 & 1934. "Would you check your archives and see if you have copies of these three years, please.

"Sure... but, I thought you were a rancher," Agnes said dryly.

Bryce shot her a lopsided grin.

"I'll check," she snickered.

Bryce plucked the 1991 Farmer's Almanac from the rack and went back to his table.

"What are you up to, now?" Bennett asked.

Bryce flipped through the almanac to the month of September. He smiled and said, "The autumnal equinox."

"More Greek?" asked Bennett.

"September 23," Bryce said, showing Bennett the page. "It's the first day of autumn—and look here—it coincides with the full moon this year.

"And what does that do for us?"

Bryce was about to explain the perigee-syzygy of the earth-sun-moon system to Bennett, but thought better of it. Instead, he quoted Sam Nightfeather again: " 'on a night when the moon shone as brightly as the sun, the beast rose.' "

"So, it's a really bright full moon?"

"Absolutely," said Bryce, "the brightest. And having a full moon on the same night as the fall equinox only happens every nineteen years."

Bennett lifted his eyebrows and nodded slowly.

Bryce quickly thumbed through the pages of the almanac,

looking at the next three months. "There's something else, too," he added. "Do you know what a blue moon is?"

"Isn't that when there are two full moons in the same month?"

Bryce smiled. "Well, that's the popular-culture version, but it's wrong. In 1946, an amateur astronomer by the name of Pruett published an article in Sky & Telescope Magazine entitled, 'Once in a Blue Moon'. The problem was, he got his facts wrong, and no one ever corrected it. Since then, two full moons during the same month has been the accepted definition for a blue moon."

"So, what *is* a blue moon, then?"

"It's a little complicated, but not too bad," Bryce began. "There's four seasons: spring, summer, fall and winter, and each season is about three months long; so, generally, each season has three full moons. However, every now and then, there are four full moons in a season. When that happens, the third of those four full moons is called a blue moon."

"I gotcha," Bennett said, nodding.

Agnes came to their table with the other almanacs. "We had all three years," she said.

"Perfect," said Bryce, "thanks, Agnes."

Bryce and Bennett flipped through the other almanacs, and found that each year was identical: a full moon that coincided with the fall equinox and a fall season with four full moons—a blue moon.

"Okay," Bennett said. "If this extra-bright full moon in September is the reason the werewolf comes out of his cave, why do the attacks always stop near the end of December?"

Bryce began looking at the December pages in each of the four almanacs. "Well, I'll be damned," Bryce said. "In every year —give or take about twelve hours—the December full moon coincides with the winter solstice—the last day of fall. That must be the werewolf's cue to go back into his cave."

Bennett cocked his head, not quite getting it.

"It's perfect," Bryce said, "don't you see? After the fall equinox, the nights grow longer and the days become shorter; but after the winter solstice, the nights become shorter again. He's hunting during the season with the longest nights and the most full moons."

"Well, I'll be . . ." Bennett said. Then he added, "How in the hell do you know all this stuff?"

Bryce just shrugged. He never liked telling people that his memory was almost photographic, and that his IQ was off-the-charts; it always felt like bragging. Instead, he just offered, "I read a lot."

"Well," Bennett chuckled. "I've never been the sharpest knife in the drawer, but, it all makes pretty good sense to me."

Bryce smiled. "Are you going to tell Sheriff Culley about all this?" he asked.

Bennett shook his head. "Neil Culley is a hardheaded old fart. He wouldn't even admit that Dalton Morrow's sketch of the footprint matches the ones we saw in The Refuge and out on the highway. He thinks a mountain lion is responsible for killing those people and he won't even discuss other possibilities."

"Well, that's just great," Bryce said sarcastically.

Bennett smiled and said, "Don't worry son, I'm gonna find this thing, and I'm gonna kill it."

"How?"

"I'm gonna set trap for it," Bennett said. "I'm gonna lure it in, and then, I'm gonna blow its damn head off."

"Do you think you'll need silver bullets?" Bryce asked. He was smiling when he said it, but he wasn't sure if he was joking. In all the old horror movies, you needed silver to kill a werewolf.

Bennett chuckled. "Well, son, I've got an old Marlin lever-action rifle that's chambered in .45-70 Government; and when I use my custom hot-load ammo in it, it'll send a 405-grain bullet downrange at about 2000 feet-per-second. At fifty yards, that bullet hits with about 3000 foot-pounds of energy; that'll stop a charging rhino. I figure, it should stop a werewolf, too—with or without silver bullets."

"I sure hope so," Bryce said. He was worried that Bennett might be getting in over his head. Killing this thing was gonna take more than a high-powered rifle. "This thing is fast, Deputy Bennett; I'm talking cheetah-fast. Judging by the size of its footprints, and the way it plowed through the forest the other night, it must weigh at least a thousand pounds, probably more. That's like, shooting at a speeding freight-train."

"Don't you worry, son," Bennett said, as he stood up from the table. "I'll get this thing." They shook hands and Bennett headed out of the library.

Bryce's face was filled with concern as he watched the deputy walk away; trying to lure the werewolf and shoot it seemed like a bad idea. He wasn't exaggerating with his speeding freight-train analogy; Bryce had done the math in his head, a thousand pounds moving at 70 mph was like having a wrecking-ball dropped on your head.

He scooped up the book by *Montague Summers* and headed to the front desk to check it out. The book would be going home with him and every word committed to memory. When Bryce asked Agnes to order everything she could find about werewolves, she didn't even bat an eyelash. Over the years, he had special-ordered books on every subject under the sun. To her, this was just another item on an endless list. Bryce tucked the book under his arm and strode resolutely out of the library; he had some studying to do.

CHAPTER 10

Blue Moon

THE DAY AFTER HIS TRIP TO THE PUBLIC LIBRARY, Bryce told Jackson and Grandpa about the meeting with Deputy Bennett, and his theory about the werewolf appearing every nineteen years. They both thought his theory seemed plausible, but Jackson had raised a few questions.

"How could an animal hibernate for nineteen years?" Jackson asked. "Wouldn't it die of starvation?"

"I thought about that, too," said Bryce, "but if you take a look at the science of how other animals hibernate, I believe it's possible.

"Some mammals, like the Alaska marmot for example, can remain asleep underground for over eight months. Their bodies produce special hormones that drastically lower their heart rate, respiration and body temperature, a hormone-induced form of hypothermia.

Their normal heart rate of about one hundred ninety beats-per-minute lowers to about thirty beats-per-minute. Respiration drops from about sixty breaths-per-minute to about two breaths-per-minute; and their body temperature falls from about 102° Fahrenheit to about 40° Fahrenheit.

"Other types of hibernating mammals, like ground squirrels, use a hormone-induced form of hypothermia, as well; but they also wake up briefly—about once per month—

to eat, drink and perform bodily functions, before returning to a state of hibernation. I think this is how the werewolf hibernates for nineteen years. There's plenty of fresh water and things to eat inside of caverns: small mammals like rats and possums or even bats, not to mention snakes and other reptiles."

Jackson and Grandpa glanced at each other. "Do you really think it could survive like that?" asked Jackson.

"Absolutely."

"Well, how do you explain the fact that this thing has been around since 1934—or even longer?" asked Jackson.

"A great number of biologists believe animals that hibernate have extended lifespans. There have been numerous studies that compared the lifespans of northern species who hibernate, with their southern counterparts who don't hibernate, and in most cases, the hibernator's lifespan was two to three times longer"—Bryce paused, and then added—"the animals in those studies only hibernated for about six months at a time; the werewolf hibernates for nineteen years. There's no telling how old this thing is."

Jackson lifted his eyebrows at the possibility. "How does it keep track of time? Nineteen years is a long time."

"Hibernation phenology and circadian rhythms have . . ." Bryce stopped talking when he saw the confused look on their faces. Instead, he turned to Jackson, and said, "Have you ever set your alarm clock when you went to bed at night, only to wake up a couple of minutes before the alarm went off the next morning?"

"Sure, all the time."

"Well, how did your body keep track of the time while you were sleeping?" asked Bryce.

Jackson shrugged.

"Every living thing has an internal clock; we don't understand *exactly* how it works—but it does."

Grandpa and Jackson looked at each other again. "How do you know all this crap?" asked Jackson.

Bryce just shrugged, smiling.

Up to this point, Grandpa had just been listening, trying to soak it all in. Finally, he said, "So, if what you're saying about this werewolf is correct, all we have to do is stay safe until after the full moon on the night of the winter solstice; after that, it'll be gone."

"That's right," said Bryce. "If my theory is correct, we should be safe after the winter solstice"—he paused, turning his head to meet each of their eyes—"but, only for the next nineteen years. After that, it'll be back."

Grandpa nodded, and then asked, "How'd you manage to come up with this theory anyway?"

"It was your idea," Bryce said, with a sly smile.

Grandpa frowned, "How's that?"

"When we were talking about seventeen-year cicadas a while back, you said, 'What if the roles were reversed? What if the cicadas were the predators?' It kind of got me thinking."

Grandpa nodded, giving a weak smile, "I think we're gonna need more than a little bug-spray to ward *this* thing off."

Bryce nodded somberly, and then said, "There's one more thing . . . Deputy Bennett told me that he was gonna set a trap for it, try to lure it in and kill it."

"You've gotta be shitting me," Jackson exclaimed.

Grandpa smacked him on the back of the head. "Language."

Jackson winced. "Sorry, Grandpa, but you gotta admit, that's nuts."

Grandpa nodded. "Not a good idea."

"That's what I tried to tell him," Bryce insisted, "but he was dead-set on trying to kill it."

Grandpa shook his head sadly. "God help him."

THE NEXT DAY at school, Bryce and Jackson learned of the missing person reports filed for a group of four individuals from USC San Diego; they had been doing research at Lake Argent and were now several days overdue.

Because of the remote location, a SAR (Search and Rescue) helicopter had been brought in and managed to locate the group's campsite. Equipment and personal possessions had been left behind; the camp deserted. There had been no signs of foul play. The search was still ongoing.

The boys already knew about the four people in The Refuge, they had feared for the group's safety over the past several days. Bryce had seen their names on the game warden's sign-in sheet and knew they were heading to Lake Argent. They also knew there was no need to continue the search—it was pointless—every person in that group was already dead.

Bryce and Jackson felt helpless. Trying to warn people about a werewolf would have been a lost cause. They made sure to watch the local newspaper, and keep an eye on the game warden's sign-in sheet. They couldn't do anything about it, but at least they'd know if someone else went missing.

Both of them had taken to keeping their deer rifles loaded and by their bedsides; no one went into the forest, or dared venture outside at night. There was only one thing left to do at this point: try to remain safe until the full moon on the winter solstice; and that was nearly eight weeks away.

DEPUTY WAYNE BENNETT had been waiting for this day for almost four weeks. It was Thursday, November 21, and tonight, there would be a full moon. Bryce McNeel had called it a blue moon; the third of four full moons in one season. He had pointed out that autumn was the season with the longest nights—and in this particular year—it had the most full moons. Bryce had shown him how this unique occurrence only took place every nineteen years; and how each time it happened—people died.

Bennett had figured that his best chance for finding and killing this predator would be on a full moon. It wasn't that he thought the thing was a werewolf—he didn't—it was because the creature hunted at night. A full moon would give him the best possible visibility to find and kill this thing, because, if he couldn't see it, he couldn't shoot it.

The plan was to hike into The Refuge, and find a good location to build a brush-blind to conceal himself. He would set a trap for the beast by using raw meat and blood as a lure. Then, when the predator showed itself, he would blow its damn head off.

Taking off work for a few days to hunt the beast hadn't been a problem; Sheriff Culley was happy to get rid of him. Over the past three weeks, Bennett had become a thorn in Culley's side. He had continually urged him to place signs at the entrance of The Refuge, warning people of a dangerous predator on the loose. Sheriff Culley had fought him every step of the way, claiming that he was overreacting.

Bennett had pointed out that three weeks ago, four people had gone missing at Lake Argent; and nine days after that three more backpackers had disappeared. Culley had argued that there wasn't any evidence linking the two incidents, and he wasn't going to scare people for no good reason.

Earlier that week, when he had requested a few days off work, Culley had jumped at the offer: *"Take the rest of the week,"* he had said—and so he did.

The day before he left for The Refuge, Bennett had headed out to do a little shopping. His first stop had been Virgil's Gun Shop to purchase some reloading supplies; he wanted to make a fresh batch of hot-load ammo for his .45-70 Government. He hadn't fired his old Marlin lever-action rifle in quite some time, or done any reloading. Bennett figured that having the freshest ammo possible would be a good idea, considering what it was that he was hunting. He also thought that adding a couple extra grains of powder to this batch of hot-loads might not be a bad idea either.

As he browsed around Virgil's shop, he had found a spray-bottle of *Old Pete's Original Indian Buck Lure*. He remembered Bryce saying that the *Buck Lure* had concealed his presence from the beast. He figured, if it had kept the predator from picking up Bryce's scent, it should work for him, too. Bennett had no doubt that this thing was just as smart as it was dangerous, and he would need to use every trick in the book to lure it in and kill it.

His next stop that day had been the local slaughterhouse, where he purchased a freshly butchered pork hindquarter and a gallon of pig's blood. When he'd asked for the blood, Bennett had raised a few eyebrows, but nobody argued much with a deputy sheriff.

That afternoon when he arrived home, Bennett began making room in the refrigerator for the large hindquarter and gallon of blood. It hadn't taken much effort to make the space; the only thing in his fridge was a bunch of old take-out boxes, and some foil-wrapped leftovers that had taken on a life of their own.

He emptied the entire fridge into the trashcan, all except for the twelve-pack of Coors Light. Then—readjusting the wire shelves—Bennett crammed the hindquarter and gallon of blood inside. Stepping back, he admired his work, grinning proudly at the offensive sight. A brief thought of his ex-wife, Joan, came to mind.

She would've had a cow, he thought, smiling, "... or a pig."

After grabbing a cold beer from the fridge, he had made his way into the living room, tossed his dirty laundry aside, and plopped down on his threadbare sofa. Prying his old, Roper boots from his feet, he clicked on the TV and took a long, well-deserved sip of icy-cold beer.

He had been divorced for almost two years, and it was plain to see he was a typical messy bachelor. Bennett was a solitary man, and rarely had any company; he didn't have any relatives in Bane County to contend with—he was originally from Texas—and it didn't bother him that his home had that, *lived-in* look.

Bennett's ex-wife, Joan, was a native of Bane County and she had convinced him to move there after their marriage in 1980. They had met each other while serving in the U.S. Army at Fort Hood, Texas. Joan had been with the Army Nurse Corps, serving at Darnall Army Community Hospital, and Bennett had been an MP with the 89th Military Police Group.

Both of their enlistments ended during 1980, so the timing had seemed perfect. Bennett had taken a position with the Bane County Sheriff's Office, and Joan went to work at Doctor Milstead's clinic in Silver Canyon. It had all come together like clockwork, and for nine years, things were great. Then, two years ago, for some reason that still eluded him, things had turned to total shit.

He chugged the dregs of his beer and headed back to the fridge for another. Tomorrow, he'd head into The Refuge to find and kill the thing Bryce McNeel had called a werewolf. Reaching into the fridge for another beer, Bennett noticed the label on the twelve-pack of Coors Light and gave a chuckle. It said, "Silver Bullet."

THE NEXT MORNING, after a large breakfast, Bennett dressed in full camouflage; he also packed his homemade hooded-poncho that he used for bow-hunting. The poncho consisted of rough-burlap and jute-string and was similar to a ghillie-suit. You simply took pieces of foliage from your surroundings and integrated them into the fabric; when done correctly, you became invisible.

Bennett took the hindquarter from the fridge and wrapped it tightly in a plastic garbage bag. He stuffed it into a large, camouflaged backpack along with the gallon of blood, a few lengths of cord and a roll of duct tape. He added a canteen, a few candy bars, and a small flashlight to the pack, and then hefted it onto his shoulder to test the weight, before hauling it outside to his truck.

After tossing the backpack into the pickup, Bennett went back inside for his rifle. He had checked the weapon the night before, and even though he hadn't fired the gun in a couple of years, it was in perfect condition. Bennett always cleaned and oiled his rifles before storing them in a soft leather case.

The rifle was a Marlin Model 1895 that Bennett had bought on a whim back in 1972. He had always wanted a rifle chambered in .45-70 Government, the same caliber used in the old ten-barrel Gatling guns the U.S. Calvary used back in the late 1800s.

The magazine tube of the old lever-action rifle only held four shots—plus, one in the chamber—but, with the knock-down power of Bennett's special hot-load ammunition, he wasn't much concerned about shot capacity.

He had made twenty of the special cartridges, enough to reload his rifle three times. He slipped the shells into a leather cartridge-belt and buckled it around his waist; he preferred the belt to a bandolier, and it fit the scabbard of his large, Bowie-style hunting knife perfectly. Having quick access to your ammo when hunting dangerous game was crucial, and for that, the belt was ideal.

Bennett thought for a moment, feeling as though he was forgetting something, then he snapped his fingers and grabbed the spray-bottle of *Buck Lure* from the kitchen counter.

Can't forget that, he thought.

Bennett drove to the entrance of the wildlife refuge, parked his truck in the lot, and then headed for the game warden's office. When he walked through the door, Bruce Fletcher was taken aback; he cocked his head at the unusual attire.

"Wayne?" Fletcher said, frowning. "What the heck are you all dressed up about?" His eyes moved to the rifle slung over Bennett's shoulder.

"Mornin', Bruce." Bennett offered a sly smile to the game warden. "How's your day going?"

"Oh, fair-to-middling," Fletcher said, still eyeing the big-bore rifle Bennett was sporting. "Have we got an elephant problem I'm unaware of?"

Bennett chuckled. "I'm heading into The Refuge," he said, "gonna see if I can solve our predator problem."

"I see," said Fletcher, cocking his head around to look at Bennett's enormous backpack. "How long you plannin' on staying?"

Bennett smiled. "Just overnight, the pack's full of raw meat—so I can lure it in."

"Ah . . . I gotcha," said Fletcher, now getting the gist of the matter. "Where's Sheriff Culley, ain't he goin' with you?"

"No . . . I'm doing this on my own time," Bennett said. "And let's keep this just between us, okay?"

"All right," Fletcher said, not wanting to pry. "So, what time should I expect you back tomorrow?"

"I'll be back a little after first light," said Bennett—he paused for a moment and then added—"if for some reason I'm not back by noon . . . then, you can call Sheriff Culley."

Fletcher gave Bennett a concerned look. "All right," he said. "You watch your ass in there, okay."

Bennett nodded and checked the sign-in sheet. "Anybody in The Refuge?" he asked. Hoping he wouldn't have to worry about some random hiker getting in his way.

"No . . . not that I know of," Fletcher said. He and Bennett both knew that people snuck into The Refuge all the time to avoid paying an entrance fee.

Bennett gave a quick wave. "All right, I'll see you in the mornin'," he said, and then headed for the door.

"Noon at the latest," Fletcher reminded.

Before heading into the wildlife refuge, Bennett sprayed his clothes with *Buck Lure* so he wouldn't leave a scent trail. It was only about 10:30 a.m., so he had plenty of time to hike into The Refuge and set his trap. He had a particular location in mind and it wasn't too far away. He was heading to a well-traveled game-trail, adjacent to several small canyons.

Bennett traveled with steady economy, working his way through the dense, rugged terrain. After about ninety minutes, he arrived at the place he was looking for—it was perfect—a small box-canyon with sheer rock walls, one-way-in, and one-way-out.

He could locate his brush-blind against the rock wall at the rear of the canyon, and place the blood-and-meat lure near the center. That way, he would only need to face forward; nothing could sneak up behind him.

Bennett hung the hindquarter from a tree limb about six feet off the ground, so smaller varmints couldn't reach it. He poured some of the blood over the raw meat, and onto the patch of grass beneath it. The rest he trailed out of the canyon, pouring it liberally onto the ground, creating a blood-trail about fifty yards long that he hoped the predator would follow. Next, he spread dried leaves and twigs all along the blood-trail and across the entire opening of the small canyon.

Nothing's coming through here without making some noise, he vowed.

Cutting small branches and bushes, Bennett began building his brush-blind. Over the years, he had made hundreds of these blinds and they always blended into their surroundings perfectly. After completing the blind, he began camouflaging his burlap poncho with grass and foliage, and when he had finished—he was invisible.

There wasn't a cloud in the sky, and he knew the full moon would give him good visibility tonight. Bennett entered his brush-blind and took his seat. He had built it around an old fallen log, so he would have a comfortable place to sit; it was going to be a long night.

He placed a large, horizontal tree-branch in front of him at shoulder-level; he would use it as a benchrest to steady his aim. He had a perfect view of the bloody hindquarter only thirty yards away, an easy shot for the iron-sights of his old Marlin rifle.

Bennett tried to stay as calm and quiet as possible. He knew that when he saw the giant predator, there would be a huge rush of adrenaline, and he needed to keep a steady hand in order to aim quickly and kill the beast.

The hours had dragged by as he hid in quietude. He glanced at his watch. In thirty more minutes, the sun would set, and the full moon would rise. Bennett cocked the hammer back on his rifle—*click-click*—making it ready to fire. He remembered Bryce saying that the beast had cleared fifty yards in less than two seconds. With an animal that fast, every second would count.

※

THE WEREWOLF SMELLED the scent of blood. Deep within the cavernous depths of his lair, the tempting aroma called to him, urging him to rise. He made his way to the surface through a twisting warren of inky-black tunnels that extended for miles in every direction. As he neared the entrance, he could see that the sun still shone in the western horizon, and the moon had yet to rise.

In the dark recesses of his hidden lair, the beast paced; a deep, rumbling growl filled his chest. He glared angrily toward the bright entrance; he was trapped by the light of day. His large, reflective eyes were made for the darkness, bright light was blinding to him, even painful.

The werewolf recognized the blood-scent that carried on the evening wind. It was the blood of a boar; but it held little interest for him—he only ate flesh that pleaded for its life.

Raising his long snout, he found another scent: this one did hold his interest. Anger and rage filled the beast; he had encountered this strange scent before—the human who had deceived him.

Drool poured from the beast's mouth at the thought of killing this man, making him suffer. He longed to savor this human's torment, as well as his flesh.

Time seemed to stand still, as the beast grew more and more impatient. Like a caged animal he paced and growled, and waited for darkness to fall. With each step, his rage grew for this human, the one who had deceived him. Soon, the feast would begin.

The light of day slowly retreated, and the first beams of moonlight crept through the entrance of his lair. The werewolf made his way outside into the night, feeling its cool embrace.

The human's strange scent was heavy in the air, and though it came from far away, he knew exactly where to go.

The werewolf tried to contain his bloodlust: the urge to run quickly toward the kill. He wanted to savor this hunt, and so, he skulked slowly and silently through the moon-painted forest. It would not be long before he found his prey. The human would be made to suffer; he would take his time with this one.

The beast followed the strange scent to the edge of a small box-canyon and peered into the deep ravine. His quarry was below him, hiding in the bushes: a rabbit cowering in a briar patch. Although the human was hidden, the beast's keen sense of smell pointed to the brush-pile as if it were a beacon.

There was another scent, as well, an oily, metallic fragrance. The werewolf had encountered this smell before; the human had a weapon. Perhaps the beast would attack quickly after all.

The cliff was too high for him to pounce, he would need to circle around, and enter through the mouth of the canyon. There would be no escape for this human; there was nowhere left to run.

THE FULL MOON ROSE and a pale-yellow light entered the small box-canyon. Bennett felt a sense of relief as his visibility improved. He was happy to see the moon's ascent into the eastern sky, though it also filled him with anxiety. The thought of what he *hoped* would happen next, was extremely disquieting.

Bennett wrinkled his nose and sniffed at the air. A terrible stench had found him. It smelled like week-old road-kill on hot summer asphalt.

The wind must have shifted, he thought.

He looked to the trees that lined the rim of the canyon. Their leaves were as still as gravestones, not a breath of wind. In fact, the entire forest had grown still; even the trilling of insects had stopped. The silence was extremely disconcerting and raised the hair on the back of his neck.

As quickly as it had arrived, the putrid odor seemed to fade away. Bennett had no idea what the smell was or where it had come from. The hideous odor of the beast was the only detail that Bryce McNeel had neglected to mention when he told Bennett of his encounter with the creature.

The sharp crack of a dried twig rose from the darkness. Bennett hunkered down and slowly raised his rifle. He peered down his barrel, across the iron sights, aiming toward the bloody hindquarter in the tree. There was just enough light to see, and he had a clear shot. He rested his rifle on the tree branch he had placed and steadied his aim. The sound of that twig had jabbed his heart with a bolt of adrenaline; he could feel it knocking in his chest.

Fear placed its lifeless hand on Bennett's shoulder and whispered an icy breath into his ear . . . *Its coming.*

He had spread dry leaves and twigs all along the blood-trail for just this purpose: to give himself a heads-up. *Nothing's coming through here without making some noise*, he had told himself. His mind pictured those giant feet; the ones that made the huge footprint by the pond, and the bloody print on the highway. Bennett now imagined those same hideous feet stepping on that twig and snapping it. An uninvited chill surrounded him.

He attempted to remain calm, but his heart wouldn't stop racing; and when he tried to take a calming breath, he noticed the foul odor had returned. Another dried twig popped loudly in the darkness, then another, and another still. Leaves crunched underfoot. Something moved in the darkness. He peered into the distance, straining to see in the wan light of the moon, but after about forty or fifty yards, his vision began to blur. Light and dark seemed to meld together, coalescing into a shadowy wall of gloom.

Bennett aimed his rifle at the darkness and listened intently. He could hear the slow and steady gait of something creeping toward him. Large clumps of bushes and briars spotted the floor of the canyon, providing cover for an animal trying to hide.

Why would it hide? He wondered. *It doesn't know I'm here.*

Bennett had poured the blood-trail along a clearing down the center of the canyon, so he would have a clear view of the animal approaching. Something wasn't right. He could hear it moving closer, but he didn't *see* anything. Bennett suddenly felt very foolish for putting himself in this position.

What the hell was I thinking?

About thirty yards away, a massive dark shadow bolted from behind a thorn-bush and rushed toward Bennett. He tried to draw-a-bead on his target, but it was moving too fast, jinking from side-to-side, dodging between bushes and large rocks. As the beast came closer, Bennett saw clearly the hideous creature that approached. With a loud gasp, he tried to wrap his mind around what he was seeing...

Fucking werewolf!

Sighting-in on the massive beast, Bennett squeezed the trigger. A fiery flash lit the night, as a tremendous blast echoed from the canyon walls. The bullet had hit the werewolf at the last possible moment—in midair—just as it pounced. The impact from the high-powered round had slammed the beast aside, sending it into a large clump of bushes.

Bennett heard a resounding *whap* when the bullet hit home; he had also heard a loud yelp. The bushes where the beast had fallen thrashed violently for a moment, but then fell as silent as a cemetery. Bennett quickly worked the lever of his rifle, loading another round.

Keeping the muzzle of his rifle trained on the dense briar, he fumbled for the small flashlight in his pocket. His heart was pounding against his ribs and he suddenly realized that he wasn't breathing. The overload of fear-pumped adrenaline made it feel as though his body was vibrating. He had never been so afraid.

He held the flashlight under the fore-stock of his rifle, gripping both in his hand. Sighting down the barrel, the beam of light followed the muzzle wherever he aimed. He played the light through the bushes where the werewolf had fallen; he couldn't see or hear anything. Cautiously, he moved closer, straining to see.

His flashlight caused a brief reflection in two amber eyes. It was the last thing he saw before he found himself flat on his back with the werewolf on top of him. His rifle and flashlight had flown out of his hands from the impact of the massive beast; they landed in the bushes behind him. The werewolf had pounced so fast, he never saw it coming.

Bennett screamed and cursed, and pounded the beast with his fists. He had forgotten about the large Bowie-knife on his belt in his panic. It was all in vain; the beast pinned him to the ground with a single clawed hand. When Bennett realized the futility of his actions, he stopped struggling and glared into the werewolf's eyes.

With every ounce of anger he could muster, he released a thunderous scream of defiance directly into the beast's face. At first, the werewolf actually seemed surprised, but then, in a furious rage, it wrapped its cavernous maw around Bennett's skull and cracked it like an egg. Bennett's provocative scream had most likely saved him a great deal of torment.

The creature devoured his brains and skull first. Bennett's body twitched and shook violently, and then slowly faded into the stillness of death. Enraged by the lack of sport, the beast fell upon him; rending him to shreds, gulping down flesh and bone in large, rapacious bites. Very little remained after the werewolf's gluttonous butchery, he had utterly devoured Bennett's body.

As he left the flesh-strewn canyon behind, the creature's blood-boltered body glistened brightly in the light of the moon. Now replete with the flesh of man, the beast reveled in the mistaken belief that he had killed the human who deceived him.

EARLY THE NEXT MORNING, a crimson-hued sky heralded the rising sun; the creature made his way into the depths of his hidden lair. The rifle bullet had torn a large hole in the werewolf's shoulder, but it was of little concern; he knew it would heal quickly. The beast had no idea why his wounds healed so rapidly—he only knew that they did.

He had no knowledge of the fibrin- and platelet-rich blood that flowed through his veins, no understanding of the unique clotting-factors that sealed his wounds almost instantly with a tough, fibrous scab that eliminated blood loss.

He was unaware of the rare, regenerative gene that his body possessed, enabling the rapid proliferation of new tissue, or that the powerful antibodies in his bloodstream could stave off even the worst infection. The werewolf only knew that his wounds would heal—and tomorrow night—he would once again hunt the flesh of men.

CHAPTER 11

Tracker

BRUCE FLETCHER looked at his watch for the hundredth time; it was a few minutes before noon. He had been pacing around his office and looking out the window for the past couple of hours.

Where the hell is he?

Bennett had said he'd be back a little after dawn, and if he wasn't back by noon to call the sheriff. Fletcher had felt concern for his friend when Bennett entered The Refuge yesterday, it seemed like a bad idea to go in there alone, but he had kept his mouth shut. Now, he had to call Sheriff Culley.

With a gusty sigh, Fletcher picked up the phone and called the sheriff's office. He disliked Sheriff Culley, thought he was a pompous, tight-assed son of a bitch, who thought *way* too much of himself.

Culley answered the phone: "Sheriff's office."

"Neil—this is Bruce, over at the game warden's office."

"Hey, Bruce," Culley said, forcing a cheerful tone. "How's it going, bud?" He didn't care much for Fletcher, either.

"Neil . . ." Fletcher said somberly, "I think we may have a problem."

Sheriff Culley was furious when the game warden relayed what Bennett had done, and that he was now missing.

"I'll be there in ten minutes," he said sharply, slamming down the receiver. He called Irene Murphy and asked her to come in early to answer the phone, he was gonna be gone the rest of the day. Then he called his wife to cancel their regular Friday-night dinner and a movie—she had *not* been happy.

Culley made his way into the equipment room and grabbed a rifle and his go-bag—a small backpack with everything needed for just such an occasion—and then he headed out the door.

It was about 12:20 p.m. when Culley parked his cruiser in The Refuge parking lot; he saw that Bennett's truck was still there. Sitting in his car for a moment, he peered through the windshield toward the dense, forbidding forest, pondering Bennett's idiocy.

Culley stepped to the rear of his car and placed his patent-leather duty-belt and revolver into the trunk. The heavy belt would weigh him down and he didn't need all the accessories. He removed his .30-30 Winchester and his go-bag, then reached down and felt the front pocket of his jeans; he wanted to make sure he had his pocketknife.

The old Barlow jackknife had belonged to his great-grandfather. His father had bequeathed it to him when he was a young boy; it was Culley's good-luck charm, and he never went anywhere without it. He slung the backpack and rifle onto his shoulder and made his way to the game warden's office.

Small talk was at a minimum when the two men met, neither had the patience for it. Their dislike for each other was set aside as they focused on finding Bennett.

"Is there anyone else in The Refuge?" Culley asked.

"No . . . not for the past three or four days," Fletcher said, glancing at the sign-in sheet.

"Good. That'll make him easier to track."

"Of course, people sneak in all the time," Fletcher pointed

out.

Culley nodded.

"He had a backpack full of raw meat with him," Fletcher added, "said he was gonna use it as a lure."

"Is that right?" Culley said. "Anything else I should know about?"

Fletcher shook his head, and then asked, "You want me to come with you? Might not be a good idea to go in there alone."

"No thanks," Culley said sharply. "I can move faster on my own. Plus, I need you to stay here and close The Refuge; just keep people out."

Fletcher frowned. "Until when?" They both knew Culley didn't have the authority to close The Refuge; it was federal property.

"Until I get back with Bennett," he snapped. Then he turned and stomped out the door.

"Asshole," Fletcher muttered.

Culley headed into the wildlife refuge and began searching for Bennett's trail. When he was a young boy, his father had taught him the art of *sign cutting*, a term that the old-timers used for tracking; and Culley could "cut the sign" with the best of them. He had also attended several NASAR (National Association for Search and Rescue) training courses, and short of a bloodhound, there wasn't a better tracker in the county.

He entered The Refuge and moved in a wide arc, searching for fresh sign. Most of the tracks were old, easily identified by their rounded edges and the debris that filled them; but two sets of tracks appeared somewhat fresh and both headed in the same direction.

Culley had a good idea which set of tracks belonged to Bennett; he would have been wearing a heavy hunting boot. The other tracks were a lightweight hiking boot; something that a tourist would wear.

He followed both sets of tracks to the point where their trails began to separate. Fortunately, one track fell atop another, and showed their age; he smiled and followed the hunting boots north.

Being all alone in the remote wilderness gave Culley time to think—and considering the current state of affairs in Bane County—he had plenty to mull over. In the past two months, eleven people had gone missing—or had been killed—and the people of Silver Canyon were frightened.

First, two backpackers had disappeared, and with the amount of blood found at the scene, Culley *knew* they were dead. Then, Wendy Walker disappeared without a trace, and two weeks later, James Clark—or what was left of him—was found dead on the highway. Soon after, four campers went missing at Lake Argent, and three more backpackers had vanished less than two weeks ago. It was crazy; Culley had never seen anything like it.

Now, Bennett's missing, he worried.

He dropped to one knee by the burbling riffles of a rock-filled mountain stream, examining one of Bennett's tracks in the muddy silt.

He forded here . . .

Seeing the deep, misshapen track near the water's edge had prickled the hair on the back of Culley's neck. It reminded him of another track that Bennett had shown him: a giant, muddy footprint at the edge of a small pond, near the campsite of two missing backpackers.

An *impossible* footprint.

It was the same footprint that Dalton Morrow had sketched on a piece of paper; the same bloody footprint that Bennett had pointed out on the highway next to James Clark's body. Culley rose and shook the crazy thoughts from his head; none of it was possible. There would be a logical explanation for everything; he just needed to find it.

Hopscotching from stone to stone, he tiptoed across the shallow, purling stream and disappeared into the verdant wilds of the thickening forest. He was closing in; the tracks were getting fresher.

He had a good idea where Bennett was heading; the trail had gone in the same basic direction since entering The Refuge. The tracks had snaked around the rugged areas, taking the easy road, but they always returned to the same heading: toward a well-used game-trail adjacent to several small canyons.

Good place to set a trap, he thought.

Culley was pissed that Bennett had pulled a stunt like this—going after a dangerous predator all alone—but he sincerely hoped to find his friend unharmed. The more he thought about it, he figured that Bennett must have injured himself—maybe he'd fallen and broken a leg—and Culley would find him trying to hobble his way back home.

What a pain in the ass that'll be, he thought. *I'll have to build a travois, and drag his sorry butt out of here.*

The coppery smell found Culley's nose at the exact same moment his eyes settled on the blood-trail at his feet. His pulse quickened at the amount of blood he saw leading into the distance.

"Bennett!" Culley shouted, his voiced echoing along the ridgeline. He listened intently, turning in a slow circle. He unslung his rifle, cocked the hammer, and fired a shot into the air. Again, he listened: hoping that Bennett would fire a shot in kind.

Nothing . . .

He worked the rifle's lever, chambering a new round, then gently lowered the hammer and continued along the trail.

While the amount of blood on the ground was disheartening, something about it didn't look right. The blood was fresh, no older than twenty-four hours; but it was partially covered with old, dry leaves that had fallen from their trees much longer ago than one day. It didn't make any sense.

Culley located one of Bennett's boot tracks; it was in a bare spot on the ground, free of grass and leaves, and made a clean impression in the soft soil. He narrowed his eyes at the boot print, peering at it intently; a faint smile played at the corner of his mouth.

The track was all wrong; most people walked in a heel-to-toe fashion, and as long as the surface of the ground was uniform—and the person wasn't jogging—the heel impression of a track would be slightly deeper. There would also be a faint, perpendicular ridge across the opposite end of the track —right behind the toe-dig—where they had pushed off with the tip of their boot. On this track, however, the toe had made the deepest impression, and there were scuff marks behind the heel.

"He was walking backward," Culley muttered.

Moving slowly along the blood-trail, he noticed that it had a slight serpentine quality, and the boot tracks were all moving backward. Culley nodded to himself; he knew exactly what Bennett had done.

He brought a bottle of blood with him.

Bennett had created a blood-trail by walking backward and pouring the blood with a slight side-to-side motion. Then, he had placed dry leaves and twigs along the trail, to create a noisy pathway. He was trying to lure the predator to a specific location.

Fletcher had mentioned to Culley that Bennett had brought a backpack full of raw meat with him, to use as a lure, but he never said *anything* about a bottle of blood.

Just like that asshole to leave out something important, Culley thought.

He continued along the blood-trail until he came to the narrow entrance of a small box-canyon; he saw that Bennett's tracks were everywhere. Culley noticed a number of fresh cut-marks on bushes and trees, as he moved along the trail. He figured Bennett must have built a brush-blind in order to hide —it only made sense—he would've needed a place to conceal himself.

The coppery smell of blood and raw flesh pervaded the air as Culley made his way deeper into the canyon. In the distance, he could hear the plangent buzzing of flies. As he rounded a large briar, he spotted the bloody hindquarter hanging in a tree. Culley nodded. *There's the raw meat he hauled in for a lure.* He was certain now; this was where Bennett had set his trap.

He continued on, past the fly-covered meat, heading toward the rear wall of the small box-canyon. He suspected he'd find Bennett's brush-blind there, and hopefully, some clue as to his whereabouts.

The blood-trail had ended beneath the hindquarter, but as Culley moved closer to the back of the canyon, he began to find more blood; not in a trail this time, but splattered all about in every direction. Rounding another briar, he spotted Bennett's brush-blind. It was at the base of a sheer rock wall, and blended perfectly into its surroundings. If it weren't for the fresh cut-marks on several large branches, he'd have never seen it.

As he drew near, Culley saw more raw meat scattered about the ground in front of the blind, and blood was everywhere; he furrowed his brow. *What the hell?* It didn't make any sense to place a lure this close to where you were hiding; you'd run the risk of the predator seeing or smelling you.

He turned and looked back at the hindquarter hanging in the tree. It was in the perfect location, no more than thirty yards from the blind; a clear and easy shot.

What the hell had he been thinking? He wondered. *Why would he place all this meat right in front of his stand?*

A glint of sunlight caught his eye, something shiny in the tall grass; he edged closer to have a look. Pushing the grass aside, Culley gasped and clamped a hand over his mouth; the blood drained from his face. He stumbled back several steps, then stooped over and retched on the canyon floor. Spitting the acrid bile from his mouth, he tried to straighten himself, but found only weak, wobbly knees; he stumbled back several more steps, and fell to the ground.

Culley sat in the grass trying to breathe, shock had stolen his breath. Eyes wide, he stared in horror at the blood-spattered ground before him; everywhere he looked, small gobbets of flesh littered the canyon floor. He wanted to stand, wanted to back away from the unspeakable gore, but his heart was pounding so hard, it forced him to clutch his chest.

The glint of sunlight Culley saw in the high grass had been Wayne Bennett's stainless-steel *Timex* watch—it rested unharmed and *still ticking*—on the wrist of his severed forearm.

The raw meat on the ground wasn't placed there by Deputy Bennett... the raw meat on the ground *was* Deputy Bennett.

Oh, sweet, Jesus, God—Bennett... what the hell?

Culley sat on the ground for several long minutes, trying to breathe and compose himself. His eyes welled at the horrible sight, and his body quaked and quivered. Until now, the remains of James Clark's body on the highway had been the most hideous thing Culley had ever seen.

This was worse—*far worse*—this was his deputy, a man he had worked with every day for the past eleven years. Sure, Bennett had been a real *ass* at times, and they didn't always see eye to eye, but this man had been Culley's partner, his friend.

He rose to his feet and balanced himself on shaky legs; his

eyes still wide with disbelief at the horror that surrounded him. He took a deep breath, aiming for clarity, and tried to pull himself together. "Okay," he whispered in a scratchy voice. "What do I do?"

My rifle was the first thought that came to his addled mind. *Protect yourself—whatever killed Bennett could still be nearby.*

The weapon had dropped from his hand at the sight of Bennett's severed arm. The tall grass had cushioned its fall, and he could see it resting there, unharmed. However, retrieving it meant he would have to look at Bennett's arm again. Culley tried to steel himself; then, clenching his jaw, he went for the Winchester.

Seeing his friend's arm for the second time was not as shocking as the first; at least this time he had been prepared. Culley realized he would need to recover Bennett's remains for a proper burial; he'd come back first thing in the morning with some help—and a body bag.

The cawing of crows drew his attention to the rim of the small box-canyon; the carrion eaters were biding their time up in the trees. Culley knew it wouldn't be long before the buzzards, and every other flesh-eating varmint in the forest arrived. He would need to protect Bennett's remains until he could return.

With grim determination, he sloughed off his backpack and pulled a pair of gloves from the pack; there was no way he could touch the remains with a bare hand. His stomach clenched into a painful knot as he gathered what was left of his friend into a small pile. It took everything he had not to puke.

Gathering large stones from the canyon floor, he piled them high over what was left of Bennett's body. The small cairn would protect his friend from scavengers until he could return and exhume the remains.

With mournful eyes, Culley stared at the makeshift grave,

his breath hitching in his throat. He felt the need to say something over his friend's brief resting place. He tried to recall a prayer or a bible verse from his childhood-days back in Sunday school. He'd never been a particularly religious man, and the only thing he could muster was part of an old Psalms.

Culley removed his hat, bowed his head and spoke with a quavering voice:

"My heart is in anguish within me

The terrors of death have fallen on me

Fear and trembling have beset me

Horror has overwhelmed me

Oh, that I had the wings of a dove

I would fly away and be at rest."

Culley's eyes had welled with unshed tears as he struggled with the words. With a faint sniffle, he replaced his hat, and finished, *"Amen."*

For some reason, reciting the short passage seemed to embolden him. The sadness and despair that filled Culley's heart melted away, replaced by a sense of strength. His sadness changed to anger—and despair became resolve. He was gonna find the animal that had killed his friend. He was gonna find it—and he was gonna kill it.

"What the hell did this to you?" Culley demanded, from the lonely pile of stones.

He turned, peering resolutely around the canyon. His jaw was set and his eyes had turned to flint. "Where the *hell* is your rifle?" he said.

Earlier, Culley had found the gore-smothered remains of Bennett's leather cartridge-belt and placed it into his grave, but he hadn't found the man's rifle. Culley took a deep breath. "Time to go to work."

He grabbed his rifle and made for Bennett's brush-blind to search his backpack. He had seen the pack earlier; it was the only thing not covered in blood. He upended the pack and dumped it onto the ground: a roll of duct tape, some cord, a canteen, a few candy wrappers, and a small spray-bottle of *Old Pete's Original Indian Buck Lure*—nothing helpful.

Shit . . .

Culley exited the blind and began searching for sign; there had to be something here that would tell him what happened. Starting at the rear of the small box-canyon, he moved in a side-to-side grid-pattern, slowly working his way forward toward the canyon mouth.

The makeup of the canyon floor consisted primarily of grass and scree; hardly a conducive substrate for finding tracks. Culley worked with slow economy, searching for any sign of the predator that committed this savage attack.

A month earlier, when he had seen the condition of James Clark's body on the side of the highway, his belief that a mountain lion was responsible had begun to wane. Now—after seeing what little remained of Bennett's body—he was certain that a big cat wasn't responsible.

Mountain lions didn't eat more than twenty or thirty pounds of meat at one sitting, and they tended to bury the rest for later. There was very little left of Bennett's body; and he'd been dead less than twenty-four hours.

In addition, a big cat wouldn't have eaten all the large bones—especially the skull—and Bennett's head was missing. There was no way a mountain lion had done this.

Culley knew that a pack of timber wolves could make short work of a carcass, but they stayed much farther north, deep in the interior of The Refuge near Lake Argent. There hadn't been a confirmed wolf attack in this county for over a hundred years, and even back then, attacks were as scarce as hen's teeth.

No, the savagery and ferocity of this attack was more like that of a large bear; and bears were well known for consuming the entire carcass of their kill—even large bones and skulls. Culley thought back to the giant footprint at the edge of the pond, and on the blood-splashed highway.

The tracks did *have a plantigrade form,* he recalled, *like those of a bear walking on the soles of its feet.*

He shook the crazy thoughts from his mind: those tracks were *not* what they had seemed. The track by the pond had been washed out by rain, and the one on the highway was nothing more than blood-splatter.

As he rounded a large briar, he saw where a few of the thorny branches had been broken; he used the barrel of his rifle to part the spiky bush and peered inside. "Well, I'll be damned," Culley muttered.

How in the hell?

Deep within the thorn-bush, was Bennett's rifle, and on the ground beneath it, a small flashlight. The gun was too deep inside the briar for Culley to reach; he would need to bring a machete in the morning to hack away the thorny branches.

A few feet away, he found an empty shell-casing on the ground. Culley picked up the brass and smelled the opening.

Freshly fired . . .

He looked at the stamp on the rim of the shell: .45-70 GOVT. The gory cartridge-belt Culley found earlier had been horrific, and he'd had no desire to look at it closely. Now that he saw the large-caliber round, he lifted an eyebrow.

Damn, Culley thought, *Bennett certainly brought a big enough gun.*

It just didn't add up. Bennett had been one hell of a good shot, and whatever he aimed at—he hit. That high-powered round he was using should have dropped anything it touched

—including a large bear.

So what the hell happened here, Culley struggled to understand, *how'd his gun end up in the goddamn bushes?*

He shook his head, frustrated, and continued on, searching for more sign. There was another large briar bush only a couple of yards ahead, and he noticed right away that it had considerable damage to its branches. It looked as though something very large had crashed through it.

The ground beneath the bush was hard-packed and covered with scree and tufts of grass, but he saw several large scuff marks in the gravelly soil. He also noticed what appeared to be holes in the ground, as though someone had been stabbing it with a pitchfork. Culley went down on one knee to examine the odd holes more closely; he began to see a pattern. The holes appeared to be in groups of five.

Claw marks? Culley wondered. *No—look at the spread—it's too big. But then again, what else could it be?*

He had seen plenty of bear tracks over the years, and their claws could leave similar holes in the ground. However, if a bear had made these holes—it would be of unimaginable size.

He noticed a small black spot on the ground, about the size of a fifty-cent piece. He touched its edge with the tip of his finger, and then pried it up from the ground. It had a flexible, almost rubbery texture, and bits of dirt and grass were adhered to its underside. It almost looked like someone had spilled paint on the ground and left it to dry.

He narrowed his eyes and held it up to the sun; it had a slight purplish hue, similar to an eggplant. Culley brought the strange find to his nose, and quickly jerked it away, grimacing; the odor was revolting. It was a foul, putrid smell, like rotting flesh.

He tossed it to the ground and wiped his hand on his jeans, then noticed several similar spots spreading across the ground; it looked a great deal like blood-splatter from a wounded animal. He frowned and rose to his feet. If this stuff was indeed blood, he'd never seen anything like it.

Maybe the animal was sick or something, Culley thought, *did rabies change the texture of an animal's blood?*

He rubbed his hand on his jeans again, disgusted by the foul substance. There was one thing he knew: if Bennett had hit this animal with that big .45-70 round, it more than likely wandered off and eventually died somewhere.

He donned his backpack and headed for the mouth of the canyon. Now that he knew what to look for—the large claw holes—he could track it with relative ease. He hoped he would find it dead; but if not, he'd put the sorry fucker out of its misery.

Culley followed the tracks around the rim of the small box-canyon to a spot overlooking Bennett's brush-blind. The high vantage point offered him a poignant and haunting tableau: a tiny stone cairn rising from the ground, encircled by a welter of blood. Whatever killed Bennett had watched him from this exact spot: sniffing and craving his tender flesh. A chill crawled the length of Culley's spine.

The tracks led through the dense forest for about a mile, then crossed an open field toward a small copse of trees. Within the brushy thicket, he found a tiny tree-lined ravine, its entrance well hidden by high weeds. Bushes were pushed aside; several snapped branches led the way; Culley cocked his rifle and proceeded cautiously.

Padding slowly into the tiny ravine, he was mindful of where he placed his feet. There was less light under the thick trees and the rocky ground was covered in a thick, green moss; he noticed that several of the large stones had been overturned, showing their lighter underbellies.

Something big came through here . . .

Rifle at the ready, he descended deeper into the darkening ravine; the dense canopy allowed very little light. Culley tried to move quietly, but gravel and dried leaves spanned the floor. Each step forward crunched noisily under his feet and seemed exceptionally loud inside the tiny ravine.

Buried within a thick layer of leaves, something caught his eye; Culley dropped to one knee and cleared the spot. It was the remains of an old ore-bucket, and next to it, the rusted head of a pickaxe.

It's not just a ravine, he realized. *It's the entrance to an old silver mine.*

He rounded a stack of rotting support-timbers that were covered in a thick, gray moss; the mouth of the mine was about twenty yards ahead, well hidden beneath a thick tangle of hanging vines.

Groundwater seeping into the tiny ravine had formed a series of small mud-puddles between Culley and the mine's entrance; as he moved closer, he spotted something shiny on the ground. He plucked the small object from the mud and rinsed it clean in a puddle.

His eyes went wide when he saw the small trinket in his hand. It was a tiny piece of jewelry: a small jade-and-silver dragonfly. Except for a missing wing, it was an exact match for the one Bennett had shown him about six weeks ago. A couple of kids had found it by Shambles Wash, claiming it belonged to Wendy Walker. "How in the hell did this get here?" Culley asked himself—his pulse quickened as he realized the answer.

Holy God . . .

His eyes widened farther as he made his way toward the mineshaft, there was a trail of footprints off to the side—large footprints. The soil was thick and moist and had a firm, clay-like texture, the perfect medium for a clear impression; and the tracks that Culley found were flawless. His heart pounded as he gaped at the giant footprints—these were *not* the tracks of a bear. "That's not fucking possible," Culley breathed.

Heart racing, he faced the forbidding mine, aiming his rifle blindly at the opening. From the stygian depths of the dark hollow, a foul odor rose to greet him: a repulsive, charnel stench. It was the smell of death.

Maybe it's dead, Culley hoped, *maybe Bennett's shot killed it.* He knew it wasn't true. No dead animal smelled that bad after only one day.

Keeping his rifle trained, he shrugged out of his backpack and let it slip to the ground. He fumbled through the pack and retrieved a flashlight. There was no way in hell he was going into that mine alone, but he at least needed to take a look; he owed Bennett that much. Moving closer, he saw more of the huge footprints, but these tracks were older, much older.

It's been living here a while...

Culley brushed the vines aside with the barrel of his rifle, and peered into absolute blackness; the smell of rotting flesh was almost overpowering. He switched on the light and trailed its beam along the long, dark tunnel; it seemed to go on forever, as the weak light slowly faded into the murky depths. "This place isn't a mine," Culley muttered, horrified, "it's a meat locker." A midden of large bones littered the floor, gnawed and cracked.

Dalton Morrow's statement about why they hadn't found any bodies came back to him: "*Well, the way I figure, it just killed more than it could eat—so, it hauled off the leftovers to its meat locker.*"

Culley squinted his eyes, struggling to see, but his light was too weak to reach any farther. At the edge of the failing light, he saw what looked like vertical support-timbers rising from the floor; they appeared to be covered with a thick, gray moss. As Culley watched, the timbers seemed to move: a gigantic gray beast emerged into the light.

For a split second, Culley thought he was imagining the shadowy image, but the glint of fiery eyes and rumbling growl erased all doubt. The flashlight slipped from his grasp and shattered. Stumbling back, an ear-splitting roar blasted from the dark pit; the sound was unlike anything he had ever heard.

Culley raised his rifle and aimed at the mine. Backing away, he had no doubt that the beast was coming for him; it would charge out of the mine any second and rip him to shreds. His thoughts turned to his wife and daughter; no one would know what happened to him.

Again, the unearthly roar rumbled from deep within the mine; it echoed along the walls of the tiny ravine. His body shook with fear as he continued backing away. The nightmarish sound awakened some baser instinct inside him. A genetic memory of primeval danger ingrained within all humans.

It was the sound of certain death . . . a sound from which, there was no escape.

He felt like a fool for following this creature back to its lair, especially after seeing what it had done to Bennett.

What the fuck was I thinking?

Sighting down the barrel of his Winchester, his aim was shaky; he ignored the backpack at his feet as he continued backing away. The entire world had grown quiet. The only sound he heard was his pounding heart.

When Culley reached the top of the ravine, he burst through the bushes and ran for about fifty yards. When he finally stopped, he turned and stood panting, staring back at the small copse of trees.

It's not coming . . . why's it not coming?

Culley stood wide-eyed and confused, heart pounding in

his chest; he was scared to death and struggling to think. He looked around in a panic to the broad open field that surrounded him; it was a bright, sunny day outside. Then—a thought occurred to him.

It only comes out at night, he hoped. *Maybe, it only comes out at night.* He prayed that it was true and a small sense of relief seemed to find him—but the solace of that prayer was short lived. He jerked his head toward the western horizon, the sun hung low in the sky.

Pulse quickening, he looked at his watch. He had entered The Refuge nearly four hours ago, and in less than two hours, it would be dark. Culley's mind raced; how long had it taken him to get to Bennett's location?

Two hours?

How much longer had it taken him to get to the ravine?

Another hour maybe?

He looked at his watch again.

Three hours total . . . Shit!

I was moving slowly, Culley assured himself, *I was searching for sign. I can shave an hour off my travel time . . . I think.*

Looking at his watch a final time, he then glanced to the falling sun. He surveyed the mountainous skyline for landmarks in order to draw the quickest line back to town. Once he had his bearing, Culley patted the good-luck charm in the front pocket of his jeans, and double-timed it across the field toward home.

THE CREATURE HAD AWAKENED TO THE SCENT OF MAN, and the sound of footsteps soon followed; they padded slowly toward his hidden lair. The beast rose from the fuliginous depths of the pit, hastening along dark and twisting pathways, harried by the redolent smell of flesh. As he neared the mouth of the mine, he saw that the light of day still lit its opening.

A man waited just outside the entrance, only a few yards away. The smell of fear surrounded the human, as the werewolf willed him to enter the mine. Slowly, the man seemed to obey, edging forward, he parted the vines and peered into the blackness, his weak eyes unable to see. A few steps farther and he would belong to the beast.

The creature knew that the human was armed, he had smelled the oily, metallic scent, but that was of no concern. The man's weapon posed little threat; last night's wound had nearly healed.

A sudden burst of light pierced the darkness; the werewolf shrank into the shadows. There was no place to hide in the long, straight tunnel; caught off guard, he was now exposed. When the man played the beam of light through the tunnel and uncovered the beast, the look on the human's face had been one of sheer terror; the light fell to the ground and disappeared, as the human backed away.

The werewolf's black heart erupted in a murderous rage; he released a savage roar that brought dust from the ceiling of the mine. The human had *seen* him, he had discovered his hidden lair; he couldn't be allowed to escape!

One of the beast's greatest strengths was that he always remained hidden, no one knew of his existence. Another resounding roar shook the ravine. The creature paced frantically near the mouth of the tunnel, unable to act. He was trapped by the light of day, and sunset was still an eternity away.

AFTER TWO HOURS OF HARD HIKING, Sheriff Neil Culley neared the entrance of the wildlife refuge. The sun had just fallen below the horizon, and in another ten or fifteen minutes, he would be back at the game warden's office having a cup of coffee with Bruce Fletcher. After everything that had transpired, the thought of Fletcher's company actually seemed inviting at this point.

The forest grew darker around him, and Culley no longer had a flashlight to guide his way. He struggled with his footing over the treacherous terrain; even during the daytime a person had to be careful, if you accidently turned an ankle, you'd be in a world of shit.

Exhaustion had claimed him; he huffed and panted, completely out of breath. He'd been moving at a steady trot—nonstop—for over two hours. He hadn't dared to slow down; not after what he'd seen in that dark mineshaft, not after what that *thing* had done to Bennett.

At forty-two-years of age, Culley was still in great shape. He'd spent his entire life hiking in the woods; but the two-hour-jog across rough terrain had taken its toll. The muscles in his legs had already passed the burning phase; now, they just felt like rubber. He had pushed through the pain, the cramps in his side, and had even thrown up at one point, but he never stopped moving; he was compelled forward by fear, and the rapid descent of the sun. "Just ten more minutes," he wheezed. Willing his feet to keep moving, he stumbled forward through the underbrush.

Dusk now owned the forest. It had enveloped Culley in a tenebrous shroud that caused his heart to beat even faster. He had no doubt that the creature was already on his trail, and depending on how fast it moved, it could be right behind him.

Over the past two hours, his mind had wandered; he thought about everything that had happened over the past two months. Wayne Bennett and Dalton Morrow had both been right; the thing that had been killing people around Bane County was some kind of monster.

A werewolf...

He felt like a fool for not listening, for being so closed-minded to everything. Even the old Gypsy woman had warned him about the creature; she said it was some kind of demon from Hell, a man-eater.

What did she call it? Culley tried to remember, *a new-ree?*

Culley's reverie ended with a loud crash; he spun around, eyes wide. The noise had come from far in the distance ... but then again, sounds could play tricks on you in The Refuge.

Again, he heard the menacing sound: wood splitting, cracking, a tree falling. *Shit!* Culley turned and ran as fast as his feet would carry him.

His heart swelled with fear, as he descended into absolute panic. He rushed headlong through the dense forest, struggling to make his way up the steep incline of a small hill. As he crested the top, he caught a glimpse of light; it winked through the thick brush at the foot of the hill: the game warden's parking lot.

A tiny glimmer of hope flitted through Culley's mind—but it disappeared completely with his next step. The loose rocks beneath his boots gave way, and his feet went right out from under him. Culley landed flat on his back atop an avalanche of loose rocks, and plunged down the steep declivity.

What had started as a back-scraping slide through a bosky darkness, soon changed into a bone-jarring, head-over-heels tumble through Hell. Culley crashed through bushes and briars, and slammed into the trunks of trees, but nothing seemed to slow his harrowing descent; not until he plowed—face first—into the ground at the bottom of the hill.

Culley struggled to lift his head and spat a mouthful of dirt.

Fuck...

He coughed and moaned, and rolled onto his back. With a

painful grunt, he strained and sat upright, then shook his head and blinked, trying to focus. His head was bursting with stars.

Even in his dazed condition, Culley hadn't forgotten why he'd been running, why he'd fallen down the hill: the crashing sounds in the forest, the *thing* that was chasing him. He grimaced and rose to his feet, the world spun, and he found himself back on the ground.

Shit...

He took a deep breath and tried again, he had to keep moving. He strained and this time managed to stay on his feet. Culley blinked repeatedly and his vision began to clear. He realized the stars in his head were actually the lights of the parking lot; the game warden's office was only about twenty-five yards away.

He glanced at the ground around him, his rifle was gone, lost somewhere during the fall. There was no time to search, he needed to move; he staggered dazedly toward the parking lot on unsteady legs.

Panting and wincing with each step forward, the bright lights of the parking lot finally surrounded him. He glanced at the Warden's office and saw that the lights were on; Fletcher was still there. Culley angled for his cruiser, the last thing he wanted to do was to talk to Bruce Fletcher; what the hell would he say?

...Oh, hi Bruce: I found what was left of Bennett's body; a werewolf ate him. I tracked it back to its hidden lair, and now it's after me. Oh, and I just fell down a mountain.

Fletcher would take one look at him and call the men in white coats, have him shipped off to a looney bin somewhere. No way was he going in there to talk with *him*.

Culley leaned wearily against the door of his car and fumbled for his keys; they jangled onto the asphalt.

Shit...

He grimaced and moaned as he stooped to retrieved them; his entire body felt like a giant raw nerve. He opened the door, slid gingerly into the seat, then closed the door and locked it. Culley took a deep breath and tried to stop shaking; he had made it, he was beat to hell, but he had made it.

Being inside a locked car, and surrounded by the bright, sodium-vapor lights of the parking lot eased Culley's fear; he looked toward the dark hillside where he'd almost lost his life. "One hell of a shortcut," he muttered giddily.

He turned and looked across the parking lot at Bennett's truck, a forlorn reminder of his lost friend; a sickening chill came over him. Images of Bennett's remains were etched into his mind forever.

I should've listened . . .

He slipped his key into the ignition and started the car; the simple act shot pain up his arm. He considered calling Doctor Milstead—go get himself checked out—but then thought better of it. Milstead's nurse was Wayne Bennett's ex-wife, Joan, and there was *no way* he could look *her* in the eye right now.

He shifted the car into DRIVE and turned on his headlights. Culley gasped and froze in horror. Near the edge of the forest —only a dozen yards away—the headlights revealed a giant gray beast hiding in the brush. It slipped into the shadows and quickly vanished, its glowing amber eyes disappearing into the night.

Culley's foot was glued to the brake pedal, he couldn't move, he was rigid with fear. Managing to take a breath, he punched the accelerator. Tires spinning, Culley swung the car around and headed toward the exit. As he approached the street, he glanced in the rearview mirror and slammed on the brakes, squealing to a halt. Bruce Fletcher was looking out the door of the warden's office, wondering who in the hell was burning rubber in his parking lot.

"Shit . . . Shit-shit-shit." Culley couldn't leave him there; what if the idiot walked out into the bushes to take a piss or something?

He threw his cruiser into REVERSE, smoke poured from his tires as he backed across the lot. He slid to a stop with his passenger door right in front of Fletcher; he reached over and flung open the door. "Get in, we gotta go!" Culley shouted.

Fletcher sneered at him. "What the hell is wrong with you?"

"Bruce, get in the damn car, now!" Culley demanded.

Fletcher jerked his thumb over his shoulder. "I gotta lock up."

"Get in the goddamn car, Fletcher, or I'll fucking arrest you!" Culley screamed.

Fletcher got in the car.

Culley took off before he'd even closed the door; the forward momentum of the vehicle slammed it shut.

"What the fuck, Neil?" Fletcher spouted angrily. Then he got a better look at Culley: his clothes were filthy, all ripped up, and his face and hands were scuffed and bloody. "What the hell happened to you?"

Culley turned onto the street and raced toward the sheriff's office. "It's a long fuckin' story," he growled. He turned and met Bruce's eyes. "And I doubt you're gonna believe a single word of it."

CHAPTER 12

Truth

BURNELL & SON FUNERAL HOME had been a family owned business in Silver Canyon since the late 1920s. Now operated by the son and grandson of the original founder, Burnell & Son had always strived to provide the families of Bane County with the utmost care and compassion during their time of loss and sorrow.

Leland Burnell Jr.—a licensed mortician and embalmer—was the current owner/operator, and preferred to be called by the more modern parlance: funeral director. His father, Leland Sr.—never being one to put on airs—had simply referred to himself as an undertaker.

Wade Burnell—Leland Jr.'s son—worked part-time for his father at the funeral home, whenever the need would arise, but he spent the majority of his days working at Reilly's IGA Grocery store as their assistant manager. When you had a small population such as Bane County, there were rarely more than one or two funerals per month. Even Leland had to supplement his income, and he did so by raising cattle.

The other hat Leland Burnell wore, was that of Bane County Coroner. It was his responsibility to collect the decedents, as well as, investigate and determine the cause of death.

In most cases, the task was straightforward; "natural causes" was the most common rationale. Although "old age" wasn't *technically* a cause of death, with an aging populace like

Bane County, it was only to be expected.

In rare instances—when something unusual transpired—Leland would call upon the expertise of Doctor Milstead to act as the Bane County Medical Examiner, relying on him to determine the cause of death, and issue the death certificate.

Such had been the case a little over a month ago with the death of James Clark; his mutilated body found by the roadside. When the sheriff's office called Leland at home that night, asking him to come collect the decedent, he hadn't been prepared for the grisly sight he'd encounter. All of his long years of experience, expertise, and exposure to working with the deceased, had gone right out the window—and splashed all over the ground.

Leland's son, Wade, hadn't fared any better; he had also left his dinner alongside that lonely highway at the sight of James Clark's body. It was the most horrible sight that either of them had ever seen.

After they had zipped the remains into a body bag, made their way back to the funeral home, and placed what was left of him into a refrigerated holding area; Leland had said a brief prayer that he'd never have to deal with such an ordeal ever again.

So, on Saturday morning, November 23, when Sheriff Neil Culley limped into the funeral home, Leland Burnell's heart sank. Culley looked like he'd been through a meat grinder. The sorrow and despair that filled his eyes told the story.

This time ... it was worse.

AFTER FORCING BRUCE FLETCHER into his cruiser the night before and spiriting him away, the two men had raced back to the safety of Culley's office.

Irene Murphy had been the first problem they encountered;

when Culley limped through the door, all bloody and battered, she refused to go home without knowing what had happened. Culley had yelled and forced her to leave; he felt bad about it later, but at the time, he didn't have any patience for it—pain always had a way of lowering a person's tolerance for such things.

Culley spent most of the evening cleaning and dressing his wounds, and trying to explain to Fletcher what the hell had happened. It had been a painful ordeal in more ways than one.

Not only was he physically injured, in need of a doctor, but the pain of losing Bennett—a trusted and longtime friend—to such a horrible, grisly death, tore at the very fabric of Culley's soul.

Trying to explain to Bruce Fletcher—a man for whom he had considerable disdain—the truth about what had transpired that afternoon; well, that had carried its own kind of pain.

The news of Bennett's death had been hard on Fletcher; he had known the man for over a decade, and considered him a close friend. When Culley had described the condition of Bennett's remains, and the fact that he had gathered and placed them under a small cairn for safekeeping, Fletcher had moved to the breakroom sink to splash water on his face. He stood there for a long moment, staring down the drain, trying to calm himself and come to terms with the horrific news.

Culley had been hesitant to share the rest of his experience; he knew how it would sound. He also knew that if he didn't tell someone ... he'd lose his damn mind.

At first, it was just as he feared; Fletcher had thought him mad. However, as Culley told of his descent into the dark ravine and his terrifying encounter with the giant gray beast, Fletcher's appearance softened, and his incredulity began to fade.

Culley pulled a case-file from the drawer of his desk and

proffered it to Fletcher; he pointed out a tiny piece of jewelry and told of its origin. Reaching into his shirt pocket, he retrieved the piece he'd found in the dark ravine. Bruce Fletcher's eyes had widened... it was a perfect match.

Fletcher locked eyes with Culley and held his gaze; he found no mendacity in his eyes. There, beneath the pain, and the sorrow, and the fear... there was only verity. Culley was telling the truth: some kind of monster had killed Wayne Bennett.

"I believe you," he said weakly. He stared at the tiny pieces of jewelry in his hand.

"No one can ever know the truth," Culley pleaded. "They'll think I'm crazy."

Fletcher looked at Culley, a perplexed frown on his face. "Why'd you tell *me* about this?" he asked. "Why in the hell did you drag *me* over here? You don't even *like* me!"

"I had no choice," he confessed.

When Culley told him about seeing the creature at the edge of The Refuge, Fletcher's face blanched, and he quickly took a seat. Though neither man spoke of it again, Fletcher knew that Culley might have saved his life.

"We can't tell anyone about this," Culley reiterated. "The entire county would panic, it'd be total mayhem; especially after what happened to James Clark."

A little over a month ago, when Doctor Milstead declared that a large predator—most likely a mountain lion—had killed James Clark, Silver Canyon had become a ghost town each evening after sundown.

News of another brutal killing could have a catastrophic effect on the populace of Bane County—especially since the person who had been killed was a well-armed deputy.

Fletcher stared at him a moment, then offered the barest nod; he figured Culley was probably right. "But we have to do something! We at least need to put signs at the entrance of The Refuge, warning of a dangerous predator—telling people not to camp overnight, and to stay out of The Refuge after sunset."

Culley nodded his agreement. "That's a good idea; let's make it happen as soon as possible."

Before he gave Fletcher a ride home, they had talked about the retrieval of Bennett's remains, a sad but necessary discussion. Culley had spent the rest of night on a cot in his office, though he never closed his eyes even once. When he'd called his wife to say he was pulling an all-nighter, the missus had *not* been happy; but at this point, he just couldn't handle another round of questions.

LELAND BURNELL had been polishing the pews in the reposing room when he looked up and saw Culley in the foyer; the sheriff looked like warmed-over death. One arm in a makeshift sling, his face scraped and bruised, and a bandage encircling his head.

His shirt had been clean—he'd had a spare at his office—but he still wore the tattered trousers from the night before; large, bloodstained holes revealed the bandages on his knees.

"Dear God," Leland exclaimed, gaping at the battered man. "What happened to you?"

Culley blinked, and gave only a faint shake of his head; he just couldn't talk about it anymore. "Leland," Culley said, struggling to keep his composure. "Wayne Bennett's been killed."

"Oh my God; how, what happened?" He sat down on a pew and motioned for Culley to join him.

Culley limped forward with a halting gait, and eased down onto the pew. He placed his hand on Leland's shoulder and met his eyes. "Leland," he said, with a weak smile. "I can't tell you everything right now, but I really need your help."

"Certainly, Neil, anything you need."

"First of all," he said. "You can't tell anyone about Bennett's death, not even your own wife; at least, not until I get things figured out."

Leland nodded hesitantly, a look of concern on his face. "But what about—"

"No one!" Culley asserted.

Leland nodded his agreement.

"I also need you to recover Bennett's body; he's in The Refuge."

"The Refuge?"

Culley nodded. "Bruce Fletcher knows where he's located, I drew him a map. He's the only other person who knows about this besides us. I'm in no condition to help, so I need you to send your son, Wade, along with Fletcher in the morning to retrieve Bennett's remains. Be sure that you swear Wade to secrecy; he can't tell anyone. Just have him call Fletcher at the game warden's office. I'm going home to get some rest."

"Don't you think we should send more than two people?" Leland asked. "Bennett was a large man, and it'll be difficult to carry him across that rough terrain."

Culley grimaced as he rose to his feet; he looked at Leland with sorrowful eyes. "It'll be okay," he assured. "They won't have any trouble carrying what's left of him."

Leland's mouth fell open as he watched Culley hobble out the door.

What's left of him?

As Culley eased his aching body onto the seat of his cruiser, he felt a certain sense of guilt and shame. While it was a fact that he wasn't in any condition to help recover Bennett's remains; the truth was—he was afraid. At this point, Culley didn't know if he'd ever go into The Refuge again.

He started the car and placed a shaking hand on the wheel. He had no idea what he was going to tell his wife; but he figured, now was as good a time as any to go find out.

※

BRYCE McNEEL yawned noisily and rolled out of bed; he made his way to the calendar on his bedroom wall. As he had done for the past five weeks, he took a marker and placed a large *X* over today's date—Monday, December 2.

"Twenty more days," he muttered.

The winter solstice—and the last full moon of the season—would both take place on December 22. Bryce hoped with all his heart that his theory about the werewolf hibernating after the winter solstice turned out to be true. If not, he had no idea what they would do.

For the past five weeks, everyone had been extremely careful. Nobody went out after dark, and even during the day, no one went into the woods alone. Bryce and Jackson kept their rifles at their sides, loaded and handy, and Grandpa's 12-gauge-pump sat next to the back door, filled with double-ought buckshot. Nobody was taking any chances.

Bryce's grandma now knew everything; it had been impossible to protect her sensibilities after she heard that howl echo through the darkness. To her credit, she had accepted the circumstances with her usual strength and grace, and seemed to be a lot less scared and more in control than either Bryce, or Grandpa.

Everyone had decided it was best not to talk about the werewolf with Jackson's parents; his mom might have believed it, but they knew his dad would think they were all nuts. It was enough that his parents thought a killer mountain lion was on the loose. They were staying out of the woods and not going outside at night, and that was good enough.

Bryce heard his grandpa whistle for Snip and then say, "Go get it." Snip was on his way to the road to retrieve the morning paper, anticipating a crispy treat; Grandpa never disappointed.

Bryce took a quick shower, dressed for school, and made his way into the kitchen; Jackson would be there soon and he wanted to grab a quick bite before school. As he tore open a buttermilk biscuit and filled it with bacon, he saw his grandma through the kitchen window; she was out back, throwing feed to her chickens.

Grandpa—who always read the morning paper at the kitchen table—was missing, however. As he wolfed down his breakfast sandwich, Bryce stepped out onto the back porch and found his grandpa sitting in his favorite rocker; the morning paper folded on his lap. The look on Grandpa's face was one of both shock and fear, and he hadn't answered when Bryce asked what was wrong; he simply proffered the morning paper.

Bryce looked at the front page and the blood drained from his face. There was a picture of Wayne Bennett with the headline: DEPUTY DIES IN LINE OF DUTY.

Bryce's knees went weak and he quickly found a chair; he couldn't believe what he was seeing. Deputy Bennett's statement at the library five weeks earlier returned to him: *"Don't worry son, I'm gonna find this thing, and I'm gonna kill it."* Bryce met Grandpa's eyes; there was no need to say anything, they both knew what had happened.

Sheriff Neil Culley had managed to keep Bennett's death quiet for ten days, though no one would realize that by reading the article; there was no mention of when he had died. In fact, there was no *actual news* to be found anywhere in the report; it was a piece of puffery, crony journalism. Cause of death, location, or any relevant facts whatsoever were nonexistent; it was nothing more than Bennett's bio, and praise for a beloved deputy.

Jackson laid on his horn and Bryce turned toward the road, the black Camaro sat waiting, idling loudly.

"Take that with you and show it to Jackson," Grandpa said, motioning to the paper. "I'll tell your grandma what happened."

Bryce tightened his lips and nodded.

Jackson revved the loud engine and Bryce headed for the road; nothing more was said between him and Grandpa.

As Bryce neared the car, Jackson mouthed the word "shit" through the driver's side window; he had seen the morning paper tucked under his arm. The last time Bryce had brought a newspaper along for the morning drive was eight weeks ago, when two backpackers were reported missing.

What the fuck happened now? Jackson wondered, shaking his head.

When he got into the car, Jackson had reached for the gearshift, but Bryce touched his hand and stopped him. The car would need to be in PARK for this news.

"Wait," Bryce said, and then he handed him the paper.

"Ho-ly shit," Jackson intoned, his eyes gone wide at the headline. He jerked his head around to meet Bryce's eyes. "You don't think that—" he paused, looked at the paper again. "How did he die?"

"It doesn't say," Bryce answered.

"Doesn't say?" Jackson frowned.

"It doesn't say jack-shit; not how he died, where, or even when."

"But why would—" he met Bryce's eyes again, and then nodded knowingly. "Those sorry sons of bitches—they're trying to cover this up!"

"I'll bet you anything that Sheriff Culley's behind this," Bryce said sharply. "Bennett told me that Culley was ignoring all the facts. Now, he's trying to hide what happened."

Jackson grimaced, "That lousy bastard."

"I think we should go have a talk with him after school," Bryce suggested.

"What—with the sheriff?" Jackson scoffed. "Are you outta your fucking mind? He'd probably throw our asses in jail."

"For what?" Bryce said. "For trying to find out the truth—for wanting an honest answer?"

"He's the sheriff; he can do whatever he wants."

"We can't let him get away with this," Bryce demanded. "People's lives are at stake. We need to know what the hell happened."

"I gotta go to work after school," Jackson hedged.

"Fine—just drop me off, and I'll talk to him myself," Bryce said stubbornly. "When I'm done, I'll walk over to Western Auto and wait for you."

Jackson shook his head, shifted the car into DRIVE and headed for school. "You're outta your cotton-picking mind."

SHERIFF NEIL CULLEY sat hunched over his desk, head bowed; Wayne Bennett's face stared back at him from the front page of the newspaper. It had been ten days, and the aches and pains of his battered body had almost faded. The pain from the loss of his friend, however, was another story; it was still acute, debilitating.

Leland Burnell and his son were true to their word; they hadn't told a soul about Bennett's death. The morning after Culley spoke to Leland at the funeral home, Bruce Fletcher and Wade Burnell had entered The Refuge to collect Bennett's remains.

The night before, Culley had explained to Fletcher how the creature wouldn't exit the mine in the light of day, and how it had shied away from the bright lights of the parking lot and the headlights of his car. Culley told him that he thought they would be safe, as long as they were out of The Refuge well before sunset. He had drawn him a map, so he'd know exactly where to go, and estimated that their roundtrip would be five or six hours. The two men left shortly after sunrise that morning, and both of them were well armed.

Culley had waited for their return at the game warden's office, scared to death that something would happen and they wouldn't come back. What frightened him even more was that *he'd* have to go into The Refuge and find them.

Six hours later, the two haggard men stumbled from The Refuge; faces drawn and pale. The horror of the near-empty body bag they carried surrounded them like a dark shroud.

While Bruce Fletcher knew the truth about Bennett's death, Wade Burnell did not. Culley figured the man would have questions about the state of the remains . . . he didn't. The only question Wade had asked after arriving back at the funeral home was, "Can I go home now?" He looked as though he would faint.

Wade's father hadn't been so accommodating; shocked by the sight of Bennett's remains, Leland wanted to know exactly what happened. Culley had stonewalled, asking for patience, and the continued silence of Leland and his son. He needed time to investigate was the excuse—and Leland hesitantly agreed.

Culley had spent the next five days trying to track down Bennett's next of kin in Texas. He couldn't very well ask the man's ex-wife, so locating his family had been quite a chore. As it turned out, his only living relative was an older brother who lived in Corpus Christi, and he hadn't spoken to Bennett in years. His brother wanted nothing to do with the funeral arrangements, apparently there had been some bad blood between them; it had been a very short phone call.

Coming up with a cover story for Bennett's death hadn't been any easier. He couldn't tell Leland Burnell to type the word WEREWOLF in the cause-of-death section of the death certificate; he needed to stall and come up with something believable, something foolproof.

The fact that Bennett had no family to speak of had made things easier; the sheriff's office would pay for the cost of a funeral. As long as Burnell and Son would keep quiet and go along with the ruse, no one would need to know about the state of Bennett's remains—or ask any questions about what might have killed him.

The last thing Culley did before reporting Bennett's death to the Silver Canyon Gazette was to convince Leland Burnell that it would be in the best interest of the community for him to cooperate; he needed to remain silent about the state of Bennett's remains.

"Imagine the level of panic it would cause," Culley had implored, "especially after what happened to poor James Clark. The rumors alone would create total chaos."

It had taken strong persuasion, but Burnell had finally agreed. They would postpone the completion and filing of Wayne Bennett's death certificate until after his burial—which would take place immediately. A memorial service for Bennett could come later. Culley would provide Leland with the cause of death at a later date—and no one would be the wiser.

"If Doctor Milstead comes nosing around," Culley had added. "Tell him his services are not needed. If he gives you any grief, just send him to me."

Leland seemed startled at the thought of Doctor Milstead, he hadn't considered that scenario; he nodded his agreement nervously. "Okay."

When he spoke with the Silver Canyon Gazette, Culley had kept his answers brief and generic; he used the oldest trick in the book. He claimed that he couldn't comment on an ongoing investigation. They published the type of article he had wanted—superficial.

Culley's reflection ended with the sound of a loud engine revving out in the street; a moment later a young man walked through the door. He recognized the boy but couldn't put a name to the face; he rose and headed over to greet him.

"Can I help you, son?" Culley asked. His voice sounded weak, so he cleared his throat.

When Bryce entered the sheriff's office, he'd been full of piss and vinegar, with every intension of being a hard-ass. He wasn't going to take any crap and he wasn't leaving until he found out *exactly* what had happened to Bennett.

However, when he saw Culley's face mottled by yellowish-brown bruises and old scabs, and the fact that he moved with a slight limp, Bryce reined in his temper.

"I'm Bryce McNeel," he said, proffering his hand.

"That's right," Culley said, gripping the boy's hand. "You're Nathan and Blanche's grandson. I thought I recognized you."

Culley had been the sheriff back in 1978 when Bryce's parents had died in a house fire. He still remembered the towheaded little boy who'd lost his parents. He had only been the sheriff for about four years at that point; it had been the first real tragedy he'd dealt with.

Bryce smiled. "If you don't mind me asking, Sheriff"—he motioned to Culley's face—"what happened?"

Culley had been asked the same question over a hundred times in the past ten days; he offered the same answer as always: "Oh, I was hiking in The Refuge and lost my footing—

fell down a dang hill."

Benjamin Franklin once wrote in *Poor Richard's Almanack* that; "Half the truth is often a great lie." Culley had taken ol' Ben's advice to heart.

"Ouch," Bryce said, frowning. "I'll bet that hurt." Secretly, he was wondering if Culley was telling the truth.

"Yeah, it smarted a bit at first," Culley said, touching his face. "But it's a lot better now"—he paused a moment—"What brings you in today, Bryce?"

"Do you mind if we sit down, Sheriff?" Bryce asked.

"Sure," Culley said, motioning toward his desk.

After they took a seat, Bryce said, "I'm a friend of"—he stopped, rephrased—"I *was* a friend of Deputy Bennett; I wanted to find out what happened to him."

A mournful darkness descended over Culley; Bennett's face looked up at him from the newspaper on his desk. Without meeting Bryce's eyes, he said, "I didn't know that you knew Bennett." He spoke quietly, never taking his eyes off the photo.

"We weren't close friends," Bryce admitted. "But we spent some time together recently, and I'd really appreciate knowing what happened to him."

Still gazing at Bennett's picture, Culley used his canned response: "I'm sorry, but I can't comment on an ongoing investigation."

Bryce's anger flared; Culley wasn't getting off that easy. Bennett was dead—lots of people were dead—and lives were still in danger. If Culley thought he was going to hide the truth behind some *bogus protocol*, he was sorely mistaken.

Bryce placed his hands on the desk and slowly rose to his feet. He leaned in toward the sheriff, and drew his eyes away from the photo—he was right in Culley's face.

When he met the boy's eyes, Culley saw that they had turned

to flint, and that his face was burning with intensity. Bryce had the look of a hunter—someone who could reach out and *snatch* the life right out of you.

Calmly and slowly, Bryce spoke through gritted teeth—threat painted every word. "I want to know . . . what happened to Bennett."

" . . . I'm sorry, but I can't—"

Wham!

Culley jumped when Bryce slammed his hand down on the desk. He stood and took a step back; Bryce didn't give him a chance to speak.

"If you think for one-damn-minute that you can hide behind some bullshit *rule of procedure*, you are dead wrong! People's lives are at stake here, Culley—my family's lives—and we don't have time for this shit.

"Bennett told me that you'd refused to look at the evidence. He laid everything right in your damn lap and you wouldn't even consider it. Well, I know what killed Bennett, I've seen it; and if you'd pull your damn head out of your ass long enough to look at the facts, you'd know what killed him, too."

Culley looked paralyzed; like a deer caught in the headlights of an oncoming car. He gaped at the young man who stood before him; red-faced, fists clenched at his side. One thing that Bryce McNeel had said stood head-and-shoulders above the rest.

" . . . You've seen it?" Culley breathed.

SHERIFF NEIL CULLEY spoke first. After Bryce told him about seeing the giant beast—just moments before it killed James Clark—Culley had been completely forthcoming about everything that had transpired over past ten days. Talking with another person who had actually seen the hideous creature had been comforting, somehow.

He told Bryce of his deputy's futile attempt to lure the beast and kill it. The gut-wrenching description of Bennett's remains had been sickening to hear. Culley's hair-raising account of his encounter with the monstrous creature and the harrowing escape that ensued had been terrifying for Bryce. The realization that the beast would've most likely caught Culley if he hadn't accidentally slipped and fallen down the mountain, had been even more frightening.

However, nothing that he had shared with Bryce had been more horrifying than the sight of a tiny jade-and-silver dragonfly. When Culley told of its discovery in the dark ravine, just outside the werewolf's lair, Bryce had turned white, and then excused himself.

As he looked into the restroom mirror, his face wet with water, Bryce recalled what Culley had said about the dark mineshaft: *"It was a meat locker—a midden of large bones littered the floor."* He turned to the toilet and threw up. He knew what the discovery of the earring meant: the werewolf had brought Wendy Walker back to his lair and devoured her. Bryce could only *hope* that Wendy was already dead when she arrived.

After pulling himself together, Bryce told Culley everything he knew about the werewolf: the history, the legend, and his theory about the beast hibernating, only to return after nineteen years during the autumn season with four full moons—a blue moon. Bryce had been as detailed as possible and Culley was amazed at how astute, well-spoken, and intelligent the boy seemed.

"So, you're saying that this thing is some kind of unknown species?" Culley clarified. "And it only comes out of its hole for three months every nineteen years?"

"That's right," Bryce insisted.

"And after December 22, it'll be gone?"

Bryce nodded. "For nineteen years."

"It just sounds too impossible," Culley doubted.

"More impossible than a werewolf chasing you back to your car the other night?" Bryce asked dryly.

Culley lifted an eyebrow and gave Bryce a lopsided grin. "Yeah . . . yeah, I guess you've got a point there."

"The real question is: what do we do now," Bryce said. "How do we keep people safe for the next twenty days?"

"Well," said Culley, "Bruce Fletcher and I placed notices at the entrance of The Refuge, warning of a dangerous predator, and recommending that people not camp overnight."

"Yeah, I've seen them," Bryce said, unimpressed. "They haven't done much good, *have* they?"

Culley frowned. "And how would you know that?"

"Because I've been keeping an eye on the sign-in sheet at The Refuge for the last eight weeks," Bryce pointed out. "And in the past seven days, two groups have entered The Refuge with extended camping permits."

"Yeah, I know," Culley said, a grim look about his face. "Fletcher told me he couldn't convince them otherwise."

"Why in the hell didn't you just close The Refuge," Bryce said, frustrated.

"Because it's federal property," Culley argued. "We don't have the authority to close it. Fletcher ran it up the chain-of-command that we had a predator problem, but they said there's no actual proof that anyone has died in The Refuge—no bodies have been found. A warning notice is the best we could do."

Bryce shook his head, disgusted. "Frigging bureaucrats."

The two sat quietly for a while, contemplating. Finally, Bryce said, "I know that you're worried about causing a panic, but what if we put a notice in the newspaper; tell people a predator is on the loose, and recommend that people stay indoors at night?"

Culley paused for a second, and then breathed a heavy sigh. "You know as well as I do how many small farms and ranches are south of town," he said. "And most of them are owned by elderly people—and some of those people live alone."

"From what I've heard about Gladys Rickman, staying behind locked doors, or even being armed, won't stop this thing—this animal seems smart, cunning. Even if we placed a notice in the newspaper and people stayed indoors, I don't think it would make any difference. This creature would just keep hunting until it found someone vulnerable. Staying inside won't stop this thing from killing people, especially if they're isolated and alone. The only thing a notice would do is cause people to live in fear."

Bryce leaned forward in his chair and placed his elbows on his knees; he hung his head, staring at nothing in particular. Unfortunately, Culley's analysis seemed sound. "We've *got* to do something," he muttered to the floor. "We need to find out as much as we can about this creature, its weaknesses, anything"—he sat up and met Culley's eyes—"do you think Dalton Morrow could tell us more about this thing? We need to find out everything we can."

Culley shook his head. "I think Dalton already shared everything he knew with me and Bennett"—he paused a moment, thinking—"but I might know someone else who can tell us something."

"Who?" Bryce asked eagerly.

Culley smiled slyly. "Are you hungry?"

CULLEY PARKED HIS CRUISER on the street alongside Cătălina's Café; the old Gypsy woman was the only person he could think of that might have more information about the creature. On the drive over, he told Bryce about the old woman's visit eight weeks earlier, and her claim that she knew what had killed the backpackers.

Culley wasn't looking forward to seeing the old woman again; he'd been rude to her at their last meeting. He wouldn't need to see a menu when he ordered *his* meal—Culley would be having the crow.

"Before we go talk to the old woman," Culley said, "let's head across the street and have a quick word with Bruce Fletcher. Except for your grandpa and Jackson, he's the only other person who knows about this thing besides us. We'll make it quick, but we need to fill him in."

When Culley walked into the game warden's office, Fletcher had been surprised that Bryce McNeel accompanied him; he'd been even more surprised at the conversation that followed.

While Culley brought Fletcher up to speed on the day's events, Bryce looked at the sign-in sheet. There were still two groups camping in The Refuge, and they wouldn't be considered overdue for another week.

Fletcher turned to Bryce. "A school project on tourism, huh?"

Bryce shrugged. "I needed to keep an eye on things. There wasn't anything I could do about it, but I needed to know"—he paused and then added—"you know they're already dead"—alluding to the sign-in sheet—"or they will be soon."

"I tried to stop them," Fletcher lamented, "but they just wouldn't listen"—he shook his head sadly—"Dumb-ass tourists."

Bryce nodded; he could see that the man was worried sick over the campers, but he'd had no choice in the matter.

While Culley explained to Fletcher about the old Gypsy

woman they were about to see, Bryce noticed the big-bore repeating rifle that leaned in the corner.

"I see you're not taking any chances," Bryce said to Fletcher. He nodded toward the lever-action rifle.

"That was Bennett's," Fletcher said despondently. "All of that stuff was his"—he pointed somberly to a box of sundries sitting on the floor by the rifle—"I didn't know what else to do with it."

Bryce moved to the box and looked inside; it was a hodgepodge of random items: a canteen, a hunting knife, a wristwatch, a flashlight, some tape and cord, all things that someone would take with them into The Refuge. One of the items, however, jumped out at Bryce: a small spray-bottle of *Old Pete's Original Indian Buck Lure*.

He removed the small bottle from the box and turned to the two men. "Bennett had this with him?" Bryce asked. His face showed concern.

"It was in his backpack," Culley replied. "Why, does it mean something to you?"

" . . . I'm not sure," Bryce admitted. He looked suspiciously at the small bottle. "I was using *Buck Lure* the evening I first saw this thing; I'm almost certain it's why the creature didn't find me. I mentioned it to Bennett the day we met at the library; he must have used it for the same reason, trying to conceal his scent."

"Makes sense," said Culley.

"Yeah, but what if," Bryce suggested, "the creature recognized the scent, somehow, and figured out that the *Buck Lure* was a trick; it would've led the werewolf right to Bennett."

Culley smiled consolingly and placed his hand on Bryce's shoulder. "There's no indication that anything like that happened," he assured him. He could see that the boy was feeling culpable somehow for Bennett's death.

"One thing's for sure," Fletcher cut in, ". . . it knows the scent now."

Bryce leered at the small bottle, and then tossed it into the trashcan. "Get rid of that," he told Fletcher; then he went into the restroom and scrubbed his hands with soap. Even touching that bottle might be risky.

Bryce and Culley left the game warden's office and headed across the street to Cătălina's Café. Sliding into a booth, they drew the attention of a statuesque young woman at the rear of the restaurant; she made her way forward toward their table.

Her long silken hair was as black as a raven and hung loosely about her slender waist; it swished gently from side to side, as she moved across the room, keeping rhythm with every step.

An elegant, off-the-shoulder blouse, embroidered with colorful flowers, accentuated her flawless olive skin and the gentle curve of her body. A colorful, coin-tasseled skirt, cradled her shape perfectly as it swept gracefully above the floor.

When the young woman arrived at their table, Culley lowered his menu, allowing her to see his face; her pale-blue eyes flashed with anger and her lips grew taut.

"*You* . . . what do *you* want?" she asked brusquely. Her face wrinkled as though she smelled something vile.

Offering a big smile, Culley said, "You're Mary . . . Mariana, right?"

She nodded, stone-faced. "Do you want to order food . . . or did you come to insult me again?" She showed no fear of the sheriff's authority.

"Ma'am," Culley said soulfully, "I am profoundly sorry about the way I acted toward you and your great-grandmother. It was wrong of me, and I sincerely apologize for my actions. Do you think you could ever find it in your heart to forgive me?"

Mariana glared at him impassively, and then a tiny smile

played at the corner of her mouth. "Okay . . . you're forgiven. Now, what do you want to eat?" She lifted her pad and pencil.

Culley smiled and rubbed his hands together. "Why don't you bring me the specialty of the house; dealer's choice, whatever you think is good."

Mariana nodded and turned to Bryce. "And what can I get for you?"

Since first entering the café, Bryce had been entranced by this beautiful young woman. She was stunning, gorgeous, and her take-no-prisoners attitude toward Culley had been mesmerizing.

"Would you like something?" Mariana tried again, cocking her head at Bryce.

The mere presence of this young woman had addled his brain and Bryce was slow to respond. Culley kicked his shin under the table.

"Oh—yes—I, I'll have what he's having." He pointed a finger across the table at Culley, a goofy smile on his face. Even though Bryce's IQ was off-the-charts, he had just become a babbling idiot.

Mariana offered a curious smile as she quickly jotted on her pad; she watched Bryce from the corner of her eye as she turned and left their table.

"Pardon me, ma'am?" Culley hollered after her. "While we're waiting, do you think it would be possible for us to speak with your great-grandmother for a moment?"

Mariana knitted her brow. "Why?" She asked, still leery of the sheriff.

Culley presented her with an "I'm-an-idiot" look, and said, "I'd like her to tell me about . . . the *new-ree*."

Mariana pursed her lips and nodded. "I-told-you-so" was written all over her face. "I will ask her," she said. "But first, you eat—then we talk." She turned and headed for the kitchen. Bryce's eyes followed her the entire way.

"That Mariana's pretty cute, huh?" Culley asked, with a sly smile; he could see that the boy was taken with the young woman.

"Gorgeous," Bryce muttered, never taking his eyes off the kitchen door where she had disappeared.

Their meal was excellent and they devoured it eagerly. Culley had treated; picking up the tab. He made certain to leave a generous gratuity for Mariana.

"Străbunică will see you now," she said, gesturing toward the beaded doorway at the rear of the room.

"Straw-boo-nee-cah?" Culley attempted.

"It means: great-grandmother," Mariana translated. "It's Romanian."

Culley offered a sheepish grin, and then they followed her to the rear of the restaurant. Making their way up the creaking stairs, Bryce and Culley entered the small apartment above the café. Cătălina Pătrașcu sat in an old upholstered chair, peering out the large picture-window that faced The Refuge. Between her ankles, a white Manx cat performed a slow figure eight, oblivious to the new intruders.

Mariana crossed the room and placed her hand on Great-grandmother's shoulder, whispering in her ear. The old woman pointed to the kitchen table and Mariana retrieved two chairs for Bryce and Culley.

Placing the chairs in front of her great-grandmother, Mariana motioned for them to sit. She hefted the large cat from the floor and took a seat on the couch. Cradling the animal as if it were a small child, she caressed it lovingly and whispered to it.

Cătălina locked eyes with Culley, fixing him with an

uncomfortable gaze. When he had met the old woman eight weeks earlier, he hadn't noticed the color and intensity of her piercing gray eyes. They were similar to those of her great-granddaughter, but the radiant, pale-blue eyes of the young woman were appealing, even alluring. Looking into the old woman's eyes, however, had raised the hair on Culley's neck. It was like peering into the limpid depths of a fathomless pool that teemed with writhing phantasms.

A wry smile blossomed on her emotionless face; Cătălina nodded knowingly at Culley. "Now you believe," she said.

Culley nodded apologetically. "Yes, ma'am . . . I do; and I'm very sorry that I didn't listen to you earlier when I had the chance."

The old woman waved away his words, forgiving him. "Who would believe such a story from a feeble old woman?" she insisted, shrugging.

"Well," Culley assured her, "I sure believe you now."

Cătălina searched his eyes, and then inhaled sharply. ". . . You have seen it," she divined. "You have seen the *Neuri*."

"Yes, ma'am, I have," he affirmed. "And so has this young man." Culley twisted in his seat to introduce him, but Bryce had failed to notice. While he appeared to be looking at Cătălina, his focus was actually on the couch behind her. He sat with a bemused look about his face, the corners of his mouth curled slightly; he was watching Mariana playing with the cat.

Smack! . . . Culley slapped the back of Bryce's head. "Pay attention."

"Yes ma'am . . . uh . . . sir . . . um, I'm sorry, what? Once again, Bryce had become a babbling idiot.

Mariana smiled secretively and continued playing with the cat.

"I was just telling Miss Cătălina that you and I have seen

this . . . *thing* that's been killing people," Culley apprised.

Bryce was embarrassed; he had been acting like a fool ever since he first laid eyes on Mariana. He reined in his teenage hormones and focused.

"Yes, ma'am," Bryce confirmed, meeting Cătălina's eyes. "I've seen it"—he paused, and then added—"It's a werewolf."

Cătălina held Bryce's gaze. "The vârcolac," she said. "A werwulf. Yes, the *Neuri* has many names."

Bryce recognized the name: *Neuri*. He had read about it in the works of *Herodotus*, a fifth-century B.C. Greek historian. Agnes Furman had provided him with over a dozen library books pertaining to werewolves over the past five weeks, and he had committed all of them to memory. The *Neuri* were said to be a tribe of people who could change into wolves. Bryce had been surprised that the old woman was familiar with Greek mythology—but then again . . . maybe she wasn't.

"Would you mind telling us what you know about the *Neuri*," Bryce asked. "Anything would be helpful."

Cătălina looked at Bryce; she saw the anxiety in his eyes. "I will tell you what I can," she agreed, "but please know—speaking of such things is unwise."

Bryce nodded; this wasn't the first time he'd been told not to talk about this creature.

"The *Neuri* is the ancient one; as old as time itself." As Cătălina spoke, she rubbed a small silver amulet that hung around her neck. "It is a demon from the underworld, spawn of *Belial*, the progeny of Hell. It is . . . the eater of men."

More than what she was saying, it was the tone of the old woman's voice and the intensity of her eyes that had caused Bryce's skin to pebble.

The old woman closed her eyes and recited a verse she had learned by rote as a small child:

"When the moons of autumn number four
And leaves cover the glen
The beast will rise from the accursed pit
To feast on the flesh of men."

Bryce's jaw dropped. *Holy shit*, he thought, *she's talking about my theory*. He gave Culley a sidelong glance and saw that his eyes, too, had gone wide; he had made the connection to Bryce's theory, as well.

Cătălina saw the surprise on their faces. "You have heard this before?" she asked.

"No," Bryce said, "not exactly. It' just sounds an awful lot like a theory that I developed."

"Thee-o-ree." The old woman wrinkled her brow.

"Speculație," Mariana translated. Even though she seemed inattentive, she was listening to every word.

"Ah"—Cătălina smiled, nodding slyly—"perhaps, you too, are a clarvăzător."

Bryce's face became confused; he was about to ask what she meant, but Mariana beat him to it. "A seer," she translated. "Clairvoyant."

"I don't know about that," Bryce said, chuckling. He paused, and then said, "Can you tell us how to stop this thing—does it have any weaknesses . . . can it be killed?"

A dour look came over her face. "The *Neuri* cannot be killed," Cătălina insisted. "It is said that its wounds heal instantly."

Culley and Bryce looked to each other. "It must have some weakness," Bryce implored.

"The *Neuri* is a creature of the night," the old women assured, "its eyes cannot abide the light of day."

"Well, that's good," said Bryce. He nodded to Culley, "At least it's something. Is there anything else you can think of?"

"Some legends say, if the *Neuri* is wounded by a weapon of silver, its wounds will heal more slowly—but I do not know if this is true."

"That's okay," said Bryce. "What else do the legends say?"

"It is said that the *Neuri* has the strength of a hundred men, and that its ears can hear a cloud floating across the night sky. It moves through the forest faster than the falcon flies, and its nose can smell the fear in men's hearts, as they lay asleep in their beds. Even in the blackest darkness of Hades' pit, the *Neuri's* eyes can see; it is a demon from the deepest bowels of Hell, and no mortal man can kill it."

Bryce's eyes had gone wide, and so had Culley's. The old woman's description was a lot scarier for people who had actually seen the giant beast. "Is there anything else?" asked Bryce.

Mariana rose from the couch, and said, "We've talked enough, Străbunică needs her rest." The look on her face showed that she would brook no argument.

Culley and Bryce both smiled kindly and rose to their feet. They thanked Cătălina and Mariana for their time and headed for the stairs.

"There is something they must know," Cătălina insisted loudly.

Culley and Bryce turned to face her. She had risen to her feet, and Mariana was holding her arm.

"The *Neuri* has always remained hidden from the eyes of man. Only those it kills have seen its face. If you have seen the beast, you are in danger . . . it will come for you."

Neither of them knew what to say. Finally, Culley said, "Okay . . . um, thank you, ma'am. We'll do our best to be careful."

"Listen for those who whisper," she added. "They will warn

you of danger."

"Those who whisper?" Culley asked, a puzzled look on his face.

Bryce's eyes went wide. He hadn't told Culley this part of the story, but he was sure he knew what the old woman meant. Sam Nightfeather had talked about lost spirits—Wanagi Nuni—when Bryce had told him about the whispering shadows he and Jackson had imagined. Bryce hadn't paid much attention to Nightfeather's statement, he didn't believe in ghosts; but now, Cătălina was talking about the same thing.

"The souls of those killed by the *Neuri* never rest," she told Culley. "They walk the earth forever as whispering shadows."

" . . . Okay," Culley said. "We'll . . . ah, keep an ear out." He said it with all sincerity. At this point, he was open to anything. They thanked both of them again and headed down the stairs.

When they walked out of the café, Culley asked Bryce how he was getting home. "Just drop me off at Western Auto," Bryce said. "Jackson gets off work in about an hour and I'm riding with him."

Culley nodded and headed for the car, but Bryce didn't move. "Can you give me just a minute?" Bryce asked. "I need to do something." He turned and went back into the restaurant.

Culley smiled, he knew what the kid was up to.

Mariana was standing at the back counter writing in a ledger; Bryce made his way across the room to talk to her.

"Excuse me," Bryce said. "I was—"

"Sure, I'd love to," Mariana interrupted. She never looked up from her ledger.

" . . . Um, w-what?" Bryce stammered.

"I said yes," Mariana repeated, still focused on her paperwork.

"But I didn't—"

"You asked me out, and I said yes," she asserted, finally meeting his eyes. "What's so hard to understand?"

He presented a big grin. "What—are you a psychic or something?" He winced and bit his tongue the very second the words left his lips. Bryce had just asked the great-granddaughter of a Gypsy fortune-teller if she was psychic.

God, I'm a complete idiot . . .

"Be here next Sunday at 2:00 p.m.," Mariana said.

"But where—"

"Just be here," she insisted, "you don't need to bring anything; we're going on a picnic. Now *leave*—I have work to do."

Bryce's mouth was open and even moving slightly, but no words were coming out. He turned and walked toward the door of the café, confused, shaking his head. He had just made a date with a gorgeous young woman, and he had *no idea* how he'd done it.

CHAPTER 13

The River

BRYCE McNEEL OPENED HIS EYES just before the alarm went off. He rolled over and looked at the calendar on the wall; there was a red circle around today's date—Sunday, December 8. He'd been looking forward to this morning for the past six days, his picnic with Mariana, the amazing young woman he'd met at Cătălina's Café.

His eyes drifted toward the bottom of the calendar, the only other day circled in red was Sunday, December 22—the winter solstice, and the last full moon of the season. Bryce rolled over, pulled the blanket up under his chin, and mused about all that had happened.

The last couple of months had been the most stressful he'd ever known; life or death situations weren't something he was accustomed to. The reality that a creature like this actually existed was more than anyone could've dealt with, and the day-to-day effort of trying to keep everyone safe had been exhausting.

The last six days, however, had felt different. While he hadn't let his guard down for even one minute, the anticipation of today's picnic with Mariana had made his life feel easier, somehow—even enjoyable. Bryce had gone out with plenty of girls over the years, but something about this young woman was different, special; no one he'd ever dated in the past had turned him into a babbling idiot.

Last Monday, when they left Cătălina's Café and drove to Western Auto to meet Jackson, he and Culley had sat in the cruiser and talked for a while.

"So what do you make of everything the old woman said," Culley had asked.

"Well, most legends contain at least a little bit of truth," Bryce said, "they just get blown out of proportion over the years. Knowing what's true and what's exaggerated is the hard part."

"So which parts do you believe?"

". . . That rhyme she recited sounded an awful lot like my theory," Bryce noted, smiling.

"Yeah, I noticed that," Culley said.

"And that part about its eyes not being able to abide bright lights and that it sees well in the dark," Bryce suggested. "Maybe that's why it didn't leave that dark mineshaft and come after you."

Culley shuddered at the memory. "Yeah," he said. "I sorta figured that part out for myself."

"That bit about the werewolf being able to hear a cloud float by, smell people's fear, and all that other jazz—my guess is: it probably just means that it has really good senses. I don't think it's faster than a falcon, but this thing does move quicker than anything I've ever seen."

Culley nodded his agreement vehemently. He knew how fast the creature had covered the same ground that had taken him over two hours. He said, "What do you think about the wounds healing instantly part, and about weapons made of silver."

Bryce knitted his brow and nodded thoughtfully. "I don't know what to think about the wounds healing instantly part," he said. "But using silver to fight evil has been associated with various mythologies and folklores for millennia"—he paused, and then added—"the name Cătălina uses for the creature: the

Neuri; that comes from Greek mythology."

"Hmm." Culley nodded. "So what's the deal with silver?"

"Well, you've heard of the whole, 'you need a silver bullet to kill a werewolf' thing, right?"

"Sure," said Culley. "Anyone who watches old horror movies has heard of that."

"Exactly," said Bryce, "it's mostly a Hollywood invention. However, there *is* some historical fact behind it. As far back as the early 1800s, silver bullets have been mentioned in literature and other writings."

"Really?"

"Mm-hmm, the renowned author and poet *Sir Walter Scott* in a personal letter to his good friend and fellow poet *George Ellis* back in 1808, called *Napoleon Bonaparte* an *evil demon*, and suggested that he needed to be shot with a silver bullet."

"No kidding?" Culley said.

"You know how in the old horror movies, vampires were afraid of mirrors and they didn't have a reflection?" Bryce asked.

"Sure."

"Well, the origin of that myth is due to the fact that the first mirrors were made from a piece of polished silver, and later on, even glass mirrors had a pure, silver-leaf backing."

"Well I'll be . . ." Culley said, fascinated.

"The historical use of silver to combat evil goes back a long way," he continued. "In ancient times, sickness and disease were thought to be caused by evil spirits and demons—even to this day, we still say, 'God bless you', when someone sneezes—even spoiled food and bad water were labeled as 'Works of the Devil'."

"Back around 400 B.C., when the ancient Greeks began using

silver containers to keep water and other liquids fresh, and silver-dust to treat infected wounds, it was thought by the masses that silver could be used to combat evil. Silver amulets were all the rage."

"Like the one the old Gypsy woman had," Culley eagerly pointed out.

"Exactly."

Culley cocked his head, puzzled. "Silver can keep water fresh and disinfect wounds?"

"You bet," said Bryce. "You know the old tradition of tossing a coin into a wishing-well?"

"Yeah."

"That began with people tossing silver coins into a village's water supply to keep it pure."

"Is that right?" said Culley, nodding.

"Back in the old west," Bryce went on, "they used to keep a solid-silver ladle inside the water-barrels on wagon trains so it would stay fresh longer; and they'd drop a silver coin inside their milk jugs to keep them from going sour."

Culley was smiling at him, amazed by the young man's knowledge.

"As far as wound-treatment is concerned," Bryce went on. "Colloidal silver was one of the most widely used bactericides available, until penicillin came into widespread use around 1940."

Culley knitted his brow and grinned. "How do you know all this stuff? My head's about to pop just trying to keep up with you."

"Sorry," Bryce said. "I kinda get off on a tangent sometimes"—he paused—"My point is: there's a whole bunch of facts—*and* folklore—about silver, and while it does have some very unique properties, I have no idea if a silver bullet would do more damage than a regular one"—Bryce shrugged, looking a little embarrassed—"I guess I should've just said that to begin with, huh?"

"Nah," Culley said indulgently. "It was all real interesting." Then he asked, "So, what do you think about the part where she said that it's gonna come after us. Do you believe that part?"

"Well, I don't buy the part about it being some kind of evil demon from Hell that's out to get us; but once a predator has your scent—yeah—it can track you. I read an article once about an African lion that tracked down the poacher who killed several members of his pride. A week later, and over fifty miles away, the lion killed the man in his own backyard."

Culley hadn't liked that explanation at all, and the look on his face showed it. He said, "What about the whispering shadows thing?"

Bryce and Jackson had convinced themselves that they'd imagined the whispering in those dark woods thirteen weeks ago, but after hearing both Sam Nightfeather and Cătălina Pătrașcu attest to their existence, he was starting to wonder. Still, Bryce shook his head, "I don't believe in ghost stories."

When Jackson walked out of Western Auto, Bryce shook Culley's hand and told him to be careful; they agreed to stay in touch. The look on Jackson's face when he saw him stepping out of Culley's cruiser had been priceless.

They hopped into the Camaro and headed for the highway. The first thing he told Jackson was that Culley had found Wendy Walker's other earring. Jackson had been horrified.

A moment later, the two boys passed over the bridge at Shambles Wash, and an icy chill enveloped them both. The knowledge of Wendy Walker's hideous death would taint that place forever.

The drive home had been too short; so after arriving at their grandparents' house, they sat in the car and finished talking. Jackson was shocked by everything Bryce had learned over the past few hours; his mouth had been slightly agape for most of the conversation. It wasn't until Bryce spoke of Mariana that Jackson's trepidation had eased, and the tension lifted from his face; a sly smile formed on his lips.

"You dog," Jackson said, nodding. "In the middle of all this shit, you manage to pick up a hottie."

A goofy grin painted Bryce's face. "She really is," he said, laughing; it was almost a giggle.

"When do I get to meet her?" Jackson asked.

"Never," he said impassively, "do you think I'm an idiot?"

They laughed. It had felt good to laugh. All the horrors of the past couple of months was enough to drive even the strongest person crazy.

His grandma's voice ended Bryce's ruminations. "I ain't runnin' a dang restaurant here," she hollered. "If you wanna eat, get your butt outta bed." There were no rainy days or Sunday morning naps on a cattle ranch; Bryce had plenty of chores to do before he met Mariana at 2:00 p.m.

AFTER HE HAD FINISHED HIS WORK, Bryce cleaned the inside of the old International Harvester and then washed it. Washing the old truck was a lot like polishing a turd. No matter how hard he rubbed . . . it was still a piece of shit.

He grabbed a shower, and then went to his closet to find something to wear. December could be quite chilly, but the weather outside today was perfect for a picnic: not a cloud in the sky and only a light, fitful breeze drifted through the trees. Bryce chose a red-and-gray long-sleeve flannel shirt, a pair of Wrangler jeans and his best Justin Roper boots. He looked in the mirror and combed his hair, frowned, and then gave up—it was what it was. He made his way to the old pickup truck and headed for Silver Canyon.

His first stop was Reilly's IGA Grocery store for a bouquet of flowers. With the exception of a corsage for formal dances at school, he had never bought flowers for someone before, but somehow, it felt completely natural. When Bryce pulled alongside Cătălina's Café and parked, he suddenly felt nervous; taking a deep breath, he left the bouquet of flowers on the bench-seat of the pickup and headed around front. As he approached the door, Bryce vowed to himself that he wouldn't mention the werewolf; today would be about Mariana.

The café was closed on Sundays, but the door was unlocked, Bryce tapped on the glass and let himself in. Mariana was a vision. She was at a table near the back of the café placing food inside two wicker picnic baskets. Bryce stood in the doorway, a smile spanning his face. Lifting his hand, he offered a quick wave—and then proceeded to trip over the floor mat with his first step forward.

God, I'm an idiot, he thought, stumbling forward.

Mariana smiled, pressing her lips together, trying not to laugh; she lifted her eyebrows sympathetically—*he's so cute*—it was like watching a clumsy puppy frolicking around the yard.

"Are you okay?" she asked, taking a step forward.

Bryce chuckled, his face reddening. "I'm fine," he said, embarrassed by the pride-erasing move.

"Do you think you can make it across the room without breaking something," she teased, "and give me a hand?"

"I make *no guarantees*..." he jested, heading across the room.

The two picnic baskets that sat atop the table were enormous, and were so packed with food that the lids stood ajar. Mariana's smile had been angelic as Bryce approached. She turned, saying that she would be right back, and disappeared into the back room. He sighed silently as he watched her move away; even in a pair of jeans and a sweater, her grace and beauty were enchanting.

As he waited for Mariana to return, an uneasy thought occurred to him: he had never introduced himself to her—she didn't even know his name.

As if on cue, Mariana entered the room carrying a large blanket in her arms. She said, "Bryce, will you please carry the baskets out to the truck?"

He hesitated briefly, surprised by his own name. "Sure," he said, smiling curiously. He hefted the large, wicker panniers and headed for the door.

How does she know my name? He wondered . . . *and how in the heck does she know I have a truck?*

They made their way outside and Bryce placed the baskets in the bed of the truck behind the cab. He jerked opened the passenger-side door with a loud, grinding squeak, and then placed Mariana's blanket in the middle of the bench-seat. With a secretive smile, he strategically positioned the bouquet of flowers atop the blanket.

He turned to Mariana, smiling. "Where to?" he asked, offering to help her up into the high truck.

One hand on her hip, she outstretched the other. "I'll drive," she said, with a determined smile.

He lifted an eyebrow at the suggestion. "This old truck is—"

"Keys," she said, thrusting her hand closer.

"Can you drive a manual trans—"

"Keys," she insisted.

It wasn't that he was being sexist; the old vehicle was just extremely hard to drive. "Its three-on-the-tree," Bryce said, explaining that the truck's transmission was a 3-speed column-shifter located behind the steering wheel.

" 'Three-on-the-tree', four-on-the-floor, whatever," Mariana said, "give me the keys!"

Bryce smiled and gave her the keys. "It's all yours."

Mariana made her way around the truck and yanked open the old creaking door. Bryce hopped in riding shotgun. Foot on the brake, she pushed in the rigid clutch and moved the shifter up, out of first gear, and then slid it forward into neutral. Inserting the key into the ignition, Mariana pushed the gas pedal halfway to the floor, pulled out the knob on the manual choke, and fired up the old engine. Revving the motor slightly, she slowly pushed in the choke knob until it purred like a kitten. Bryce lifted an eyebrow; he hadn't thought she'd be able to start the old truck, but Mariana had gone through the motions with flawless economy, better than he himself could have done.

She glanced at the flowers next to her on the seat. "Are those for me?" she asked, with a captivating smile.

Bryce grinned. He had an a*w-shucks* look about his face, pleased with his efforts.

"You're sweet," she said, touching his hand. Pushing in the clutch, she moved the shifter back-and-down, and dropped it into first gear. Giving the old truck a little gas, she eased away from the curb flawlessly. Maneuvering the stiff steering wheel, she skillfully manhandled the old vehicle around the block, and then headed south along Main Street, picking up speed.

Mariana double-clutched the old truck as she shifted into second gear, using two separate but fluid motions. Working the old clutch, she moved the shifter up-and-forward into neutral, then revving the engine slightly, she clutched again, pushing the shifter forward-and-up into second gear. It was perfect—smoother than a politician's tongue on Election Day.

Bryce's mouth dropped open slightly, even he and Grandpa ground the gears most of the time when they shifted the old International into second gear. Mariana's driving was impeccable.

"Where did you learn to drive?" Bryce asked, amazed by the young woman's skill.

"Oh, here and there," she said, shrugging, as if it were nothing.

As they left Silver Canyon and headed south on Highway 50, Bryce asked where they would be picnicking.

"I know a beautiful spot right on the river," she replied. "It's not too far from here."

Bryce smiled cheerfully, and watched the green countryside roll by his window; but as they passed over the bridge at Shambles Wash, his face became severe.

"Is something wrong?" Mariana asked intuitively.

"No, not at all," Bryce said, feigning a smile.

"You knew the girl who went missing here," she said.

Bryce wasn't sure if she was asking, or making a statement. Mariana seemed to know a lot more about him than he did about her.

"Yeah, I knew her," he said, gazing out the window despondently. She could tell he didn't want to discuss it; nothing more was said.

After another mile or so, Mariana slowed the truck and turned off the highway onto a dirt road. They crossed over the metal grid of a teeth-rattling cattle-guard, and then headed across the open pasture toward a heavily forested tree line in the distance.

"Whose land is this?" Bryce asked.

"Străbunică's."

"Your great-grandmother's," he said, remembering.

Mariana looked at Bryce, offering a pleased smile. "Not much farther," she said.

They followed the twisting turns of the bumpy dirt road for about two miles, moving through deep gullies and thickly-wooded hills. The road was treacherous and slow to traverse, not much more than a cow trail through the brush. It was a beautiful piece of property, however, and reminded Bryce greatly of his grandparents' ranch.

After about fifteen minutes, the shadowy woods receded and they found themselves at the top of a steep hill that overlooked a bright, verdant glade. Bryce noticed a small, cottage-style house nestled amongst a grove of large maple trees.

"Is that your great-grandmother's house?" he asked, pointing across the green field.

"Mm-hmm," she said, "but she lives in the apartment above the restaurant most of the time—it's easier for her—but I prefer to stay here, it's peaceful."

"It's beautiful," Bryce said, admiring the picturesque setting. "And you have goats." As they coasted down the tall hill, Bryce had noticed several white goats grazing in the field below.

They're Saanen goats, for milking," Mariana said. "We make cheese from their milk and use it at the café."

"Really," said Bryce. "Do *you* milk them?"

"Every afternoon," she said. "Well, except for today. I milked them earlier this morning so we could have our picnic."

"I don't think I've ever tried goat cheese."

"Well, then, you're in for a treat. I brought plenty."

The sonorous barking of a large dog drew Bryce's attention back toward the house. A large, black fur-ball strolled out into the field. "What kind of dog is that?"

"He's a mutt," she said, "mostly Chow. He keeps an eye on the place."

"Yeah, I can see that," said Bryce. "What's his name?"

"Stufos—it means, ah ... bushy."

"Good name," he said, chuckling.

Mariana pointed to the unfrequented trail ahead. It was nothing more than two wheel-ruts heading into the brush, a beaten and bowered pathway. "The river's just ahead," she assured, heading for the secluded trail, "about a half-mile."

Bryce smiled, admiring her spirit and initiative. She was amazing, and he couldn't get over how capable and self-assured she seemed.

They exited the dense tree line atop a long, grassy slope; the vista from the high vantage point was breathtaking. Beneath them in the distance lay a scenic bend of the Little Carantina River, cutting a sinuous swath through the verdurous countryside.

Putting the old truck into neutral, Mariana slowly edged forward, letting gravity do all the work. She gently pumped the brakes, descending the precipitous hill in a switchback fashion, carefully choosing her route. Bryce was awestruck at how adeptly the young woman maneuvered the vehicle around the hairpin turns of the strenuous, serpentine path. The shocks and springs of the old International squeaked and popped as they bounced over the rugged terrain.

About two-thirds of the way down the steep escarpment, Mariana parked the pickup perpendicular to the hill's slope. The high grass near the bottom of the hill concealed large rocks, and it wasn't safe to drive any farther. The final hundred yards to the river's edge would be traveled on foot.

Mariana took the large blanket, and her bouquet of flowers, and headed down the steep, grassy slope. She moved cautiously, mindful of the large rocks hidden in the knee-high grass. Hefting the two large picnic baskets, Bryce followed her closely. While he was also being mindful, it wasn't due to the hidden rocks; the gentle curve and graceful flow of Mariana's form had captivated *his* attention.

As they reached the river's edge, Bryce saw why Mariana had chosen this particular location. A huge sandstone ledge jutted out into the river about a foot above water level. Its top was perfectly flat, and it formed a natural pier that extended out from the riverbank about thirty feet.

"This is awesome," Bryce said, as they made their way out onto the rock formation. He put down the heavy baskets and flexed his hands.

Mariana smiled graciously. "I found it a few months ago," she said, handing her bouquet to Bryce. She unfolded the large blanket and gave it a quick flick of her wrists; with a loud snap, it opened flawlessly and floated down, spreading over the sandstone. Bryce marveled at her; everything she did was graceful.

Walking to the edge of the rock, Bryce dropped to one knee; he reached down and cupped a handful of water. "Too bad its cold," he commented, staring into the murky depths, "this would be a great place to swim."

Mariana didn't respond; she was busy unpacking the picnic baskets. "Are you hungry, Bryce?"

He rose to his feet and walked toward her, smiling. "How is it that you know my name?" he asked playfully. "I never told you my name."

"Small town," she shrugged, not meeting his eyes, still unpacking the baskets.

Bryce took a seat on the blanket next to her, looking at all the food. "Think you brought enough?" he quipped.

Mariana elbowed him in the ribs playfully. "I like to eat," she said, smiling. "Plus, I thought you might like to try a little bit of everything."

"Hey, I'm not complaining," Bryce said, chuckling. "I'm starved. Breakfast was a long time ago."

Mariana held what looked like a deviled egg up to Bryce's mouth. "Open," she demanded, and then shoveled it in.

"Mm," he mumbled around the huge mouthful, "'at's gweat"—he finished chewing and swallowed—"What was that?"

She already had bite number two ready to go, some kind of dumpling or something. "Open." This time Mariana giggled as she shoved the entire thing into his mouth.

Bryce cupped his hand over his mouth, trying not to laugh. "'at's gweat, too," he mumbled unintelligibly.

Mariana had bite number three ready, but Bryce stopped her. "How about we try a plate?" he said, chuckling, trying to swallow his last bite.

Mariana stuck out her lower lip, feigning disappointment, then prepared him a paper plate filled with a little of everything.

They laughed and talked, Bryce devoured the food, commenting constantly that everything was delicious, especially the goat cheese; they couldn't have asked for a more beautiful day, and the location Mariana had chosen was beyond compare.

"You know," said Bryce, "I've lived here my entire life, how is it I've never met you before?"

"I've only lived here for about six months."

"Ah, well, that explains it," he said. "And since I haven't seen you around school—I'm guessing that you've already graduated?"

"Last June," she affirmed.

"Not many people move '*to*' Bane County—*especially* young people," he pointed out. "Most can't wait to leave"—he chuckled—"what brought you *here* of all places?"

Bryce noticed Mariana seemed to stiffen slightly at the question; she hesitated, and there was a hint of sadness in her eyes. He quickly interjected: "I'm sorry. I'm being too nosy—I ask too many questions—bad habit of mine."

"No, no, it's okay, I just"—she paused, taking a breath—"when I was fifteen-years-old I lost my mother to cancer. It was an extremely hard time in my life, but eventually, I learned to live with it. My father, however, couldn't deal with the loss; he started drinking too much. We tried everything to help him, but"—she took another breath. Bryce could see her eyes welling—"just after Christmas, last year, he ran his car off the highway one night . . . drunk . . . he died."

Bryce placed his hand atop hers. "I am *so* sorry . . . I didn't mean to dredge up those bad memories."

"It's okay," she said, forcing a smile. "Talking's good. It helps you heal"—she squeezed his hand—"anyway, I finished out the school year, graduated, and moved here to help my great-grandmother. She needs the help, and I really needed a change of scenery."

"Well," Bryce said. "I feel terrible about the circumstances that brought you here—but . . . I'm glad you're here."

"Thanks." She smiled and kissed his cheek.

Trying to lift the somber mood, Bryce said, "I'm gonna put my feet in the water." He yanked off his boots and socks, with a silly grin on his face, and rolled his jeans up to his knees. The bright sun had heated the sandstone beneath them and it radiated warmth.

Mariana watched with a big smile about her face as Bryce moved to the edge of the rock formation; sitting down, he dunked his feet and legs into the cold river. "Yikes, that's cold!"

Mariana laughed, and then said, "Okay." She peeled off her shoes and socks, and joined him.

Sitting abreast, hips touching, splashing their feet in the cold water, they talked and laughed, and nudged shoulders as they bantered with each other.

"So how'd you know how to drive my grandpa's old International?" Bryce asked.

Mariana shrugged, acting secretive. "It's no big deal," she finally admitted. "My grandfather taught me how to drive in an old truck much like that one."

"Ah, I gotcha," he said.

"Do you live with your grandparents?" she asked.

Bryce nodded. "Yeah, I lost my parents, too; but I was only four, so I really don't remember much."

"I'm sorry," she said, taking his hand. "What happened?"

"My parents worked for the U.S. Fish and Wildlife Service—they were biologists," he added proudly. "They were working up at Lake Argent, doing some water testing, or something. The U.S. Fish and Wildlife Service had an old cabin up there by the lake for their employees to use. From what I understand, there was a leak in the propane system—it exploded . . . the cabin burnt to the ground."

"My God, that's horrible," she said, squeezing his hand.

Bryce nodded. His lips were taut. "It was a long time ago—1978. I was only four . . . I barely remember."

"Still," Mariana said, laying her head on his shoulder. "What were their names?"

Bryce smiled wistfully. "Brian—Brian and Lori McNeel."

"That's nice," she said.

Changing the subject, Bryce asked, "Didn't I see a radio in one of those baskets?"

Mariana smiled and retrieved the radio; spinning the dial, she stopped on an easy-listening station. *Bryan Adams* sang,

"Everything I do—I do it for you."

She held out her hand. "Dance with me."

"I'm not very good," he confessed.

Bryce had never been one to believe in love-at-first-site; but gazing into Mariana's pale-blue eyes, he felt as though he'd known her his entire life. She was gorgeous, mysterious, and yet, it was like spending time with an old friend. Bryce had no doubt; he was falling for her.

Holding each other close, dancing away the afternoon, they talked and kissed, and then laid lazily atop their sun-warmed blanket, holding hands, and gazing into the dusty-blue heavens.

As the ever-changing shapes of billowy-white clouds scudded across the late-afternoon sky, Bryce and Mariana pointed, and remarked as to their imagined likenesses—until at last, they slowly drifted off to sleep.

THE SUN FELL BELOW THE HORIZON, setting the western sky ablaze with a warm orange glow. Bryce and Mariana sat bolt upright, something had awakened them—a sound. They looked at each other, eyes wide, realizing they had fallen asleep—and now, night had arrived.

A metallic scraping sound reached their ears; they turned, lifting their eyes up the steep hill. There, in front of the old pickup, stood a gigantic gray beast, its clawed hand resting atop the truck's hood. Again, the creature scraped its taloned fingers across the metal, announcing its presence.

Hearts pounding, enveloped by fear, they stood atop their blanket, paralyzed.

"Bryce?" Mariana whimpered—it was enough to snap him out of his fear-laced trance.

Why didn't I bring a gun?

He glanced frantically for a weapon; the only thing they had was a flimsy, blunt-tipped bread knife. He looked up and down the riverbank, searching for a tree they could climb; the closest one was over fifty yards away . . . there was nowhere to run, no way to fight—they were trapped, defenseless.

"Bryce," she whimpered again, her voice quavering with fear.

He turned to Mariana, his eyes were filled with sorrow; there was nothing he could do. Forcing a wan smile, he pulled her close and kissed her. As Mariana's pale-blue eyes filled with tears, Bryce knew there was one final thing he needed to say to her—and this would be his last chance. Taking a breath, he uttered those three-little-words into her ear . . . those three little life-changing words that would make all the difference . . . "Can you swim?"

Bryce didn't wait for the answer. He jumped into the cold dark river yanking Mariana behind him. "Swim!" he yelled.

The river was wide, nearly a hundred yards across, but the middle of the bend was strewn with large boulders; tiny rock islands covered with tufts of weed and grass.

"Swim for the rocks!" he shouted. They were side by side, swimming like mad; Mariana motioned that she understood. Even though they were barefoot, trying to swim in jeans and shirts was extremely grueling, and they fought feverishly against the brutal current.

Over the sounds of their flailing limbs and frantic splashing, Bryce could hear the werewolf rushing down the steep hill. The thunderous sounds of pounding feet, and the avalanche of rocks that followed, had been more chilling than the cold water in which he swam. He didn't dare look back. Bryce knew that any second he would hear the tumultuous *splash* of the giant beast crashing into the river after them.

As Bryce reached the stony islands, a blood-curdling roar

rent the air. He clambered up the rock, reaching back to pull Mariana along with him. Making their way to the top of a large boulder, they chanced a brief glance at the riverbank. The giant creature stood atop the sandstone ledge, baring its teeth and claws, huge yellow eyes gleaming angrily in the fading twilight.

Those fiery eyes had horrified Bryce. It was as though Hell itself burned within those bulging black globes. He wondered if Mariana's great-grandmother had been right. Maybe this amber-eye beast *was* some kind of demon.

"*It will come for you,*" the old woman had told him.

Again, the beast roared; it kicked one of the picnic baskets into the river, and then proceeded to rip everything else to shreds in a fit of rage. Mariana buried her face in Bryce's chest, shivering from both the cold water and the sight of the hideous creature.

The werewolf leapt from the end of the rocky outcropping to the sandy bank of the river; Bryce's mouth fell open, the creature had cleared almost forty feet in a single bound. With another vicious roar, the beast made his way into the dark water—Bryce tensed and his eyes went wide.

Oh, shit, here it comes . . .

The beast waded into the river, bearing its teeth and claws; but then stopped as the water reached its thighs. It stood there glaring, growling, swaying in the water; then slowly, it slogged back up the riverbank, stalking back and forth at the water's edge like a caged animal.

"What's it doing?" Mariana asked. Her voice trembled from the cold.

" . . . I'm not sure."

"It's just toying with us."

. . . Maybe not, Bryce thought. He was looking at the physical

structure of the creature. It was at least eight-feet-tall, and had a heavily muscled, lanky frame. Other than its exceptionally long legs, the body was much like that of a chimpanzee or gorilla.

"It's some kind of hominid," Bryce muttered, speculating.

"What?"

"I don't think it can swim," he said.

"Wolves can swim," Mariana insisted. She was staring at the creature's huge, wolf-like head as it stalked up and down the riverbank.

"It's not a wolf," Bryce said, "it just looks like one. I think it's some kind of primate."

"What—you mean . . . like a monkey?"

"Well, more like one of the great apes, a simian. But—yeah."

"Apes can't swim?" she questioned.

"None of the higher primates can swim," Bryce said, "not even humans. People have to be taught to swim, they don't have a natural ability—and neither do apes. In the wild, large primates have a natural fear of the water."

The werewolf roared viciously and tromped back into the river until the water reached its waist.

"It doesn't look afraid to me," Mariana said, her eyes wide.

"No . . . it doesn't."

As Bryce and Mariana watched nervously, the giant creature once again exited the water and paced the riverbank, growling. Bryce looked at the werewolf's enormous clawed hands; they hung to the beast's knees. Its long, spindly fingers and immense hooked claws were unlike anything he had ever seen.

Those aren't just the claws of a predator, Bryce thought, *those are the claws of a burrower—something that lives underground—like a mole, or a gopher.*

After a while, the monstrous beast made its way toward the dense tree line, and then disappeared into the shadowy forest.

"Do you think it's leaving?" she asked.

"... I don't think so."

"... Me either."

"At least we're safe," Bryce said. *Hopefully.*

Twilight quickly turned to dusk, and dusk into night. Yesterday had been a new moon, and tonight . . . darkness would reign. They sat atop the cold, hard rock, wet and shivering. Bryce took off his flannel shirt and wrung it out the best he could.

"You need to do the same," he told Mariana, "I'll turn my back. It's going to get cold tonight, and we're not going anywhere"—he paused—"We should wring out our jeans, too."

They got undressed and dried their clothing the best they could, it was too cold to be bashful; they huddled together in a tight knot, sharing their body heat.

"Can you see anything?" Mariana asked.

"No, it's too dark; I can't even see the riverbank anymore."

As if on cue, a crunch of leaves and the snap of a twig filled the darkness. Bryce caught a glimpse of fiery eyes across the river, and a horrible stench filled the air.

That's strange, he thought, *there's not enough light to reflect in the creature's eyes.* A shudder went down his spine, and it wasn't due to the cold night air.

"What is it?" she asked, intuitively.

"It's back," he whispered softly, though he didn't know why he bothered; he figured the creature could see them as plain as day. It was nocturnal, a night hunter, its eyes were made for the darkness. An angry growl affirmed his belief.

Mariana gripped him tighter.

"I never thought I'd end up spending the night in the middle of the Little Carantina River," Bryce scoffed.

It's a *stupid* name for a river," Mariana insisted, shivering.

Why's that?"

"Do you know what Carantina means?"

"Growing up here, I guess I never really thought about it," Bryce admitted. "I just figured it was probably named after some old Spanish explorer or something."

"Oh, no, it's not Spanish," she assured. "Carantina is Romanian."

"Romanian?"

"Yes. Carantina means: Quarantine."

"Quarantine?"

"Mm-hmm. The Little 'Quarantine' River," she scoffed, "stupid name." She held him closer, shivering.

...*Maybe it isn't stupid*, Bryce wondered.

Something Sam Nightfeather said suddenly occurred to him: "*swimming keeps you alive.*" Bryce thought back to the rickety pier that barely supported his weight. If the werewolf tried to walk on that pier, its immense size would've caused it to collapse. The beast would've fallen into the river—the "Quarantine" River—the river that completely encircled Bane County.

Then, something else that Nightfeather had said occurred to Bryce; something that made him shudder, "*If you utter the name of the beast, you risk summoning it.*" Perhaps it had been a bad idea to talk about this creature after all.

Regardless, Bryce thought angrily, *Nightfeather knew a hell of a lot more about this thing than he told me.*

Time stretched and the evening grew cold; neither of them slept. A fiery-eyed monster lurked in the dark, tormenting them endlessly. Bryce trembled at the thought of what Străbunică had said, *"Even in the blackest darkness of Hades' pit, the Neuri's eyes can see."*

The next morning, they waited until the sun was well above the horizon before making their way to shore; it had been the coldest and most painful swim of their young lives.

They drove quickly to Străbunică's house, filled a bathtub with warm water, and jumped in wearing their clothes. It was extremely painful at first, but after a while, it became heavenly. Mariana slipped into some dry clothes, while Bryce borrowed her bright, flowery robe; he tossed his jeans and shirt into the clothes dryer. Even after the horrors of last night, Mariana offered a slight giggle when she saw him in the robe. Bryce just rolled his eyes.

While she boiled water for hot tea, he used the phone to call his grandparents; they had been worried sick. He gave Grandpa a quick summary and said he'd be home a little later to explain in detail.

Grandpa said he'd call the school, to say that Bryce was out sick, and would leave a message for Jackson, telling him that everything was fine. Jackson had been extremely worried this morning when Bryce missed his ride to school.

Mariana needed to check on her great-grandmother, so they finished their tea and Bryce pulled his clothes from the dryer. She would decide later if Străbunică needed to know about last night's brush with death; she was very old, and Mariana didn't want to upset her.

One thing was certain, however. Mariana would no longer be spending her nights at Great-grandmother's house in the woods.

CHAPTER 14

Dime Store Cowboys

JACKSON CAMPBELL PEEKED AROUND THE CORNER. Mr. Burrows, the school principal, stood at the other end of the long corridor trying to wipe some graffiti off of a locker. *Aimee loves Jimmy inside a heart with an arrow through it—or some such thing*, Jackson figured. He smiled slyly and padded out the side door of the high school as quietly as possible.

Keeping his head low, he skirted the long hedgerow next to the building and worked his way to the parking lot. He glanced furtively over his shoulder, then hopped into his Camaro and started the loud engine. The deep rumble of the side-exit exhaust system made him cringe. *Shit! Everybody in the building just heard that*, he thought. *Fuck it. They'll know I'm gone next period anyway.* He roared out of the parking lot.

As he turned onto Main Street, Jackson glanced to his rearview mirror; Mr. Burrows came running out the front door of the building. Jackson grinned and offered a quick wave as the car squealed around the corner.

When he found out that Bryce hadn't come home last night after his date with Mariana, and that no one knew where they were, Jackson hadn't wanted to go to school this morning, but Grandpa insisted. A few hours later, when the school's office manager gave him a message saying that Bryce was at home sick, and that he was doing fine, Jackson decided to ditch school and find out what the hell was going on. He knew he'd get in trouble for skipping, but he didn't care at this point. Something big was up; Bryce didn't do this kind of thing. He hadn't missed a day of school in his entire life. Jackson popped *Led Zeppelin IV* into the deck, floored it, and roared down the highway.

When he arrived at his grandparents' house, he headed toward the door, but then saw Bryce out back, sitting under the old maple tree. The first thing he noticed was that he didn't have a book in his hands. He had found his cousin sitting beneath that old tree hundreds of times in the past; it was his favorite spot to read. Today, however, Bryce was just sitting there, staring ahead at nothing in particular, and his face was drawn and pale.

"Bryce?" Jackson said softly, "You okay, man?"

Bryce looked at him as if he didn't understand the words, as though Jackson wasn't speaking English. Finally, he gave the barest shake of his head. "No . . . no, I'm not."

"What happened?" Jackson questioned gently. He could see that his cousin wasn't well. His eyes were glassy and red, and his nose was runny; he looked as though he was coming down with a cold. Beneath the surface, however, Jackson noticed something else: fear. Bryce was scared, horrified. Again, he urged gently, "Tell me what happened, man."

Bryce told him—told him everything that had taken place the night before—and when he had finished, Jackson, too, was horrified.

"I was wrong," Bryce continued. He offered Jackson a grave look.

"About what?"

"About this thing being . . . an animal, some kind of unknown species."

"What do you mean?"

Bryce locked eyes with him. "This thing is evil, Jackson. It really is some kind of monster."

He was shocked to hear Bryce say something like this, he was the most logical and grounded person on the planet. "I'm sorry," Jackson said jokingly, trying to lighten the mood. "I was looking for Bryce McNeel—you know, *the scientist?*—he looks a lot like you, but—he's not out of his *friggin'* mind."

He ignored Jackson's lame attempt at humor. "You weren't there," he said. "You didn't see it. This thing didn't act like an animal—like a predator."

"What did it do?"

"Predators are efficient killers," Bryce pointed out. "They sneak up on their prey, jump out and grab it by the throat—go for the quick kill—it's all about food. We were asleep, Jackson; it could have easily walked right up and killed us, but it didn't. This thing *wanted* us to know it was there, it *wanted* us to be afraid, it wanted us to *know* we were about to die; and then, when we escaped—it went completely insane. Animals don't act like that; they don't have the mental capacity for complex emotions. The type of extreme fury that this thing exhibited, the way it behaved, it was almost . . . human."

"Human?" Jackson shot him a disbelieving look.

"I'm not saying it's a person who turned into a werewolf," Bryce clarified. "I'm just saying it's not . . . an animal."

"Well, what the hell is it then?"

Bryce sneezed and blew his nose on a paper towel that he had stuffed in his shirt pocket. Sitting on that cold rock all night in damp clothing had taken its toll on his health.

"God bless you," Jackson said.

Bryce met his eyes. "You believe in God?"

"You know I do," said Jackson. "Maybe not some old guy with a long white beard floating around up in the sky watching over us, but"—he motioned to the world around them—"all this didn't happen by accident."

"... Do you believe in the Devil?"

"Where are you going with this, man?"

"I think Mariana's great-grandmother might've been right," he said. "I think this thing is some kind of—demon."

Jackson didn't know how to respond to that. He opened his mouth, he even moved his lips, but no words would come out. Finally, he managed, "Why?"

"... Its eyes."

"Its eyes? What—I don't..."

"They glowed in the dark," Bryce said, "like they were on fire."

"Lots of animals have eyes that shine in the dark," said Jackson. "You know that. I don't see what the big de—"

"There was no light," Bryce interrupted. "It was a new moon. It was pitch-black outside."

Jackson looked at him, not fully understanding.

"You need some kind of light source to create eyeshine," Bryce insisted. "It reflects off the tapetum lucidum behind the retina."

"The *what?*"

"The tapetu—" Bryce took a breath. "The shiny coating on the back of an animal's eyes that reflects light; it helps them see in the dark. The coating only reflects light, Jackson; it doesn't create it. This thing's eyes glowed as if they were on fire—in complete darkness. I sat on that rock all night, watching, and the only thing I could see in the blackness ... were those fiery eyes."

"Jesus," Jackson said, the hair prickled on the back of his neck. He had no reason to doubt Bryce; he was the smartest person he knew. Hell, he was the smartest person that anyone knew; but, a demon? That was a little hard to process. He swallowed hard and said, "What are we gonna do?"

"I don't know, man." Bryce shook his head despondently. "... I just don't know."

EVEN THOUGH HE HAD A COLD, and felt like crap, Bryce went to school the next day. His first stop had been Mr. Burrows' office, with Jackson in tow. He wanted to see if he could help his cousin out of the trouble that he'd gotten himself into for cutting class. Grandpa had written Jackson a note, so he wouldn't need to involve his parents; it simply said that there had been a family emergency and to please excuse him. That, and the fact that Mr. Burrows really liked Bryce, had helped Jackson dodge the bullet. He got off with a stern warning about school policy on leaving campus without permission. It hadn't hurt that Jackson was wearing a plain gray T-shirt, without some type of offensive depiction emblazoned on it. Moreover, it still had its sleeves attached—Bryce's idea.

After school, Jackson dropped off Bryce at Cătălina's Café and then headed to work at Western Auto.

"I get off work at 6:00 p.m.," Jackson said.

"Okay, I'll walk down and meet you," said Bryce.

Bryce hadn't spoken with Mariana since he dropped her off at the café yesterday morning, and wanted to make sure she was okay. The horrors of their night on the river were still fresh in his mind and he feared that it would be the same for her. He entered the café and asked a waiter if he could speak with Mariana; the man told him to take a seat and then disappeared into the back room. A moment later, he motioned for Bryce and told him that he could go upstairs.

Mariana sat on the sofa wrapped in a warm shawl sipping

a mug of hot tea; the entire apartment smelled of homemade chicken soup. The look on her face, and the pile of used tissues in the wastebasket at her feet, answered his first question.

"You got sick, too, huh?" he said, sniffling.

Mariana offered a weak smile and nodded. She patted the sofa beside her. "Come, sit—want some tea, or some soup?"

Bryce sat next to her on the sofa. "No thanks, I'm fine."

"I feel rotten," she said, laying her head on his shoulder.

"Yeah, me too," he said. "Have you gotten any sleep?"

"No, not really—nightmares."

Bryce put his arm around her. "Yeah, me too."

Mariana sneezed. "Sorry," she reached for the tissues and blew her nose, then offered the box to Bryce.

"Thanks," he said, blowing his nose. "Where's your great-grandmother?"

"She went with Uncle Felix to care for the goats."

Bryce offered her a grave look.

"Don't worry," she said. "They know to be back before sundown."

"So, you told her what happened to us?"

"She already knew; I just gave her the details."

"Already knew?" Bryce said, lifting an eyebrow.

Mariana nodded but offered no explanation.

Bryce didn't push the issue. "Where's that big cat of yours?" he said, changing the subject.

"Pisicuta?" she said, smiling. "He went with Străbunică and Uncle Felix. He always goes—he hunts for rats in the barn."

Something suddenly registered in Bryce's brain. He said, "Uncle *Felix?* You don't mean the old man that owns Pat's gas station out on Highway 50, do you?"

"Mm-hmm, he's my great-uncle—Străbunică's son. 'Pat' is short for Pătrașcu."

"Well, what do you know," Bryce said, smiling. Then he added, "The same as your last name."

Mariana furrowed her brow. "I never told you my last name."

Bryce shrugged slyly. "Small town."

Mariana smirked and elbowed him in the ribs.

Bryce kissed the top of her head and stood. "I better go, you need your rest. I just wanted to drop by real quick to check on you."

Mariana sneezed. "Thank you." Her cold seemed much worse than his.

"I guess I don't have to tell you to stay here at night, do I?" he asked.

"I don't know if I'll ever spend the night at Străbunică's house again."

"Listen," Bryce said, "if my theory is correct, this thing will be gone after the next full moon, twelve days from now."

Mariana blew her nose, she looked miserable. "Really? Why?"

"I'll explain later," said Bryce. "For now, just get some rest, and stay inside at night." He kissed her atop the head again and took a couple tissues for the road.

When he exited the café, he looked across the street toward the game warden's office; Sheriff Culley's cruiser was parked next the building. Bryce glanced at his watch; he still had a while before Jackson got off work, so he made his way across the street.

Culley was sitting across the desk from Fletcher when Bryce came through the door; both men had dour looks about their faces. Bryce knew what was wrong.

"The campers?" Bryce asked. He knew there had been two groups in The Refuge.

"Both groups were due back yesterday," Fletcher said. He shook his head sadly. "... Five people."

"Damn," Bryce said, although it was no real surprise. All of them had feared that the campers would never return.

"Two more days before we can start looking for them," Culley said. He was dreading going back into The Refuge with a search party. One thing was certain; he sure as hell wouldn't be searching after sundown.

"You look like Hell," Fletcher said to Bryce. "Are you sick?"

"... Yeah, I've got a cold," he said, blowing his nose. Then he told them how he'd caught it.

Both men were horrified that the creature had chased Bryce and Mariana into the river, barely escaping with their lives. "So, it can't swim?" Culley said.

"I guess not," Bryce replied. "Otherwise, we'd be dead."

"Je-sus Christ," said Fletcher. "You're damn lucky, kid."

Bryce didn't feel lucky, he felt like crap. He was sick and wasn't in the mood for any chitchat. He said his goodbyes and headed toward Western Auto to meet Jackson.

As he passed the Buckhorn Café the smell of food found him; he looked at his watch. It was still over an hour before Jackson got off work, so he stopped for a bowl of Adelaide's homemade chicken soup. He entered the café and took a seat at the lunch counter. His body felt chilled—he had a mild fever—and the chrome and red-vinyl stool felt cold against his body. Even the red Formica countertop felt icy beneath his palms.

"Dang, boy; you look like you've been rode hard and put up wet," Adelaide quipped. "You sick?"

"Yeah, I feel rotten," Bryce said. "Got any chicken soup?"

"You betcha; we'll get you fixed right up."

She returned shortly with a steaming bowl of soup and a large mug of hot tea. "If you were a little older, I would've put some bourbon in that tea, but you'll have to settle for honey and lemon."

Bryce smiled. "Thanks, Adelaide." He breathed in the hot steam that wafted from the bowl, trying to clear his stuffy nose. Chicken soup always made everything better.

After finishing his meal, he sat sipping his tea; his body still had a slight chill, but he felt better after the soup. He held the hot mug tightly in both hands, warming them.

"More soup, Bryce?" Adelaide asked.

He shook his head. "No, I'm full, thanks."

"Well, bless your heart," she said. "You feel better now, okay?" She placed a ticket next to his bowl.

"Thank you," Bryce said, then he glanced at the bill—three dollars and twenty cents. He took a five from his wallet and slid it across the counter. Adelaide turned to the register to make change.

"Here you go," she said, "a buck-eighty."

Bryce chuckled.

"What's so funny?"

"Oh, nothing; I was just thinking about a movie I saw a while back." He looked down at the change: a dollar bill, two quarters, and three dimes. He lifted an eyebrow; one of the dimes looked old and dull. He picked it up and checked the date. "1961," he said.

"Oh, that's a good one," said Adelaide, "anything before 1965 is pure silver."

A bell went off in Bryce's head and his eyes went wide. " . . . Ninety percent, actually," he muttered, staring at the old dime intently. "Ninety-two point-five percent is sterling."

"What's that?" Adelaide said, "I couldn't hear you."

"Oh, nothing," he said, smiling. "I was just thinking out loud." He dropped the old dime into his shirt pocket, and pushed the rest of the change across the counter to Adelaide as a tip. "Thanks; see you later." Then he hurried out the door.

"Feel better," she hollered after him.

Bryce walked briskly down the sidewalk toward Western Auto, a sly smile on his face. He couldn't wait to tell Jackson that he'd just figured out how to make silver bullets.

IT WAS WELL AFTER MIDNIGHT WHEN GRANDPA McNEEL awoke and stumbled blearily to the bathroom. *Getting old is hell,* he thought. Standing in front of the toilet, looking down, he argued with his hesitant bladder. "Come on, already—you're the one who woke *me* up."

Flushing the toilet, he glanced out the window; the light in the barn was on. "What the—who in the *hell* left the light on?" Grandpa McNeel's biggest pet peeve was wasting electricity. Whenever he would find that the lights had been left on in the guest bedroom unnecessarily, he would always shout: "Is *Claude Rains* visiting us this week?"

Wearing only a pair of faded-blue boxer shorts—the ones that never quite closed in the front—he slipped into his wife's quilted, pink housecoat that was hanging on the bathroom door. He didn't have a robe of his own; real cowboys didn't wear robes, only sissies wore robes.

He padded across the kitchen's cold linoleum floor in his bare feet, and then stepped into an oversized pair of black, knee-high rubber boots that he kept by the back door in case of rain; the rubber was icy-cold against his bare skin, and sent a shiver up his spine.

From his dog-bed in the living room, Snip lifted his head and offered a questioning whimper. "No, you stay here," said Grandpa. "I'll be right back."

Stomping across the backyard toward the barn in his squeaky footwear and tiny, hot-pink housecoat, he grumbled to himself the entire way. "Who the *hell* do these people think I am—*Tom Bodett?*—'We'll leave the light on for you,' " he said, mocking the *Motel 6* radio spot.

When he reached the door, he heard the faint *whir* of an electric motor from inside the barn. *What the—?* He flung opened the barn door to find Bryce sitting on a stool at the workbench, with a power drill in his hand.

"Bryce?" Grandpa said, surprised to see the boy.

Bryce spun around, dropping the drill on the benchtop, his hand now resting on the 12-gauge-pump at his side, eyes wide. "Grandpa?" A wide grin formed on his face. "Is that Grandma's housecoat?"

Feeling a bit flustered, and somewhat embarrassed, Grandpa said, "N-never mind that, what are you doing out here, it's after midnight."

Bryce was trying not to laugh at the sight of his grandpa in what was, essentially, a pink mini-skirt. His snow-white, bandy legs, naked as a jaybird, disappearing into those knee-high, black boots was more than Bryce could take; he burst out laughing.

Earlier that evening, when he had met Jackson at Western Auto, Bryce had been extremely excited. However, when he told him that he'd figured out how to make silver bullets, as usual, his cousin had a few questions.

"How do you know it'll even work," Jackson had asked. "I mean, it was just a movie for Chrissake. Your shotgun might explode in your hands."

"It'll work."

"How do you know?"

"I just do."

"... You really believe it's some kind of monster, don't you?" Jackson said.

"... I don't know," said Bryce.

"Do you think silver will kill it?

"I don't know—but there's twelve more days until the last full moon of the season; and if this thing shows up at one of our houses, wouldn't you like to have silver bullets, just in case?"

"... Yeah," Jackson said. "Yeah, I guess so."

"Look," Bryce said. "As soon as we get home, we'll talk with Grandpa, and then we'll make up a test-shell and try it out, okay?"

"Okay."

When they arrived home, they were surprised to find that Grandpa knew all about shooting dimes from a shotgun. He said that—like them—he too, had seen it in a movie once.

"It was 1973," Grandpa said to Bryce. "Your parents were newlyweds, and we all went down to the Rialto to see *Pat Garrett & Billy the Kid*. It starred *Kris Kristofferson* and *James Coburn,* and there was a scene where *Billy the Kid* shoots Deputy Bob Ollinger with a shotgun filled with dimes; then Billy says, 'Keep the change, Bob.' It was a dang good movie."

Grandpa walked to the corner, retrieved his old Ithaca model 37, and checked the safety. The 12-gauge-pump had been sitting in the corner by the back door for the past six weeks, loaded with double-ought buckshot. "Well, if we're gonna do this, let's get to it; supper's almost ready."

"Fried chicken with mashed potatoes and gravy," Grandma added, from the kitchen. She had been listening to every word. Together they made their way to Grandpa's workshop out in the barn and went to work.

"Bryce," Grandpa said, pointing to the shelves. "You go through my coin collection and pick out some dimes." There were dozens of quart-size Mason-jars filled with old coins lining the shelves of Grandpa's workshop. "And Jackson, you go look through that pile of scrap-lumber. Find a big piece of three-quarter-inch plywood that we can use for a target."

While the boys set about their tasks, Grandpa readied the shotgun. Working the pump, he unloaded the weapon, placing the five shells on the workbench. Then he removed the choke-tube from the gun's muzzle, replacing the full-choke with a cylinder-bore. Increasing the bore's diameter would ensure the dimes' flight through the barrel would be unrestricted.

Bryce brought a large handful of silver dimes to the workbench, piling them on top. To double-check that they would fit properly through the bore, Grandpa dropped a dime into the open chamber of the shotgun and tilted the muzzle downward; it slid through the barrel easily and fell to the ground.

Jackson returned with a half-sheet of three-quarter-inch plywood. He took a can of spray-paint and made a small circle in the center of the sheet, then leaned the piece of wood against a large stack of hay bales; the hay would provide a bulletproof backstop. It was already dark outside, so their test would need to be conducted indoors.

"Okay," Grandpa said, "let's make a silver bullet." He took a seat on the stool in front of his shotgun-shell reloading press. "Jackson, hand me one of those used hulls." He pointed to a large cardboard box under the workbench that was filled with the hulls of used shotgun shells. Whenever they went bird hunting, they always recovered their spent shells for reloading.

Grandpa inspected the hull for defects, and then placed it into the first station of the reloading press. Working the lever, he popped out the old primer and reshaped the hull; then moving to the second station, he inserted a new primer, worked the lever again, and seated it in place.

Inspecting his work, Grandpa placed the hull into the third station. He worked the lever and added the proper amount of powder to charge the hull with a magnum load. "Bryce, hand me one of those plastic wads." He pointed to a large bag at the end of the workbench.

Studying the wad intently, Grandpa said, "We're gonna need to remove the shot-cup from this wad to make the dimes fit." He pulled out his pocketknife and trimmed the plastic petals from the end of the wad; placing it into the hull, he again worked the lever, seating the plastic wad atop the powder.

"All right," Grandpa said. "We're ready for the dimes." One by one, he carefully placed the dimes into the hull, tamping each one into place with a small wooden dowel. When he had finished, there was a total of eighteen silver dimes.

"A buck-eighty," Jackson said, smiling.

Grandpa placed the shell back on the loading press, and moved it through the final two stations, crimping and then sealing the newly made shell. He held it out to Bryce with a smile. "Here you go—one silver bullet."

Bryce met Grandpa's smile with his own, and took the shell in his hand, hefting its weight. "Let's see what this baby can do." He took up the shotgun and slid the shell into its magazine tube. Checking the safety, he worked the pump, racking the round into the chamber, and then took a position about ten yards from the target.

"It's gonna be loud as Hell inside this barn," Grandpa said. He handed Bryce a pair of foam earplugs. "Jackson and I can just use our fingers."

Bryce stuffed the plugs into his ears and took aim at the target. Jackson and Grandpa stepped behind him and plugged their ears. "Fire in the hole," Bryce said, flicking off the safety; then he squeezed the trigger. Inside the huge barn, the sound was deafening, resounding off the roof and walls.

Together they trotted quickly to the plywood to survey the damage.

"What the hell?" said Jackson. "That ain't worth a shit!"

Grandpa smacked him on the back of the head for cursing.

"Ow! Sorry, Grandpa," Jackson said, rubbing his head. "But it isn't worth a . . . crap."

Jackson was right. The dimes had created a large shot-pattern, considering how close Bryce had been to the target, and only a few of the coins actually penetrated the sheet of plywood. Most of the dimes were embedded in the wood, and some had just made a dent and bounced off.

"Apparently, the ballistic-coefficient of a dime ain't worth two-cents," Grandpa quipped, attempting to lighten the mood; he could see that Bryce was crestfallen.

"Guess you can't believe everything you see in the movies," Jackson added.

"Damn," Bryce muttered. "It was like shooting a bunch of miniature Frisbees."

"Well, it was worth a try," Grandpa said. He clapped Bryce on the shoulder. "Come on; let's head in, your grandma's got supper ready."

Bryce hung his head and shuffled out of the barn . . . *Damn*.

"You stayin' for supper, Jackson?" Grandpa asked.

"Heck yeah!" he said. "Fried chicken."

All throughout dinner, and the rest of the evening, Bryce had been quiet and reserved. Grandpa knew that he was disheartened over the failure of his silver bullet idea, and probably needed some space, so he had just left him alone.

Though it may have seemed as though Bryce was sulking over a failure—something a person with his level of intelligence would be unaccustomed to—in actuality, he was just thinking. He had gone into his *problem-solving* mode, and he couldn't turn it off until he had a solution.

Late that night, lying awake in bed, staring at the ceiling, the answer suddenly came to him. Bryce hopped out of bed and got dressed, then padded quietly through the dark house. Taking his grandpa's shotgun from the corner by the back door, he headed back to the barn, and Grandpa's workshop; he had some work to do. However, before Bryce could finish his task, he'd had an unexpected visitor . . .

"Ha-ha-ha," Grandpa mocked loudly, "Real funny. Now what the heck are you doing out here?"

Bryce did his best to rein in his laughter; he would've paid a hundred bucks for a camera. Seeing his grandpa in that hot-pink, quilted housecoat—that was half his size—was definitely one for the scrapbooks.

" . . . I couldn't sleep," Bryce finally managed. "And I figured out how to make the dimes work."

Grandpa made his way over to the workbench, his bare feet squeaking loudly inside the over-sized rubber boots with each step forward. Bryce pressed his lips together, trying not to laugh. If Snip were here, he'd be running circles around the man, thinking that he had a squeaky-toy.

"What are you up to?" Grandpa said grumpily. He could see that Bryce had been drilling tiny holes in the center of each dime.

"Solid silver slugs," Bryce said. He offered a sly smile. "I drilled a one-eighth-inch hole in the center of each dime, and then threaded them onto a one-eight-inch stainless-steel machine screw. Then, I tightened them down with a nut"— he handed one of his silver slugs to Grandpa—"eighteen silver dimes, bolted together, a solid silver slug."

Grandpa hefted the weight in his hand, smiling, it was indeed, a solid silver slug. "This'll work," he said, nodding, "No doubt about it"—he met Bryce's eyes and winked—"damn fine job, son."

Bryce grinned proudly.

"Now, it's late—we'll finish this tomorrow, okay? It's time for bed."

"Okay," said Bryce. "Sorry I woke you."

"Ah, it's all right," Grandpa said, heading for the door. Then he turned and added, "And don't forget to turn out the dang light!"

AFTER THE BOYS LEFT FOR SCHOOL the next morning, Grandpa took a few hours from his busy schedule and made ten silver slugs. He loaded five of the shells into his old Ithaca model 37—four in the magazine tube, and one in the chamber. The other five shells he put aside for Jackson to take home.

When Jackson had picked up Bryce for school, he said he didn't have to work that afternoon. Grandpa told them to come straight home after school, so they could test one of Bryce's silver slugs; both boys had seemed extremely excited. Grandpa, on the other hand, just prayed they would never have a cause to use them.

Grandpa went about his daily chores: feeding cattle, mending fences, and the thousand other tasks he did each day to keep his cattle ranch running. A little before 4:00 p.m., he heard the loud rumble of Jackson's Camaro coming down Ranch-Road 11. "He ought to put a muffler on that damn car."

He waved at them when they drove up and motioned them

out to the barn; they both hurried back to meet him. Grandpa stood next to his workbench with a big grin on his face. He handed each of them a silver slug. They looked the same as any other shotgun shell, but the weight seemed different, more solid, and a little heavier maybe.

"These five shells are yours," Grandpa told Jackson. "Stick'em in your pocket."

"All right, thanks!" Jackson said, stuffing them into his jeans.

"Bryce; grab that plywood target," Grandpa said. "Let's take it out behind the barn and give one of these slugs a try."

Checking the safety, Grandpa took his shotgun off the workbench, and Bryce grabbed the target; together they made their way to the field behind the barn. "Lean that sheet of plywood up against that fence post over there," Grandpa said, pointing. Bryce trotted over to the barbed-wire fence, positioning the target against the cedar fence post, and then hurried back.

"There's one in the chamber," Grandpa said, handing the gun to Bryce; he nodded and took the weapon, then positioned himself about twenty yards from the target.

"Well," Bryce said. "Let's see how they work." He aimed, flicked off the safety, and squeezed the trigger. A loud *boom* echoed through the countryside.

Wood splinters exploded violently from the rear of the target, and the top three strands of barbed wire suddenly drooped. The sheet of plywood tilted forward and fell flat to the ground. Behind it, they saw the top-half of a severed fence post dangling in midair, suspended only by the strands of wire.

"Ho-ly shit!" Jackson exclaimed. He tensed, waiting for a slap to his head, but it never came. Grandpa stood stunned, eyes wide, mouth open.

Bryce lowered the gun, speechless.

"... I'd say they work pretty well," Grandpa finally managed.

From behind them, "What the *heck* did you do?" Grandma hollered. Together they spun around, meeting her eyes. All three of them had a look about their faces as if they'd just been caught with a dead body. "Are y'all outta your cotton-picking minds?" she continued. "Look at *my fence!*"

Anything that was near the house, belonged to Grandma: *her* trees, *her* grass, *her* shrubs, and—*her fence!* The only thing near the house that belonged to Grandpa was the barn—as in, go clean up *your* barn, it's a mess!

"Those cows are gonna get in here and destroy *my yard!*" she said, tromping angrily toward them. The look on her face was scary as Hell, and none of them had uttered a single word; they were shell-shocked.

Jackson and Grandpa each backed away from Bryce—the person who was holding the gun—because *that* seemed to be where Grandma was heading. "Give me that dang shotgun," she barked. "Before you haul-off and *blow a hole* in something else."

She snatched the gun from his hands, set the safety, and pointed the muzzle at the ground. Grandma knew weapons as well as any of them. "I want that fence fixed before sundown, do you hear me?" She glared at them, meeting each of their eyes. It was like negotiating with a five-foot-tall ball of fire.

"Yes ma'am," they all said in unison.

"Of all the *stupid*, idiotic, pea-brained . . ." She stomped off toward the house shaking her head and grumbling to herself; she was madder than a wet hen.

She stopped, turned around and hollered back at them, "I'm puttin' this gun in the corner by the back door, and nobody better touch it unless somethin' needs killing! Do you understand me?"

"Yes ma'am," they all said again.

When she was finally gone, everyone took a breath, and then Jackson said, "... Shit."

Grandpa swatted him.

"Hey?" he said, frowning, rubbing his head.

Bryce said, "That was a bad idea. She's really pissed."

Grandpa chuckled. "I'd say we got off easy."

Jackson started edging away. "I, uh . . . gotta get going," he said.

Grandpa looked at him. "You ain't going nowhere, buster. We got a fence to mend. Now go get a posthole digger."

He frowned and turned toward the barn, mumbling. "Damn it."

Smack!

"Ow! What the *hell*?"

Smack!!

CHAPTER 15

The Clarion Call

A ROSY-HUED GLOW lit the morning sky. A shy horizon blushed at the sun's brazen advance. The day they had all been waiting for had finally arrived—Sunday, December 22, 1991—the winter solstice, and the last full moon of the season.

Over the past eleven days, Sheriff Neil Culley had led several search parties into The Refuge, looking for the two groups of missing campers. Culley had made certain that the searches only took place during daylight hours, and that everyone was safely back in town before dark. His efforts had been fruitless, he'd found nothing but dead-end trails.

During the same period, Bruce Fletcher had been unable to dissuade two additional groups of campers from entering The Refuge. One of the two groups was due back tomorrow, and the other later in the week; no one held hope that they would ever be seen again.

Over the past three months, fourteen tourists and one local person (Wendy Walker) had gone missing, and not a single body had been found. The only proof the public had that some type of predator existed was the body of James Clark; and that had been ruled a mountain lion attack.

Deputy Wayne Bennett's *true* cause of death had been covered up and forgotten. It was a sad ending to a brave and honest man's life. There had been a total of seventeen people, dead or missing, in only three months, and that didn't include the four new campers still inside The Refuge. While the citizens of Bane County were wary and apprehensive, they had no real grasp of the *true* danger; life carried on as usual for many of them.

Jackson Campbell spent the day working at Western Auto, one of the few businesses in Silver Canyon open on Sundays; he worked the majority of his hours on weekends. Bryce McNeel and Grandpa spent the day working around the ranch; it was the best time for them to tackle major projects, since Bryce was at school during the week. Staying busy with work was comforting in a way, it occupied their minds and kept them from dwelling on the horror they knew was lurking in the darkness.

As the day ended, and the sun dropped below the treetops of the neighboring forest, Bryce washed his hands and took his place at the kitchen table. As he waited for supper, his grandma and grandpa began their evening banter session.

"Nathan," Grandma barked. "If I catch that egg-sucking-dog of yours chasing my chickens again, I'm gonna jerk a knot in his tail and hang him from the clothesline."

Straight-faced, Grandpa replied, "He doesn't have a tail, Blanche—that's why we call him Snip."

She wrinkled her face, glaring at him, and was about to respond, when the phone rang—two long rings. Grandma moved to answer it.

"Saved by the bell," Grandpa muttered to Bryce.

"Hello," Grandma answered. "Yes, it is . . . all right, just a minute"—she covered the receiver's mouthpiece with her hand—"Bryce, its Mariana . . . she seems really upset."

A cloud of fear came over Bryce as he moved quickly to the phone and answered, "Mariana?"

What she told him, nearly stopped his heart.

THAT MORNING, as Mariana Pătrașcu prepared brunch for Străbunică and herself, it had seemed like any other Sunday morning. The restaurant was closed—it was her only day off—and she had lounged lazily in bed until around 10:30 a.m., before moving to the kitchen to start the coffee.

The other days of the week were always busy; she would rise early, preparing the restaurant for lunch. Their doors opened at 11:00 a.m. and they were generally busy until around 2:00 p.m. After that, business slowed until the dinner crowd arrived around 5:30 p.m.

It was during this slow period each day that Mariana would change into her jeans, and go to her great-grandmother's farm to care for the animals. Her large Manx cat, Pisicuta, would always accompany her; she would release him into the barn while she went about her chores. The big Manx was a ruthless mouser—or in this case, a ratter—and he always kept the farm's rat population in check.

While Pisicuta went about his work in the barn, Mariana would gather the goats and bring them into the milking shed. She would pour their feed into a long trough—to keep them occupied—and then set about the task of milking them. They were tame and docile animals, and enjoyed being milked, mostly because they associated it with their favorite feed. Mariana would pour their milk into a large stainless-steel can that she then brought back to the café, where Joseph, their head cook, would process it into a variety of delicious cheeses and other dairy products.

When the milking was complete, she would move to the henhouse and gather the eggs—which were also used at the café—and then spread feed for the chickens. If there was time to spare after feeding and watering all the animals, Mariana would work on other chores, but she always made certain she was gone before sundown. The thought of the hideous creature still horrified her, and there was no way she would stay at the farm alone after dark. Besides, she was needed back at the café to work the dinner crowd.

That morning, after she and Străbunică had finished their brunch, Mariana started a load of laundry and curled up on the sofa with a new *Stephen King* novel, "Needful Things." Sipping her cup of herbal tea, still in her jammies, she relaxed and entered the creepy small town of Castle Rock.

After three loads of laundry, and a couple hundred pages, Mariana looked at the clock—*2:13 p.m.*—and saw it was time to leave for the farm. The goats needed to be fed and milked each afternoon, and they didn't care if it was her only day off. The chickens needed tending to as well, so Mariana slipped out of her jammies and into her jeans.

Grabbing her purse and car keys from the coffee table, she headed downstairs to the café's kitchen. She took one of the stainless-steel milk cans from under the counter, and some empty cartons for the eggs, and then made her way to the base of the stairs to call the cat.

"Here kitty-kitty-kitty." The large Manx bounded down the stairs and ran straight to the front door of the restaurant, mewing loudly, ready for the hunt.

Mariana opened the door and the cat scurried to her truck, a 1983 Ford Bronco II. He waited impatiently, turning circles, as she opened the door. The cat leapt inside, and as usual, he sat in the driver's seat. Mariana shooed him over to the passenger side. "Move it fatso, I'm driving. When you get a license, then we'll talk. "

Starting the motor, she let the truck idle for a moment, warming up. She revved the engine a couple of times. "Purring like a Pisicuta," she told the cat. Then she dropped it into gear, and headed south out of town.

A few minutes later, she turned off the highway, crossing over the bone-jarring cattle-guard onto Străbunică's property; she followed the dirt road across an open field toward the thickly wooded hills. It was always slow going along the tightly twisting road; it rose and fell severely through the steep hills and gullies.

Mariana gripped the steering wheel tightly as her Ford Bronco bounced wildly down the bumpy road. It was a lot like riding a real bronco, she thought. Pisicuta dug his claws into the upholstery, flattening his ears and yowling, as he held on for dear life. They plodded along slowly for a couple of miles and then crested the final hill. Great-grandmother's house lay below in a green glade wreathed by tall, swaying trees. A susurrant north wind had arrived, bringing with it the sounds and crisp fragrances of winter.

She trundled slowly down the long slope and then followed the dirt road into the field. As Mariana made her way toward the house, she tapped on the truck's horn, sounding the dinner bell. On cue, white goats appeared from the edge of the woods, trotting happily toward the vehicle, forming a line behind her like a brood of obedient ducklings.

She parked near the barn and opened the door, Pisicuta scrambled across her lap, not waiting for her to alight. "Hey! Watch those claws, mister," she warned, rubbing her thighs. He went straight to the barn door, yowling to be let in.

Mariana smirked at him and opened the door. "Here you go, psycho; happy hunting." The big Manx bolted into the large barn, and quickly disappeared behind a large stack of feedbags. She left the door open, he liked to drag his kills out into the yard, bragging. Later, when Mariana would dig a hole and bury the rats, the cat always looked appalled and offended by the senseless act.

It was a bright and sunny afternoon; feathery wisps of clouds dusted a lofty blue sky, and a fitful wind blew from the north. It felt good to be outside in the cool crisp air; the world smelled fresh and clean, new. Shaking a feedbag noisily, she gathered the goats into the milking shed and began her daily chores.

The afternoon went by quickly, and about thirty minutes before sundown, Mariana loaded the milk and eggs into the Bronco for the trip home. She had already buried two large rats that Pisicuta had killed, but the cat was still inside the barn hunting. She went to the door and called for him. "Here kitty-kitty-kitty," but the cat didn't come. She called again with the same result.

Mariana entered the dark barn to search for the stubborn cat. "Come here you little shit. Where the heck are you? Here kitty-kitty-kitty." She called and called, looking everywhere, but he wasn't there. "Pisicuta? Damn it!"

She went outside and walked the perimeter of the large barn, calling and searching the tall grass, but the cat was nowhere to be found. Mariana looked to the western horizon, the sun was falling fast, and it was time to go. "Sorry, kitty," she said. "Looks like you're spending the night." Mariana loved her cat, but there was no way she was staying there after sundown. The cat had stayed outside at night plenty of times in the past. "He'll be fine," she muttered.

She started her truck, making her way across the field to the dense tree line, and then turned up the long, steep hill. Mariana switched on her headlights for good measure. She could still see without them, the sun was still up, but it was darker under the thick canopy

As the hill steepened, she gunned the engine; with a slight squeal, the vehicle powered up the sharp incline with little effort. Reaching the top, she worked her way around a sharp curve, turning the steering wheel as tightly as she could, until it whined in protest. Then straightening out the truck, she wound her way down the other side of the darkening hill.

After about a mile, she came to another steep gradient, the Bronco plodded its way up the hill with ease. Near the top of the rise, the road became excessively steep; Mariana downshifted and revved the engine. The motor squealed loudly, and the Bronco lunged up the hill. As it cleared the crest, the squealing stopped and there was a loud clattering sound. Mariana slammed on the brakes and stopped, thinking she had hit something.

The clattering stopped, and the engine seemed to run normally, although the idle was a little fast. The acrid stench of burnt rubber reached her nose. "Eww, God, what is *that*?" She wrinkled her face and rolled down the window; the smell was as bad outside as in.

Mariana put the truck into gear and slowly moved forward; the engine sounded a little strange, but the nasty smell was dissipating, and the truck seemed to be running fine. However, when she came to the next curve and tried to turn, the steering wheel felt as though it weighed a thousand pounds; it took every ounce of her strength to maneuver the truck around the corner.

Shit...

She stopped the truck, set the parking brake, and shifted into neutral. Mariana wanted to pop the hood and have a look, but was afraid to shut off the engine for fear it wouldn't start again. She reached down, pulled the hood release and hopped out of the Bronco.

As she made her way to the front of the vehicle and lifted the hood, Mariana realized how dark it had become. Even though the headlights lit the road, it was dark inside the engine compartment, she couldn't see a thing, and to make matters worse, she didn't have a flashlight.

The acrid scent of burnt rubber wafted from under the hood and the engine was radiating an excessive amount of heat. She went back to the cab of the truck and looked at the dashboard;

the temperature gauge was pointing to *H*.

Damn it!

Though she didn't know it at the time, the engine belt for the power-steering- and water-pump had snapped.

Mariana was an exceptional driver, but wasn't well versed when it came to engines. She knew how to check and fill all of the fluids, and how to change a flat and keep the proper air pressure in her tires, but that was about the limit of her mechanical skills. One thing she did know, however: never let an engine overheat, it could cause serious damage to the motor. She reached for the key and turned off the ignition; the engine sputtered and then clunked to a stop.

While the Bronco's headlights still lit the road, and the dark woods in front of her, Mariana was suddenly engulfed by a tomb-like silence. It was at that exact moment . . . that fear finally found her.

She had been so absorbed with her engine problems that she had forgotten all about the rapidly setting sun. She looked behind her at the dark, forbidding woods; she was stranded. The highway was at least a mile away, and even if she reached it, she might not be able to flag down a car. There was a dearth of traffic on Highway 50 in the evenings.

Her only option was to return to Străbunică's house and use the phone to call for help. Mariana looked down the long, lonely road. The taillights of her Bronco cast an eerie, crimson glow that slowly faded into the distance. Great-grandmother's house was about a mile behind. She steeled her courage, and then briskly strode down the dark, wooded hill.

Darkness gathered. The sun had set, and dusk was upon her; the sounds of night filled the woods. Up ahead, an opening in the thick canopy allowed a small circle of light. Mariana gazed into the eastern sky. A luminous full moon offered a telling glow through the bony, interlaced branches of a dead tree; a small island of light within an ominous black sea. A shuddering chill washed over her as she quickly hastened her gait.

Try though she might, Mariana couldn't expel the portentous visions that haunted her mind—a sibylline gift that was her legacy.

Moving fatefully along her chosen path, Mariana feared that she would never see the light of day again.

B RYCE GRIPPED THE PHONE IN HORROR. "I'll be right there. Just stay inside and lock the doors." Slamming down the phone, he turned to his grandparents, eyes wide. "Mariana's car broke down. She's at her great-grandmother's farm. Alone!"

Grandpa moved quickly to the corner and retrieved the shotgun. "Let's go get her," he said excitedly.

"No," Bryce said. He took the shotgun from his grandpa's hands. "You need to stay here and watch after Grandma. Go get my deer rifle."

"I can watch after myself," Grandma barked. She reached inside the large cookie jar on the countertop and pulled out Grandpa's .45 Long Colt revolver. Both of them lifted an eyebrow at her.

"Look, we don't have time to argue about this," Bryce demanded. "Just stay here!" Then he grabbed the keys and ran out the door.

The speedometer on Grandpa's 1966 International Harvester went to 100 mph, but its top speed was only about 75 mph. Bryce had the accelerator pinned to the floor the entire way. He came close to missing the turn for Străbunică's house; the entrance was hard to see. He slammed on the brakes, burning long, black stripes into the asphalt, then flew across the cattle-guard and headed for the tree line.

He knew that once he entered the woods he would need to slow his speed; the brush-choked road could be treacherous even during the day, and the last thing he needed was to run off the side and crash, or get the truck stuck somewhere. Gripping the wheel so tightly his knuckles turned white, Bryce focused intently on the road before him, he rarely shifted the old truck out of first gear as he wound through the rugged hills; the journey seemed to go on forever.

Up ahead in the distance, the forest was aglow. Around the next corner he found Mariana's Bronco; it was blocking the narrow road ahead. The hood was up and its headlights were starting to fade, as the battery slowly lost its charge. Bryce moved to the edge of the brush-lined road, steering cautiously around the stranded vehicle. Thick brush scraped noisily at the side of the truck, as sharp branches clawed at the metal. The high-pitched squeal was like nails on a chalkboard, and prickled the hairs on Bryce's skin. His eyes flitted to the large claw marks that still marred the hood of the truck as he continued along the dark and twisting road.

At last, he reached the crest of the tall hill overlooking the farm. The full moon lit the countryside brightly and he could see everything with surprising detail. As he raced down the long, steep hill, Bryce looked across the open field toward the farm—the house was dark; no light shone through the windows, not even a light on the porch. An overwhelming feeling of dread found him.

Reaching the bottom of the hill, Bryce turned into the field and floored the accelerator, careening recklessly across the bumpy pasture until he reached the house. He slammed on the brakes, sliding wildly to a stop, and then jumped out of the truck, shotgun in hand. Bryce was about to scream Mariana's name—when he saw the door.

The full moon lit the front of the house—the door was gone, destroyed; only a small, triangular-shaped piece of wood remained, hanging from the top hinge.

No...

He stumbled numbly toward the house, his horror growing with each step forward. The front porch was bathed in blood; it spilled across the floor like a thick burgundy wine, shining darkly in the moonlight.

No...

Bryce stopped at the edge of the porch, unable to go any farther. The wall near the doorway was scarred with huge claw marks, and the porch-light had been smashed; the broken fixture dangled precariously by its wires. Though the house was dark, the moon was low in the sky, and shone brightly into the open doorway.

The house was a shambles; furniture destroyed, strewn everywhere—blood and flesh painted the room. Bryce looked on in horror: skeins of Mariana's long, raven-black hair lay matted in blood, her clothing ripped to shreds.

No... Mariana, No...

Bryce shook his head; it wasn't true, he backed away from the house, trying to distance himself from the nightmarish scene that lay before him. Finally, he fell to his knees in the tall grass beside the truck... and wept.

A loud crash came from inside the house. Bryce bolted to his feet. "Mariana?" he yelled, hoping, praying. He took a step forward.

A gigantic dark shadow moved inside the house; Bryce's heart jolted, as adrenaline flooded his body. A huge, blood-soaked hand reached through the doorway, its large claws grasping the doorframe; the towering creature ducked its head and stalked outside into the moonlight. A hideous stench pervaded the air as the beast stepped off the porch.

Large jagged teeth filled its bloody mouth, and it almost

seemed to smile as it cocked its head. The werewolf appeared to derive great pleasure from Bryce's fear.

Its glowing yellow eyes burned brightly in the moonlight as it slowly moved forward, savoring and prolonging its kill. It was a creature risen from the fiery pits of Hell.

Bryce raised his shotgun and leveled it at the werewolf's chest; he could see that its hair was soaked with blood—Mariana's blood. His body quaked with rage and fear as he flicked off the gun's safety.

"Die you fucker," Bryce snarled. Then he squeezed the trigger.

Nothing happened.

The gun didn't fire—there wasn't even a click.

Oh my God . . .

Bryce's heart froze in his chest. His mind flashed back to the day he had shot the fence post. Grandma had taken the gun away from him before he had ejected the spent shell and loaded a new one. The gun had been sitting in the corner for the past eleven days without a live round in the chamber.

Fuck . . .

The beast was right on top of him, clawed hands reaching out, hot rancid breath in his face. Bryce quickly worked the pump. An empty hull flew from the chamber as he racked a live round into place. He fired into the beast's chest at point-blank range.

The sound was deafening. The giant creature stumbled back several steps, but it didn't go down. Bryce could see where the silver slug had hit the werewolf's chest. A large chunk of thick hide had been blown away, and beneath it, he could see a yellowy-white breastbone. He racked another shell into the chamber.

The beast growled angrily and came for him. Bryce aimed

and fired, sending another slug into the open wound. The giant creature reeled back, stumbling; this time it lost its footing and went down. Bryce worked the pump, racking in another round.

With an ear-splitting roar, the werewolf sprang to his feet. Bryce could see that the wound was much larger now and the breastbone had been shattered. The beast lunged forward and Bryce fired. This time, the shot stopped the creature in its tracks; it staggered back on wobbly legs. Bryce could see that the slug had penetrated the werewolf's sternum. There was a large hole in the yellowy-white breastbone, and black blood poured from the wound. The beast swayed on its feet for a moment, and then tilted back, collapsing like a felled tree.

The giant creature slammed into the ground with such force that the earth shook beneath Bryce's feet. He worked the shotgun's pump a final time, loading his last silver slug into the chamber. He approached slowly, aiming at the gigantic beast. Bryce could see the subtle rise and fall of the werewolf's chest, as puffs of hot breath condensed into the cold night air—it was still alive.

The creature suddenly shuddered and Bryce jumped back, gasping; he nearly pulled the trigger on his weapon. A wheezing death-rattle came from the beast's throat, and then it lay still; its chest no longer moving. It seemed to be dead, but Bryce was wary; at any second, it could leap to its feet and rip him to shreds. He kept up his guard.

Still aiming at the giant creature, he edged closer, its odor was nauseating, almost unbearable; he couldn't believe what he was looking at. The thing was enormous, the size of a Kodiak bear, or even larger, and its skin was unlike anything he had ever seen: rugose and leathery, and unbelievably thick. It looked like the hide of an elephant, or a rhino, at least three-inches-thick—extremely tough.

Damn thing's bulletproof, Bryce thought. *If you shot it with a small-caliber weapon, it wouldn't even penetrate the skin.*

He looked at the large hole in its chest; a huge patch of skin had been blown away, revealing the bone underneath. Black blood had clotted around the outside of the wound, forming a hard, rubbery mass. Using the muzzle of his shotgun, Bryce prodded the area, wary that the creature might still be alive. The breastbone was unnaturally thick, at least two inches, and appeared to cover the entire chest area.

It doesn't have ribs, Bryce thought, as he prodded its side—*just a big, bony breastplate to protect its vital organs.*

"It's like friggin' body armor," he muttered—and then the creature moved.

Bryce gasped, recoiling quickly, his finger tight against the trigger. After a long, nervous moment, he said, ". . . Just death throes." Something that Mariana's great-grandmother had said suddenly occurred to him, *"It is said that their wounds heal instantly. It is a demon from the deepest bowels of Hell, and no mortal man can kill it."* He looked toward the blood-drenched house.

Mariana . . .

Rage filled him. He pointed the shotgun at the beast's head and looked into its bulbous eyes. They were enormous, the size of a large plum, and seemed to stare right back at him. The eyes still glowed brightly, as if alive, reflecting in the light of the moon. He targeted the large, amber eye and tightened his finger on the trigger. Then, just as he was about to fire, he noticed something remarkable.

Bryce stepped forward and pushed the muzzle of his gun against the creature's eye. A tiny shimmer of light appeared at the inner edge, where the tear duct would be.

Holy shit . . .

A translucent third eyelid moved horizontally across the large eye. Which, in itself, wasn't that unusual; numerous animals had a third eyelid—or nictitating membrane—

including nocturnal primates and canines. This one, however—was *glowing*... like the tail of a firefly.

"Bioluminescence," Bryce breathed. He was stunned. "That's how it's able to see in pitch-black."

No mammal was known to be bioluminescent. Other than bacteria and fungi, only insects, fish and other marine invertebrates had that quality. Bryce wondered if this thing was even a mammal, he had seen hot breath coming from its mouth; it must be warm blooded. He dropped to one knee and hesitantly reached out a hand, touching its skin, and then quickly pulled back, surprised and repulsed. Its skin was as cold as ice.

What the hell?

Though he was still curious, he had seen all he wanted to see. Bryce rose and looked toward the blood-drenched porch, his anger rising once again. Mariana was gone, slaughtered, devoured by this—this *thing*. He gritted his teeth, rammed the muzzle of his gun into the creature's eye socket, and pulled the trigger. Its head exploded like a ripe melon. Skull and brains scattered across the field.

"Let's see you heal *that*, fucker!" He turned, walking back to the truck and tossed the empty shotgun onto the seat; then he reached over and turned off the ignition. The old International sputtered and died; it had been idling loudly this entire time, ever since he'd first arrived and jumped out of the truck. Silence surrounded him; Bryce had never known that a night could be so quiet. His eyes filled with unshed tears. He looked up into the star-filled heavens; he felt extremely small—tiny. It didn't seem real. How could all this be happening?

...Meow...

Bryce looked toward the house, listening. Again, he heard it, the faint mewing of a cat—Mariana's cat. He moved closer to the house, listening.

"Kitty-kitty-kitty?"

Nothing...

He moved a little closer, continuing to call. He thought he heard something.

...Meow...

"Here Kitty-kitty-kitty...come on kitty...here kitty."

Silence...

"Kitty-kitty-kitty? Damn it, what the *hell* was that cat's name?"

"...Pisicuta," a voice said from inside the dark house. Mariana stepped through the doorway. The moon lit her face like that of an angel. "It means...kitten."

"Mariana?" Bryce breathed. He thought he was seeing a ghost. His heart was pounding in his chest. "How—I thought—but, where?"

She moved toward him, tears were streaming down her face; the large Manx cat was cradled in her arms. She seemed fine, unharmed.

Bryce looked at the blood-covered porch behind her, not understanding. "...The blood?"

Mariana broke down, crying uncontrollably. "...Stufos," she sobbed.

The dog—*Jesus*—the large, black fur-ball he had seen two weeks ago. Bryce moved forward, taking her into his arms, holding her. The cat hissed and jumped to the ground. "I'm so sorry," he said, trying to comfort her. "...I thought I'd lost you."

She looked at the carcass of the giant beast. "You killed it."

"Yeah...I blew its damn head off."

"Good," Mariana said firmly, glaring at the dead creature; she looked as though she would spit on its corpse. "It killed Stufos..." and again, she sobbed.

Bryce held her close for a long moment, kissing the top of her head. Finally, he asked, " . . . What happened? Where were you?"

Taking a deep breath, Mariana tried to calm herself. She wiped the tears from her cheeks, and said, "After my truck broke down, I walked back here as fast as I could. *That* little shit"—she pointed to the cat sitting at her feet—"and Stufos were waiting for me on the front porch. We all went inside and I locked the door—that's when I called you—then I drew the curtains over the windows, and waited. I don't know how much time passed, maybe fifteen or twenty minutes, it seemed like forever, and then, Stufos started growling and sniffing at the door. I knew it wasn't you, I hadn't heard your truck drive up. I was afraid to pull back the curtains and look. Then, there was a loud *crash*, and the porch light went out."

"Jesus," Bryce said. Even though it was over, he still looked horrified.

"Stufos went crazy. I tried to call him back, away from the door, but he wouldn't listen—that's when the horrible scraping sounds began. I could hear it . . . clawing at the walls. I grabbed Pisicuta, ran to the back hallway, and opened the access door to the attic. I called for Stufos . . . but he wouldn't come."

She was speaking quickly now, breathing hard, and Bryce could tell she was reliving the horror. Her eyes welled and Bryce held her again.

Mariana wiped her eyes. "Even if he *had* come," she confessed, "I don't think I could've carried Stufos up the ladder. He weighs over—" she paused, breath hitching in her throat. " . . . he *weighed* over a hundred pounds."

"I'm so sorry," Bryce said, meeting her eyes. He squeezed her hands, offering a weak smile. "He was protecting you."

She nodded, eyes welling. "I know." She took another deep breath. "When I heard the front door crash open, I pulled up the ladder and shut the hatch. It was horrible. There was a huge fight: growling, crashing . . . yelping, it went on forever. Then it was quiet . . . I could hear the creature moving down the hallway, sniffing. It stopped right beneath me—it *knew* I was there. It started to claw at the ceiling . . . but then it stopped. That's when I heard your truck. I was so scared." She began to sob again.

"You're okay," Bryce said, gently rocking her in his arms.

"I was scared for *you*," she said. "I thought it was going to kill you"—she wiped away her tears—"I heard the gunshots, but you never came for me. I thought you were dead."

"I thought *you* were dead," said Bryce. "When I saw"—he paused—"the torn clothing." He didn't want to mention the blood, or the dog's long, black hair; he knew she was anguishing over the animal's horrible death.

Mariana glance to the house, her body trembling. "The coat rack," she said. "It was by the door, full of my clothes."

Bryce nodded, understanding now.

"After the gunshots, Pisicuta started yowling, and pacing around, he wanted out of the attic. I tried to make him be quiet . . . but then, I heard you calling for him," she said, trying to smile. "And I knew you were okay."

"We're *both* okay," Bryce said, returning her smile, ". . . and that *thing* is dead"—He motioned to the bloody carcass—"It'll never hurt anyone again."

Mariana kissed his lips and held him tight. "It's over," she said.

"Yeah, it's over," Bryce said, kissing the top of her head. "It's finally ov—"

A thunderous howl rent the cold night air—a mournful dirge of rage. The entire world fell silent.

Mariana and Bryce froze, gripped by fear, their breath seizing in their lungs. The nightmarish howl had stolen their ability to move.

"Bryce," Mariana said. Her voice quavered, no louder than a whisper.

"Get in the truck," he said quietly, eyes fixed on the dark forest in the distance.

Mariana didn't move; she was rigid, trembling, feet rooted to the ground.

"Get in the truck!" he said frantically—and then he ran—pulling her along behind him.

"My cat!" she said, pointing to the animal.

"I'll get the damn cat—just get in the truck!"

Bryce snatched Pisicuta by the scruff of the neck, and flung the hissing cat into the truck; one lost pet tonight was enough. He jumped in and tried to start the engine, but it wouldn't fire. "Shit!"

Another ungodly howl split the night; it was closer, more furious.

"Use the choke!" Mariana urged, as she tried to control the pissed off cat. Bryce's rough treatment had turned him into a fifteen-pound-ball of fur and claws.

"Damn it." He pulled the choke and the engine started. Dropping into gear, he floored the accelerator, tires spinning, and cutting deep ruts through the grass. They bounded across the field and started up the steep hill.

Over the loud engine, and the rattling of steel and springs, another resounding howl reached their ears: an ululant wail of anguish that seemed to rise from the depths of Hell. It was a sound heard only in nightmares.

Cresting the hill, the road became more treacherous; the next two miles would have to be traveled at a snail's pace, winding slowly through the dark forest. Bryce slowed the truck and tightened his grip on the wheel, trying to focus on the narrow, brush-lined road. His heart pounded in his chest like a jackhammer. Moving at this slow speed was a death sentence.

Still breathless, Mariana said, "What *was* that?"

Bryce didn't answer; he just focused on the road, trying to drive as quickly as possible.

"Is there another one?" she asked franticly.

He didn't answer.

"Bryce?"

"I don't know," he snapped. Then more calmly, "I'm sorry . . . yeah . . . there must be two of them."

". . . What do we do?"

"We get the hell out of here."

A branch scraped noisily against the side of the truck and Mariana screamed; Bryce offered a yelp, as well; more frightened by her cry than the noise.

"It's just a bush," he said, breathing hard, eyes wide. "It's okay . . . we're okay."

They both watched the dark forest as they drove, expecting something unspeakable to pounce at any moment. Bryce's eyes continually flitted to the rearview mirror and the crimson-hued darkness that followed them. He imagined a giant, hairy beast emerging from the gloom, trotting along behind the truck, hell-bent on exacting its bloody revenge.

Each time brush clawed at the side of the truck they both tensed. Ominous black shadows filled the dense woods, and seemed to follow them as they drove. Everywhere they looked, the forest seemed to move, something lurking in the darkness. Their anxiety grew with each twisting turn of the slow, unending road, and they feared they would never reach the highway.

When they finally exited the tree line, Bryce gunned the engine and raced across the open field toward the highway. He never slowed until they reached the sheltering lights of Main Street. They parked at the café, sitting in the truck for a long moment, holding each other, trying to calm their fears. The yowling of an angry cat wasn't helpful.

"Ingrate," Mariana scolded, sneering at the fat feline.

"I better go," said Bryce. "I need to go check on my grandparents, and tell them what happened"—He walked her to the door and gave her a quick kiss—"I'll call you tomorrow, okay?"

Mariana smiled weakly and nodded; she looked exhausted. "Okay," she said.

Driving back down Main Street, Bryce passed the Western Auto store and saw that it was closed. Jackson would be at home now and that was exactly where he was heading. His cousin still had five silver slugs, and while Bryce knew it was unlikely, he feared that before the night was over . . . they might need them.

THERE WAS NO SCHOOL THE NEXT DAY, Christmas break had started, and they were off until after the first of the year. Jackson had spent the night at Bryce's house, and they hadn't slept a wink. When Bryce explained what happened, nobody at the McNeel house had been able to sleep; the realization of a second creature was just too horrifying.

Later that morning, Bryce and Jackson took Grandpa's truck and headed to the Pătrașcu farm; Jackson wanted to see the creature's carcass, and Bryce needed another look, as well.

Jackson carried a double-barrel 12-gauge, an old Rossi coach-gun with twenty-inch barrels that he had loaded with the silver slugs. He gave the other three slugs to Bryce to reload the

Ithaca pump. Even though the sun was up, fear still reigned, and they were unwilling to take any chances.

As Bryce turned north onto the highway, Jackson asked, "Are you *sure* that you heard another one?"

"Yeah," Bryce said. "It was the same as that howl we heard on the first day of deer season."

"But you didn't see it."

"I didn't *need* to see it," Bryce said firmly. "Trust me, there's another one."

"Shit," Jackson muttered. He paused and then added, "I thought you said this shit would be over after the winter solstice."

"I know what I said."

"Well?"

"Well what?"

"Is it over?"

"We need to wait and see," Bryce said.

"Wait and see what?"

Bryce met Jackson's eyes. "Wait and see if anybody else dies," he said.

Jackson raised an eyebrow, but didn't respond. *That's a hell of an indicator*, he thought.

After a few minutes, they turned off the highway and made their way into the forest, following the narrow winding road toward the farm. As they crested another hill, Jackson asked, "Do you think they were a pair?"

"What?" Bryce said, knitting his brow.

"You know, a pair—mates—male and female," Jackson said.

Bryce offered him a grave look; he hadn't considered that possibility, he had never thought of the creature as being male or female. "I don't know," Bryce said. "I guess . . . it's possible."

"I sure hope not," said Jackson.

"Why is that?" he asked.

He offered Bryce a worried look. "Because," Jackson said. "If you killed my mate . . . I'd be *really* fuckin' pissed."

"Jesus," Bryce said, returning the worried look. Jackson had a point.

As they crested the final hill, Jackson pointed across the field. "Is that her house?"

"Yeah," Bryce said. "That's it." The hair stood on the back of his neck at the thought of seeing the giant creature again. They coasted down the hill and made their way across the field, stopping in front of the house.

"Shit!" Bryce yelled. His eyes had gone wide.

"What?"

"It's gone!"

"You're fuckin' kidding me!" said Jackson. They hopped out of the truck and moved quickly into the tall grass.

"It was right here!" Bryce insisted. They could see where the creature had fallen. The grass was crushed flat and something that looked like dried black paint covered the ground; the stench was almost unbearable.

"Are you sure it was dead?"

"You damn right it was dead!" Bryce shouted. "I blew its friggin' head off—brains went everywhere."

Jackson moved around to the other side, looking in the grass. "Tracks," he said. Bryce joined him. You could see where large, heavy feet had flattened the grass.

"Did it walk through this area," Jackson asked.

"No, I don't think so. It came from inside the house." Bryce said. They did a quick sweep of the area, and found the trail the creature had made through the tall grass when it first approached the house. Then they found a second trail, coming from a different direction. It made its way to where the first creature had fallen, and then returned to the dense forest.

"No doubt," Jackson said. "There were two of them."

"I told you."

They stood for a long moment staring at the large, black spot in the grass. Jackson dropped to one knee, picked up a stick and poked at the strange substance. "Is this shit dried blood," he asked, disgusted. "It looks more like, melted plastic or something."

Bryce squatted down beside him and picked up a stick of his own, prodding. "Yeah, it's weird, right?" Bryce said. "Last night when I shot this thing, its blood clotted almost instantly around the outside of the wound. I've never seen anything like it." He thought back again to what Mariana's great-grandmother had said about its wounds healing instantly.

"God, this shit stinks," Jackson said. He stood and took a step back.

"You know," Bryce said, pondering. "One of the leading causes of death from traumatic injury is uncontrolled blood loss. A lot of the time, the wound itself is minor, but people bleed-out and die before help arrives."

"Your point?" said Jackson.

"My point is that this creature's blood is very unique. It can clot a wound exceptionally fast, and then seals it with a tough, rubbery scab. When you add the fact that its skin is harder and thicker than a rhino, and that its vital organs are protected behind a two-inch-thick plate of solid bone; what you end up with is a creature that is virtually unstoppable."

"Great," Jackson said. He stretched the word sarcastically —then he noticed something shiny within the black, bloody mass. "Hey what's that?" He pointed.

Bryce followed his gaze and scraped at the shiny object with his stick. "It's a dime," he said. "The slug must've broken apart." He picked it up, holding it between his thumb and forefinger. It was dripping with wet blood.

"Why is *that* blood still wet?" asked Jackson.

"That's a damn good question," Bryce muttered.

As blood dripped off of the dime and ran across Bryce's skin, he saw that it clotted instantly. The blood that remained on the dime, however, stayed wet. "Holy shit," he said. "It's the silver."

"What are you talking about?" asked Jackson.

"The silver—there's something about the silver." Bryce said excitedly. "It's having some kind of chemical reaction with the blood—it's preventing it from clotting."

"No shit?" said Jackson. "Huh? I guess the old horror movies were right. It takes silver to kill a werewolf."

"Something Mariana's great-grandmother had said occurred to Bryce: *"Some legends say, if the Neuri is wounded by a weapon of silver, its wounds will heal more slowly."*

"I don't know if it'll kill it," said Bryce. "But—sure as hell—it'll make it bleed."

Jackson nodded and offered a big smile; it was good news. He looked at the black goo on Bryce's fingers. "You know you're not getting back into the truck until you wash your hands, right? That shit's disgusting."

Bryce laughed and together they made their way over to the water hose. One question still remained unanswered.

"So where the hell do you think it went?" Jackson asked.

"I wish I knew," Bryce said. " . . . I wish I knew."

EPILOGUE

Returning Moon

IT WAS JUNE. Six months had passed since the horrors of last fall, and life in Bane County had returned to normal. The citizens of Silver Canyon went about their daily lives as usual: children played outside, day or night; families went on picnics in the woods. No one was afraid to go camping, or of taking long hikes in remote areas. Tourists ventured deep into The Refuge for extended periods without worry or incident. All thoughts of killer mountain lions and raving lunatics had faded away. It seemed as though the missing people and grisly deaths had never occurred.

Bryce McNeel and Jackson Campbell had been astonished by their community's uncanny ability to dismiss the strange occurrences of last fall and carry on with their lives. No one spoke of the macabre events, and if the subject were accidently raised, it was quickly changed. It was as though the entire town had been cast in some surreal production of *life in a small town*, and the set designer had used a *Thomas J. Wright* painting from *Rod Serling's* "Night Gallery" for the backdrop, and then painted over it with a Rockwellesque scene, with only a trace of the ghostly pentimento visible. Everyone played his or her role perfectly.

The four campers who had entered The Refuge a week before the winter solstice never returned, which had been no great surprise. Sheriff Neil Culley had hired a new deputy, Deacon

Edmund—or "Deke" as he preferred—and in the weeks that followed, they had searched for the missing campers; even though the sheriff knew it was pointless. Culley hadn't shared with Deke his knowledge of the werewolf; it would have been counterproductive for obvious reasons. The four lost campers had brought the total to twenty-one people, missing or dead, in only three months' time—and yet—life went on. People forgot —and no one spoke of it again.

Bryce, on the other hand, thought frequently of his encounter with the werewolf. He was still baffled as to what had happened to the creature's carcass, and didn't think he'd ever know for sure. When he told Sheriff Culley and Bruce Fletcher what had taken place, and that the body had disappeared, they seemed even more confused than he was.

Bryce knew there were only two scenarios that could explain the strange disappearance: one was logical, and the other, illogical. The problem was, however, that the logical scenario lent a great deal of credence to the illogical one—creating a catch-22 situation.

Bryce's stance that the werewolf was a supernatural being —a demon from Hell as Cătălina Pătrașcu had put it—had stemmed from his unsettling experience with the creature's luminous eyes. Later, when he discovered the bioluminescent quality of the beast's third eyelid, however, his point of view had changed, somewhat—though not entirely; there was still the question of the werewolf's preternatural behavior to be considered.

Animals just didn't have the mental capacity for the complex emotions that this creature exhibited. It had gone to painstaking lengths to instill the highest possible level of fear into its victims, and seemed to derive an enormous amount of pleasure from their horror. The murderous hatred and extreme fury that the werewolf displayed was completely non-existent within the animal kingdom—save for one species:

man.

This unprecedented, human-like behavior made the werewolf seem supernatural in a way, and led to the illogical possibility that it had somehow healed itself after having its head blown off—and then... just walked away.

Bryce couldn't bring himself to believe that the creature possessed some kind of *demonic power* it used to heal itself. He preferred to believe the more logical scenario for the missing carcass: that the second werewolf had retrieved the body of its fallen companion and carried it away. The problem with this scenario, however, was that animals didn't behave in that fashion. Caring for the remains of the dead was strictly a human trait.

In addition, Bryce had asked himself another question: why had the carcass been removed? Something that Sam Nightfeather had said provided the answer: *"The beast always remained hidden; no one who saw him had ever lived. In fact, his greatest strength was that no one knew he existed."* If the other werewolf had removed the body, it had done so for one reason: to conceal the evidence—and *that* was not the work of a mere animal.

Whether the creature miraculously healed itself, or its body had been carried away, Bryce knew it made little difference. Either way, he still had *no idea* what it was they were dealing with. Fortunately, for him, however, he had over eighteen years to figure it out.

High school graduation day for Bryce and Jackson had taken place on a Friday. There were no classes that day and the ceremony hadn't started until noon, so there was plenty of time for them to prepare. The graduating class of 1992 stood jammed into the narrow hallway outside the assembly hall, sweltering in their caps and gowns, complaining, and awaiting their cue.

Bryce had been named valedictorian—no great surprise—

and would be giving the valedictory at the end of the day's proceedings. He wanted to foist the responsibility onto someone else—he hated being singled out—but the principle, Mr. Burrows, would brook no argument on the issue, so he was stuck with it.

Bryce stood on his toes, craning his neck above the jabbering din of excited seniors, scanning the crowded hallway for Jackson.

"Where the heck is he," Bryce muttered. His cousin had disappeared about a half-hour ago and the ceremony was about to start.

"Where's who?" the person next to him asked.

Bryce turned, he recognized the voice, but it took a moment for his eyes to register who was speaking. "Ho-ly shit," he said. It was Jackson. He had been standing right next to him, but Bryce hadn't noticed—because Jackson . . . was bald.

Jackson grinned and removed his cap. His head was shaved, high-and-tight, all the way up to his short stubbly crown—a Ranger cut.

Bryce was speechless. He just stood there, eyes wide, mouth agape. Finally, he said, "What did you do?"

Jackson replaced his cap and said, "I joined the Army."

"What?" Bryce blurted. "I—wh-when?"

"Last month. When I turned eighteen."

"But, wh-why didn't you—"

"I've been planning this for almost a year," Jackson admitted. "It's just something I have to do."

After a brief moment of shock, a smile slowly formed on Bryce's lips; he was proud of his cousin. "All right," he said. Then a little louder, "Well, all right!" He gave him a rough hug, clapping him on the back.

"Hey, watch the gown," Jackson said prissily, feigning concern.

"So, when do you have to leave?" Bryce asked.

"Tomorrow."

"What!" Bryce exclaimed. "What the hell do you mean, *'tomorrow'*?"

"I have to report to Fort Benning, Georgia in five days," Jackson said. "And it's a hell of a long drive."

"Shit."

"Hey, man," Jackson said, "you're leaving for college in a few weeks anyway."

"I know," Bryce said glumly, "but I thought we'd at least . . . I don't know."

The music started; it was their cue. "Come on, man," Jackson said. "Let's get this bullshit over with—then—we're gonna fucking party!"

"All right," Bryce said, smiling. "Let's do it."

"Who knows," Jackson said in a smart-ass tone, "you might even *drink a beer* tonight."

Smack!

"Hey! Watch the cap."

THE NEXT MORNING, Bryce and Jackson woke with a hangover. Jackson had managed to get his hands on a case of beer and they had gone to Grandpa's cabin for the night. They built a large bonfire at the edge of the Carantina River and spent the night laughing, reminiscing, and getting drunker than *Cooter Brown*. Now, they were paying for it.

Bryce peeled open an eyelid; he was sprawled on a small settee, legs dangling over the armrest. He squinted toward the invading morning light. Right outside the window, a mourning dove sat in a tree, cooing like a *screaming* banshee. "If I had a suppressor, I'd shoot that nerve-rackin' son of a bitch," Bryce muttered, slurring his words. His mouth was drier than a desert, and tasted like a camel had just taken a dump in it. His head was splitting; even the sound of his own breath was louder than the roar of the ocean.

Jackson rose from the couch and stretched. "If you think that's bad," he said. "You should've heard the mouse that came stomping through here about an hour ago."

Bryce chuckled. "Ow! Don't make me laugh . . . I'm never drinking again."

Jackson searched through the sea of empty beer cans that covered the coffee table, shaking each one hopefully. Smiling, he lifted the remains of a near-full can and chugged it down. Crumpling the can, he released a loud, endless belched. "Hair of the dog," he said, and then belched again.

"You're insane."

"Certifiable," Jackson agreed. " . . . I'm hungry. Let's go get Grandma to make us some breakfast."

"Blech, how can you even think about eating?" Bryce asked. "I feel like I swallowed a brick."

"Come on light-weight, we're outta here."

"Not until we clean up this mess," Bryce demanded.

"Okay—Mom."

They went back to their grandparents' house and Grandma made them a feast. She could see that they'd been drinking, but didn't say anything. Jackson ate heartily, scoffing down plate after plate, while Bryce showed less enthusiasm, his stomach still in full revolt.

After several cups of strong black coffee, Jackson said he had to leave; he had a long trip ahead of him and needed to get going. As he and Bryce headed out the door, Grandma handed Jackson an envelope containing five hundred dollars cash.

"It's your graduation present," Grandma said. She gave him a big hug and a kiss, told him that she loved him and to be careful. Grandpa shook his hand, gave him a hug, and said that he was proud of him. Jackson was touched by the loving gestures and his eyes welled as he hugged them goodbye.

It was odd walking Jackson to his car, not knowing when they would see each other again; Bryce had to take a deep breath to keep from getting emotional.

"So . . . off to Georgia," Bryce said.

"Yep, Fort Benning."

"How long is boot camp?"

"I think basic training lasts somewhere around ten or twelve weeks," Jackson said. "But that's just the beginning."

"What do you mean?"

"After basic, I'm volunteering for jump school."

"Jump school?"

"Airborne," Jackson said. "Then after that, I'll volunteer for Ranger school. In all, I hope to be done in about six or seven months."

"Then what?"

"Then I volunteer for the 75th Ranger Regiment," Jackson said, with a pleased smile. "They're the best—the elite."

"Sounds like a plan," Bryce said. He shook Jackson's hand and gave him a tight hug. "I'm gonna miss you, brother."

"Me too," Jackson said, clapping Bryce on the back. Then he hopped into the Camaro through the T-top and fired up the loud motor. He hung his head out the window. "Love ya, man."

"You too, man" Bryce said, sketching a wave. It felt so strange to say goodbye; they had spent their entire lives together.

Jackson returned his wave and then headed for the road.

"Hey, Jackson!" Bryce hollered after him.

He stopped, hung his head back out the window and lifted his chin. "What?"

"Don't get your ass shot off, okay?"

Jackson smiled and offered a wink . . . and then he was gone.

THE NEXT FEW WEEKS went by quickly. Bryce worked on the ranch with his grandpa, as always, and prepared to leave for college. He had chosen Stanford University for their exceptional biology department. Both Harvard and MIT had also accepted Bryce, but Stanford seemed like a better fit. He would be leaving tomorrow in order to rent an apartment and give himself plenty of time to take in the sights and acclimate to his new surroundings before the autumn quarter began.

Funding for Bryce's future education wouldn't be a problem; his grandparents had created a college fund for him in 1978, using the money from his parents' life insurance policies. Together, the two policies had totaled five hundred thousand, and after thirteen years of earning interest, Bryce was now financially independent.

His body was filled with nervous excitement as he lay in bed that night, and he had trouble falling asleep; he couldn't believe he was leaving for California in the morning. He thought of all the things that had happened over the past year; it seemed like a dream, or more to the point, a nightmare; he would carry the memories for the rest of his life.

He rubbed a silver dime between his thumb and forefinger as he mused about the past. Bryce had kept the coin that he'd found in the werewolf's blood, threading it onto a beaded chain he now wore around his neck. It had become his good-luck charm.

He thought of Mariana and it made him smile. Over the past six months, they had become fast friends. After all that had happened, they both realized they made better friends than lovers; their relationship had remained purely platonic.

Bryce thought of Jackson, and wondered how he was faring. He worried about his cousin and figured he would probably be starting jump school in the next month or so. He couldn't believe that Jackson actually *wanted* to jump out of perfectly good airplanes. With thoughts of California and the new life that lay ahead, Bryce eventually drifted off to sleep; and for the first time in a long time, he didn't have any nightmares.

The next morning, he devoured a large breakfast, with an extra helping of biscuits and gravy; he was going to miss his grandma's cooking. Bryce's bags were packed and ready, sitting by the back door. Grandpa would be driving him to the bus station soon.

As he rinsed his plate and placed it into the sink, Bryce heard a car drive up outside; he poked his head out the door to see who it was. He didn't recognize the vehicle, but when the driver exited, he saw that it was Doc Waggner, so he walked out to greet him.

"Hey, Doc," Bryce said, smiling. "Is that a new truck?"

"It sure is," Doc said, with his crooked grin, "1992 Chevy Blazer."

"Nice," Bryce said, nodding. "Good color, too. Blue's my favorite."

"Is that right?" Doc said.

Grandpa walked out of the house and joined them. "Mornin', Doc."

"Nathan."

"So, that's it, huh?"

"Yep, there she is."

"Well, come on in for some coffee, and then we'll go give Happy Jack a look-see. I'll give you a ride back to town a little later."

It took a moment for that last part to sink in. Bryce looked at the two old codgers. They were both grinning like a possum eating persimmons. "A ride back to town?" he said, knitting his brows.

Grandpa motioned for Doc to toss Bryce the keys. He caught them, and then his mouth fell open; his name was on the keychain.

"What?"

Grandma had come outside to enjoy the show. "That's your graduation present from me and your grandpa," she said, putting her arm around Grandpa's waist.

Bryce was thunderstruck, speechless. He looked at the keys in his hand, his face beaming. "I don't know what to—"

"You don't need to say anything," Grandma said, waving away his words. "You deserve it."

Bryce opened the door, sliding into the driver's seat; it was amazing. He took a deep breath.

New car smell . . .

The next hour was spent saying goodbye and was very emotional for everyone. As Bryce loaded his suitcases into his new Blazer, there was another round of hugs, kisses and tears.

"I got this for you," Grandma said. She handed him a leather-bound journal. "So you can keep track of what you do each day."

"Thank you, Grandma"—he kissed her cheek—"it's perfect."

"I expect a letter from you each month, telling me about everything you're doing," she said.

"Every month," Bryce promised.

"And don't forget to call."

"I won't."

After more hugs and tears, Bryce headed for the highway, turning south, toward his new life. When he reached the bridge at the Carantina River, he slowed and pulled onto the verge. Parking his new Blazer, he alighted for a final look at the rolling green hills of Bane County.

He smiled fondly at the picturesque countryside that he knew so well, his childhood there had been nearly perfect. It was July now, and next month Bryce would turn eighteen; he mused about what the *next* eighteen years might bring.

The cloud-tipped mountains of The Refuge drew his gaze, looming ominously in the distance. He knew that at least one of the two creatures was still alive, and that fact made a chill crawl down his spine. Somewhere within the cavernous depths of those rugged mountains—the werewolf slept. Waiting, growing hungry, and longing for its time to rise.

Bryce slid into the driver's seat and opened his new journal; he jotted down a quick note and then tossed it aside. With an expectant smile, he crossed the long bridge over the Carantina River—and left Bane County far behind.

The note Bryce scribbled in his journal had been a date: September 22, 2010. Beneath it, he had written two words: returning moon. He would be thirty-six-years-old when the creature emerged again—and *that* was a lifetime away.

Printed in Great Britain
by Amazon